The Strange Case of
Dr. Jekyll and Mr. Hyde
and Other Stories

ROBERT LOUIS STEVENSON

The Strange Case of Dr. Jekyll and Mr. Hyde and Other Stories

Illustrations by
JOSEPH CIARDIELLO

Afterword by
SCOTT RUSSELL SANDERS

THE WORLD'S BEST READING
The Reader's Digest Association, Inc.
Pleasantville, N.Y. · Montreal · Sydney · Auckland

The Strange Case of Dr. Jekyll and Mr. Hyde
and Other Stories

This Reader's Digest edition contains the complete text of
Robert Louis Stevenson's *The Strange Case of Dr. Jekyll and Mr. Hyde*,
first published in 1886, and other selected stories.

Library of Congress Catalog Card Number 90-63831
ISBN 0-89577-384-8

Printed in the United States of America

Contents

Illustrations

The Strange Case of Dr. Jekyll and Mr. Hyde

Story of the Door

M R. UTTERSON THE lawyer was a man of a rugged countenance that was never lighted by a smile; cold, scanty and embarrassed in discourse; backward in sentiment; lean, long, dusty, dreary and yet somehow lovable. At friendly meetings, and when the wine was to his taste, something eminently human beaconed from his eye; something indeed which never found its way into his talk, but which spoke not only in these silent symbols of the after-dinner face, but more often and loudly in the acts of his life. He was austere with himself; drank gin when he was alone, to mortify a taste for vintages; and though he enjoyed the theatre, had not crossed the doors of one for twenty years. But he had an approved tolerance for others; sometimes wondering, almost with envy, at the high pressure of spirits involved in their misdeeds; and in any extremity inclined to help rather than to reprove. "I incline to Cain's heresy," he used to say quaintly: "I let my brother go to the devil in his own way." In this character, it was frequently his fortune to be the last reputable acquaintance and the last good influence in the lives of downgoing men. And to such as these, so long as they came about his chambers, he never marked a shade of change in his demeanour.

No doubt the feat was easy to Mr. Utterson; for he was undemonstrative at the best, and even his friendship seemed to be founded in a similar catholicity of good nature. It is the mark of a modest man to accept his friendly circle ready-made from the hands of opportunity; and that was the lawyer's way. His friends were those of his own blood or those whom he had known the longest; his affections, like ivy, were the growth of time, they implied no aptness in the object. Hence, no doubt, the bond that united him to Mr. Richard Enfield, his distant kinsman, the well-known man about town. It was a nut to crack for many, what these two could see in each other, or what subject they could find in common. It was reported by those who encountered them in their Sunday walks, that they said nothing, looked singularly dull, and would hail with obvious relief the appearance of a friend. For all that, the two men put the greatest store by these excursions, counted them the chief jewel of each week, and not only set aside occasions of pleasure, but even resisted the calls of business, that they might enjoy them uninterrupted.

It chanced on one of these rambles that their way led them down a bystreet in a busy quarter of London. The street was small and what is called quiet, but it drove a thriving trade on the weekdays. The inhabitants were all doing well, it seemed, and all emulously hoping to do better still, and laying out the surplus of their gains in coquetry; so that the shop fronts stood along that thoroughfare with an air of invitation, like rows of smiling saleswomen. Even on Sunday, when it veiled its more florid charms and lay comparatively empty of passage, the street shone out in contrast to its dingy neighbourhood, like a fire in a forest; and with its freshly painted shutters, well-polished brasses, and general cleanliness and gaiety of note, instantly caught and pleased the eye of the passenger.

Two doors from one corner, on the left hand going east, the line was broken by the entry of a court; and just at that point, a certain sinister block of building thrust forward its gable on the street. It was two storeys high; showed no window, nothing but a door on the lower storey and a blind forehead of discoloured wall on the upper; and bore in every feature the marks of prolonged and sordid negligence. The door, which was equipped with neither bell nor knocker, was blistered and distained. Tramps slouched into the recess and struck matches on the panels; children kept shop upon the steps; the schoolboy had tried his knife on the mouldings; and for close on a generation, no one had appeared to drive away these random visitors or to repair their ravages.

Mr. Enfield and the lawyer were on the other side of the bystreet; but when they came abreast of the entry, the former lifted his cane and pointed.

"Did you ever remark that door?" he asked; and when his companion had replied in the affirmative, "It is connected in my mind," added he, "with a very odd story."

"Indeed?" said Mr. Utterson, with a slight change of voice, "and what was that?"

"Well, it was this way," returned Mr. Enfield: "I was coming home from someplace at the end of the world, about three o'clock of a black winter morning, and my way lay through a part of town where there was literally nothing to be seen but lamps. Street after street, and all the folks asleep—street after street, all lighted up as if for a procession and all as empty as a church—till at last I got into that state of mind when a man listens and listens and begins to long for the sight of a policeman. All at once, I saw two figures: one a little man who was stumping along eastward at a good walk, and the other a girl of maybe eight or ten who was running as hard as she was able down a cross street. Well, sir, the two ran into one another naturally enough at the corner; and then came the horrible part of the thing; for the man trampled calmly over the child's body and left her screaming on the ground. It sounds nothing to hear, but it was hellish to see. It wasn't like a man; it was like some damned juggernaut. I gave a view halloa, took to my heels, collared my gentleman, and brought him back to where there was already quite a group about the screaming child. He was perfectly cool and made no resistance, but gave me one look so ugly that it brought out the sweat on me like running. The people who had turned out were the girl's own family; and pretty soon, the doctor, for whom she had been sent, put in his appearance. Well, the child was not much the worse, more frightened, according to the sawbones; and there you might have supposed would be an end to it. But there was one curious circumstance. I had taken a loathing to my gentleman at first sight. So had the child's family, which was only natural. But the doctor's case was what struck me. He was the usual cut-and-dry apothecary, of no particular age and colour, with a strong Edinburgh accent, and about as emotional as a bagpipe. Well, sir, he was like the rest of us; every time he looked at my prisoner, I saw that sawbones turn sick and white with the desire to kill him. I knew what was in his mind, just as he knew what was in mine; and killing being out of the question, we did the next best. We told the man we could and would make such a scandal out of this, as should make his name stink from one end of London to the other. If he had any friends or any credit, we undertook that he should lose them. And all the time, as we were pitching it in red-hot, we were keeping the women off him as best we could, for they were as wild as harpies. I never saw a circle of such hateful faces; and there was the man in the middle, with a kind of black, sneering coolness—frightened too, I could see that— but carrying it off, sir, really like Satan. 'If you choose to make capital out of this accident,' said he, 'I am naturally helpless. No gentleman but wishes to avoid a scene,' says he. 'Name your figure.' Well, we screwed him up to a hundred pounds for the child's family; he would have clearly liked to stick out; but there was something about the lot of us that meant mischief, and at last he struck. The next thing was to get the money; and where do you think he carried us but to that place with the door?—whipped out a key, went in, and presently came back with the matter of ten pounds in gold and a cheque for the balance on Coutts's, drawn payable to bearer and signed with a name that I can't mention, though it's one of the points of my story, but it was a name at least very well known and often printed. The figure was stiff; but the signature was good for more than that, if it was only genuine. I took the liberty of pointing out to my gentleman that the whole business looked apocryphal, and that a man does not, in real life, walk into a cellar door at four in the morning and come out of it with another man's cheque for close upon a hundred pounds. But he was quite easy and sneering. 'Set your mind at rest,' says he,, 'I will stay with you till the banks open and cash the cheque myself.' So we all set off, the doctor, and the child's father, and our friend and myself, and passed the rest of the night in my chambers; and next day, when we had breakfasted, went in a body to the bank. I gave in the cheque myself, and said I had every reason to believe it was a forgery. Not a bit of it. The cheque was genuine."

"Tut-tut," said Mr. Utterson.

"I see you feel as I do," said Mr. Enfield. "Yes, it's a bad story. For my man was a fellow that nobody could have to do with, a really damnable man; and the person that drew the cheque is the very pink of the proprieties, celebrated too, and (what makes it worse) one of your fellows who do what they call good. Blackmail, I suppose; an honest man paying through the nose for some of the capers of his youth. Blackmail House is what I call that place with the door, in consequence. Though even that, you know, is far from explaining all," he added, and with the words fell into a vein of musing.

From this he was recalled by Mr. Utterson asking rather suddenly: "And you don't know if the drawer of the cheque lives there?"

"A likely place, isn't it?" returned Mr. Enfield. "But I happen to have noticed his address; he lives in some square or other."

"And you never asked about the—place with the door?" said Mr. Utterson.

"No, sir: I had a delicacy," was the reply. "I feel very strongly about putting questions; it partakes too much of the style of the day of judgment. You start a question, and it's like starting a stone. You sit quietly on the top of a hill; and away the stone goes, starting others; and presently some bland old bird (the last you would have thought of) is knocked on the head in his own back garden and the family have to change their name. No sir, I make it a rule of mine: the more it looks like Queer Street, the less I ask."

"A very good rule, too," said the lawyer.

"But I have studied the place for myself," continued Mr. Enfield. "It seems scarcely a house. There is no other door, and nobody goes in or out of that one but, once in a great while, the gentleman of my adventure. There are three windows looking on the court on the first floor; none below; the windows are always shut but they're clean. And then there is a chimney which is generally smoking; so somebody must live there. And yet it's not so sure; for the buildings are so packed together about that court, that it's hard to say where one ends and another begins."

The pair walked on again for a while in silence; and then "Enfield," said Mr. Utterson, "that's a good rule of yours."

"Yes, I think it is," returned Enfield.

"But for all that," continued the lawyer, "there's one point I want to ask: I want to ask the name of that man who walked over the child."

"Well," said Mr. Enfield, "I can't see what harm it would do. It was a man of the name of Hyde."

"Hm," said Mr. Utterson. "What sort of a man is he to see?"

"He is not easy to describe. There is something wrong with his appearance; something displeasing, something downright detestable. I never saw a man I so disliked, and yet I scarce know why. He must be deformed somewhere; he gives a strong feeling of deformity, although I couldn't specify the point. He's an extraordinary looking man, and yet I really can name nothing out of the way. No, sir; I can make no hand of it; I can't describe him. And it's not want of memory; for I declare I can see him this moment."

Mr. Utterson again walked some way in silence and obviously under a weight of consideration. "You are sure he used a key?" he inquired at last.

"My dear sir . . ." began Enfield, surprised out of himself.

"Yes, I know," said Utterson; "I know it must seem strange. The fact is, if I do not ask you the name of the other party, it is because I know it already. You see, Richard, your tale has gone home. If you have been inexact in any point, you had better correct it."

"I think you might have warned me," returned the other with a touch of sullenness. "But I have been pedantically exact, as you call it. The fellow had a key; and what's more, he has it still. I saw him use it, not a week ago."

Mr. Utterson sighed deeply but said never a word; and the young man presently resumed. "Here is another lesson to say nothing," said he. "I am ashamed of my long tongue. Let us make a bargain never to refer to this again."

"With all my heart," said the lawyer. "I shake hands on that, Richard."

Search for Mr. Hyde

THAT EVENING MR. UTTERSON came home to his bachelor house in sombre spirits and sat down to dinner without relish. It was his custom of a Sunday, when this meal was over, to sit close by the fire, a volume of some dry divinity on his reading desk, until the clock in the neighbouring church rang out the hour of twelve, when he would go soberly and gratefully to bed. On this night, however, as soon as the cloth was taken away, he took up a candle and went into his business room. There he opened his safe, took from the most private part of it a document endorsed on the envelope as Dr. Jekyll's Will, and sat down with a clouded brow to study its contents. The will was holograph, for Mr. Utterson, though he took charge of it now that it was made, had refused to lend the least assistance in the making of it; it provided not only that, in case of the decease of Henry Jekyll, M.D., D.C.L., L.L.D., F.R.S., etc., all his possessions were to pass into the hands of his "friend and benefactor Edward Hyde," but that in case of Dr. Jekyll's "disappearance or unexplained absence for any period exceeding three calendar months," the said Edward Hyde should step into the said Henry Jekyll's shoes without further delay and free from any burthen or obligation beyond the payment of a few small sums to the members of the doctor's household. This document had long been the lawyer's eyesore. It offended him both as a lawyer and as a lover of the sane and customary sides of life, to whom the fanciful was the immodest. And hitherto it was his ignorance of Mr. Hyde that had swelled his indignation; now, by a sudden turn, it was his knowledge. It was already bad enough when the name was but a name of which he could learn no more. It was worse when it began to be clothed upon with detestable attributes; and out of the shifting, insubstantial mists that had so long baffled his eye, there leaped up the sudden, definite presentment of a fiend.

"I thought it was madness," he said, as he replaced the obnoxious paper in the safe, "and now I begin to fear it is disgrace."

With that he blew out his candle, put on a greatcoat, and set forth in the direction of Cavendish Square, that citadel of medicine, where his friend, the great Dr. Lanyon, had his house and received his crowding patients. "If anyone knows, it will be Lanyon," he had thought.

The solemn butler knew and welcomed him; he was subjected to no stage of delay, but ushered direct from the door to the dining room where Dr. Lanyon sat alone over his wine. This was a hearty, healthy, dapper, red-faced gentleman, with a shock of hair prematurely white, and a boisterous and decided manner. At sight of Mr. Utterson, he sprang up from his chair and welcomed him with both hands. The geniality, as was the way of the man, was somewhat theatrical to the eye; but it reposed on genuine feeling. For these two were old friends, old mates both at school and college, both thorough respecters of themselves and of each other, and, what does not always follow, men who thoroughly enjoyed each other's company.

After a little rambling talk, the lawyer led up to the subject which so disagreeably preoccupied his mind.

"I suppose, Lanyon," said he, "you and I must be the two oldest friends that Henry Jekyll has?"

"I wish the friends were younger," chuckled Dr. Lanyon. "But I suppose we are. And what of that? I see little of him now."

"Indeed!" said Utterson. "I thought you had a bond of common interest."

"We had," was the reply. "But it is more than ten years since Henry Jekyll became too fanciful for me. He began to go wrong, wrong in mind; and though of course I continue to take an interest in him for old sake's sake, as they say, I see and I have seen devilish little of the man. Such unscientific balderdash," added the doctor, flushing suddenly purple, "would have estranged Damon and Pythias."

This little spirt of temper was somewhat of a relief to Mr. Utterson.

"They have only differed on some point of science," he thought; and being a man of no scientific passions (except in the matter of conveyancing), he even added: "It is nothing worse than that!" He gave his friend a few seconds to recover his composure, and then approached the question he had come to put. "Did you ever come across a protégé of his—one Hyde?" he asked.

"Hyde?" repeated Lanyon. "No. Never heard of him. Since my time."

That was the amount of information that the lawyer carried back with him to the great, dark bed on which he tossed to and fro until the small hours of the morning began to grow large. It was a night of little ease to his toiling mind, toiling in mere darkness and besieged by questions.

Six o'clock struck on the bells of the church that was so conveniently near to Mr. Utterson's dwelling, and still he was digging at the problem. Hitherto it had touched him on the intellectual side alone; but now his imagination also was engaged, or rather enslaved; and as he lay and tossed in the gross darkness of the night and the curtained room, Mr. Enfield's tale went by before his mind in a scroll of lighted pictures. He would be aware of the great field of lamps of a nocturnal city; then of the figure of a man walking swiftly; then of a child running from the doctor's; and then these met, and that human juggernaut trod the child down and passed on regardless of her screams. Or else he would see a room in a rich house, where his friend lay asleep, dreaming and smiling at his dreams; and then the door of that room would be opened, the curtains of the bed plucked apart, the sleeper recalled, and lo! there would stand by his side a figure to whom power was given, and even at that dead hour, he must rise and do its bidding. The figure in these two phases haunted the lawyer all night; and if at any time he dozed over, it was but to see it glide more stealthily through sleeping houses, or move the more swiftly and still the more swiftly, even to dizziness, through wider labyrinths of lamplighted city, and at every street corner crush a child and leave her screaming. And still the figure had no face by which he might know it; even in his dreams, it had no face, or one that baffled him and melted before his eyes; and thus it was that there sprang up and grew apace in the lawyer's mind a singularly strong, almost an inordinate, curiosity to behold the features of the real Mr.

Hyde. If he could but once set eyes on him, he thought the mystery would lighten and perhaps roll altogether away, as was the habit of mysterious things when well examined. He might see a reason for his friend's strange preference or bondage (call it which you please) and even for the startling clause of the will. At least it would be a face worth seeing: the face of a man who was without bowels of mercy: a face which had but to show itself to raise up, in the mind of the unimpressionable Enfield, a spirit of enduring hatred.

From that time forward, Mr. Utterson began to haunt the door in the bystreet of shops. In the morning before office hours, at noon when business was plenty, and time scarce, at night under the face of the fogged city moon, by all lights and at all hours of solitude or concourse, the lawyer was to be found on his chosen post.

"If he be Mr. Hyde," he had thought, "I shall be Mr. Seek."

And at last his patience was rewarded. It was a fine dry night; frost in the air; the streets as clean as a ballroom floor; the lamps, unshaken by any wind, drawing a regular pattern of light and shadow. By ten o'clock, when the shops were closed, the bystreet was very solitary and, in spite of the low growl of London from all round, very silent. Small sounds carried far; domestic sounds out of the houses were clearly audible on either side of the roadway; and the rumour of the approach of any passenger preceded him by a long time. Mr. Utterson had been some minutes at his post, when he was aware of an odd, light footstep drawing near. In the course of his nightly patrols, he had long grown accustomed to the quaint effect with which the footfalls of a single person, while he is still a great way off, suddenly spring out distinct from the vast hum and clatter of the city. Yet his attention had never before been so sharply and decisively arrested; and it was with a strong, superstitious prevision of success that he withdrew into the entry of the court.

The steps drew swiftly nearer, and swelled out suddenly louder as they turned the end of the street. The lawyer, looking forth from the entry, could soon see what manner of man he had to deal with. He was small and very plainly dressed, and the look of him, even at that distance, went somehow strongly against the watcher's inclination. But he made straight for the door, crossing the roadway to save time; and as he came, he drew a key from his pocket like one approaching home.

Mr. Utterson stepped out and touched him on the shoulder as he passed. "Mr. Hyde, I think?"

Mr. Hyde shrank back with a hissing intake of the breath. But his fear was only momentary; and though he did not look the lawyer in the face, he answered coolly enough: "That is my name. What do you want?"

"I see you are going in," returned the lawyer. "I am an old friend of Dr. Jekyll's—Mr. Utterson of Gaunt Street—you must have heard of my name; and meeting you so conveniently, I thought you might admit me."

"You will not find Dr. Jekyll; he is from home," replied Mr. Hyde, blowing in the key. And then suddenly, but still without looking up, "How did you know me?" he asked.

"On your side," said Mr. Utterson, "will you do me a favour?"

"With pleasure," replied the other. "What shall it be?"

"Will you let me see your face?" asked the lawyer.

Mr. Hyde appeared to hesitate, and then, as if upon some sudden reflection, fronted about with an air of defiance; and the pair stared at each other pretty fixedly for a few seconds. "Now I shall know you again," said Mr. Utterson. "It may be useful."

"Yes," returned Mr. Hyde, "it is as well we have met; and *à propos*, you should have my address." And he gave a number of a street in Soho.

"Good God!" thought Mr. Utterson, "can he, too, have been thinking of the will?" But he kept his feelings to himself and only grunted in acknowledgment of the address.

"And now," said the other, "how did you know me?"

"By description," was the reply.

"Whose description?"

"We have common friends," said Mr. Utterson.

"Common friends?" echoed Mr. Hyde, a little hoarsely. "Who are they?"

"Jekyll, for instance," said the lawyer.

"He never told you," cried Mr. Hyde, with a flush of anger. "I did not think you would have lied."

"Come," said Mr. Utterson, "that is not fitting language."

The other snarled aloud into a savage laugh; and the next moment, with extraordinary quickness, he had unlocked the door and disappeared into the house.

The lawyer stood awhile when Mr. Hyde had left him, the picture of disquietude. Then he began slowly to mount the street, pausing every step or two and putting his hand to his brow like a man in mental perplexity. The problem he was thus debating as he walked was one of a class that is rarely solved. Mr. Hyde was pale and dwarfish, he gave an impression of deformity without any nameable malformation, he had a displeasing smile, he had borne himself to the lawyer with a sort of murderous mixture of timidity and boldness, and he spoke with a husky, whispering and somewhat broken voice; all these were points against him, but not all of these together could explain the hitherto unknown disgust, loathing and fear with which Mr. Utterson regarded him. "There must be something else," said the perplexed gentleman. "There *is* something more, if I could find a name for it. God bless me, the man seems hardly human! Something troglodytic, shall we say? Or can it be the old story of Dr. Fell? Or is it the mere radiance of a foul soul that thus transpires through, and transfigures, its clay continent? The last, I think; for, O my poor old Harry Jekyll, if ever I read Satan's signature upon a face, it is on that of your new friend."

Round the corner from the bystreet, there was a square of ancient, handsome houses, now for the most part decayed from their high estate and let in flats and chambers to all sorts and conditions of men; map engravers, architects, shady lawyers and the agents of obscure enterprises. One house, however, second from the corner, was still occupied entire; and at the door of this, which wore a great air of wealth and comfort, though it was now plunged in darkness except for the fanlight, Mr. Utterson stopped and knocked. A well-dressed, elderly servant opened the door.

"Is Dr. Jekyll at home, Poole?" asked the lawyer.

"I will see, Mr. Utterson," said Poole, admitting the visitor, as he spoke, into a large, low-roofed, comfortable hall, paved with flags, warmed (after the fashion of a country house) by a bright, open fire, and furnished with costly cabinets of oak. "Will you wait here by the fire, sir? Or shall I give you a light in the dining room?"

"Here, thank you," said the lawyer, and he drew near and leaned on the tall fender. This hall, in which he was now left alone, was a pet fancy of his friend the doctor's; and Utterson himself was wont to speak of it as the pleasantest room in London. But tonight there was a shudder in his blood; the face of Hyde sat heavy on his memory; he felt (what was rare with him) a nausea and distaste of life; and in the gloom of his spirits, he seemed to read a menace in the flickering of the firelight on the polished cabinets and the uneasy starting of the shadow on the roof. He was ashamed of his relief, when Poole presently returned to announce that Dr. Jekyll was gone out.

"I saw Mr. Hyde go in by the old dissecting-room door, Poole," he said. "Is that right, when Dr. Jekyll is from home?"

"Quite right, Mr. Utterson, sir," replied the servant. "Mr. Hyde has a key."

"Your master seems to repose a great deal of trust in that young man, Poole," resumed the other musingly.

"Yes, sir, he do indeed," said Poole. "We have all orders to obey him."

"I do not think I ever met Mr. Hyde?" asked Utterson.

"O, dear no, sir. He never *dines* here," replied the butler. "Indeed we see very little of him on this side of the house; he mostly comes and goes by the laboratory."

"Well, good night, Poole."

"Good night, Mr. Utterson."

And the lawyer set out homeward with a very heavy heart. "Poor Harry Jekyll," he thought, "my mind misgives me he is in deep waters! He was wild when he was young; a long while ago to be sure; but in the law of God, there is no statute of limitations. Ay, it must be that; the ghost of some old sin, the cancer of some concealed disgrace: punishment coming, *pede claudo*, years after memory has forgotten and self-love condoned the fault." And the lawyer, scared by the thought, brooded awhile on his own past, groping in all the corners of memory, lest by chance some jack-in-the-box of an old iniquity should leap to light there. His past was fairly blameless; few men could read the rolls of their life with less apprehension; yet he was humbled to the dust by the many ill things he had done, and raised up again into a sober and fearful gratitude by the many he had come so near to doing, yet avoided. And then by a return on his former subject, he conceived a spark of hope. "This Master Hyde, if he were studied," thought he, "must have secrets of his own; black secrets, by the look of him; secrets compared to which poor Jekyll's worst would be like sunshine. Things cannot continue as they are. It turns me cold to think of this creature stealing like a thief to Harry's bedside; poor Harry, what a wakening! And the danger of it; for if this Hyde suspects the existence of the will, he may grow impatient to inherit. Ay, I must put my shoulder to the wheel—if Jekyll will but let me," he added, "if Jekyll will only let me." For once more he saw before his mind's eye, as clear as transparency, the strange clauses of the will.

Dr. Jekyll Was Quite at Ease

A FORTNIGHT LATER, by excellent good fortune, the doctor gave one of his pleasant dinners to some five or six old cronies, all intelligent, reputable men and all judges of good wine; and Mr. Utterson so contrived that he remained behind after the others had departed. This was no new arrangement, but a thing that had befallen many scores of times. Where Utterson was liked, he was liked well. Hosts loved to detain the dry lawyer, when the lighthearted and loose-tongued had already their foot on the threshold; they liked to sit awhile in his unobtrusive company, practicing for solitude, sobering their minds in the man's rich silence after the expense and strain of gaiety. To this rule, Dr. Jekyll was no exception; and as he now sat on the opposite side of the fire—a large, well-made, smooth-faced man of fifty, with something of a slyish cast perhaps, but every mark of capacity and kindness—you could see by his looks that he cherished for Mr. Utterson a sincere and warm affection.

"I have been wanting to speak to you, Jekyll," began the latter. "You know that will of yours?"

A close observer might have gathered that the topic was distasteful; but the doctor carried it off gaily. "My poor Utterson," said he, "you are unfortunate in such a client. I never saw a man so distressed as you were by my will; unless it were that hidebound pedant, Lanyon, at what he called my scientific heresies. O, I know he's a good fellow—you needn't frown—an excellent fellow, and I always mean to see more of him; but a hidebound pedant for all that; an ignorant, blatant pedant. I was never more disappointed in any man than Lanyon."

"You know I never approved of it," pursued Utterson, ruthlessly disregarding the fresh topic.

"My will? Yes, certainly, I know that," said the doctor, a trifle sharply. "You have told me so."

"Well, I tell you so again," continued the lawyer. "I have been learning something of young Hyde."

The large handsome face of Dr. Jekyll grew pale to the very lips, and there came a blackness about his eyes. "I do not care to hear more," said he. "This is a matter I thought we had agreed to drop."

"What I heard was abominable," said Utterson.

"It can make no change. You do not understand my position," returned the doctor, with a certain incoherency of manner. "I am painfully situated, Utterson; my position is a very strange—a very strange one. It is one of those affairs that cannot be mended by talking."

"Jekyll," said Utterson, "you know me: I am a man to be trusted. Make a clean breast of this in confidence; and I make no doubt I can get you out of it."

"My good Utterson," said the doctor, "this is very good of you, this is downright good of you, and I cannot find words to thank you in. I believe you fully; I would trust you before any man alive, ay, before myself, if I could make the choice; but indeed it isn't what you fancy; it is not as bad as that; and just to put your good heart at rest, I will tell you one thing: the moment I choose, I can be rid of Mr. Hyde. I give you my hand upon that; and I thank you again and again; and I will just add one little word, Utterson, that I'm sure you'll take in good part: this is a private matter, and I beg of you to let it sleep."

Utterson reflected a little, looking in the fire.

"I have no doubt you are perfectly right," he said at last, getting to his feet.

"Well, but since we have touched upon this business, and for the last time I hope," continued the doctor, "there is one point I should like you to understand. I have really a very great interest in poor Hyde. I know you have seen him; he told me so; and I fear he was rude. But I do sincerely take a great, a very great interest in that young man; and if I am taken away, Utterson, I wish you to promise me that you will bear with him and get his rights for him. I think you would, if you knew all; and it would be a weight off my mind if you would promise."

"I can't pretend that I shall ever like him," said the lawyer.

"I don't ask that," pleaded Jekyll, laying his hand upon the other's arm; "I only ask for justice; I only ask you to help him for my sake, when I am no longer here."

Utterson heaved an irrepressible sigh. "Well," said he, "I promise."

The Carew Murder Case

NEARLY A YEAR LATER, in the month of October, 18—, London was startled by a crime of singular ferocity and rendered all the more notable by the high position of the victim. The details were few and startling. A maidservant living alone in a house not far from the river had gone upstairs to bed about eleven. Although a fog rolled over the city in the small hours, the early part of the night was cloudless, and the lane, which the maid's window overlooked, was brilliantly lit by the full moon. It seems she was romantically given, for she sat down upon her box, which stood immediately under the window, and fell into a dream of musing. Never (she used to say, with streaming tears, when she narrated that experience), never had she felt more at peace with all men or thought more kindly of the world. And as she so sat she became aware of an aged beautiful gentleman with white hair, drawing near along the lane; and advancing to meet him, another and very small gentleman, to whom at first she paid less attention. When they had come within speech (which was just under the maid's eyes) the older man bowed and accosted the other with a very pretty manner of politeness. It did not seem as if the subject of his address were of great importance; indeed, from his pointing, it sometimes appeared as if he were only inquiring his way; but the moon shone on his face as he spoke, and the girl was pleased to watch it, it seemed to breathe such an innocent and old-world kindness of disposition, yet with something high too, as of a well-founded self-content. Presently her eye wandered to the other, and she was surprised to recognise in him a certain Mr. Hyde, who had once visited her master and for whom she had conceived a dislike. He had in his hand a heavy cane, with which he was trifling; but he answered never a word, and seemed to listen with an ill-contained impatience. And then all of a sudden he broke out in a great flame of anger, stamping with his foot, brandishing the cane, and carrying on (as the maid described it) like a madman. The old gentleman took a step back, with the air of one very much surprised and a trifle hurt; and at that Mr. Hyde broke out of all bounds and clubbed him to the earth. And next moment, with ape-like fury, he was trampling his victim under foot and hailing down a storm of blows, under which the bones were audibly shattered and the body jumped upon the roadway. At the horror of these sights and sounds, the maid fainted.

It was two o'clock when she came to herself and called for the police. The murderer was gone long ago; but there lay his victim in the middle of the lane, incredibly mangled. The stick with which the deed had been done, although it was of some rare and very tough and heavy wood, had broken in the middle under the stress of this insensate cruelty; and one splintered half had rolled in the neighbouring gutter—the other, without doubt, had been carried away by the murderer. A purse and gold watch were found upon the victim: but no cards or papers, except a sealed and stamped envelope, which he had been probably carrying to the post, and which bore the name and address of Mr. Utterson.

This was brought to the lawyer the next morning, before he was out of bed; and he had no sooner seen it, and been told the circumstances, than he shot out a solemn lip. "I shall say nothing till I have seen the body," said he; "this may be very serious. Have the kindness to wait while I dress." And with the same grave countenance he hurried through his breakfast and drove to the police station, whither the body had been carried. As soon as he came into the cell, he nodded.

"Yes," said he, "I recognise him. I am sorry to say that this is Sir Danvers Carew."

"Good God, sir," exclaimed the officer, "is it possible?" And the next moment his eye lighted up with professional ambition. "This will make a deal of noise," he said. "And perhaps you can help us to the man." And he briefly narrated what the maid had seen, and showed the broken stick.

Mr. Utterson had already quailed at the name of Hyde; but when the stick was laid before him, he could doubt no longer; broken and battered as it was, he recognised it for one that he had himself presented many years before to Henry Jekyll.

"Is this Mr. Hyde a person of small stature?" he inquired. "Particularly small and particularly wicked-looking, is what the maid calls him," said the officer.

Mr. Utterson reflected; and then, raising his head, "If you will come with me in my cab," he said, "I think I can take you to his house."

It was by this time about nine in the morning, and the first fog of the season. A great chocolate-coloured pall lowered over heaven, but the wind was continually charging and routing these embattled vapours; so that as the cab crawled from street to street, Mr. Utterson beheld a marvelous number of degrees and hues of twilight; for here it would be dark like the back end of evening; and there would be a glow of a rich, lurid brown, like the light of some strange conflagration; and here, for a moment, the fog would be quite broken up, and a haggard shaft of daylight would glance in between the swirling wreaths. The dismal quarter of Soho seen under these changing glimpses, with its muddy ways, and slatternly passengers, and its lamps, which had never been extinguished or had been kindled afresh to combat this mournful reinvasion of darkness, seemed, in the lawyer's eyes, like a district of some city in a nightmare. The thoughts of his mind, besides, were of the gloomiest dye; and when he glanced at the companion of his drive, he was conscious of some touch of that terror of the law and the law's officers which may at times assail the most honest.

As the cab drew up before the address indicated, the fog lifted a little and showed him a dingy street, a gin palace, a low French eating house, a shop for the retail of penny numbers and twopenny salads, many ragged children huddled in the doorways, and many women of many different nationalities passing out, key in hand, to have a morning glass; and the next moment the fog settled down again upon that part, as brown as umber, and cut him off from his blackguardly surroundings. This was the home of Henry Jekyll's favourite; of a man who was heir to a quarter of a million sterling.

An ivory-faced and silvery-haired old woman opened the door. She had an evil face, smoothed by hypocrisy: but her manners were excellent. Yes, she said, this was Mr. Hyde's, but he was not at home; he had been in that night very late, but he had gone away again in less than an hour; there was nothing strange in that; his habits were very irregular, and he was often absent; for instance, it was nearly two months since she had seen him till yesterday.

"Very well, then, we wish to see his rooms," said the lawyer; and when the woman began to declare it was impossible, "I had better tell you who this person is," he added. "This is Inspector Newcomen of Scotland Yard."

A flash of odious joy appeared upon the woman's face. "Ah!" said she, "he is in trouble! What has he done?"

Mr. Utterson and the inspector exchanged glances. "He don't seem a very popular character," observed the latter. "And now, my good woman, just let me and this gentleman have a look about us."

In the whole extent of the house, which but for the old woman remained otherwise empty, Mr. Hyde had only used a couple of rooms; but these were furnished with luxury and good taste. A closet was filled with wine; the plate was of silver, the napery elegant; a good picture hung upon the wall, a gift (as Utterson supposed) from Henry Jekyll, who was much of a connoisseur; and the carpets were of many piles and agreeable in colour. At this moment, however, the rooms bore every mark of having been recently and hurriedly ransacked; clothes lay about the floor, with their pockets inside out; lock-fast drawers stood open; and on the hearth there lay a pile of grey ashes, as though many papers had been burned. From these embers the inspector disinterred the butt end of a green chequebook, which had resisted the action of the fire; the other half of the stick was found behind the door; and as this clinched his suspicions, the officer declared himself delighted. A visit to the bank, where several thousand pounds were found to be lying to the murderer's credit, completed his gratification.

"You may depend upon it, sir," he told Mr. Utterson: "I have him in my hand. He must have lost his head, or he never would have left the stick or, above all, burned the chequebook. Why, money's life to the man. We have nothing to do but wait for him at the bank, and get out the handbills."

This last, however, was not so easy of accomplishment; for Mr. Hyde had numbered few familiars—even the master of the servantmaid had only seen him twice; his family could nowhere be traced; he had never been photographed; and the few who could describe him differed widely, as common observers will. Only on one point were they agreed; and that was the haunting sense of unexpressed deformity with which the fugitive impressed his beholders.

Incident of the Letter

IT WAS LATE IN the afternoon, when Mr. Utterson found his way to Dr. Jekyll's door, where he was at once admitted by Poole, and carried down by the kitchen offices and across a yard which had once been a garden, to the building which was indifferently known as the laboratory or dissecting rooms. The doctor had bought the house from the heirs of a celebrated surgeon; and his own tastes being rather chemical than anatomical, had changed the destination of the block at the bottom of the garden. It was the first time that the lawyer had been received in that part of his friend's quarters; and he eyed the dingy, windowless structure with curiosity, and gazed round with a distasteful sense of strangeness as he crossed the theatre, once crowded with eager students and now lying gaunt and silent, the tables laden with chemical apparatus, the floor strewn with crates and littered with packing straw, and the light falling dimly through the foggy cupola. At the further end, a flight of stairs mounted to a door covered with red baize; and through this, Mr. Utterson was at last received into the doctor's cabinet. It was a large room fitted round with glass presses, furnished, among other things, with a cheval glass and a business table, and looking out upon the court by three dusty windows barred with iron. The fire burned in the grate; a lamp was set lighted on the chimney shelf, for even in the houses the fog began to lie thickly; and there, close up to the warmth, sat Dr. Jekyll, looking deadly sick. He did not rise to meet his visitor, but held out a cold hand and bade him welcome in a changed voice.

"And now," said Mr. Utterson, as soon as Poole had left them, "you have heard the news?"

The doctor shuddered. "They were crying it in the square," he said. "I heard them in my dining room."

"One word," said the lawyer. "Carew was my client, but so are you, and I want to know what I am doing. You have not been mad enough to hide this fellow?"

"Utterson, I swear to God," cried the doctor, "I swear to God I will never set eyes on him again. I bind my honour to you that I am done with him in this world. It is all at an end. And indeed he does not want my help; you do not know him as I do; he is safe, he is quite safe; mark my words, he will never more be heard of."

The lawyer listened gloomily; he did not like his friend's feverish manner. "You seem pretty sure of him," said he; "and for your sake, I hope you may be right. If it came to a trial, your name might appear."

"I am quite sure of him," replied Jekyll; "I have grounds for certainty that I cannot share with anyone. But there is one thing on which you may advise me. I have — I have received a letter; and I am at a loss whether I should show it to the police. I should like to leave it in your hands, Utterson; you would judge wisely, I am sure; I have so great a trust in you."

"You fear, I suppose, that it might lead to his detection?" asked the lawyer.

"No," said the other. "I cannot say that I care what becomes of Hyde; I am quite done with him. I was thinking of my own character, which this hateful business has rather exposed."

Utterson ruminated awhile; he was surprised at his friend's selfishness, and yet relieved by it. "Well," said he, at last, "let me see the letter."

The letter was written in an odd, upright hand and signed "Edward Hyde": and it signified, briefly enough, that the writer's benefactor, Dr. Jekyll, whom he had long so unworthily repaid for a thousand generosities, need labour under no alarm for his safety, as he had means of escape on which he placed a sure dependence. The lawyer liked this letter well enough; it put a better colour on the intimacy than he had looked for; and he blamed himself for some of his past suspicions.

"Have you the envelope?" he asked.

"I burned it," replied Jekyll, "before I thought what I was about. But it bore no postmark. The note was handed in."

"Shall I keep this and sleep upon it?" asked Utterson.

"I wish you to judge for me entirely," was the reply. "I have lost confidence in myself."

"Well, I shall consider," returned the lawyer. "And now one word more: it was Hyde who dictated the terms in your will about that disappearance?"

The doctor seemed seized with a qualm of faintness; he shut his mouth tight and nodded.

"I knew it," said Utterson. "He meant to murder you. You had a fine escape."

"I have had what is far more to the purpose," returned the doctor solemnly: "I have had a lesson—O God, Utterson, what a lesson I have had!" And he covered his face for a moment with his hands.

On his way out, the lawyer stopped and had a word or two with Poole. "By the bye," said he, "there was a letter handed in today: what was the messenger like?" But Poole was positive nothing had come except by post; "and only circulars by that," he added.

This news sent off the visitor with his fears renewed. Plainly the letter had come by the laboratory door; possibly, indeed, it had been written in the cabinet; and if that were so, it must be differently judged, and handled with the more caution. The newsboys, as he went, were crying themselves hoarse along the footways: "Special edition. Shocking murder of an M.P." That was the funeral oration of one friend and client; and he could not help a certain apprehension lest the good name of another should be sucked down in the eddy of the scandal. It was, at least, a ticklish decision that he had to make; and self-reliant as he was by habit, he began to cherish a longing for advice. It was not to be had directly; but perhaps, he thought, it might be fished for.

Presently after, he sat on one side of his own hearth, with Mr. Guest, his head clerk, upon the other, and midway between, at a nicely calculated distance from the fire, a bottle of a particular old wine that had long dwelt unsunned in the foundations of his house. The fog still slept on the wing above the drowned city, where the lamps glimmered like carbuncles; and through the muffle and smother of these fallen clouds, the procession of the town's life was still rolling in through the great arteries with a sound as of a mighty wind. But the room was gay with firelight. In the bottle the acids were long ago resolved; the imperial dye had softened with time, as the colour grows richer in stained windows, and the glow of hot autumn afternoons on hillside vineyards was ready to be set free and to disperse the fogs of London. Insensibly the lawyer melted. There was no man from whom he kept fewer secrets than Mr. Guest; and he was not always sure that he kept as many as he meant. Guest had often been on business to the doctor's; he knew Poole; he could scarce have failed to hear of Mr. Hyde's familiarity about the house; he might draw conclusions: was it not as well, then, that he should see a letter which put that mystery to rights? and above all since Guest, being a great student and critic of handwriting, would consider the step natural and obliging? The clerk, besides, was a man of counsel; he could scarce read so strange a document without dropping a remark; and by that remark Mr. Utterson might shape his future course.

"This is a sad business about Sir Danvers," he said.

"Yes, sir, indeed. It has elicited a great deal of public feeling," returned Guest. "The man, of course, was mad."

"I should like to hear your views on that," replied Utterson. "I have a document here in his handwriting; it is between ourselves, for I scarce know what to do about it; it is an ugly business at the best. But there it is; quite in your way: a murderer's autograph."

Guest's eyes brightened, and he sat down at once and studied it with passion. "No sir," he said: "not mad; but it is an odd hand."

"And by all accounts a very odd writer," added the lawyer.

Just then the servant entered with a note.

"Is that from Dr. Jekyll, sir?" inquired the clerk. "I thought I knew the writing. Anything private, Mr. Utterson?"

"Only an invitation to dinner. Why? Do you want to see it?"

"One moment. I thank you, sir"; and the clerk laid the two sheets of paper alongside and sedulously compared their contents. "Thank you, sir," he said at last, returning both; "it's a very interesting autograph."

There was a pause, during which Mr. Utterson struggled with himself. "Why did you compare them, Guest?" he inquired suddenly.

"Well, sir," returned the clerk, "there's a rather singular resemblance; the two hands are in many points identical: only differently sloped."

"Rather quaint," said Utterson.

"It is, as you say, rather quaint," returned Guest.

"I wouldn't speak of this note, you know," said the master.

"No, sir," said the clerk. "I understand."

But no sooner was Mr. Utterson alone that night, than he locked the note into his safe, where it reposed from that time forward. "What!" he thought. "Henry Jekyll forge for a murderer!" And his blood ran cold in his veins.

Remarkable Incident of Dr. Lanyon

TIME RAN ON; thousands of pounds were offered in reward, for the death of Sir Danvers was resented as a public injury; but Mr. Hyde had disappeared out of the ken of the police as though he had never existed. Much of his past was unearthed, indeed, and all disreputable: tales came out of the man's cruelty, at once so callous and violent; of his vile life, of his strange associates, of the hatred that seemed to have surrounded his career; but of his present whereabouts, not a whisper. From the time he had left the house in Soho on the morning of the murder, he was simply blotted out; and gradually, as time drew on, Mr. Utterson began to recover from the hotness of his alarm, and to grow more at quiet with himself. The death of Sir Danvers was, to his way of thinking, more than paid for by the disappearance of Mr. Hyde. Now that that evil influence had been withdrawn, a new life began for Dr. Jekyll. He came out of his seclusion, renewed relations with his friends, became once more their familiar guest and entertainer; and whilst he had always been known for charities, he was now no less distinguished for religion. He was busy; he was much in the open air, he did good; his face seemed to open and brighten, as if with an inward consciousness of service; and for more than two months, the doctor was at peace.

On the 8th of January Utterson had dined at the doctor's with a small party; Lanyon had been there; and the face of the host had looked from one to the other as in the old days when the trio were inseparable friends. On the 12th, and again on the 14th, the door was shut against the lawyer. "The doctor was confined to the house," Poole said, "and saw no one." On the 15th, he tried again, and was again refused; and having now been used for the last two months to see his friend almost daily, he found this return of solitude to weigh upon his spirits. The fifth night he had in Guest to dine with him; and the sixth he betook himself to Dr. Lanyon's.

There at least he was not denied admittance; but when he came in, he was shocked at the change which had taken place in the doctor's appearance. He had his death warrant written legibly upon his face. The rosy man had grown pale; his flesh had fallen away; he was visibly balder and older; and yet it was not so much these tokens of a swift physical decay that arrested the lawyer's notice, as a look in the eye and quality of manner that seemed to testify to some deep-seated terror of the mind. It was unlikely that the doctor should fear death; and yet that was what Utterson was tempted to suspect. "Yes," he thought; "he is a doctor, he must know his own state and that his days are counted; and the knowledge is more than he can bear." And yet when Utterson remarked on his ill looks, it was with an air of great firmness that Lanyon declared himself a doomed man.

"I have had a shock," he said, "and I shall never recover. It is a question of weeks. Well, life has been pleasant; I liked it; yes, sir, I used to like it. I sometimes think if we knew all, we should be more glad to get away."

"Jekyll is ill, too," observed Utterson. "Have you seen him?"

But Lanyon's face changed, and he held up a trembling hand. "I wish to see or hear no more of Dr. Jekyll," he said in a loud, unsteady voice. "I am quite done with that person; and I beg that you will spare me any allusion to one whom I regard as dead."

"Tut-tut," said Mr. Utterson; and then after a considerable pause, "Can't I do anything?" he inquired. "We are three very old friends, Lanyon; we shall not live to make others."

"Nothing can be done," returned Lanyon; "ask himself."

"He will not see me," said the lawyer.

"I am not surprised at that," was the reply. "Someday, Utterson, after I am dead, you may perhaps come to learn the right and wrong of this. I cannot tell you. And in the meantime, if you can sit and talk with me of other things, for God's sake, stay and do so; but if you cannot keep clear of this accursed topic, then in God's name, go, for I cannot bear it."

As soon as he got home, Utterson sat down and wrote to Jekyll, complaining of his exclusion from the house, and asking the cause of this unhappy break with Lanyon; and the next day brought him a long answer, often very pathetically worded, and sometimes darkly mysterious in drift. The quarrel with Lanyon was incurable. "I do not blame our old friend," Jekyll wrote, "but I share his view that we must never meet. I mean from henceforth to lead a life of extreme seclusion; you must not be surprised, nor must you doubt my friendship, if my door is often shut even to you. You must suffer me to go my own dark way. I have brought on myself a punishment and a danger that I cannot name. If I am the chief of sinners, I am the chief of sufferers also. I could not think that this earth contained a place for sufferings and terrors so unmanning; and you can do but one thing, Utterson, to lighten this destiny, and that is to respect my silence." Utterson was amazed; the dark influence of Hyde had been withdrawn, the doctor had returned to his old tasks and amities; a week ago, the prospect had smiled with every promise of a cheerful and an honoured age; and now in a moment, friendship, and peace of mind, and the whole tenor of his life were wrecked. So great and unprepared a change pointed to madness; but in view of Lanyon's manner and words, there must lie for it some deeper ground.

A week afterwards Dr. Lanyon took to his bed, and in something less than a fortnight he was dead. The night after the funeral, at which he had been sadly affected, Utterson locked the door of his business room, and sitting there by the light of a melancholy candle, drew out and set before him an envelope addressed by the hand and sealed with the seal of his dead friend. "PRIVATE: for the hands of G.J. Utterson ALONE, and in case of his predecease *to be destroyed unread*," so it was emphatically superscribed; and the lawyer dreaded to behold the contents. "I have buried one friend today," he thought: "what if this should cost me another?" And then he condemned the fear as a disloyalty, and broke the seal. Within there was another enclosure, likewise sealed, and marked upon the cover as "not to be opened till the death or disappearance of Dr. Henry Jekyll." Utterson could not trust his eyes. Yes, it was disappearance; here again, as in the mad will which he had long ago restored to its author, here again were the idea of a disappearance and the name of Henry Jekyll bracketted. But in the will, that idea had sprung from the sinister suggestion of the man Hyde; it was set there with a purpose all too plain and horrible. Written by the hand of Lanyon, what should it mean? A great curiosity came on the trustee to disregard the prohibition and dive at once to the bottom of these mysteries; but professional honour and faith to his dead friend were stringent obligations; and the packet slept in the inmost corner of his private safe.

It is one thing to mortify curiosity, another to conquer it; and it may be doubted if, from that day forth, Utterson desired the society of his surviving friend with the same eagerness. He thought of him kindly; but his thoughts were disquieted and fearful. He went to call indeed; but he was perhaps relieved to be denied admittance; perhaps, in his heart, he preferred to speak with Poole upon the doorstep and surrounded by the air and sounds of the open city, rather than to be admitted into that house of voluntary bondage, and to sit and speak with its inscrutable recluse. Poole had, indeed, no very pleasant news to communicate. The doctor, it appeared, now more than ever confined himself to the cabinet over the laboratory, where he would sometimes even sleep; he was out of spirits, he had grown very silent, he did not read; it seemed as if he had something on his mind. Utterson became so used to the unvarying character of these reports that he fell off little by little in the frequency of his visits.

Incident at the Window

I T CHANCED ON Sunday, when Mr. Utterson was on his usual walk with Mr. Enfield, that their way lay once again through the bystreet; and that when they came in front of the door, both stopped to gaze on it.

"Well," said Enfield, "that story's at an end at least. We shall never see more of Mr. Hyde."

"I hope not," said Utterson. "Did I ever tell you that I once saw him, and shared your feeling of repulsion?"

"It was impossible to do the one without the other," returned Enfield. "And by the way, what an ass you must have thought me, not to know that this was a back way to Dr. Jekyll's! It was partly your own fault that I found it out, even when I did."

"So you found it out, did you?" said Utterson. "But if that be so, we may step into the court and take a look at the windows. To tell you the truth, I am uneasy about poor Jekyll; and even outside, I feel as if the presence of a friend might do him good."

The court was very cool and a little damp, and full of premature twilight, although the sky, high up overhead, was still bright with sunset. The middle one of the three windows was halfway open; and sitting close beside it, taking the air with an infinite sadness of mien, like some disconsolate prisoner, Utterson saw Dr. Jekyll.

"What! Jekyll!" he cried. "I trust you are better."

"I am very low, Utterson," replied the doctor drearily, "very low. It will not last long, thank God."

"You stay too much indoors," said the lawyer. "You should be out, whipping up the circulation like Mr. Enfield and me. (This is my cousin—Mr. Enfield—Dr. Jekyll.) Come now; get your hat and take a quick turn with us."

"You are very good," sighed the other. "I should like to very much; but no, no, no, it is quite impossible; I dare not. But indeed, Utterson, I am very glad to see you; this is really a great pleasure; I would ask you and Mr. Enfield up, but the place is really not fit."

"Why then," said the lawyer, good-naturedly, "the best thing we can do is to stay down here and speak with you from where we are."

"That is just what I was about to venture to propose," returned the doctor with a smile. But the words were hardly uttered, before the smile was struck out of his face and succeeded by an expression of such abject terror and despair as froze the very blood of the two gentlemen below. They saw it but for a glimpse for the window was instantly thrust down; but that glimpse had been sufficient, and they turned and left the court without a word. In silence, too, they traversed the bystreet; and it was not until they had come into a neighbouring thoroughfare, where even upon a Sunday there were still some stirrings of life, that Mr. Utterson at last turned and looked at his companion. They were both pale; and there was an answering horror in their eyes.

"God forgive us, God forgive us," said Mr. Utterson.

But Mr. Enfield only nodded his head very seriously, and walked on once more in silence.

The Last Night

MR. UTTERSON WAS sitting by his fireside one evening after dinner when he was surprised to receive a visit from Poole.

"Bless me, Poole, what brings you here?" he cried; and then taking a second look at him, "What ails you?" he added; "is the doctor ill?"

"Mr. Utterson," said the man, "there is something wrong."

"Take a seat, and here is a glass of wine for you," said the lawyer. "Now, take your time, and tell me plainly what you want."

"You know the doctor's ways, sir," replied Poole, "and how he shuts himself up. Well, he's shut up again in the cabinet; and I don't like it, sir—I wish I may die if I like it. Mr. Utterson, sir, I'm afraid."

"Now, my good man," said the lawyer, "be explicit. What are you afraid of?"

"I've been afraid for about a week," returned Poole, doggedly disregarding the question, "and I can bear it no more."

The man's appearance amply bore out his words; his manner was altered for the worse; and except for the moment when he had first announced his terror, he had not once looked the lawyer in the face. Even now, he sat with the glass of wine untasted on his knee, and his eyes directed to a corner of the floor. "I can bear it no more," he repeated.

"Come," said the lawyer, "I see you have some good reason, Poole; I see there is something seriously amiss. Try to tell me what it is."

"I think there's been foul play," said Poole, hoarsely.

"Foul play!" cried the lawyer, a good deal frightened and rather inclined to be irritated in consequence. "What foul play? What does the man mean?"

"I daren't say, sir," was the answer; "but will you come along with me and see for yourself?"

Mr. Utterson's only answer was to rise and get his hat and greatcoat; but he observed with wonder the greatness of the relief that appeared upon the butler's face, and perhaps with no less, that the wine was still untasted when he set it down to follow.

It was a wild, cold, seasonable night of March, with a pale moon lying on her back as though the wind had tilted her, and a flying wrack of the most diaphanous and lawny texture. The wind made talking difficult, and flecked the blood into the face. It seemed to have swept the streets unusually bare of passengers, besides; for Mr. Utterson thought he had never seen that part of London so deserted. He could have wished it otherwise; never in his life had he been conscious of so sharp a wish to see and touch his fellow creatures; for struggle as he might, there was borne in upon his mind a crushing anticipation of calamity. The square, when they got there, was full of wind and dust, and the thin trees in the garden were lashing themselves along the railing. Poole, who had kept all the way a pace or two ahead, now pulled up in the middle of the pavement, and in spite of the biting weather, took off his hat and mopped his brow with a red pocket handkerchief. But for all the hurry of his coming, these were not the dews of exertion that he wiped away, but the moisture of some strangling anguish; for his face was white and his voice, when he spoke, harsh and broken.

"Well, sir," he said, "here we are, and God grant there be nothing wrong."

"Amen, Poole," said the lawyer.

Thereupon the servant knocked in a very guarded manner; the door was opened on the chain; and a voice asked from within, "Is that you, Poole?"

"It's all right," said Poole. "Open the door."

The hall, when they entered it, was brightly lighted up; the fire was built high; and about the hearth the whole of the servants, men and women, stood huddled together like a flock of sheep. At the sight of Mr. Utterson, the housemaid broke into hysterical whimpering; and the cook, crying out "Bless God! It's Mr. Utterson," ran forward as if to take him in her arms.

"What, what? Are you all here?" said the lawyer peevishly. "Very irregular, very unseemly; your master would be far from pleased."

"They're all afraid," said Poole.

Blank silence followed, no one protesting; only the maid lifted up her voice and now wept loudly.

"Hold your tongue!" Poole said to her, with a ferocity of accent that testified to his own jangled nerves; and indeed, when the girl had so suddenly raised the note of her lamentation, they had all started and turned towards the inner door with faces of dreadful expectation. "And now," continued the butler, addressing the knife boy, "reach me a candle, and we'll get this through hands at once." And then he begged Mr. Utterson to follow him, and led the way to the back garden.

"Now, sir," said he, "you come as gently as you can. I want you to hear, and I don't want you to be heard. And see here, sir, if by any chance he was to ask you in, don't go."

Mr. Utterson's nerves, at this unlooked-for termination, gave a jerk that nearly threw him from his balance; but he recollected his courage and followed the butler into the laboratory building and through the surgical theatre, with its lumber of crates and bottles, to the foot of the stair. Here Poole motioned him to stand on one side and listen; while he himself, setting down the candle and making a great and obvious call on his resolution, mounted the steps and knocked with a somewhat uncertain hand on the red baize of the cabinet door.

"Mr. Utterson, sir, asking to see you," he called; and even as he did so, once more violently signed to the lawyer to give ear.

A voice answered from within: "Tell him I cannot see anyone," it said complainingly.

"Thank you, sir," said Poole, with a note of something like triumph in his voice; and taking up his candle, he led Mr. Utterson back across the yard and into the great kitchen, where the fire was out and the beetles were leaping on the floor.

"Sir," he said, looking Mr. Utterson in the eyes, "was that my master's voice?"

"It seems much changed," replied the lawyer, very pale, but giving look for look.

"Changed? Well, yes, I think so," said the butler. "Have I been twenty years in this man's house, to be deceived about his voice? No, sir; master's made away with; he was made away with eight days ago, when we heard him cry out upon the name of God; and *who's* in there instead of him, and *why* it stays there, is a thing that cries to Heaven, Mr. Utterson!"

"This is a very strange tale, Poole; this is rather a wild tale, my man," said Mr. Utterson, biting his finger. "Suppose it were as you suppose, supposing Dr. Jekyll to have been—well, murdered, what could induce the murderer to stay? That won't hold water; it doesn't commend itself to reason."

"Well, Mr. Utterson, you are a hard man to satisfy, but I'll do it yet," said Poole. "All this last week (you must know) him, or it, whatever it is that lives in that cabinet, has been crying night and day for some sort of medicine and cannot get it to his mind. It was sometimes his way—the master's, that is—to write his orders on a sheet of paper and throw it on the stair. We've had nothing else this week back; nothing but papers, and a closed door, and the very meals left there to be smuggled in when nobody was looking. Well, sir, every day, ay, and twice and thrice in the same day, there have been orders and complaints, and I have been sent flying to all the wholesale chemists in town. Every time I brought the stuff back, there would be another paper telling me to return it, because it was not pure, and another order to a different firm. This drug is wanted bitter bad, sir, whatever for."

"Have you any of these papers?" asked Mr. Utterson.

Poole felt in his pocket and handed out a crumpled note, which the lawyer, bending nearer to the candle, carefully examined. Its contents ran thus: "Dr. Jekyll presents his compliments to Messrs. Maw. He assures them that their last sample is impure and quite useless for his present purpose. In the year 18—, Dr. J. purchased a somewhat large quantity from Messrs. M. He now begs them to search with most sedulous care, and should any of the same quality be left, to forward it to him at once. Expense is no consideration. The importance of this to Dr. J. can hardly be exaggerated." So far the letter had run composedly enough, but here with a sudden splutter of the pen, the writer's emotions had broken loose. "For God's sake," he added, "find me some of the old."

"This is a strange note," said Mr. Utterson; and then sharply, "How do you come to have it open?"

"The man at Maw's was main angry, sir, and he threw it back to me like so much dirt," returned Poole.

"This is unquestionably the doctor's hand, do you know?" resumed the lawyer.

"I thought it looked like it," said the servant rather sulkily; and then, with another voice, "But what matters hand of write?" he said. "I've seen him!"

"Seen him?" repeated Mr. Utterson. "Well?"

"That's it!" said Poole. "It was this way. I came suddenly into the theatre from the garden. It seems he had slipped out to look for this drug or whatever it is; for the cabinet door was open, and there he was at the far end of the room digging among the crates. He looked up when I came in, gave a kind of cry, and whipped upstairs into the cabinet. It was but for one minute that I saw him, but the hair stood upon my head like quills. Sir, if that was my master, why had he a mask upon his face? If it was my master, why did he cry out like a rat, and run from me? I have served him long enough. And then . . ." The man paused and passed his hand over his face.

"These are all very strange circumstances," said Mr. Utterson, "but I think I begin to see daylight. Your master, Poole, is plainly seized with one of those maladies that both torture and deform the sufferer; hence, for aught I know, the alteration of his voice; hence the mask and the avoidance of his friends; hence his eagerness to find this drug, by means of which the poor soul retains some hope of ultimate recovery—God grant that he be not deceived! There is my explanation; it is sad enough, Poole, ay, and appalling to consider; but it is plain and natural, hangs well together, and delivers us from all exorbitant alarms."

"Sir," said the butler, turning to a sort of mottled pallor, "that thing was not my master, and there's the truth. My master"—here he looked round him and began to whisper—"is a tall, fine build of a man, and this was more of a dwarf." Utterson attempted to protest. "O, sir," cried Poole, "do you think I do not know my master after twenty years? Do you think I do not know where his head comes to in the cabinet door, where I saw him every morning of my life? No, sir, that thing in the mask was never Dr. Jekyll—God knows what it was, but it was never Dr. Jekyll; and it is the belief of my heart that there was murder done."

"Poole," replied the lawyer, "if you say that, it will become my duty to make certain. Much as I desire to spare your master's feelings, much as I am puzzled by this note which seems to prove him to be still alive, I shall consider it my duty to break in that door."

"Ah, Mr. Utterson, that's talking!" cried the butler.

"And now comes the second question," resumed Utterson: "Who is going to do it?"

"Why, you and me, sir," was the undaunted reply.

"That's very well said," returned the lawyer; "and whatever comes of it, I shall make it my business to see you are no loser."

"There is an axe in the theatre," continued Poole; "and you might take the kitchen poker for yourself."

The lawyer took that rude but weighty instrument into his hand, and balanced it. "Do you know, Poole," he said, looking up, "that you and I are about to place ourselves in a position of some peril?"

"You may say so, sir, indeed," returned the butler.

"It is well, then, that we should be frank," said the other. "We both think more than we have said; let us make a clean breast. This masked figure that you saw, did you recognise it?"

"Well, sir, it went so quick, and the creature was so doubled up, that I could hardly swear to that," was the answer. "But if you mean, was it Mr. Hyde?—why, yes, I think it was! You see, it was much of the same bigness; and it had the same quick, light way with it; and then who else could have got in by the laboratory door? You have not forgot, sir, that at the time of the murder he had still the key with him? But that's not all. I don't know, Mr. Utterson, if you ever met this Mr. Hyde?"

"Yes," said the lawyer, "I once spoke with him."

"Then you must know as well as the rest of us that there was something queer about that gentleman—something that gave a man a turn—I don't know rightly how to say it, sir, beyond this: that you felt in your marrow kind of cold and thin."

"I own I felt something of what you describe," said Mr. Utterson.

"Quite so, sir," returned Poole. "Well, when that masked thing like a monkey jumped from among the chemicals and whipped into the cabinet, it went down my spine like ice. O, I know it's not evidence, Mr. Utterson; I'm book-learned enough for that; but a man has his feelings, and I give you my bible word it was Mr. Hyde!"

"Ay, ay," said the lawyer. "My fears incline to the same point. Evil, I fear, founded—evil was sure to come—of that connection. Ay truly, I believe you; I believe poor Harry is killed; and I believe his murderer (for what purpose, God alone can tell) is still lurking in his victim's room. Well, let our name be vengeance. Call Bradshaw."

The footman came at the summons, very white and nervous.

"Pull yourself together, Bradshaw," said the lawyer. "This suspense, I know, is telling upon all of you; but it is now our intention to make an end of it. Poole, here, and I are going to force our way into the cabinet. If all is well, my shoulders are broad enough to bear the blame. Meanwhile, lest anything should really be amiss, or any malefactor seek to escape by the back, you and the boy must go round the corner with a pair of good sticks and take your post at the laboratory door. We give you ten minutes to get to your stations."

As Bradshaw left, the lawyer looked at his watch. "And now, Poole, let us get to ours," he said; and taking the poker under his arm, led the way into the yard. The scud had banked over the moon, and it was now quite dark. The wind, which only broke in puffs and draughts into that deep well of building, tossed the light of the candle to and fro about their steps, until they came into the shelter of the theatre, where they sat down silently to wait. London hummed solemnly all around; but nearer at hand, the stillness was only broken by the sounds of a footfall moving to and fro along the cabinet floor.

"So it will walk all day, sir," whispered Poole; "ay, and the better part of the night. Only when a new sample comes from the chemist, there's a bit of a break. Ah, it's an ill conscience that's such an enemy to rest! Ah, sir, there's blood foully shed in every step of it! But hark again, a little closer—put your heart in your ears, Mr. Utterson, and tell me, is that the doctor's foot?"

The steps fell lightly and oddly, with a certain swing, for all they went so slowly; it was different indeed from the heavy creaking tread of Henry Jekyll. Utterson sighed. "Is there never anything else?" he asked.

Poole nodded. "Once," he said. "Once I heard it weeping!"

"Weeping? How that?" said the lawyer, conscious of a sudden chill of horror.

"Weeping like a woman or a lost soul," said the butler. "I came away with that upon my heart, that I could have wept too."

But now the ten minutes drew to an end. Poole disinterred the axe from under a stack of packing straw; the candle was set upon the nearest table to light them to the attack; and they drew near with bated breath to where that patient foot was still going up and down, up and down, in the quiet of the night. "Jekyll," cried Utterson, with a loud voice, "I demand to see you." He paused a moment, but there came no reply. "I give you fair warning, our suspicions are aroused, and I must and shall see you," he resumed; "if not by fair means, then by foul—if not of your consent, then by brute force!"

"Utterson," said the voice, "for God's sake, have mercy!"

"Ah, that's not Jekyll's voice—it's Hyde's!" cried Utterson. "Down with the door, Poole!"

Poole swung the axe over his shoulder; the blow shook the building, and the red baize door leaped against the lock and hinges. A dismal screech, as of mere animal terror, rang from the cabinet. Up went the axe again, and again the panels crashed and the frame bounded; four times the blow fell; but the wood was tough and the fittings were of excellent workmanship; and it was not until the fifth that the lock burst and the wreck of the door fell inwards on the carpet.

The besiegers, appalled by their own riot and the stillness that had succeeded, stood back a little and peered in. There lay the cabinet before their eyes in the quiet lamplight, a good fire glowing and chattering on the hearth, the kettle singing its thin strain, a drawer or two open, papers neatly set forth on the business table, and nearer the fire, the things laid out for tea; the quietest room, you would have said, and, but for the glazed presses full of chemicals, the most commonplace that night in London.

Right in the midst there lay the body of a man sorely contorted and still twitching. They drew near on tiptoe, turned it on its back and beheld the face of Edward Hyde. He was dressed in clothes far too large for him, clothes of the doctor's bigness; the cords of his face still moved with a semblance of life, but life was quite gone: and by the crushed phial in the hand and the strong smell of kernels that hung upon the air, Utterson knew that he was looking on the body of a self-destroyer.

"We have come too late," he said sternly, "whether to save or punish. Hyde is gone to his account; and it only remains for us to find the body of your master."

The far greater proportion of the building was occupied by the theatre, which filled almost the whole ground storey and was lighted from above, and by the cabinet, which formed an upper storey at one end and looked upon the court. A corridor joined the theatre to the door on the bystreet; and with this the cabinet communicated separately by a second flight of stairs. There were, besides, a few dark closets and a spacious cellar. All these they now thoroughly examined. Each closet needed but a glance, for all were empty, and all, by the dust that fell from their doors, had stood long unopened. The cellar, indeed, was filled with crazy lumber, mostly dating from the times of the surgeon who was Jekyll's predecessor; but even as they opened the door they were advertised of the uselessness of further search, by the fall of a perfect mat of cobweb which had for years sealed up the entrance. Nowhere was there any trace of Henry Jekyll, dead or alive.

Poole stamped on the flags of the corridor. "He must be buried here," he said, hearkening to the sound.

"Or he may have fled," said Utterson, and he turned to examine the door in the bystreet. It was locked; and lying nearby on the flags, they found the key, already stained with rust.

"This does not look like use," observed the lawyer.

"Use!" echoed Poole. "Do you not see, sir, it is broken?—much as if a man had stamped on it."

"Ay," continued Utterson, "and the fractures, too, are rusty." The two men looked at each other with a scare. "This is beyond me, Poole," said the lawyer. "Let us go back to the cabinet."

They mounted the stair in silence, and still with an occasional awestruck glance at the dead body, proceeded more thoroughly to examine the contents of the cabinet. At one table, there were traces of chemical work, various measured heaps of some white salt being laid on glass saucers, as though for an experiment in which the unhappy man had been prevented.

"That is the same drug that I was always bringing him," said Poole; and even as he spoke, the kettle with a startling noise boiled over.

This brought them to the fireside, where the easy chair was drawn cosily up, and the tea things stood ready to the sitter's elbow, the very sugar in the cup. There were several books on a shelf; one lay beside the

There lay the body of a man sorely contorted
and still twitching.

tea things open, and Utterson was amazed to find it a copy of a pious work, for which Jekyll had several times expressed a great esteem, annotated, in his own hand, with startling blasphemies.

Next, in the course of their review of the chamber, the searchers came to the cheval glass, into whose depths they looked with an involuntary horror. But it was so turned as to show them nothing but the rosy glow playing on the roof, the fire sparkling in a hundred repetitions along the glazed front of the presses, and their own pale and fearful countenances stooping to look in.

"This glass has seen some strange things, sir," whispered Poole.

"And surely none stranger than itself," echoed the lawyer in the same tone. "For what did Jekyll" — he caught himself up at the word with a start, and then conquering the weakness — "what could Jekyll want with it?" he said.

"You may say that!" said Poole.

Next they turned to the business table. On the desk, among the neat array of papers, a large envelope was uppermost, and bore, in the doctor's hand, the name of Mr. Utterson. The lawyer unsealed it, and several enclosures fell to the floor. The first was a will, drawn in the same eccentric terms as the one which he had returned six months before, to serve as a testament in case of death and as a deed of gift in case of disappearance; but in place of the name of Edward Hyde, the lawyer, with indescribable amazement, read the name of Gabriel John Utterson. He looked at Poole, and then back at the paper, and last of all at the dead malefactor stretched upon the carpet.

"My head goes round," he said. "He has been all these days in possession; he had no cause to like me; he must have raged to see himself displaced; and he has not destroyed this document."

He caught up the next paper; it was a brief note in the doctor's hand and dated at the top. "O Poole!" the lawyer cried, "he was alive and here this day. He cannot have been disposed of in so short a space; he must be still alive, he must have fled! And then, why fled? And how? And in that case, can we venture to declare this suicide? O, we must be careful. I foresee that we may yet involve your master in some dire catastrophe."

"Why don't you read it, sir?" asked Poole.

"Because I fear," replied the lawyer solemnly. "God grant I have no cause for it!" And with that he brought the paper to his eyes and read as follows:

My dear Utterson—When this shall fall into your hands, I shall have disappeared, under what circumstances I have not the penetration to foresee, but my instinct and all the circumstances of my nameless situation tell me that the end is sure and must be early. Go then, and first read the narrative which Lanyon warned me he was to place in your hands; and if you care to hear more, turn to the confession of
                    Your unworthy and unhappy friend,
                              HENRY JEKYLL.

"There was a third enclosure?" asked Utterson.

"Here, sir," said Poole, and gave into his hands a considerable packet sealed in several places.

The lawyer put it in his pocket. "I would say nothing of this paper. If your master has fled or is dead, we may at least save his credit. It is now ten; I must go home and read these documents in quiet; but I shall be back before midnight, when we shall send for the police."

They went out, locking the door of the theatre behind them; and Utterson, once more leaving the servants gathered about the fire in the hall, trudged back to his office to read the two narratives in which this mystery was now to be explained.

Dr. Lanyon's Narrative

ON THE NINTH OF January, now four days ago, I received by the evening delivery a registered envelope, addressed in the hand of my colleague and old school companion, Henry Jekyll. I was a good deal surprised by this; for we were by no means in the habit of correspondence; I had seen the man, dined with him, indeed, the night before; and I could imagine nothing in our intercourse that should justify formality of registration. The contents increased my wonder; for this is how the letter ran:

10th December, 18——.

Dear Lanyon——You are one of my oldest friends; and although we may have differed at times on scientific questions, I cannot remember, at least on my side, any break in our affection. There was never a day when, if you had said to me, "Jekyll, my life, my honour, my reason, depend upon you," I would not have sacrificed my left hand to help you. Lanyon, my life, my honour, my reason, are all at your mercy; if you fail me tonight, I am lost. You might suppose, after this preface, that I am going to ask you for something dishonourable to grant. Judge for yourself.

I want you to postpone all other engagements for tonight——ay, even if you were summoned to the bedside of an emperor; to take a cab, unless your carriage should be actually at the door; and with this letter in your hand for consultation, to drive straight to my house. Poole, my butler, has his orders; you will find him waiting your arrival with a locksmith. The door of my cabinet is then to be forced: and you are to go in alone; to open the glazed press (letter E) on the left hand, breaking the lock if it be shut; and to draw out, with all its contents as they stand, *the fourth drawer from the top or (which is the same thing) the third from the bottom. In my extreme distress of mind, I have a morbid fear of misdirecting you; but even if I am in error, you may know the right drawer by its contents: some powders, a phial and a paper book. This drawer I beg of you to carry back with you to Cavendish Square exactly as it stands.*

That is the first part of the service: now for the second. You should be back, if you set out at once on the receipt of this, long before midnight; but I will leave you that amount of margin, not only in the fear of one of those obstacles that can neither be prevented nor foreseen, but because an hour when your servants are in bed is to be preferred for what will then remain to do. At midnight, then, I have to ask you to be alone in your consulting room, to admit with your own hand into the house a man who will present himself in my name, and to place in his hands the drawer that you will have brought with you from my cabinet. Then you will have played your part and earned my gratitude completely. Five minutes afterwards, if you insist upon an explanation, you will have understood that these arrangements are of capital importance; and that by the neglect of one of them, fantastic as they must appear, you might have charged your conscience with my death or the shipwreck of my reason.

Confident as I am that you will not trifle with this appeal, my heart sinks and my hand trembles at the bare thought of such a possibility. Think of me at this hour, in a strange place, labouring under a blackness of distress that no fancy can exaggerate, and yet well aware that, if you will but punctually serve me, my troubles will roll away like a story that is told. Serve me, my dear Lanyon, and save

Your friend,
H. J.

P.S. I had already sealed this up when a fresh terror struck upon my soul. It is possible that the post office may fail me, and this letter not come into your hands until tomorrow morning. In that case, dear Lanyon, do my errand when it shall be most convenient for you in the course of the day; and once more expect my messenger at midnight. It may then already be too late; and if that night passes without event, you will know that you have seen the last of Henry Jekyll.

Upon the reading of this letter, I made sure my colleague was insane; but till that was proved beyond the possibility of doubt, I felt bound to do as he requested. The less I understood of this farrago, the less I was in a position to judge of its importance; and an appeal so worded could not be set aside without a grave responsibility. I rose accordingly from table, got into a hansom, and drove straight to Jekyll's house. The butler was awaiting my arrival; he had received by the same post as mine a registered letter of instruction, and had sent at once for a locksmith and a carpenter. The tradesmen came while we were yet speaking; and we moved in a body to old Dr. Denman's surgical theatre, from which (as you are doubtless aware) Jekyll's private cabinet is most conveniently entered. The door was very strong, the lock excellent; the carpenter avowed he would have great trouble and have to do much damage, if force were to be used; and the locksmith was near despair. But this last was a handy fellow, and after two hours' work, the door stood open. The press marked E was unlocked; and I took out the drawer, had it filled up with straw and tied in a sheet, and returned with it to Cavendish Square.

Here I proceeded to examine its contents. The powders were neatly enough made up, but not with the nicety of the dispensing chemist; so that it was plain they were of Jekyll's private manufacture: and when I opened one of the wrappers I found what seemed to me a simple crystalline salt of a white colour. The phial, to which I next turned my attention, might have been about half-full of a bloodred liquor, which was highly pungent to the sense of smell and seemed to me to contain phosphorus and some volatile ether. At the other ingredients I could make no guess. The book was an ordinary version book and contained little but a series of dates. These covered a period of many years, but I observed that the entries ceased nearly a year ago and quite abruptly. Here and there a brief remark was appended to a date, usually no more than a single word: "double" occurring perhaps six times in a total of several hundred entries; and once very early in the list and followed by several marks of exclamation, "total failure!!!" All this, though it whetted my curiosity, told me little that was definite. Here were a phial of some tincture, a paper of some salt, and the record of a series of experiments that had led (like too many of Jekyll's investigations) to no end of practical usefulness. How could the presence of these articles in my house affect either the honour, the sanity, or the life of my flighty colleague? If his messenger could go to one place, why could he not go to another? And even granting some impediment, why was this gentleman to be received by me in secret? The more I reflected the more convinced I grew that I was dealing with a case of cerebral disease; and though I dismissed my servants to bed, I loaded an old revolver, that I might be found in some posture of self-defence.

Twelve o'clock had scarce rung out over London, ere the knocker sounded very gently on the door. I went myself at the summons, and found a small man crouching against the pillars of the portico.

"Are you come from Dr. Jekyll?" I asked.

He told me "yes" by a constrained gesture; and when I had bidden him enter, he did not obey me without a searching backward glance into the darkness of the square. There was a policeman not far off, advancing with his bull's eye open; and at the sight, I thought my visitor started and made greater haste.

These particulars struck me, I confess, disagreeably; and as I followed him into the bright light of the consulting room, I kept my hand ready on my weapon. Here, at last, I had a chance of clearly seeing him. I had never set eyes on him before, so much was certain. He was small, as I have said; I was struck besides with the shocking expression of his face, with his remarkable combination of great muscular activity and great apparent debility of constitution, and—last but not least—with the odd, subjective disturbance caused by his neighbourhood. This bore some resemblance to incipient rigour, and was accompanied by a marked sinking of the pulse. At the time, I set it down to some idiosyncratic, personal distaste, and merely wondered at the acuteness of the symptoms; but I have since had reason to believe the cause to lie much deeper in the nature of man, and to turn on some nobler hinge than the principle of hatred.

This person (who had thus, from the first moment of his entrance, struck in me what I can only describe as a disgustful curiosity) was dressed in a fashion that would have made an ordinary person laughable; his clothes, that is to say, although they were of rich and sober fabric, were enormously too large for him in every measurement—the trousers hanging on his legs and rolled up to keep them from the ground, the waist of the coat below his haunches, and the collar sprawling wide upon his shoulders. Strange to relate, this ludicrous accoutrement was far from moving me to laughter. Rather, as there was something abnormal and misbegotten in the very essence of the creature that now faced me— something seizing, surprising and revolting—this fresh disparity seemed but to fit in with and to reinforce it; so that to my interest in the man's nature and character, there was added a curiosity as to his origin, his life, his fortune and status in the world.

These observations, though they have taken so great a space to be set down in, were yet the work of a few seconds. My visitor was, indeed, on fire with sombre excitement.

"Have you got it?" he cried. "Have you got it?" And so lively was his impatience that he even laid his hand upon my arm and sought to shake me.

I put him back, conscious at his touch of a certain icy pang along my blood. "Come, sir," said I. "You forget that I have not yet the pleasure of your acquaintance. Be seated, if you please." And I showed him an example, and sat down myself in my customary seat and with as fair an imitation of my ordinary manner to a patient, as the lateness of the hour, the nature of my preoccupations, and the horror I had of my visitor would suffer me to muster.

"I beg your pardon, Dr. Lanyon," he replied civilly enough. "What you say is very well founded; and my impatience has shown its heels to my politeness. I come here at the instance of your colleague, Dr. Henry Jekyll, on a piece of business of some moment; and I understood . . ." He paused and put his hand to his throat, and I could see, in spite of his collected manner, that he was wrestling against the approaches of the hysteria—"I understood, a drawer . . ."

But here I took pity on my visitor's suspense, and some, perhaps, on my own growing curiosity.

"There it is, sir," said I, pointing to the drawer, where it lay on the floor behind a table and still covered with the sheet.

He sprang to it, and then paused, and laid his hand upon his heart: I could hear his teeth grate with the convulsive action of his jaws; and his face was so ghastly to see that I grew alarmed both for his life and reason.

"Compose yourself," said I.

He turned a dreadful smile to me, and as if with the decision of despair, plucked away the sheet. At sight of the contents, he uttered one loud sob of such immense relief that I sat petrified. And the next moment, in a voice that was already fairly well under control, "Have you a graduated glass?" he asked.

I rose from my place with something of an effort and gave him what he asked.

He thanked me with a smiling nod, measured out a few minims of the red tincture and added one of the powders. The mixture, which was at first of a reddish hue, began, in proportion as the crystals melted, to brighten in colour, to effervesce audibly, and to throw off small fumes of vapour. Suddenly and at the same moment, the ebullition ceased and the compound changed to a dark purple, which faded again more slowly to a watery green. My visitor, who had watched these metamorphoses with a keen eye, smiled, set down the glass upon the table, and then turned and looked upon me with an air of scrutiny.

"And now," said he, "to settle what remains. Will you be wise? Will you be guided? Will you suffer me to take this glass in my hand and to go forth from your house without further parley? Or has the greed of curiosity too much command of you? Think before you answer, for it shall be done as you decide. As you decide, you shall be left as you were before, and neither richer nor wiser, unless the sense of service rendered to a man in mortal distress may be counted as a kind of riches of the soul. Or, if you shall so prefer to choose, a new province of knowledge and new avenues to fame and power shall be laid open to you, here, in this room, upon the instant; and your sight shall be blasted by a prodigy to stagger the unbelief of Satan."

"Sir," said I, affecting a coolness that I was far from truly possessing, "you speak enigmas, and you will perhaps not wonder that I hear you with no very strong impression of belief. But I have gone too far in the way of inexplicable services to pause before I see the end."

"It is well," replied my visitor. "Lanyon, you remember your vows: what follows is under the seal of our profession. And now, you who have so long been bound to the most narrow and material views, you who have denied the virtue of transcendental medicine, you who have derided your superiors—behold!"

He put the glass to his lips and drank at one gulp. A cry followed; he reeled, staggered, clutched at the table and held on, staring with injected eyes, gasping with open mouth; and as I looked there came, I thought, a change—he seemed to swell—his face became suddenly black and the features seemed to melt and alter—and the next moment, I had sprung to my feet and leaped back against the wall, my arm raised to shield me from that prodigy, my mind submerged in terror.

"O God!" I screamed, and "O God!" again and again; for there before my eyes—pale and shaken, and half-fainting, and groping before him with his hands, like a man restored from death—there stood Henry Jekyll!

What he told me in the next hour, I cannot bring my mind to set on paper. I saw what I saw, I heard what I heard, and my soul sickened at it; and yet now when that sight has faded from my eyes, I ask myself if I believe it, and I cannot answer. My life is shaken to its roots; sleep has left me; the deadliest terror sits by me at all hours of the day and night; and I feel that my days are numbered, and that I must die; and yet I shall die incredulous. As for the moral turpitude that man unveiled to me, even with tears of penitence, I cannot, even in memory, dwell on it without a start of horror. I will say but one thing, Utterson, and that (if you can bring your mind to credit it) will be more than enough. The creature who crept into my house that night was, on Jekyll's own confession, known by the name of Hyde and hunted for in every corner of the land as the murderer of Carew.

HASTIE LANYON

Henry Jekyll's Full Statement of the Case

I WAS BORN IN the year 18— to a large fortune, endowed besides with excellent parts, inclined by nature to industry, fond of the respect of the wise and good among my fellowmen, and thus, as might have been supposed, with every guarantee of an honourable and distinguished future. And indeed the worst of my faults was a certain impatient gaiety of disposition, such as has made the happiness of many, but such as I found it hard to reconcile with my imperious desire to carry my head high, and wear a more than commonly grave countenance before the public. Hence it came about that I concealed my pleasures; and that when I reached years of reflection, and began to look round me and take stock of my progress and position in the world, I stood already committed to a profound duplicity of life. Many a man would have even blazoned such irregularities as I was guilty of; but from the high views that I had set before me, I regarded and hid them with an almost morbid sense of shame. It was thus rather the exacting nature of my aspirations than any particular degradation in my faults that made me what I was, and, with even a deeper trench than in the majority of men, severed in me those provinces of good and ill which divide and compound man's dual nature. In this case, I was driven to reflect deeply and inveterately on that hard law of life, which lies at the root of religion and is one of the most plentiful springs of distress. Though so profound a double dealer, I was in no sense a hypocrite; both sides of me were in dead earnest; I was no more myself when I laid aside restraint and plunged in shame, than when I laboured, in the eye of day, at the furtherance of knowledge or the relief of sorrow and suffering. And it chanced that the direction of my scientific studies, which led wholly towards the mystic and the transcendental, reacted and shed a strong light on this consciousness of the perennial war among my members. With every day, and from both sides of my intelligence, the moral and the intellectual, I thus drew steadily nearer to that truth by whose partial discovery I have been doomed to such a dreadful shipwreck: that man is not truly one, but truly two. I say two, because the state of my own knowledge does not pass beyond that point. Others will follow, others will outstrip me on the same lines; and I hazard the guess that man will be ultimately known for a mere polity of multifarious, incongruous and independent denizens. I, for my part, from the nature of my life, advanced infallibly in one direction and in one direction only. It was on the moral side, and in my own person, that I learned to recognize the thorough and primitive duality of man; I saw that, of the two natures that contended in the field of my consciousness, even if I could rightly be said to be either, it was only because I was radically both; and from an early date, even before the course of my scientific discoveries had begun to suggest the most naked possibility of such a miracle, I had learned to dwell with pleasure, as a beloved daydream, on the thought of the separation of these elements. If each, I told myself, could be housed in separate identities, life would be relieved of all that was unbearable; the unjust might go his way, delivered from the aspirations and remorse of his more upright twin; and the just could walk steadfastly and securely on his upward path, doing the good things in which he found his pleasure, and no longer exposed to disgrace and penitence by the hands of this extraneous evil. It was the curse of mankind that these incongruous faggots were thus bound together—that in the agonised womb of consciousness, these polar twins should be continuously struggling. How, then, were they dissociated?

I was so far in my reflection when, as I have said, a sidelight began to shine upon the subject from the laboratory table. I began to perceive more deeply than it has ever yet been stated, the trembling immateriality, the mist-like transience, of this seemingly so solid body in which we walk attired. Certain agents I found to have the power to shake and pluck back that fleshly vestment, even as a wind might toss the curtains of a pavilion. For two good reasons, I will not enter deeply into this scientific branch of my confession. First, because I have been made to learn that the doom and burthen of our life is bound forever on man's shoulders, and when the attempt is made to cast it off, it but returns upon us with more unfamiliar and more awful pressure. Second, because, as my narrative will make, alas! too evident, my discoveries were incomplete. Enough, then, that I not only recognized my natural body from the mere aura and effulgence of certain of the powers that made up my spirit, but managed to compound a drug by which these powers should be dethroned from their supremacy, and a second form and countenance substituted, none the less natural to me because they were the expression, and bore the stamp of lower elements in my soul.

I hesitated long before I put this theory to the test of practice. I knew well that I risked death; for any drug that so potently controlled and shook the very fortress of identity, might, by the least scruple of an overdose or at the least inopportunity in the moment of exhibition, utterly blot out that immaterial tabernacle which I looked to it to change. But the temptation of a discovery so singular and profound at last overcame the suggestions of alarm. I had long since prepared my tincture; I purchased at once, from a firm of wholesale chemists, a large quantity of a particular salt which I knew, from my experiments, to be the last ingredient required; and late one accursed night, I compounded the elements, watched them boil and smoke together in the glass, and when the ebullition had subsided, with a strong glow of courage, drank off the potion.

The most racking pangs succeeded: a grinding in the bones, deadly nausea, and a horror of the spirit that cannot be exceeded at the hour of birth or death. Then these agonies began swiftly to subside, and I came to myself as if out of a great sickness. There was something strange in my sensations, something indescribably new and, from its very novelty, incredibly sweet. I felt younger, lighter, happier in body; within, I was conscious of a heady recklessness, a current of disordered sensual images running like a millrace in my fancy, a solution of the bonds of obligation, an unknown but not an innocent freedom of the soul. I knew myself, at the first breath of this new life, to be more wicked, tenfold more wicked, sold a slave to my original evil; and the thought, in that moment, braced and delighted me like wine. I stretched out my hands, exulting in the freshness of these sensations; and in the act, I was suddenly aware that I had lost in stature.

There was no mirror at that date, in my room; that which stands beside me as I write was brought there later on and for the very purpose of these transformations. The night, however, was far gone into the morning—the morning, black as it was, was nearly ripe for the conception of the day—the inmates of my house were locked in the most rigorous hours of slumber; and I determined, flushed as I was with hope and triumph, to venture in my new shape as far as to my bedroom. I crossed the yard, wherein the constellations looked down upon me, I could have thought, with wonder, the first creature of that sort that their unsleeping vigilance had yet disclosed to them; I stole through the corridors, a stranger in my own house; and coming to my room, I saw for the first time the appearance of Edward Hyde.

I must here speak by theory alone, saying not that which I know, but that which I suppose to be most probable. The evil side of my nature, to which I had now transferred the stamping efficacy, was less robust and less developed than the good which I had just deposed. Again, in the course of my life, which had been, after all, nine-tenths a life of effort, virtue and control, it had been much less exercised and much less exhausted. And hence, as I think, it came about that Edward Hyde was so much smaller, slighter and younger than Henry Jekyll. Even as good shone upon the countenance of the one, evil was written broadly and plainly on the face of the other. Evil besides (which I must still believe to be the lethal side of man) had left on that body an imprint of deformity and decay. And yet when I looked upon that ugly idol in the glass, I was conscious of no repugnance, rather of a leap of welcome. This, too, was myself. It seemed natural and human. In my eyes it bore a livelier image of the spirit, it seemed more express and single, than the imperfect and divided countenance I had been hitherto accustomed to call mine. And insofar I was doubtless right. I have observed that when I wore the semblance of Edward Hyde, none could come near to me at first without a visible misgiving of the flesh. This, as I take it, was because all human beings, as we meet them, are commingled out of good and evil: and Edward Hyde, alone in the ranks of mankind, was pure evil.

I lingered but a moment at the mirror: the second and conclusive experiment had yet to be attempted; it yet remained to be seen if I had lost my identity beyond redemption and must flee before daylight from a house that was no longer mine; and hurrying back to my cabinet, I once more prepared and drank the cup, once more suffered the pangs of dissolution, and came to myself once more with the character, the stature and the face of Henry Jekyll.

That night I had come to the fatal crossroads. Had I approached my discovery in a more noble spirit, had I risked the experiment while under the empire of generous or pious aspirations, all must have been other-wise, and from these agonies of death and birth, I had come forth an angel instead of a fiend. The drug had no discriminating action; it was neither diabolical nor divine; it but shook the doors of the prisonhouse of my disposition; and like the captives of Philippi, that which stood within ran forth. At that time my virtue slumbered; my evil, kept awake by ambition, was alert and swift to seize the occasion; and the thing that was projected was Edward Hyde. Hence, although I had now two characters as well as two appearances, one was wholly evil, and the other was still the old Henry Jekyll, that incongruous compound of whose reformation and improvement I had already learned to despair. The movement was thus wholly toward the worse.

Even at that time, I had not yet conquered my aversion to the dryness of a life of study. I would still be merrily disposed at times; and as my pleasures were (to say the least) undignified, and I was not only well-known and highly considered, but growing towards the elderly man, this incoherency of my life was daily growing more unwelcome. It was on this side that my new power tempted me until I fell in slavery. I had but to drink the cup, to doff at once the body of the noted professor, and to assume, like a thick cloak, that of Edward Hyde. I smiled at the notion; it seemed to me at the time to be humorous; and I made my preparations with the most studious care. I took and furnished that house in Soho, to which Hyde was tracked by the police; and engaged as a housekeeper a creature whom I knew well to be silent and unscrupulous. On the other side, I announced to my servants that a Mr. Hyde (whom I described) was to have full liberty and power about my house in the square; and to parry mishaps, I even called and made myself a familiar object in my second character. I next drew up that will to which you so much objected; so that if anything befell me in the person of Dr. Jekyll, I could enter on that of Edward Hyde without pecuniary loss. And thus fortified, as I supposed, on every side, I began to profit by the strange immunities of my position.

Men have before hired bravos to transact their crimes, while their own person and reputation sat under shelter. I was the first that ever did so for his pleasures. I was the first that could thus plod in the public eye with a load of genial respectability, and in a moment, like a schoolboy, strip off these lendings and spring headlong into the sea of liberty. But for me, in my impenetrable mantle, the safety was complete. Think of it—I did not even exist! Let me but escape into my laboratory door, give me but a second or two to mix and swallow the draught that I had always standing ready; and whatever he had done, Edward Hyde would pass away like the stain of breath upon a mirror; and there in his stead, quietly at home, trimming the midnight lamp in his study, a man who could afford to laugh at suspicion, would be Henry Jekyll.

The pleasures which I made haste to seek in my disguise were, as I have said, undignified; I would scarce use a harder term. But in the hands of Edward Hyde, they soon began to turn towards the monstrous. When I would come back from these excursions, I was often plunged into a kind of wonder at my vicarious depravity. This familiar that I called out of my own soul, and sent forth alone to do his good pleasure, was a being inherently malign and villainous; his every act and thought centred on self; drinking pleasure with bestial avidity from any degree of torture to another; relentless like a man of stone. Henry Jekyll stood at times aghast before the acts of Edward Hyde; but the situation was apart from ordinary laws, and insidiously relaxed the grasp of conscience. It was Hyde, after all, and Hyde alone, that was guilty. Jekyll was no worse; he woke again to his good qualities seemingly unimpaired; he would even make haste, where it was possible, to undo the evil done by Hyde. And thus his conscience slumbered.

Into the details of the infamy at which I thus connived (for even now I can scarce grant that I committed it) I have no design of entering; I mean but to point out the warnings and the successive steps with which my chastisement approached. I met with one accident which, as it brought on no consequence, I shall no more than mention. An act of cruelty to a child aroused against me the anger of a passer-by, whom I recognised the other day in the person of your kinsman; the doctor and the child's family joined him; there were moments when I feared for my life; and at last, in order to pacify their too just resentment, Edward Hyde had to bring them to the door, and pay them in a cheque drawn in the name of Henry Jekyll. But this danger was easily eliminated from the future, by opening an account at another bank in the name of Edward Hyde himself; and when, by sloping my own hand backwards, I had supplied my double with a signature, I thought I sat beyond the reach of fate.

Some two months before the murder of Sir Danvers, I had been out for one of my adventures, had returned at a late hour, and woke the next day in bed with somewhat odd sensations. It was in vain I looked about me; in vain I saw the decent furniture and tall proportions of my room in the square; in vain that I recognised the pattern of the bed curtains and the design of the mahogany frame; something still kept insisting that I was not where I was, that I had not wakened where I seemed to be, but in the little room in Soho where I was accustomed to sleep in the body of Edward Hyde. I smiled to myself, and, in my psychological way, began lazily to inquire into the elements of this illusion, occasionally, even as I did so, dropping back into a comfortable morning doze. I was still so engaged when, in one of my more wakeful moments, my eyes fell upon my hand. Now the hand of Henry Jekyll (as you have often remarked) was professional in shape and size: it was large, firm, white and comely. But the hand which I now saw, clearly enough, in the yellow light of a mid-London morning, lying half-shut on the bedclothes, was lean, corded, knuckly, of a dusky pallor and thickly shaded with a swart growth of hair. It was the hand of Edward Hyde.

I must have stared upon it for near half a minute, sunk as I was in the mere stupidity of wonder, before terror woke up in my breast as sudden and startling as the crash of cymbals; and bounding from my bed, I rushed to the mirror. At the sight that met my eyes, my blood was changed into something exquisitely thin and icy. Yes, I had gone to bed Henry Jekyll, I had awakened Edward Hyde. How was this to be explained? I asked myself; and then, with another bound of terror—how was it to be remedied? It was well on in the morning; the servants were up; all my drugs were in the cabinet—a long journey down two pairs of stairs, through the back passage, across the open court and through the anatomical theatre, from where I was then standing horror-struck. It might indeed be possible to cover my face; but of what use was that, when I was unable to conceal the alteration in my stature? And then with an overpowering sweetness of relief, it came back upon my mind that the servants were already used to the coming and going of my second self. I had soon dressed, as well as I was able, in clothes of my own size: had soon passed through the house, where Bradshaw stared and drew back at seeing Mr. Hyde at such an hour and in such a strange array; and ten minutes later, Dr. Jekyll had returned to his own shape and was sitting down, with a darkened brow, to make a feint of breakfasting.

Small indeed was my appetite. This inexplicable incident, this reversal of my previous experience, seemed, like the Babylonian finger on the wall, to be spelling out the letters of my judgment; and I began to reflect more seriously than ever before on the issues and possibilities of my double existence. That part of me which I had the power of projecting had lately been much exercised and nourished; it had seemed to me of late as though the body of Edward Hyde had grown in stature, as though (when I wore that form) I were conscious of a more generous tide of blood; and I began to spy a danger that, if this were much prolonged, the balance of my nature might be permanently overthrown, the power of voluntary change be forfeited, and the character of Edward Hyde become irrevocably mine. The power of the drug had not been always equally displayed. Once, very early in my career, it had totally failed me; since then I had been obliged on more than one occasion to double, and once, with infinite risk of death, to treble the amount; and these rare uncertainties had cast hitherto the sole shadow on my contentment. Now, however, and in the light of that morning's accident, I was led to remark that whereas, in the beginning, the difficulty had been to throw off the body of Jekyll, it had of late gradually but decidedly transferred itself to the other side. All things therefore seemed to point to this; that I was slowly losing hold of my original and better self, and becoming slowly incorporated with my second and worse.

Between these two, I now felt I had to choose. My two natures had memory in common, but all other faculties were most unequally shared between them. Jekyll (who was composite) now with the most sensitive apprehensions, now with a greedy gusto, projected and shared in the pleasures and adventures of Hyde; but Hyde was indifferent to Jekyll, or but remembered him as the mountain bandit remembers the cavern in which he conceals himself from pursuit. Jekyll had more than a father's interest; Hyde had more than a son's indifference. To cast in my lot with Jekyll was to die to those appetites which I had long secretly indulged and had of late begun to pamper. To cast it in with Hyde was to die to a thousand interests and aspirations, and to become, at a blow and forever, despised and friendless. The bargain might appear unequal; but there was still another consideration in the scales; for while Jekyll would suffer smartingly in the fires of abstinence, Hyde would be not even conscious of all that he had lost. Strange as my circumstances were, the terms of this debate are as old and commonplace as man; much the same inducements and alarms cast the die for any tempted and trembling sinner; and it fell out with me, as it falls with so vast a majority of my fellows, that I chose the better part and was found wanting in the strength to keep to it.

Yes, I preferred the elderly and discontented doctor, surrounded by friends and cherishing honest hopes; and bade a resolute farewell to the liberty, the comparative youth, the light step, leaping impulses and secret pleasures, that I had enjoyed in the disguise of Hyde. I made this choice perhaps with some unconscious reservation, for I neither gave up the house in Soho, nor destroyed the clothes of Edward Hyde, which still lay ready in my cabinet. For two months, however, I was true to my determination; for two months, I led a life of such severity as I had never before attained to, and enjoyed the compensations of an approving conscience. But time began at last to obliterate the freshness of my alarm; the praises of conscience began to grow into a thing of course; I began to be tortured with throes and longings, as of Hyde struggling after freedom; and at last, in an hour of moral weakness, I once again compounded and swallowed the transforming draught.

I do not suppose that, when a drunkard reasons with himself upon his vice, he is once out of five hundred times affected by the dangers that he runs through his brutish, physical insensibility; neither had I, long as I had considered my position, made enough allowance for the complete moral insensibility and insensate readiness to evil which were the leading characters of Edward Hyde. Yet it was by these that I was punished. My devil had been long caged, he came out roaring. I was conscious, even when I took the draught, of a more unbridled, a more furious propensity to ill. It must have been this, I suppose, that stirred in my soul that tempest of impatience with which I listened to the civilities of my unhappy victim; I declare, at least, before God, no man morally sane could have been guilty of that crime upon so pitiful a provocation; and that I struck in no more reasonable spirit than that in which a sick child may break a plaything. But I had voluntarily stripped myself of all those balancing instincts by which even the worst of us continues to walk with some degree of steadiness among temptations; and in my case, to be tempted, however slightly, was to fall.

Instantly the spirit of hell awoke in me and raged. With a transport of glee, I mauled the unresisting body, tasting delight from every blow; and it was not till weariness had begun to succeed that I was suddenly, in the top fit of my delirium, struck through the heart by a cold thrill of terror. A mist dispersed; I saw my life to be forfeit; and fled from the scene of these excesses, at once glorying and trembling, my lust of evil gratified and stimulated, my love of life screwed to the topmost peg. I ran to the house in Soho, and (to make assurance doubly sure) destroyed my papers; thence I set out through the lamplit streets, in the same divided ecstasy of mind, gloating on my crime, light-headedly devising others in the future, and yet still hastening and still hearkening in my wake for the steps of the avenger. Hyde had a song upon his lips as he compounded the draught, and as he drank it, pledged the dead man. The pangs of transformation had not done tearing him, before Henry Jekyll, with streaming tears of gratitude and remorse, had fallen upon his knees and lifted his clasped hands to God. The veil of self-indulgence was rent from head to foot. I saw my life as a whole: I followed it up from the days of childhood, when I had walked with my father's hand, and through the self-denying toils of my professional life, to arrive again and again, with the same sense of unreality, at the damned horrors of the evening. I could have screamed aloud; I sought with tears and prayers to smother down the crowd of hideous images and sounds with which my memory swarmed against me; and still, between the petitions, the ugly face of my iniquity stared into my soul. As the acuteness of this remorse began to die away, it was succeeded by a sense of joy. The problem of my conduct was solved. Hyde was thenceforth impossible; whether I would or not, I was now confined to the better part of my existence; and O, how I rejoiced to think of it! With what willing humility I embraced anew the restrictions of natural life! With what sincere renunciation I locked the door by which I had so often gone and come, and ground the key under my heel!

The next day came the news that the murder had been overlooked, that the guilt of Hyde was patent to the world, and that the victim was a man high in public estimation. It was not only a crime, it had been a tragic folly. I think I was glad to know it; I think I was glad to have my better impulses thus buttressed and guarded by the terrors of the scaffold. Jekyll was now my city of refuge; let but Hyde peep out an instant, and the hands of all men would be raised to take and slay him.

I resolved in my future conduct to redeem the past; and I can say with honesty that my resolve was fruitful of some good. You know yourself how earnestly, in the last months of the last year, I laboured to relieve suffering; you know that much was done for others, and that the days passed quietly, almost happily for myself. Nor can I truly say that I wearied of this beneficent and innocent life; I think instead that I daily enjoyed it more completely; but I was still cursed with my duality of purpose; and as the first edge of my penitence wore off, the lower side of me, so long indulged, so recently chained down, began to growl for licence. Not that I dreamed of resuscitating Hyde; the bare idea of that would startle me to frenzy: no, it was in my own person that I was once more tempted to trifle with my conscience; and it was as an ordinary secret sinner that I at last fell before the assaults of temptation.

There comes an end to all things; the most capacious measure is filled at last; and this brief condescension to my evil finally destroyed the balance of my soul. And yet I was not alarmed; the fall seemed natural, like a return to the old days before I had made my discovery. It was a fine, clear, January day, wet underfoot where the frost had melted, but cloudless overhead; and the Regent's Park was full of winter chirrupings and sweet with spring odours. I sat in the sun on a bench; the animal within me licking the chops of memory; the spiritual side a little drowsed, promising subsequent penitence, but not yet moved to begin. After all, I reflected, I was like my neighbours; and then I smiled, comparing myself with other men, comparing my active good will with the lazy cruelty of their neglect. And at the very moment of that vainglorious thought, a qualm came over me, a horrid nausea and the most deadly shuddering. These passed away, and left me faint; and then as, in turn, faintness subsided, I began to be aware of a change in the temper of my thoughts, a greater boldness, a contempt of danger, a solution of the bonds of obligation. I looked down; my clothes hung formlessly on my shrunken limbs; the hand that lay on my knee was corded and hairy. I was once more Edward Hyde. A moment before I had been safe of all men's respect, wealthy, beloved—the cloth laying for me in the dining room at home; and now I was the common quarry of mankind, hunted, houseless, a known murderer, thrall to the gallows.

My reason wavered, but it did not fail me utterly. I have more than once observed that, in my second character, my faculties seemed sharpened to a point and my spirits more tensely elastic; thus it came about that, where Jekyll perhaps might have succumbed, Hyde rose to the importance of the moment. My drugs were in one of the presses of my cabinet; how was I to reach them? That was the problem that (crushing my temples in my hands) I set myself to solve. The laboratory door I had closed. If I sought to enter by the house, my own servants would consign me to the gallows. I saw I must employ another hand, and thought of Lanyon. How was he to be reached? How persuaded? Supposing that I escaped capture in the streets, how was I to make my way into his presence? And how should I, an unknown and displeasing visitor, prevail on the famous physician to rifle the study of his colleague, Dr. Jekyll? Then I remembered that of my original character, one part remained to me: I could write my own hand; and once I had conceived that kindling spark, the way that I must follow became lighted up from end to end.

Thereupon, I arranged my clothes as best I could, and summoning a passing hansom, drove to an hotel in Portland Street, the name of which I chanced to remember. At my appearance (which was indeed comical enough, however tragic a fate these garments covered) the driver could not conceal his mirth. I gnashed my teeth upon him with a gust of devilish fury; and the smile withered from his face—happily for him— yet more happily for myself, for in another instant I had certainly dragged him from his perch. At the inn, as I entered, I looked about me with so black a countenance as made the attendants tremble; not a look did they exchange in my presence; but obsequiously took my orders, led me to a private room, and brought me wherewithal to write. Hyde in danger of his life was a creature new to me; shaken with inordinate anger, strung to the pitch of murder, lusting to inflict pain. Yet the creature was astute; mastered his fury with a great effort of the will; composed his two important letters, one to Lanyon and one to Poole; and that he might receive actual evidence of their being posted, sent them out with directions that they should be registered. Thenceforward, he sat all day over the fire in the private room, gnawing his nails; there he dined, sitting alone with his fears, the waiter visibly quailing before his eye; and thence, when the night was fully come, he set forth in the corner of a closed cab, and was driven to and fro about the streets of the city. He, I say—I cannot say, I. That child of Hell had nothing human; nothing lived in him but fear and hatred. And when at last, thinking the driver had begun to grow suspicious, he discharged the cab and ventured on foot, attired in his misfitting clothes, an object marked out for observation, into the midst of the nocturnal passengers, these two base passions raged within him like a tempest. He walked fast, hunted by his fears, chattering to himself, skulking through the less frequented thoroughfares, counting the minutes that still divided him from midnight. Once a woman spoke to him, offering, I think, a box of lights. He smote her in the face, and she fled.

When I came to myself at Lanyon's, the horror of my old friend perhaps affected me somewhat: I do not know; it was at least but a drop in the sea to the abhorrence with which I looked back upon these hours. A change had come over me. It was no longer the fear of the gallows, it was the horror of being Hyde that racked me. I received Lanyon's condemnation partly in a dream; it was partly in a dream that I came home to my own house and got into bed. I slept after the prostration of the day, with a stringent and profound slumber which not even the nightmares that wrung me could avail to break. I awoke in the morning shaken, weakened, but refreshed. I still hated and feared the thought of the brute that slept within me, and I had not of course forgotten the appalling dangers of the day before; but I was once more at home, in my own house and close to my drugs; and gratitude for my escape shone so strong in my soul that it almost rivalled the brightness of hope.

I was stepping leisurely across the court after breakfast, drinking the chill of the air with pleasure, when I was seized again with those indescribable sensations that heralded the change; and I had but the time to gain the shelter of my cabinet before I was once again raging and freezing with the passions of Hyde. It took on this occasion a double dose to recall me to myself; and alas! six hours after, as I sat looking sadly in the fire, the pangs returned, and the drug had to be readministered. In short, from that day forth it seemed only by a great effort, as of gymnastics, and only under the immediate stimulation of the drug, that I was able to wear the countenance of Jekyll. At all hours of the day and night, I would be taken with the premonitory shudder; above all, if I slept, or even dozed for a moment in my chair, it was always as Hyde that I awakened. Under the strain of this continually impending doom and by the sleeplessness to which I now condemned myself, ay, even beyond what I had thought possible to man, I became, in my own person, a creature eaten up and emptied by fever, languidly weak both in body and mind, and solely occupied by one thought: the horror of my other self. But when I slept, or when the virtue of the medicine wore off, I would leap almost without transition (for the pangs of transformation grew daily less marked) into the possession of a fancy brimming with images of terror, a soul boiling with causeless hatreds, and a body that seemed not strong enough to contain the raging energies of life. The powers of Hyde seemed to have grown with the sickliness of Jekyll. And certainly the hate that now divided them was equal on each side. With Jekyll, it was a thing of vital instinct. He had now seen the full deformity of that creature that shared with him some of the phenomena of consciousness, and was co-heir with him to death: and beyond these links of community, which in themselves made the most poignant part of his distress, he thought of Hyde, for all his energy of life, as of something not only hellish but inorganic. This was the shocking thing; that the slime of the pit seemed to utter cries and voices; that the amorphous dust gesticulated and sinned; that what was dead, and had no shape, should usurp the offices of life. And this again, that that insurgent horror was knit to him closer than a wife, closer than an eye, lay caged in his flesh, where he heard it mutter and felt it struggle to be born; and at every hour of weakness, and in the confidence of slumber, prevailed against him, and deposed him out of life. The hatred of Hyde for Jekyll was of a different order. His terror of the gallows drove him continually to commit temporary suicide, and return to his subordinate station of a part instead of a person; but he loathed the necessity, he loathed the despondency into which Jekyll was now fallen, and he resented the dislike with which he was himself regarded. Hence the ape-like tricks that he would play me, scrawling in my own hand blasphemies on the pages of my books, burning the letters and destroying the portrait of my father; and indeed, had it not been for his fear of death, he would long ago have ruined himself in order to involve me in the ruin. But his love of life is wonderful; I go further: I, who sicken and freeze at the mere thought of him, when I recall the abjection and passion of this attachment, and when I know how he fears my power to cut him off by suicide, I find it in my heart to pity him.

It is useless, and the time awfully fails me, to prolong this description; no one has ever suffered such torments, let that suffice; and yet even to these, habit brought—no, not alleviation—but a certain callousness of soul, a certain acquiescence of despair; and my punishment might have gone on for years, but for the last calamity which has now fallen, and which has finally severed me from my own face and nature. My provision of the salt, which had never been renewed since the date of the first experiment, began to run low. I sent out for a fresh supply and mixed the draught; the ebullition followed, and the first change of colour, not the second; I drank it and it was without efficiency. You will learn from Poole how I have had London ransacked; it was in vain; and I am now persuaded that my first supply was impure, and that it was that unknown impurity which lent efficacy to the draught.

About a week has passed, and I am now finishing this statement under the influence of the last of the old powders. This, then, is the last time, short of a miracle, that Henry Jekyll can think his own thoughts or see his own face (now how sadly altered!) in the glass. Nor must I delay too long to bring my writing to an end; for if my narrative has hitherto escaped destruction, it has been by a combination of great prudence and great good luck. Should the throes of change take me in the act of writing it, Hyde will tear it in pieces; but if some time shall have elapsed after I have laid it by, his wonderful selfishness and circumscription to the moment will probably save it once again from the action of his

This, then, is the last time that Henry Jekyll can think his own thoughts or see his own face.

ape-like spite. And indeed the doom that is closing on us both has already changed and crushed him. Half an hour from now, when I shall again and forever reindue that hated personality, I know how I shall sit shuddering and weeping in my chair, or continue, with the most strained and fearstruck ecstasy of listening, to pace up and down this room (my last earthly refuge) and give ear to every sound of menace. Will Hyde die upon the scaffold? Or will he find courage to release himself at the last moment? God knows; I am careless; this is my true hour of death, and what is to follow concerns another than myself. Here then, as I lay down the pen and proceed to seal up my confession, I bring the life of that unhappy Henry Jekyll to an end.

The Bottle Imp

THERE WAS A MAN in the island of Hawaii, whom I shall call Keawe; for the truth is, he still lives, and his name must be kept secret; but the place of his birth was not far from Honaunau, where the bones of Keawe the Great lie hidden in a cave. This man was poor, brave, and active; he could read and write like a schoolmaster; he was a first-rate mariner besides, sailed for some time in the island steamers, and steered a whaleboat on the Hamakua coast. At length it came in Keawe's mind to have a sight of the great world and foreign cities, and he shipped on a vessel bound to San Francisco.

This is a fine town, with a fine harbour, and rich people uncountable; and, in particular, there is one hill which is covered with palaces. Upon

Notes.—Any student of that very unliterary product, the English drama of the early part of the century, will here recognise the name and the root idea of a piece once rendered popular by the redoubtable O. Smith. The root idea is there, and identical, and yet I believe I have made it a new thing. And the fact that the tale has been designed and written for a Polynesian audience may lend it some extraneous interest nearer home.—R. L. S.

this hill Keawe was one day taking a walk, with his pocket full of money, viewing the great houses upon either hand with pleasure. "What fine houses they are!" he was thinking, "and how happy must these people be who dwell in them, and take no care for the morrow!" The thought was in his mind when he came abreast of a house that was smaller than some others, but all finished and beautified like a toy; the steps of that house shone like silver, and the borders of the garden bloomed like garlands, and the windows were bright like diamonds; and Keawe stopped and wondered at the excellence of all he saw. So stopping, he was aware of a man that looked forth upon him through a window, so clear that Keawe could see him as you see a fish in a pool upon the reef. The man was elderly, with a bald head and a black beard; and his face was heavy with sorrow, and he bitterly sighed. And the truth of it is, that as Keawe looked in upon the man, and the man looked out upon Keawe, each envied the other.

All of a sudden the man smiled and nodded, and beckoned Keawe to enter, and met him at the door of the house.

"This is a fine house of mine," said the man, and bitterly sighed. "Would you not care to view the chambers?"

So he led Keawe all over it, from the cellar to the roof, and there was nothing there that was not perfect of its kind, and Keawe was astonished.

"Truly," said Keawe, "this is a beautiful house; if I lived in the like of it, I should be laughing all day long. How comes it, then, that you should be sighing?"

"There is no reason," said the man, "why you should not have a house in all points similar to this, and finer, if you wish. You have some money, I suppose?"

"I have fifty dollars," said Keawe, "but a house like this will cost more than fifty dollars."

The man made a computation. "I am sorry you have no more," said he, "for it may raise you trouble in the future; but it shall be yours at fifty dollars."

"The house?" asked Keawe.

"No, not the house," replied the man; "but the bottle. For, I must tell you, although I appear to you so rich and fortunate, all my fortune, and this house itself and its garden, came out of a bottle not much bigger than a pint. This is it."

And he opened a lock-fast place, and took out a round-bellied bottle with a long neck; the glass of it was white like milk, with changing rainbow colours in the grain. Withinsides something obscurely moved, like a shadow and a fire.

"This is the bottle," said the man; and, when Keawe laughed, "You do not believe me?" he added. "Try, then, for yourself. See if you can break it."

So Keawe took the bottle up and dashed it on the floor till he was weary; but it jumped on the floor like a child's ball, and was not injured.

"This is a strange thing," said Keawe. "For by the touch of it, as well as by the look, the bottle should be of glass."

"Of glass it is," replied the man, sighing more heavily than ever; "but the glass of it was tempered in the flames of hell. An imp lives in it, and that is the shadow we behold there moving; or so I suppose. If any man buys this bottle the imp is at his command; all that he desires—love, fame, money, houses like this house, ay, or a city like this city—all are his at the word uttered. Napoleon had this bottle, and by it he grew to be the king of the world; but he sold it at the last and fell. Captain Cook had this bottle, and by it he found his way to so many islands; but he, too, sold it, and was slain upon Hawaii. For, once it is sold, the power goes and the protection; and unless a man remain content with what he has, ill will befall him."

"And yet you talk of selling it yourself?" Keawe said.

"I have all I wish, and I am growing elderly," replied the man. "There is one thing the imp cannot do—he cannot prolong life; and it would not be fair to conceal from you there is a drawback to the bottle; for if a man die before he sells it, he must burn in hell forever."

"To be sure, that is a drawback and no mistake," cried Keawe. "I would not meddle with the thing. I can do without a house, thank God; but there is one thing I could not be doing with one particle, and that is to be damned."

"Dear me, you must not run away with things," returned the man.

"All you have to do is to use the power of the imp in moderation, and then sell it to someone else, as I do to you, and finish your life in comfort."

"Well, I observe two things," said Keawe. "All the time you keep sighing like a maid in love, that is one; and, for the other, you sell this bottle very cheap."

"I have told you already why I sigh," said the man. "It is because I fear my health is breaking up; and, as you said yourself, to die and go to the devil is a pity for anyone. As for why I sell so cheap, I must explain to you there is a peculiarity about the bottle. Long ago, when the devil brought it first upon earth, it was extremely expensive, and was sold first of all to Prester John for many millions of dollars; but it cannot be sold at all, unless sold at a loss. If you sell it for as much as you paid for it, back it comes to you again like a homing pigeon. It follows that the price has kept falling in these centuries, and the bottle is now remarkably cheap. I bought it myself from one of my great neighbours on this hill, and the price I paid was ninety dollars. I could sell it for as high as eighty-nine dollars and ninety-nine cents, but not a penny dearer, or back the thing must come to me. Now, about this there are two bothers. First, when you offer a bottle so singular for eighty-odd dollars, people suppose you to be jesting. And second—but there is no hurry about that—and I need not go into it. Only remember it must be coined money that you sell it for."

"How am I to know that this is all true?" asked Keawe.

"Some of it you can try at once," replied the man. "Give me your fifty dollars, take the bottle, and wish your fifty dollars back into your pocket. If that does not happen, I pledge you my honour I will cry off the bargain and restore your money."

"You are not deceiving me?" said Keawe.

The man bound himself with a great oath.

"Well, I will risk that much," said Keawe, "for that can do no harm," and he paid over his money to the man, and the man handed him the bottle.

"Imp of the bottle," said Keawe, "I want my fifty dollars back." And sure enough, he had scarce said the word before his pocket was as heavy as ever.

"To be sure this is a wonderful bottle," said Keawe.

"And now good morning to you, my fine fellow, and the devil go with you for me," said the man.

"Hold on," said Keawe, "I don't want anymore of this fun. Here, take your bottle back."

"You have bought it for less than I paid for it," replied the man, rubbing his hands. "It is yours now; and, for my part, I am only concerned to see the back of you." And with that he rang for his Chinese servant, and had Keawe shown out of the house.

Now, when Keawe was in the street, with the bottle under his arm, he began to think. "If all is true about this bottle, I may have made a losing bargain," thinks he. "But, perhaps the man was only fooling me." The first thing he did was to count his money; the sum was exact— forty-nine dollars American money, and one Chili piece. "That looks like the truth," said Keawe. "Now I will try another part."

The streets in that part of the city were as clean as a ship's decks, and though it was noon, there were no passengers. Keawe set the bottle in the gutter and walked away. Twice he looked back, and there was the milky, round-bellied bottle where he left it. A third time he looked back, and turned a corner; but he had scarce done so, when something knocked upon his elbow, and behold! it was the long neck sticking up; and as for the round belly, it was jammed into the pocket of his pilot coat.

"And that looks like the truth," said Keawe.

The next thing he did was to buy a corkscrew in a shop, and go apart into a secret place in the fields. And there he tried to draw the cork, but as often as he put the screw in, out it came again, and the cork was as whole as ever.

"This is some new sort of cork," said Keawe, and all at once he began to shake and sweat, for he was afraid of that bottle.

On his way back to the port side he saw a shop where a man sold shells and clubs from the wild islands, old heathen deities, old coined money, pictures from China and Japan, and all manner of things that sailors bring in their sea chests. And here he had an idea. So he went in and offered the bottle for a hundred dollars. The man of the shop laughed at him at first, and offered him five, but, indeed, it was a curious bottle, such glass was never blown in any human glassworks, so prettily the

81

colours shone under the milky white, and so strangely the shadow hovered in the midst; so, after he had disputed a while after the manner of his kind, the shopman gave Keawe sixty silver dollars for the thing and set it on a shelf in the midst of his window.

"Now," said Keawe, "I have sold that for sixty which I bought for fifty—or, to say truth, a little less, because one of my dollars was from Chili. Now I shall know the truth upon another point."

So he went back on board his ship, and when he opened his chest, there was the bottle, and had come more quickly than himself. Now Keawe had a mate on board whose name was Lopaka.

"What ails you?" said Lopaka, "that you stare in your chest?"

They were alone in the ship's forecastle, and Keawe bound him to secrecy, and told all.

"This is a very strange affair," said Lopaka; "and I fear you will be in trouble about this bottle. But there is one point very clear—that you are sure of the trouble, and you had better have the profit in the bargain. Make up your mind what you want with it; give the order, and if it is done as you desire, I will buy the bottle myself; for I have an idea of my own to get a schooner, and go trading through the island."

"That is not my idea," said Keawe; "but to have a beautiful house and garden on the Kona Coast where I was born, the sun shining in at the door, flowers in the garden, glass in the windows, pictures on the walls, and toys and fine carpets on the table, for all the world like the house I was in this day—only a story higher, and with balconies all about like the King's palace; and to live there without care and make merry with my friends and relatives."

"Well," said Lopaka, "let us carry it back with us to Hawaii; and if all comes true, as you suppose, I will buy the bottle, as I said, and ask a schooner."

Upon that they were agreed, and it was not long before the ship returned to Honolulu, carrying Keawe and Lopaka, and the bottle. They were scarce come ashore when they met a friend upon the beach, who began at once to condole with Keawe.

"I do not know what I am to be condoled about," said Keawe.

"Is it possible you have not heard," said the friend, "your uncle—that good old man—is dead, and your cousin—that beautiful boy—was drowned at sea?"

Keawe was filled with sorrow, and, beginning to weep and to lament, he forgot about the bottle. But Lopaka was thinking to himself, and presently, when Keawe's grief was a little abated, "I have been thinking," said Lopaka, "had not your uncle lands in Hawaii, in the district of Kaü?"

"No," said Keawe; "not in Kaü: they are on the mountainside—a little be-south Hookena."

"These lands will now be yours?" asked Lopaka.

"And so they will," says Keawe, and began again to lament for his relatives.

"No," said Lopaka, "do not lament at present. I have a thought in my mind. How if this should be the doing of the bottle? For here is the place ready for your house."

"If this be so," cried Keawe, "it is a very ill way to serve me by killing my relatives. But it may be, indeed; for it was in just such a station that I saw the house with my mind's eye."

"The house, however, is not yet built," said Lopaka.

"No, nor like to be!" said Keawe; "for though my uncle has some coffee and ava and bananas, it will not be more than will keep me in comfort; and the rest of that land is the black lava."

"Let us go to the lawyer," said Lopaka; "I have still this idea in my mind."

Now, when they came to the lawyer's, it appeared Keawe's uncle had grown monstrous rich in the last days, and there was a fund of money.

"And here is the money for the house!" cried Lopaka.

"If you are thinking of a new house," said the lawyer, "here is the card of a new architect of whom they tell me great things."

"Better and better!" cried Lopaka. "Here is all made plain for us. Let us continue to obey orders."

So they went to the architect, and he had drawings of houses on his table.

"You want something out-of-the-way?" said the architect. "How do you like this?" and he handed a drawing to Keawe.

Now, when Keawe set eyes on the drawing, he cried out aloud, for it was the picture of his thought exactly drawn.

"I am in for this house," thought he. "Little as I like the way it comes to me, I am in for it now, and I may as well take the good along with the evil."

So he told the architect all that he wished, and how he would have that house furnished, and about the pictures on the wall and the knickknacks on the tables; and he asked the man plainly for how much he would undertake the whole affair.

The architect put many questions, and took his pen and made a computation; and when he had done he named the very sum that Keawe had inherited.

Lopaka and Keawe looked at one another and nodded.

"It is quite clear," thought Keawe, "that I am to have this house, whether or no. It comes from the devil, and I fear I will get little good by that; and of one thing I am sure, I will make no more wishes as long as I have this bottle. But with the house I am saddled, and I may as well take the good along with the evil."

So he made his terms with the architect, and they signed a paper; and Keawe and Lopaka took ship again and sailed to Australia; for it was concluded between them they should not interfere at all, but leave the architect and the bottle imp to build and to adorn the house at their own pleasure.

The voyage was a good voyage, only all the time Keawe was holding in his breath, for he had sworn he would utter no more wishes and take no more favours from the devil. The time was up when they got back. The architect told them that the house was ready, and Keawe and Lopaka took a passage in the *Hall*, and went down Kona way to view the house, and see if all had been done fitly according to the thought that was in Keawe's mind.

Now, the house stood on the mountainside, visible to ships. Above, the forest ran up into the clouds of rain; below, the black lava fell in cliffs, where the kings of old lay buried. A garden bloomed about that house with every hue of flowers; and there was an orchard of papaia on the one hand and an orchard of breadfruit on the other, and right in front, towards the sea, a ship's mast had been rigged up and bore a flag. As for the house, it was three stories high, with great chambers and broad balconies on each. The windows were of glass, so excellent that it was clear as water and as bright as day. All manner of furniture adorned the chambers. Pictures hung upon the wall in golden frames—pictures of ships, and men fighting, and of the most beautiful women, and of singular places; nowhere in the world are these pictures of so bright a colour as those Keawe found hanging in his house. As for the knick-knacks, they were extraordinarily fine: chiming clocks and musical boxes, little men with nodding heads, books filled with pictures, weapons of price from all quarters of the world, and the most elegant puzzles to entertain the leisure of a solitary man. And as no one would care to live in such chambers, only to walk through and view them, the balconies were made so broad that a whole town might have lived upon them in delight; and Keawe knew not which to prefer, whether the back porch, where you get the land breeze and looked upon the orchards and the flowers, or the front balcony, where you could drink the wind of the sea, and look down the steep wall of the mountain and see the *Hall* going by once a week or so between Hookena and the hills of Pele, or the schooners plying up the coast for wood and ava and bananas.

When they had viewed all, Keawe and Lopaka sat on the porch.

"Well," asked Lopaka, "is it all as you designed?"

"Words cannot utter it," said Keawe. "It is better than I dreamed, and I am sick with satisfaction."

"There is but one thing to consider," said Lopaka, "all this may be quite natural, and the bottle imp have nothing whatever to say to it. If I were to buy the bottle, and got no schooner after all, I should have put my hand in the fire for nothing. I gave you my word, I know; but yet I think you would not grudge me one more proof."

"I have sworn I would take no more favours," said Keawe. "I have gone already deep enough."

"This is no favour I am thinking of," replied Lopaka. "It is only to see the imp himself. There is nothing to be gained by that, and so nothing to be ashamed of, and yet, if I once saw him, I should be sure of the whole matter. So indulge me so far, and let me see the imp; and, after that, here is the money in my hand, and I will buy it."

"There is only one thing I am afraid of," said Keawe. "The imp may be very ugly to view, and if you once set eyes upon him you might be very undesirous of the bottle."

"I am a man of my word," said Lopaka. "And here is the money betwixt us."

"Very well," replied Keawe, "I have a curiosity myself. So come, let us have one look at you, Mr. Imp."

Now as soon as that was said, the imp looked out of the bottle, and in again, swift as a lizard; and there sat Keawe and Lopaka turned to stone. The night had quite come before either found a thought to say or voice to say it with; and then Lopaka pushed the money over and took the bottle.

"I am a man of my word," said he, "and had need to be so, or I would not touch this bottle with my foot. Well, I shall get my schooner and a dollar or two for my pocket; and then I will be rid of this devil as fast as I can. For to tell you the plain truth, the look of him has cast me down."

"Lopaka," said Keawe, "do not you think any worse of me than you can help; I know it is night, and the roads bad, and the pass by the tombs an ill place to go by so late, but I declare since I have seen that little face, I cannot eat or sleep or pray till it is gone from me. I will give you a lantern, and a basket to put the bottle in, and any picture or fine thing in all my house that takes your fancy; and be gone at once, and go sleep at Hookena with Nahinu."

"Keawe," said Lopaka, "many a man would take this ill; above all, when I am doing you a turn so friendly as to keep my word and buy the bottle; and for that matter, the night and the dark and the way by the tombs must be all tenfold more dangerous to a man with such a sin upon his conscience and such a bottle under his arm. But for my part, I am so extremely terrified myself, I have not the heart to blame you. Here I go then; and I pray God you may be happy in your house, and I fortunate with my schooner, and both get to heaven in the end in spite of the devil and his bottle."

So Lopaka went down the mountain; and Keawe stood in his front balcony, and listened to the clink of the horse's shoes, and watched the lantern go shining down the path, and along the cliff of caves where the old dead are buried; and all the time he trembled and clasped his hands, and prayed for his friend, and gave glory to God that he himself was escaped out of that trouble.

But the next day came very brightly, and that new house of his was so delightful to behold that he forgot his terrors. One day followed another, and Keawe dwelt there in perpetual joy. He had his place on the back porch; it was there he ate and lived, and read the stories in the Honolulu newspapers; but when anyone came by they would go in and view the chambers and the pictures. And the fame of the house went far and wide; it was called *Ka-Hale Nui*—the Great House—in all Kona; and sometimes the Bright House, for Keawe kept a Chinaman, who was all day dusting and furbishing; and the glass, and the gilt, and the fine stuffs, and the pictures, shone as bright as the morning. As for Keawe himself, he could not walk in the chambers without singing, his heart was so enlarged; and when ships sailed by upon the sea, he would fly his colours on the mast.

So time went by, until one day Keawe went upon a visit as far as Kailua to certain of his friends. There he was well feasted; and left as soon as he could the next morning, and rode hard, for he was impatient to behold his beautiful house; and, besides, the night then coming on was the night in which the dead of old days go abroad in the sides of Kona; and having already meddled with the devil, he was the more chary of meeting with the dead. A little beyond Honaunau, looking far ahead, he was aware of a woman bathing in the edge of the sea; and she seemed a well-grown girl, but he thought no more of it. Then he saw her white shift flutter as she put it on, and then her red holoku; and by the time he came abreast of her she was done with her toilet, and had come up from the sea, and stood by the trackside in her red holoku, and she was all freshened with the bath, and her eyes shone and were kind. Now Keawe no sooner beheld her than he drew rein.

"I thought I knew everyone in this country," said he. "How comes it that I do not know you?"

"I am Kokua, daughter of Kiano," said the girl, "and I have just returned from Oahu. Who are you?"

"I will tell you who I am in a little," said Keawe, dismounting from his horse, "but not now. For I have a thought in my mind, and if you knew who I was, you might have heard of me, and would not give me a true answer. But tell me, first of all, one thing: are you married?"

At this Kokua laughed out aloud. "It is you who asks questions," she said. "Are you married yourself?"

"Indeed, Kokua, I am not," replied Keawe, "and never thought to be until this hour. But here is the plain truth. I have met you here at the roadside, and I saw your eyes, which are like the stars, and my heart went to you as swift as a bird. And so now, if you want none of me, say so, and I will go on to my own place; but if you think me no worse than any other young man, say so, too, and I will turn aside to your father's for the night, and tomorrow I will talk with the good man."

Kokua said never a word, but she looked at the sea and laughed.

"Kokua," said Keawe, "if you say nothing, I will take that for the good answer; so let us be stepping to your father's door."

She went on ahead of him, still without speech; only sometimes she glanced back and glanced away again, and she kept the strings of her hat in her mouth.

Now, when they had come to the door, Kiano came out on his verandah, and cried out and welcomed Keawe by name. At that the girl looked over, for the fame of the great house had come to her ears; and, to be sure, it was a great temptation. All that evening they were very merry together; and the girl was as bold as brass under the eyes of her parents, and made a mock of Keawe, for she had a quick wit. The next day he had a word with Kiano, and found the girl alone.

"Kokua," said he, "you made a mock of me all the evening; and it is still time to bid me go. I would not tell you who I was, because I have so fine a house, and I feared you would think too much of that house and too little of the man that loves you. Now you know all, and if you wish to have seen the last of me, say so at once."

"No," said Kokua, but this time she did not laugh, nor did Keawe ask for more.

This was the wooing of Keawe; things had gone quickly; but so an arrow goes, and the ball of a rifle swifter still, and yet both may strike the target. Things had gone fast, but they had gone far also, and the thought of Keawe rang in the maiden's head; she heard his voice in the breach of the surf upon the lava, and for this young man that she had seen but twice she would have left father and mother and her native islands. As for Keawe himself, his horse flew up the path of the mountain under the cliff of tombs, and the sound of the hoofs, and the sound of Keawe singing to himself for pleasure, echoed in the caverns of the dead. He came to the Bright House, and still he was singing. He sat and ate in the broad balcony, and the Chinaman wondered at his master, to hear how he sang between the mouthfuls. The sun went down into the sea, and the night came; and Keawe walked the balconies by lamplight, high on the mountains, and the voice of his singing startled men on ships.

"Here am I now upon my high place," he said to himself. "Life may be no better; this is the mountaintop; and all shelves about me towards the worse. For the first time I will light up the chambers, and bathe in my fine bath with the hot water and the cold, and sleep alone in the bed of my bridal chamber."

So the Chinaman had word, and he must rise from sleep and light the furnaces; and as he walked below, beside the boilers, he heard his master singing and rejoicing above him in the lighted chambers. When the water began to be hot the Chinaman cried to his master: and Keawe went into the bathroom; and the Chinaman heard him sing as he filled the marble basin; and heard him sing, and the singing broken, as he undressed; until of a sudden, the song ceased. The Chinaman listened, and listened; he called up the house to Keawe to ask if all were well, and Keawe answered him "Yes," and bade him go to bed; but there was no more singing in the Bright House; and all night long the Chinaman heard his master's feet go round and round the balconies without repose.

Now, the truth of it was this: as Keawe undressed for his bath, he spied upon his flesh a patch like a patch of lichen on a rock, and it was then that he stopped singing. For he knew the likeness of that patch, and knew that he was fallen in the Chinese Evil.[1]

Now, it is a sad thing for any man to fall into this sickness. And it

[1]Leprosy.

89

would be a sad thing for anyone to leave a house so beautiful and so commodious, and depart from all his friends to the north coast of Molokai, between the mighty cliff and the sea breakers. But what was that to the case of the man Keawe, he who had met his love but yesterday and won her but that morning, and now saw all his hopes break, in a moment, like a piece of glass?

A while he sat upon the edge of the bath, then sprang, with a cry, and ran outside; and to and fro, to and fro, along the balcony, like one despairing.

"Very willingly could I leave Hawaii, the home of my fathers," Keawe was thinking. "Very lightly could I leave my house, the high-placed, the many-windowed, here upon the mountains. Very bravely could I go to Molokai, to Kalaupapa by the cliffs, to live with the smitten and to sleep there, far from my fathers. But what wrong have I done, what sin lies upon my soul, that I should have encountered Kokua coming cool from the seawater in the evening? Kokua, the soul ensnarer! Kokua, the light of my life! Her may I never wed, her may I look upon no longer, her may I no more handle with my loving hand; and it is for this, it is for you, O Kokua! that I pour my lamentations!"

Now you are to observe what sort of a man Keawe was, for he might have dwelt there in the Bright House for years, and no one been the wiser of his sickness; but he reckoned nothing of that, if he must lose Kokua. And again he might have wed Kokua even as he was; and so many would have done, because they have the soul of pigs; but Keawe loved the maid manfully, and he would do her no hurt and bring her in no danger.

A little beyond the midst of the night, there came in his mind the recollection of that bottle. He went round the back porch, and called to memory the day when the devil had looked forth; and at the thought ice ran in his veins.

"A dreadful thing is the bottle," thought Keawe, "and dreadful is the imp, and it is a dreadful thing to risk the flames of hell. But what other hope have I to cure my sickness or to wed Kokua? What!" he thought, "would I beard the devil once, only to get me a house, and not face him again to win Kokua?"

Thereupon he called to mind it was the next day the *Hall* went by on her return to Honolulu. "There must I go first," he thought, "and see ·Lopaka. For the best hope that I have now is to find that same bottle I was so pleased to be rid of."

Never a wink could he sleep; the food stuck in his throat; but he sent a letter to Kiano, and about the time when the steamer would be coming, rode down beside the cliff of the tombs. It rained; his horse went heavily, he looked up at the black mouths of the caves, and he envied the dead that slept there and were done with trouble; and called to mind how he had galloped by the day before, and was astonished. So he came down to Hookena, and there was all the country gathered for the steamer as usual. In the shed before the store they sat and jested and passed the news; but there was no matter of speech in Keawe's bosom, and he sat in their midst and looked without on the rain falling on the houses, and the surf beating among the rocks, and the sighs arose in his throat.

"Keawe of the Bright House is out of spirits," said one to another. Indeed, and so he was, and little wonder.

Then the *Hall* came, and the whaleboat carried him on board. The after part of the ship was full of Haoles[2] —who had been to visit the volcano, as their custom is; and the midst was crowded with Kanakas, and the fore part with wild bulls from Hilo and horses from Kaü; but Keawe sat apart from all in his sorrow, and watched for the house of Kiano. There it sat low upon the shore in the black rocks, and shaded by the cocoa palms, and there by the door was a red holoku, no greater than a fly, and going to and fro with a fly's busyness. "Ah, queen of my heart," he cried, "I'll venture my dear soul to win you!"

Soon after, darkness fell and the cabins were lit up, and the Haoles sat and played at the cards and drank whiskey as their custom is; but Keawe walked the deck all night; and all the next day, as they steamed under the lee of Maui or of Molokai, he was still pacing to and fro like a wild animal in a menagerie.

Towards evening they passed Diamond Head, and came to the pier

[2] Whites.

91

of Honolulu. Keawe stepped out among the crowd and began to ask for Lopaka. It seemed he had become the owner of a schooner—none better in the islands—and was gone upon an adventure as far as Pola-Pola or Kahiki; so there was no help to be looked for from Lopaka. Keawe called to mind a friend of his, a lawyer in the town (I must not tell his name), and inquired of him. They said he was grown suddenly rich, and had a fine new house upon Waikiki shore; and this put a thought in Keawe's head, and he called a hack and drove to the lawyer's house.

The house was all brand new, and the trees in the garden no greater than walking sticks, and the lawyer, when he came, had the air of a man well pleased.

"What can I do to serve you?" said the lawyer.

"You are a friend of Lopaka's," replied Keawe, "and Lopaka purchased from me a certain piece of goods that I thought you might enable me to trace."

The lawyer's face became very dark. "I do not profess to misunderstand you, Mr. Keawe," said he, "though this is an ugly business to be stirring in. You may be sure I know nothing, but yet I have a guess, and if you would apply in a certain quarter I think you might have news."

And he named the name of a man, which, again, I had better not repeat. So it was for days, and Keawe went from one to another, finding everywhere new clothes and carriages, and fine new houses and men everywhere in great contentment, although, to be sure, when he hinted at his business their faces would cloud over.

"No doubt I am upon the track," thought Keawe. "The new clothes and carriages are all the gifts of the little imp, and these glad faces are the faces of men who have taken their profit and got rid of the accursed thing in safety. When I see pale cheeks and hear sighing, I shall know that I am near the bottle."

So it befell at last he was recommended to a Haole in Beritania Street. When he came to the door, about the hour of the evening meal, there were the usual marks of the new house, and the young garden, and the electric light shining in the windows; but when the owner came, a shock of hope and fear ran through Keawe; for here was a young man, white as a corpse, and black about the eyes, the hair shedding from his head, and such a look in his countenance as a man may have when he is waiting for the gallows.

"Here it is, to be sure," thought Keawe, and so with this man he noways veiled his errand. "I am come to buy the bottle," said he.

At the word, the young Haole of Beritania Street reeled against the wall.

"The bottle!" he gasped. "To buy the bottle!" Then he seemed to choke, and seizing Keawe by the arm, carried him into a room and poured out wine in two glasses.

"Here is my respects," said Keawe, who had been much about with Haoles in his time. "Yes," he added, "I am come to buy the bottle. What is the price by now?"

At that word the young man let his glass slip through his fingers, and looked upon Keawe like a ghost.

"The price," says he; "the price! You do not know the price?"

"It is for that I am asking you," returned Keawe. "But why are you so much concerned? Is there anything wrong about the price?"

"It has dropped a great deal in value since your time, Mr. Keawe," said the young man, stammering.

"Well, well, I shall have the less to pay for it," says Keawe. "How much did it cost you?"

The young man was as white as a sheet. "Two cents," said he.

"What?" cried Keawe, "two cents? Why, then, you can only sell it for one. And he who buys it——" The words died upon Keawe's tongue; he who bought it could never sell it again, the bottle and the bottle imp must abide with him until he died, and when he died must carry him to the red end of hell.

The young man of Beritania Street fell upon his knees. "For God's sake, buy it!" he cried. "You can have all my fortune in the bargain. I was mad when I bought it at that price. I had embezzled money at my store; I was lost else; I must have gone to jail."

"Poor creature," said Keawe, "you would risk your soul upon so desperate an adventure, and to avoid the proper punishment of your own disgrace; and you think I could hesitate with love in front of me.

93

Give me the bottle, and the change which I make sure you have all ready. Here is a five-cent piece."

It was as Keawe supposed; the young man had the change ready in a drawer; the bottle changed hands, and Keawe's fingers were no sooner clasped upon the stalk than he had breathed his wish to be a clean man. And, sure enough, when he got home to his room, and stripped himself before a glass, his flesh was whole like an infant's. And here was the strange thing: he had no sooner seen this miracle than his mind was changed within him, and he cared naught for the Chinese Evil, and little enough for Kokua; and had but the one thought, that here he was bound to the bottle imp for time and for eternity, and had no better hope but to be a cinder forever in the flames of hell. Away ahead of him he saw them blaze with his mind's eye, and his soul shrank, and darkness fell upon the light.

When Keawe came to himself a little, he was aware it was the night when the band played at the hotel. Thither he went, because he feared to be alone; and there, among happy faces, walked to and fro, and heard the tunes go up and down, and saw Berger beat the measure, and all the while he heard the flames crackle and saw the red fire burning in the bottomless pit. Of a sudden the band played *Hiki-ao-ao*; that was a song that he had sung with Kokua, and at the strain courage returned to him.

"It is done now," he thought, "and once more let me take the good along with the evil."

So it befell that he returned to Hawaii by the first steamer, and as soon as it could be managed he was wedded to Kokua, and carried her up the mountainside to the Bright House.

Now it was so with these two, that when they were together Keawe's heart was stilled; but as soon as he was alone he fell into a brooding horror, and heard the flames crackle, and saw the red fire burn in the bottomless pit. The girl, indeed, had come to him wholly; her heart leaped in her side at sight of him, her hand clung to his; and she was so fashioned, from the hair upon her head to the nails upon her toes, that none could see her without joy. She was pleasant in her nature. She had the good word always. Full of song she was, and went to and fro in the Bright House, the brightest thing in its three storeys, carolling like the birds. And Keawe beheld and heard her with delight, and then must shrink upon one side, and weep and groan to think upon the price that he had paid for her; and then he must dry his eyes, and wash his face, and go and sit with her on the broad balconies, joining in her songs, and, with a sick spirit, answering her smiles.

There came a day when her feet began to be heavy and her songs more rare; and now it was not Keawe only that would weep apart, but each would sunder from the other and sit in opposite balconies with the whole width of the Bright House betwixt. Keawe was so sunk in his despair, he scarce observed the change, and was only glad he had more hours to sit alone and brood upon his destiny, and was not so frequently condemned to pull a smiling face on a sick heart. But one day, coming softly through the house, he heard the sound of a child sobbing, and there was Kokua rolling her face upon the balcony floor, and weeping like the lost.

"You do well to keep in this house, Kokua," he said. "And yet I would give the head off my body that you (at least) might have been happy."

"Happy!" she cried. "Keawe, when you lived alone in your Bright House you were the word of the island for a happy man; laughter and song were in your mouth, and your face was as bright as the sunrise. Then you wedded poor Kokua; and the good God knows what is amiss in her—but from that day you have not smiled. Oh!" she cried, "what ails me? I thought I was pretty, and I knew I loved him. What ails me, that I throw this cloud upon my husband?"

"Poor Kokua," said Keawe. He sat down by her side, and sought to take her hand; but that she plucked away. "Poor Kokua," he said again. "My poor child—my pretty. And I had thought all this while to spare you! Well, you shall know all. Then, at least, you will pity poor Keawe; then you will understand how much he loved you in the past—that he dared hell for your possession—and how much he loves you still (the poor condemned one), that he can yet call up a smile when he beholds you."

With that he told her all, even from the beginning.

"You have done this for me?" she cried. "Ah, well, then what do I care!" and she clasped and wept upon him.

"Ah, child!" said Keawe; "and yet, when I consider of the fire of hell, I care a good deal!"

"Never tell me," said she, "no man can be lost because he loved Kokua, and no other fault. I tell you, Keawe, I shall save you with these hands, or perish in your company. What! you loved me and gave your soul, and you think I will not die to save you in return?"

"Ah, my dear, you might die a hundred times, and what difference would that make?" he cried, "except to leave me lonely till the time comes for my damnation."

"You know nothing," said she. "I was educated in a school in Honolulu, I am no common girl. And I tell you I shall save my lover. What is this you say about a cent? But all the world is not American. In England they have a piece they call a farthing, which is about half a cent. Ah! sorrow!" she cried, "that makes it scarcely better, for the buyer must be lost, and we shall find none so brave as my Keawe! But, then, there is France; they have a small coin there which they call a centime, and these go five to the cent, or thereabout. We could not do better. Come, Keawe, let us go to the French islands; let us go to Tahiti, as fast as ships can bear us. There we have four centimes, three centimes, two centimes, one centime; four possible sales to come and go on; and two of us to push the bargain. Come, my Keawe! kiss me, and banish care. Kokua will defend you."

"Gift of God!" he cried. "I cannot think that God will punish me for desiring aught so good. Be it as you will, then, take me where you please: I put my life and my salvation in your hands."

Early the next day Kokua went about her preparations. She took Keawe's chest that he went with sailoring; and first she put the bottle in a corner, and then packed it with the richest of their clothes and the bravest of the knickknacks in the house. "For," said she, "we must seem to be rich folks, or who would believe in the bottle?" All the time of her preparation she was as gay as a bird; only when she looked upon Keawe the tears would spring in her eye, and she must run and kiss him. As for Keawe, a weight was off his soul; now that he had his secret shared, and some hope in front of him, he seemed like a new man, his feet went lightly on the earth, and his breath was good to him again. Yet was terror still at his elbow; and ever and again, as the wind blows out a taper, hope died in him, and he saw the flames toss and red fire burn in hell.

It was given out in the country they were gone pleasuring to the States, which was thought a strange thing, and yet not so strange as the truth, if any could have guessed it. So they went to Honolulu in the *Hall*, and thence in the *Umatilla* to San Francisco with a crowd of Haoles, and at San Francisco took their passage by the mail brigantine, the *Tropic Bird*, for Papeete, the chief place of the French in the south islands. Thither they came, after a pleasant voyage, on a fair day of the trade wind, and saw the reef with the surf breaking and Motuiti with its palms, and the schooner riding withinside, and the white houses of the town low down along the shore among green trees, and overhead the mountains and the clouds of Tahiti, the wise island.

It was judged the most wise to hire a house, which they did according- ly, opposite the British Consul's, to make a great parade of money, and themselves conspicuous with carriages and horses. This it was very easy to do, so long as they had the bottle in their possession; for Kokua was more bold than Keawe, and whenever she had a mind, called on the imp for twenty or a hundred dollars. At this rate they soon grew to be remarked in the town; and the strangers from Hawaii, their riding and their driving, the fine holokus, and the rich lace of Kokua, became the matter of much talk.

They got on well after the first with the Tahitian language, which is indeed like to the Hawaiian, with a change of certain letters; and as soon as they had any freedom of speech, began to push the bottle. You are to consider it was not an easy subject to introduce; it was not easy to persuade people you are in earnest, when you offer to sell them for four centimes the spring of health and riches inexhaustible. It was necessary besides to explain the dangers of the bottle; and either people disbe- lieved the whole thing and laughed, or they thought the more of the darker part, became overcast with gravity, and drew away from Keawe and Kokua as from persons who had dealings with the devil. So far from gaining ground, these two began to find they were avoided in the town; the children ran away from them screaming, a thing intolerable to

Kokua; Catholics crossed themselves as they went by; and all persons began with one accord to disengage themselves from their advances.

Depression fell upon their spirits. They would sit at night in their new house, after a day's weariness, and not exchange one word, or the silence would be broken by Kokua bursting suddenly into sobs. Sometimes they would pray together; sometimes they would have the bottle out upon the floor, and sit all evening watching how the shadow hovered in the midst. At such times they would be afraid to go to rest. It was long ere slumber came to them, and, if either dozed off, it would be to wake and find the other silently weeping in the dark, or, perhaps, to wake alone, the other having fled from the house and the neighbourhood of that bottle, to pace under the bananas in the little garden, or to wander on the beach by moonlight.

One night it was so when Kokua awoke. Keawe was gone. She felt in the bed and his place was cold. Then fear fell upon her, and she sat up in bed. A little moonshine filtered through the shutters. The room was bright, and she could spy the bottle on the floor. Outside it blew high, the great trees of the avenue cried aloud, and the fallen leaves rattled in the verandah. In the midst of this Kokua was aware of another sound; whether of a beast or of man she could scarce tell, but it was as sad as death, and cut her to the soul. Softly she arose, set the door ajar, and looked forth into the moonlit yard. There, under the bananas, lay Keawe, his mouth in the dust, and as he lay he moaned.

It was Kokua's first thought to run forward and console him; her second potently withheld her. Keawe had borne himself before his wife like a brave man; it became her little in the hour of weakness to intrude upon his shame. With the thought she drew back into the house.

"Heaven," she thought, "how careless have I been—how weak! It is he, not I, that stands in this eternal peril; it was he, not I, that took the curse upon his soul. It is for my sake, and for the love of a creature of so little worth and such poor help, that he now beholds so close to him the flames of hell—ay, and smells the smoke of it, lying without there in the wind and moonlight. Am I so dull of spirit that never till now I surmised my duty, or have I seen it before and turned aside? But now, at least, I take up my soul in both the hands of my affection; now I say farewell to the white steps of heaven and the waiting faces of my friends. A love for a love, and let mine be equalled with Keawe's! A soul for a soul, and be it mine to perish!"

She was a deft woman with her hands, and was soon apparelled. She took in her hands the change—the precious centimes they kept ever at their side; for this coin is little used, and they had made provision at a government office. When she was forth in the avenue clouds came on the wind, and the moon was blackened. The town slept, and she knew not whither to turn till she heard one coughing in the shadow of the trees.

"Old man," said Kokua, "what do you here abroad in the cold night?"

The old man could scarce express himself for coughing, but she made out that he was old and poor, and a stranger in the island.

"Will you do me a service?" said Kokua. "As one stranger to another, and as an old man to a young woman, will you help a daughter of Hawaii?"

"Ah," said the old man. "So you are the witch from the Eight Islands, and even my old soul you seek to entangle. But I have heard of you, and defy your wickedness."

"Sit down here," said Kokua, "and let me tell you a tale." And she told him the story of Keawe from the beginning to the end.

"And now," said she, "I am his wife, whom he bought with his soul's welfare. And what should I do? If I went to him myself and offered to buy it, he will refuse. But if you go, he will sell it eagerly; I will await you here; you will buy it for four centimes, and I will buy it again for three. And the Lord strengthen a poor girl!"

"If you meant falsely," said the old man, "I think God would strike you dead."

"He would!" cried Kokua. "Be sure he would. I could not be so treacherous; God would not suffer it."

"Give me the four centimes and await me here," said the old man.

Now, when Kokua stood alone in the street, her spirit died. The wind roared in the trees, and it seemed to her the rushing of the flames of hell; the shadows towered in the light of the streetlamp, and they seemed to her the snatching hands of evil ones. If she had had the strength, she must have run away, and if she had had the breath, she must have screamed aloud; but, in truth, she could do neither, and stood and trembled in the avenue, like an affrighted child.

Then she saw the old man returning, and he had the bottle in his hand.

"I have done your bidding," said he, "I left your husband weeping like a child; tonight he will sleep easy." And he held the bottle forth.

"Before you give it me," Kokua panted, "take the good with the evil—ask to be delivered from your cough."

"I am an old man," replied the other, "and too near the gate of the grave to take a favour from the devil. But what is this? Why do you not take the bottle? Do you hesitate?"

"Not hesitate!" cried Kokua. "I am only weak. Give me a moment. It is my hand resists, my flesh shrinks back from the accursed thing. One moment only!"

The old man looked upon Kokua kindly. "Poor child!" said he, "you fear: your soul misgives you. Well, let me keep it. I am old, and can never more be happy in this world, and as for the next——"

"Give it me!" gasped Kokua. "There is your money. Do you think I am so base as that? Give me the bottle."

"God bless you, child," said the old man.

Kokua concealed the bottle under her holoku, said farewell to the old man, and walked off along the avenue, she cared not whither. For all roads were now the same to her, and led equally to hell. Sometimes she walked, and sometimes ran; sometimes she screamed out loud in the night, and sometimes lay by the wayside in the dust and wept. All that she had heard of hell came back to her; she saw the flames blaze, and she smelled the smoke, and her flesh withered on the coals.

Near day she came to her mind again, and returned to the house. It was even as the old man said—Keawe slumbered like a child. Kokua stood and gazed upon his face.

"Now, my husband," said she, "it is your turn to sleep. When you wake it will be your turn to sing and laugh. But for poor Kokua, alas! that meant no evil—for poor Kokua no more sleep, no more singing, no more delight, whether in earth or heaven."

With that she lay down in the bed by his side, and her misery was so extreme that she fell in a deep slumber instantly.

Late in the morning her husband woke her and gave her the good news. It seemed he was silly with delight, for he paid no heed to her distress, ill though she dissembled it. The words stuck in her mouth, it mattered not; Keawe did the speaking. She ate not a bite, but who was to observe it? For Keawe cleared the dish. Kokua saw and heard him, like some strange thing in a dream; there were times when she forgot or doubted, and put her hands to her brow; to know herself doomed and hear her husband babble seemed so monstrous.

All the while Keawe was eating and talking, and planning the time of their return, and thanking her for saving him and fondling her, and calling her the true helper after all. He laughed at the old man that was fool enough to buy that bottle.

"A worthy old man he seemed," Keawe said. "But no one can judge by appearances. For why did the old reprobate require the bottle?"

"My husband," said Kokua, humbly, "his purpose may have been good."

Keawe laughed like an angry man.

"Fiddle-de-dee!" cried Keawe. "An old rogue, I tell you; and an old ass to boot. For the bottle was hard enough to sell at four centimes; and at three it will be quite impossible. The margin is not broad enough, the thing begins to smell of scorching—brrr!" said he, and shuddered. "It is true I bought it myself at a cent, when I knew not there were smaller coins. I was a fool for my pains; there will never be found another, and whoever has that bottle now will carry it to the pit."

"O my husband!" said Kokua. "Is it not a terrible thing to save oneself by the eternal ruin of another? It seems to me I could not laugh. I would be humbled. I would be filled with melancholy. I would pray for the poor holder."

Then Keawe, because he felt the truth of what she said, grew the more angry. "Heighty-teighty!" cried he. "You may be filled with melancholy if you please. It is not the mind of a good wife. If you thought at all of me, you would sit shamed."

Thereupon he went out, and Kokua was alone.

What chance had she to sell that bottle at two centimes? None, she perceived. And if she had any, here was her husband hurrying her away to a country where there was nothing lower than a cent. And here—on the morrow of her sacrifice—was her husband leaving her and blaming her.

She would not even try to profit by what time she had, but sat in the house, and now had the bottle out and viewed it with unutterable fear, and now, with loathing, hid it out of sight.

"My husband, I am ill," she said. "I am out of heart. Excuse me, I can take no pleasure."

Then was Keawe more wroth than ever. With her, because he thought she was brooding over the case of the old man; and with himself, because he thought she was right and was ashamed to be so happy.

"This is your truth," cried he, "and this your affection! Your husband is just saved from eternal ruin, which he encountered for the love of you—and you can take no pleasure! Kokua, you have a disloyal heart."

He went forth again furious, and wandered in the town all day. He met friends, and drank with them; they hired a carriage and drove into the country, and there drank again. All the time Keawe was ill at ease, because he was taking this pastime while his wife was sad, and because he knew in his heart that she was more right than he; and the knowledge made him drink the deeper.

Now there was an old brutal Haole drinking with him, one that had been a boatswain of a whaler—a runaway, a digger in gold mines, a convict in prisons. He had a low mind and a foul mouth; he loved to drink and to see others drunken; and he pressed the glass upon Keawe. Soon there was no more money in the company.

"Here, you!" says the boatswain, "you are rich, you have been always saying. You have a bottle or some foolishness."

"Yes," says Keawe, "I am rich; I will go back and get some money from my wife, who keeps it."

"That's a bad idea, mate," said the boatswain. "Never you trust a petticoat with dollars. They're all as false as water; you keep an eye on her."

Now this word struck in Keawe's mind; for he was muddled with what he had been drinking.

"I should not wonder but she was false, indeed," thought he. "Why else should she be so cast down at my release? But I will show her I am not the man to be fooled. I will catch her in the act."

Accordingly, when they were back in town, Keawe bade the boatswain wait for him at the corner, by the old calaboose, and went forward up the avenue alone to the door of his house. The night had come again; there was a light within, but never a sound; and Keawe crept about the corner, opened the back door softly, and looked in.

There was Kokua on the floor, the lamp at her side; before her was a milk-white bottle, with a round belly and a long neck; and as she viewed it, Kokua wrung her hands.

A long time Keawe stood and looked in the doorway. At first he was struck stupid; and then fear fell upon him that the bargain had been made amiss, and the bottle had come back to him as it came at San Francisco; and at that his knees were loosened, and the fumes of the wine departed from his head like mists off a river in the morning. And then he had another thought; and it was a strange one, that made his cheeks to burn.

"I must make sure of this," thought he.

So he closed the door, and went softly round the corner again, and then came noisily in, as though he were but now returned. And, lo! by the time he opened the front door no bottle was to be seen; and Kokua sat in a chair and started up like one awakened out of sleep.

"I have been drinking all day and making merry," said Keawe. "I have been with good companions, and now I only come back for money, and return to drink and carouse with them again."

Both his face and voice were as stern as judgment, but Kokua was too troubled to observe.

"You do well to use your own, my husband," said she, and her words trembled.

"Oh, I do well in all things," said Keawe, and he went straight to the chest and took out money. But he looked besides in the corner where they kept the bottle, and there was no bottle there.

At that the chest heaved upon the floor like a sea-billow, and the house span about him like a wreath of smoke, for he saw he was lost now, and there was no escape. "It is what I feared," he thought. "It was she who has bought it."

And then he came to himself a little and rose up; but the sweat streamed on his face as thick as the rain and as cold as the well-water.

"Kokua," said he, "I said to you today what ill became me. Now I return to carouse with my jolly companions," and at that he laughed a little quietly. "I will take more pleasure in the cup if you forgive me."

She clasped his knees in a moment; she kissed his knees with flowing tears.

"Oh," she cried, "I ask but a kind word!"

"Let us never one think hardly of the other," said Keawe, and was gone out of the house.

Now, the money that Keawe had taken was only some of that store of centime pieces they had laid in at their arrival. It was very sure he had no mind to be drinking. His wife had given her soul for him, now he must give his for hers; no other thought was in the world with him.

At the corner, by the old calaboose, there was the boatswain waiting.

"My wife has the bottle," said Keawe, "and, unless you help me to recover it, there can be no more money and no more liquor tonight."

"You do not mean to say you are serious about that bottle?" cried the boatswain.

"There is the lamp," said Keawe. "Do I look as if I was jesting?"

"That is so," said the boatswain. "You look as serious as a ghost."

"Well, then," said Keawe, "here are two centimes; you must go to my wife in the house, and offer her these for the bottle, which (if I am not much mistaken) she will give you instantly. Bring it to me here, and I will buy it back from you for one; for that is the law with this bottle, that it still must be sold for a less sum. But whatever you do, never breathe a word to her that you have come from me."

"Mate, I wonder are you making a fool of me?" asked the boatswain.

"It will do you no harm if I am," returned Keawe.

"That is so, mate," said the boatswain.

"And if you doubt me," added Keawe, "you can try. As soon as you are clear of the house, wish to have your pocket full of money, or a bottle of the best rum, or what you please, and you will see the virtue of the thing."

"Very well, Kanaka," says the boatswain. "I will try; but if you are having your fun out of me, I will take my fun out of you with a belaying pin."

So the whalerman went off up the avenue; and Keawe stood and

Before her was a milk-white bottle, with
a round belly and a long neck.

waited. It was near the same spot where Kokua had waited the night before; but Keawe was more resolved, and never faltered in his purpose; only his soul was bitter with despair.

It seemed a long time he had to wait before he heard a voice singing in the darkness of the avenue. He knew the voice to be the boatswain's; but it was strange how drunken it appeared upon a sudden.

Next the man himself came stumbling into the light of the lamp. He had the devil's bottle buttoned in his coat; another bottle was in his hand; and even as he came in view he raised it to his mouth and drank.

"You have it," said Keawe. "I see that."

"Hands off!" cried the boatswain, jumping back. "Take a step near me, and I'll smash your mouth. You thought you could make a catspaw of me, did you?"

"What do you mean?" cried Keawe.

"Mean?" cried the boatswain. "This is a pretty good bottle, this is; that's what I mean. How I got it for two centimes I can't make out; but I am sure you shan't have it for one."

"You mean you won't sell?" gasped Keawe.

"No, sir," cried the boatswain. "But I'll give you a drink of the rum, if you like."

"I tell you," said Keawe, "the man who has that bottle goes to hell."

"I reckon I'm going anyway," returned the sailor; "and this bottle's the best thing to go with I've struck yet. No sir!" he cried again, "this is my bottle now, and you can go and fish for another."

"Can this be true?" Keawe cried. "For your own sake, I beseech you, sell it me!"

"I don't value any of your talk," replied the boatswain. "You thought I was a flat, now you see I'm not; and there's an end. If you won't have a swallow of the rum, I'll have one myself. Here's your health, and good night to you!"

So off he went down the avenue towards town, and there goes the bottle out of the story.

But Keawe ran to Kokua light as the wind; and great was their joy that night; and great, since then, has been the peace of all their days in the Bright House.

Markheim

"Y"ES," SAID THE dealer, "our windfalls are of various kinds. Some customers are ignorant, and then I touch a dividend of my superior knowledge. Some are dishonest," and here he held up the candle, so that the light fell strongly on his visitor, "and in that case," he continued, "I profit by my virtue."

Markheim had but just entered from the daylight streets, and his eyes had not yet grown familiar with the mingled shine and darkness in the shop. At these pointed words, and before the near presence of the flame, he blinked painfully and looked aside.

The dealer chuckled. "You come to me on Christmas Day," he resumed, "when you know that I am alone in my house, put up my shutters, and make a point of refusing business. Well, you will have to pay for that; you will have to pay for my loss of time, when I should be balancing my books; you will have to pay, besides, for a kind of manner that I remark in you today very strongly. I am the essence of discretion, and ask no awkward questions; but when a customer cannot look me in the eye, he has to pay for it." The dealer once more chuckled; and then, changing to his usual business voice, though still with a note of irony, "You can give, as usual, a clear account of how you came into the possession of the object?" he continued. "Still your uncle's cabinet? A remarkable collector, sir!"

And the little pale, round-shouldered dealer stood almost on tiptoe, looking over the top of his gold spectacles, and nodding his head with every mark of disbelief. Markheim returned his gaze with one of infinite pity, and a touch of horror.

"This time," said he, "you are in error. I have not come to sell, but to buy. I have no curios to dispose of; my uncle's cabinet is bare to the wainscot; even were it still intact, I have done well on the Stock Exchange, and should more likely add to it than otherwise, and my errand today is simplicity itself. I seek a Christmas present for a lady," he continued, waxing more fluent as he struck into the speech he had prepared; "and certainly I owe you every excuse for thus disturbing you upon so small a matter. But the thing was neglected yesterday; I must produce my little compliment at dinner; and, as you very well know, a rich marriage is not a thing to be neglected."

There followed a pause during which the dealer seemed to weigh this statement incredulously. The ticking of many clocks among the curious lumber of the shop and the faint rushing of the cabs in a near thoroughfare filled up the interval of silence.

"Well, sir," said the dealer, "be it so. You are an old customer, after all; and if, as you say, you have the chance of a good marriage, far be it from me to be an obstacle.—Here is a nice thing for a lady now," he went on, "this hand glass—fifteenth century, warranted; comes from a good collection, too; but I reserve the name, in the interests of my customer, who was just like yourself, my dear sir, the nephew and sole heir of a remarkable collector."

The dealer, while he thus ran on in his dry and biting voice, had stooped to take the object from its place; and, as he had done so, a shock had passed through Markheim, a start both of hand and foot, a sudden leap of many tumultuous passions to the face. It passed as swiftly as it came, and left no trace beyond a certain trembling of the hand that now received the glass.

"A glass," he said hoarsely, and then paused, and repeated it more clearly. "A glass? For Christmas? Surely not?"

"And why not?" cried the dealer. "Why not a glass?"

Markheim was looking upon him with an indefinable expression. "You ask me why not?" he said. "Why, look here—look in it—look at yourself! Do you like to see it? No! nor I—nor any man."

The little man had jumped back when Markheim had so suddenly confronted him with the mirror; but now, perceiving there was nothing worse on hand, he chuckled. "Your future lady, sir, must be pretty hard-favoured," said he.

"I ask you," said Markheim, "for a Christmas present, and you give me this—this damned reminder of years, and sins and follies—this hand-conscience! Did you mean it? Had you a thought in your mind? Tell me. It will be better for you if you do. Come, tell me about yourself. I hazard a guess now, that you are in secret a very charitable man?"

The dealer looked closely at his companion. It was very odd, Markheim did not appear to be laughing; there was something in his face like an eager sparkle of hope, but nothing of mirth.

"What are you driving at?" the dealer asked.

"Not charitable?" returned the other, gloomily. "Not charitable; not pious; not scrupulous; unloving, unbeloved; a hand to get money, a safe to keep it. Is that all? Dear God, man, is that all?"

"I will tell you what it is," began the dealer, with some sharpness, and then broke off again into a chuckle. "But I see this is a love match of yours, and you have been drinking the lady's health."

"Ah!" cried Markheim, with a strange curiosity. "Ah, have you been in love? Tell me about that."

"I," cried the dealer. "I in love! I never had the time, nor have I the time today for all this nonsense. Will you take the glass?"

"Where is the hurry?" returned Markheim. "It is very pleasant to stand here talking; and life is so short and insecure that I would not hurry away from any pleasure—no, not even from so mild a one as this. We should rather cling, cling to what little we can get, like a man at a cliff's edge. Every second is a cliff, if you think upon it—a cliff a mile high—high enough, if we fall, to dash us out of every feature of humanity. Hence it is best to talk pleasantly. Let us talk of each other; why should we wear this mask? Let us be confidential. Who knows we might become friends?"

"I have just one word to say to you," said the dealer. "Either make your purchase, or walk out of my shop."

"True, true," said Markheim. "Enough fooling. To business. Show me something else."

The dealer stooped once more, this time to replace the glass upon the shelf, his thin blond hair falling over his eyes as he did so. Markheim moved a little nearer, with one hand in the pocket of his greatcoat; he drew himself up and filled his lungs; at the same time many different emotions were depicted together on his face—terror, horror, and resolve, fascination and a physical repulsion; and through a haggard lift of his upper lip, his teeth looked out.

"This, perhaps, may suit," observed the dealer; and then, as he began to re-arise, Markheim bounded from behind upon his victim. The long, skewer-like dagger flashed and fell. The dealer struggled like a hen, striking his temple on the shelf, and then tumbled on the floor in a heap.

Time had some score of small voices in that shop, some stately and slow as was becoming to their great age; others garrulous and hurried. All these told out the seconds in an intricate chorus of tickings. Then the passage of a lad's feet, heavily running on the pavement, broke in upon these smaller voices and startled Markheim into the consciousness of his surroundings. He looked about him awfully. The candle stood on the counter, its flame solemnly wagging in a draught; and by that inconsiderable movement, the whole room was filled with noiseless bustle and kept heaving like a sea: the tall shadows nodding, the gross blots of darkness swelling and dwindling as with respiration, the faces of the portraits and the china gods changing and wavering like images in water. The inner door stood ajar, and peered into that leaguer of shadows with a long slit of daylight like a pointing finger.

From these fear-stricken rovings, Markheim's eyes returned to the body of his victim, where it lay both humped and sprawling, incredibly small and strangely meaner than in life. In these poor, miserly clothes, in that ungainly attitude, the dealer lay like so much sawdust. Markheim had feared to see it, and, lo! it was nothing. And yet, as he gazed, this bundle of old clothes and pool of blood began to find eloquent voices. There it must lie; there was none to work the cunning hinges or direct the miracle of locomotion—there it must lie till it was found. Found! ay, and then? Then would this dead flesh lift up a cry that would ring over England, and fill the world with the echoes of pursuit. Ay, dead or not, this was the enemy. "Time was that when the brains were out," he thought; and the first word struck into his mind. Time, now that the deed was accomplished—time, which had closed for the victim, had become instant and momentous for the slayer.

The thought was yet in his mind, when, first one and then another, with every variety of pace and voice—one deep as the bell from a cathedral turret, another ringing on its treble notes the prelude of a waltz—the clocks began to strike the hour of three in the afternoon.

The sudden outbreak of so many tongues in that dumb chamber staggered him. He began to bestir himself, going to and fro with the candle, beleaguered by moving shadows, and startled to the soul by chance reflections. In many rich mirrors, some of home designs, some from Venice or Amsterdam, he saw his face repeated and repeated, as it were an army of spies; his own eyes met and detected him; and the sound of his own steps, lightly as they fell, vexed the surrounding quiet. And still, as he continued to fill his pockets, his mind accused him, with a sickening iteration, of the thousand faults of his design. He should have chosen a more quiet hour; he should have prepared an alibi; he should not have used a knife; he should have been more cautious, and only bound and gagged the dealer, and not killed him; he should have been more bold, and killed the servant also; he should have done all things otherwise; poignant regrets, weary, incessant toiling of the mind to change what was unchangeable, to plan what was now useless, to be the architect of the irrevocable past. Meanwhile, and behind all this activity, brute terrors, like the scurrying of rats in a deserted attic, filled the more remote chambers of his brain with riot; the hand of the constable would fall heavy on his shoulder, and his nerves would jerk like a hooked fish;

or he beheld, in galloping defile, the dock, the prison, the gallows and the black coffin.

Terror of the people in the street sat down before his mind like a besieging army. It was impossible, he thought, but that some rumour of the struggle must have reached their ears and set on edge their curiosity; and now, in all the neighbouring houses, he divined them sitting motionless and with uplifted ear—solitary people, condemned to spend Christmas dwelling alone on memories of the past, and now startlingly recalled from that tender exercise; happy family parties, struck into silence round the table, the mother still with raised finger; every degree and age and humour, but all, by their own hearts, prying and hearkening and weaving the rope that was to hang him. Sometimes it seemed to him he could not move too softly; the clink of the tall Bohemian goblets rang out loudly like a bell; and alarmed by the bigness of the ticking, he was tempted to stop the clocks. And then, again, with a swift transition of his terrors, the very silence of the place appeared a source of peril, and a thing to strike and freeze the passerby; and he would step more boldly, and bustle aloud among the contents of the shop, and imitate, with elaborate bravado, the movements of a busy man at ease in his own house.

But he was now so pulled about by different alarms that, while one portion of his mind was still alert and cunning, another trembled on the brink of lunacy. One hallucination in particular took a strong hold on his credulity. The neighbour hearkening with white face beside his window, the passerby arrested by a horrible surmise on the pavement—these could at worst suspect, they could not know; through the brick walls and shuttered windows only sounds could penetrate. But here, within the house, was he alone? He knew he was; he had watched the servant set forth sweethearting, in her poor best, "out for the day" written in every ribbon and smile. Yes, he was alone, of course; and yet, in the bulk of empty house above him, he could surely hear a stir of delicate footing—he was surely conscious, inexplicably conscious of some presence. Ay, surely; to every room and corner of the house his imagination followed it; and now it was a faceless thing, and yet had eyes to see with; and again it was a shadow of himself; and yet again beheld the image of the dead dealer, reinspired with cunning and hatred.

At times, with a strong effort, he would glance at the open door which still seemed to repel his eyes. The house was tall, the skylight small and dirty, the day blind with fog; and the light that filtered down to the ground storey was exceedingly faint, and showed dimly on the threshold of the shop. And yet, in that strip of doubtful brightness, did there not hang wavering a shadow?

Suddenly, from the street outside, a very jovial gentleman began to beat with a staff on the shop door, accompanying his blows with shouts and railleries in which the dealer was continually called upon by name. Markheim, smitten into ice, glanced at the dead man. But no! he lay quite still; he was fled away far beyond earshot of these blows and shoutings; he was sunk beneath seas of silence; and his name, which would once have caught his notice above the howling of a storm, had become an empty sound. And presently the jovial gentleman desisted from his knocking and departed.

Here was a broad hint to hurry what remained to be done, to get forth from this accusing neighbourhood, to plunge into a bath of London multitudes, and to reach, on the other side of day, that haven of safety and apparent innocence—his bed. One visitor had come: at any moment another might follow and be more obstinate. To have done the deed, and yet not to reap the profit would be too abhorrent a failure. The money, that was now Markheim's concern; and as a means to that, the keys.

He glanced over his shoulder at the open door, where the shadow was still lingering and shivering; and with no conscious repugnance of the mind, yet with a tremor of the belly, he drew near the body of his victim. The human character had quite departed. Like a suit half-stuffed with bran, the limbs lay scattered, the trunk doubled, on the floor; and yet the thing repelled him. Although so dingy and inconsiderable to the eye, he feared it might have more significance to the touch. He took the body by the shoulders, and turned it on its back. It was strangely light and supple, and the limbs, as if they had been broken, fell into the oddest postures. The face was robbed of all expression; but it was as pale as wax, and shockingly smeared with blood about one temple. That was, for

Markheim, the one displeasing circumstance. It carried him back, upon the instant, to a certain fair day in a fishers' village: a grey day, a piping wind, a crowd upon the street, the blare of brasses, the booming of drums, the nasal voice of a ballad singer; and a boy going to and fro, buried overhead in the crowd and divided between interest and fear, until coming out upon the chief place of concourse, he beheld a booth and a great screen with pictures, dismally designed, garishly coloured: Brownrigg with her apprentice; the Mannings with their murdered guest; Weare in the death grip of Thurtell; and a score besides of famous crimes. The thing was as clear as an illusion; he was once again that little boy; he was looking once again, and with the same sense of physical revolt, at these vile pictures; he was still stunned by the thumping of the drums. A bar of that day's music returned upon his memory; and at that, for the first time, a qualm came over him, a breath of nausea, a sudden weakness of the joints, which he must instantly resist and conquer.

He judged it more prudent to confront than to flee from these considerations; looking the more hardily in the dead face, bending his mind to realise the nature and greatness of his crime. So little a while ago that face had moved with every change of sentiment, that pale mouth had spoken, that body had been all on fire with governable energies; and now, and by his act, that piece of life had been arrested, as the horologist, with interjected finger, arrests the beating of the clock. So he reasoned in vain; he could rise to no more remorseful consciousness; the same heart which had shuddered before the painted effigies of crime looked on its reality unmoved. At best, he felt a gleam of pity for one who had been endowed in vain with all those faculties that can make the world a garden of enchantment, one who had never lived and who was now dead. But of penitence, no, not a tremor.

With that, shaking himself clear of these considerations, he found the keys and advanced towards the open door of the shop. Outside, it had begun to rain smartly; and the sound of the shower upon the roof had banished silence. Like some dripping cavern, the chambers of the house were haunted by an incessant echoing which filled the ear and mingled with the ticking of the clocks. And, as Markheim approached the door, he seemed to hear, in answer to his own cautious tread, the steps of another foot withdrawing up the stair. The shadow still palpitated loosely on the threshold. He threw a ton's weight of resolve upon his muscles, and drew back the door.

The faint, foggy daylight glimmered dimly on the bare floor and stairs; on the bright suit of armour posted, halbert in hand, upon the landing; and on the dark wood carvings and framed pictures that hung against the yellow panels of the wainscot. So loud was the beating of the rain through all the house that, in Markheim's ears, it began to be distinguished into many different sounds. Footsteps and sighs, the tread of regiments marching in the distance, the chink of money in the counting, and the creaking of doors held stealthily ajar, appeared to mingle with the patter of the drops upon the cupola and the gushing of the water in the pipes. The sense that he was not alone grew upon him to the verge of madness. On every side he was haunted and begirt by presences. He heard them moving in the upper chambers; from the shop, he heard the dead man getting to his legs; and as he began with a great effort to mount the stairs, feet fled quietly before him and followed stealthily behind. If he were but deaf, he thought, how tranquilly he would possess his soul. An then again, and hearkening with ever fresh attention, he blessed himself for that unresting sense which held the outposts and stood a trusty sentinel upon his life. His head turned continually on his neck; his eyes, which seemed starting from their orbits, scouted on every side, and on every side were half-rewarded as with the tail of something nameless vanishing. The four-and-twenty steps to the first floor were four-and-twenty agonies.

On that first storey, the doors stood ajar, three of them like three ambushes, shaking his nerves like the throats of cannon. He could never again, he felt, be sufficiently immured and fortified from men's observing eyes; he longed to be home, girt in by walls, buried among bedclothes, and invisible to all but God. And at that thought he wondered a little, recollecting tales of other murderers and the fear they were said to entertain of heavenly avengers. It was not so, at least, with him. He feared the laws of nature, lest, in their callous and immutable procedure, they should preserve some damning evidence of his crime. He feared tenfold more, with a slavish, superstitious terror, some scission in the continuity of man's experience, some wilful illegality of nature. He played a game of skill, depending on the rules, calculating consequence from cause; and what if nature, as the defeated tyrant overthrew the chessboard, should break the mould of their succession? The like had befallen Napoleon (so writers said) when the winter changed the time of its appearance. The like might befall Markheim: the solid walls might become transparent and reveal his doings like those of bees in a glass hive; the stout planks might yield under his foot like quicksands and detain him in their clutch; ay, and there were soberer accidents that might destroy him; if, for instance, the house should fall and imprison him beside the body of his victim; or the house next door should fly on fire, and the firemen invade him from all sides. These things he feared; and, in a sense, these things might be called the hands of God reached forth against sin. But about God himself he was at ease; his act was doubtless exceptional, but so were his excuses, which God knew; it was there, and not among men, that he felt sure of justice.

When he had got safe into the drawing room, and shut the door behind him, he was aware of a respite from alarms. The room was quite dismantled, uncarpeted besides, and strewn with packing cases and incongruous furniture; several great pier glasses, in which he beheld himself at various angles, like an actor on a stage; many pictures, framed and unframed, standing, with their faces to the wall; a fine Sheraton sideboard, a cabinet of marquetry, and a great old bed, with tapestry hangings. The windows opened to the floor; but by great good fortune the lower part of the shutters had been closed, and this concealed him from the neighbours. Here, then, Markheim drew in a packing case before the cabinet, and began to search among the keys. It was a long business, for there were many; and it was irksome, besides; for, after all, there might be nothing in the cabinet, and time was on the wing. But the closeness of the occupation sobered him. With the tail of his eye he saw the door—even glanced at it from time to time directly, like a besieged commander pleased to verify the good estate of his defences. But in truth he was at peace. The rain falling in the street sounded natural and pleasant. Presently, on the other side, the notes of a piano were wakened to the music of a hymn, and the voices of many children took up the air and words. How stately, how comfortable was the melody! How fresh the youthful voices! Markheim gave ear to it smilingly, as he sorted out the keys; and his mind was thronged with answerable ideas and images; churchgoing children and the pealing of the high organ; children afield, bathers by the brookside, ramblers on the brambly common, kite-fliers in the windy and cloud-navigated sky; and then, at another cadence of the hymn, back again to church, and the somnolence of summer Sundays, and the high genteel voice of the parson (which he smiled a little to recall) and the painted Jacobean tombs, and the dim lettering of the Ten Commandments in the chancel.

And as he sat thus, at once busy and absent, he was startled to his feet. A flash of ice, a flash of fire, a bursting gush of blood, went over him, and then he stood transfixed and thrilling. A step mounted the stair slowly and steadily, and presently a hand was laid upon the knob, and the lock clicked, and the door opened.

Fear held Markheim in a vice. What to expect he knew not, whether the dead man walking, or the official ministers of human justice, or some chance witness blindly stumbling in to consign him to the gallows. But when a face was thrust into the aperture, glanced round the room, looked at him, nodded and smiled as if in friendly recognition, and then withdrew again, and the door closed behind it, his fear broke loose from his control in a hoarse cry. At the sound of this the visitant returned.

"Did you call me?" he asked, pleasantly and with that he entered the room and closed the door behind him.

Markheim stood and gazed at him with all his eyes. Perhaps there was a film upon his sight, but the outlines of the newcomer seemed to change and waver like those of the idols in the wavering candlelight of the shop; and at times he thought he knew him; and at times he thought he bore a likeness to himself; and always, like a lump of living terror, there lay in his bosom the conviction that this thing was not of the earth and not of God.

And yet the creature had a strange air of the commonplace, as he stood looking on Markheim with a smile; and when he added: "You are looking for the money, I believe?" it was in the tones of everyday politeness.

Markheim made no answer.

"I should warn you," resumed the other, "that the maid has left her sweetheart earlier than usual and will soon be here. If Mr. Markheim be found in this house, I need not describe to him the consequences."

"You know me?" cried the murderer.

The visitor smiled. "You have long been a favourite of mine," he said; "and I have long observed and often sought to help you."

"What are you?" cried Markheim. "The devil?"

"What I may be," returned the other, "cannot affect the service I propose to render you."

"It can," cried Markheim; "it does! Be helped by you? No, never; not by you! You do not know me yet; thank God, you do not know me!"

"I know you," replied the visitant, with a sort of kind severity or rather firmness. "I know you to the soul."

"Know me!" cried Markheim. "Who can do so? My life is but a travesty and slander on myself. I have lived to belie my nature. All men do; all men are better than this disguise that grows about and stifles them. You see each dragged away by life, like one whom bravos have seized and muffled in a cloak. If they had their own control—if you could see their faces, they would be altogether different, they would shine out for heroes and saints! I am worse than most; myself is more overlaid; my excuse is known to me and God. But, had I the time, I could disclose myself."

"To me?" inquired the visitant.

"To you before all," returned the murderer. "I supposed you were intelligent. I thought—since you exist—you would prove a reader of the heart. And yet you would propose to judge me by my acts! Think of it; my acts! I was born and I have lived in a land of giants; giants have dragged me by the wrists since I was born out of my mother—the giants of circumstance. And you would judge me by my acts! But can you not look within? Can you not understand that evil is hateful to me? Can you not see within me the clear writing of conscience, never blurred by any wilful sophistry, although too often disregarded? Can you not read me for a thing that surely must be common as humanity—the unwilling sinner?"

"All this is very feelingly expressed," was the reply, "but it regards me not. These points of consistency are beyond my province, and I care not in the least by what compulsion you may have been dragged away, so as you are but carried in the right direction. But time flies; the servant delays, looking in the faces of the crowd and at the pictures on the hoardings, but still she keeps moving nearer; and remember, it is as if the gallows itself was striding towards you through the Christmas streets! Shall I help you; I, who know all? Shall I tell you where to find the money?"

"For what price?" asked Markheim.

"I offer you the service for a Christmas gift," returned the other.

Markheim could not refrain from smiling with a kind of bitter triumph. "No," said he, "I will take nothing at your hands; if I were dying of thirst, and it was your hand that put the pitcher to my lips, I should find the courage to refuse. It may be credulous, but I will do nothing to commit myself to evil."

"I have no objection to a deathbed repentance," observed the visitant.

"Because you disbelieve their efficacy!" Markheim cried.

"I do not say so," returned the other; "but I look on these things from a different side, and when the life is done my interest falls. The man has lived to serve me, to spread black looks under colour of religion, or to sow tares in the wheat field, as you do, in a course of weak compliance with desire. Now that he draws so near to his deliverance, he can add but one act of service—to repent, to die smiling, and thus to build up in confidence and hope the more timorous of my surviving followers. I am not so hard a master. Try me. Accept my help. Please yourself in life as you have done hitherto; please yourself more amply, spread your elbows at the board; and when the night begins to fall and the curtains to be drawn, I tell you, for your greater comfort, that you will find it even easy to compound your quarrel with your conscience, and to make a truckling peace with God. I came but now from such a deathbed, and the room was full of sincere mourners, listening to the man's last words: and when I looked into that face, which had been set as a flint against mercy, I found it smiling with hope."

"And do you, then, suppose me such a creature?" asked Markheim.

"Do you think I have no more generous aspiration than to sin, and sin, and sin, and, at last, sneak into heaven? My heart rises at the thought. Is this, then, your experience of mankind? Or is it because you find me with red hands that you presume such baseness? And is this crime of murder indeed so impious as to dry up the very springs of good?"

"Murder is to me no special category," replied the other. "All sins are murder, even as all life is war. I behold your race, like starving mariners on a raft, plucking crusts out of the hands of famine and feeding on each other's lives. I follow sins beyond the moment of their acting; I find in all that the last consequence is death; and to my eyes, the pretty maid who thwarts her mother with such taking graces on a question of a ball, drips no less visibly with human gore than such a murderer as yourself. Do I say that I follow sins? I follow virtues also; they differ not by the thickness of a nail, they are both scythes for the reaping angel of Death. Evil, for which I live, consists not in action but in character. The bad man is dear to me; not the bad act, whose fruits, if we could follow them far enough down the hurtling cataract of the ages, might yet be found more blessed than those of the rarest virtues. And it is not because you have killed a dealer, but because you are Markheim, that I offered to forward your escape."

"I will lay my heart open to you," answered Markheim. "This crime on which you find me is my last. On my way to it I have learned many lessons; itself is a lesson, a momentous lesson. Hitherto I have been driven with revolt to what I would not; I was a bondslave to poverty, driven and scourged. There are robust virtues that can stand in these temptations; mine was not so: I had a thirst of pleasure. But today, and out of this deed, I pluck both warning and riches—both the power and a fresh resolve to be myself. I become in all things a free actor in the world; I begin to see myself all changed, these hands the agents of good, this heart at peace. Something comes over me out of the past; something of what I have dreamed on Sabbath evenings to the sound of the church organ, of what I forecast when I shed tears over noble books, or talked, an innocent child, with my mother. There lies my life; I have wandered a few years, but now I see once more my city of destination."

"You are to use this money on the Stock Exchange, I think?" remarked the visitor; "and there, if I mistake not, you have already lost some thousands?"

"Ah," said Markheim, "but this time I have a sure thing."

"This time, again, you will lose," replied the visitor quietly.

"Ah, but I keep back the half!" cried Markheim.

"That also you will lose," said the other.

The sweat started upon Markheim's brow. "Well, then, what matter?" he exclaimed. "Say it be lost, say I am plunged again in poverty, shall one part of me, and that the worst, continue until the end to override the better? Evil and good run strong in me, haling me both ways. I do not love the one thing, I love all. I can conceive great deeds, renunciations, martyrdoms; and though I be fallen to such a crime as murder, pity is no stranger to my thoughts. I pity the poor; who knows their trials better than myself? I pity and help them; I prize love, I love honest laughter; there is no good thing nor true thing on earth but I love it from my heart. And are my vices only to direct my life, and my virtues to lie without effect, like some passive lumber of the mind? Not so; good, also, is a spring of acts."

But the visitant raised his finger. "For six-and-thirty years that you have been in this world," said he, "through many changes of fortune and varieties of humour, I have watched you steadily fall. Fifteen years ago you would have started at a theft. Three years back you would have blenched at the name of murder. Is there any crime, is there any cruelty or meanness, from which you still recoil? — five years from now I shall detect you in the fact! Downward, downward, lies your way; nor can anything but death avail to stop you."

"It is true," Markheim said huskily, "I have in some degree complied with evil. But it is so with all: the very saints, in the mere exercise of living, grow less dainty and take on the tone of their surroundings."

"I will propound to you one simple question," said the other; "and as you answer, I shall read to you your moral horoscope. You have grown in many things more lax; possibly you do right to be so; and at any account, it is the same with all men. But granting that, are you in any one particular, however trifling, more difficult to please with your own conduct, or do you go in all things with a looser rein?"

"In any one?" repeated Markheim, with an anguish of consideration. "No," he added, with despair, "in none! I have gone down in all."

"Then," said the visitor, "content yourself with what you are, for you will never change; and the words of your part on this stage are irrevocably written down."

Markheim stood for a long while silent, and indeed it was the visitor who first broke the silence. "That being so," he said, "shall I show you the money?"

"And grace?" cried Markheim.

"Have you not tried it?" returned the other. "Two or three years ago, did I not see you on the platform of revival meetings, and was not your voice the loudest in the hymn?"

"It is true," said Markheim; "and I see clearly what remains for me by way of duty. I thank you for these lessons from my soul; my eyes are opened, and I behold myself at last for what I am."

At this moment, the sharp note of the doorbell rang through the house; and the visitant, as though this were some concerted signal for which he had been waiting, changed at once in his demeanour. "The maid!" he cried. "She has returned, as I forewarned you, and there is now before you one more difficult passage. Her master, you must say, is ill; you must let her in, with an assured but rather serious countenance—no smiles, no overacting, and I promise you success! Once the girl is within, and the door closed, the same dexterity that has already rid you of the dealer will relieve you of this last danger in your path. Thenceforward you have the whole evening—the whole night, if needful—to ransack the treasures of the house and to make good your safety. This is help that comes to you with the mask of danger. Up!" he cried: "up, friend; your life hangs trembling in the scales: up, and act!"

Markheim steadily regarded his counsellor. "If I be condemned to evil acts," he said, "there is still one door of freedom open—I can cease from action. If my life be an ill thing, I can lay it down. Though I be, as you say truly, at the beck of every small temptation, I can yet, by one decisive gesture, place myself beyond the reach of all. My love of good is damned to barrenness; it may, and let it be! But I have still my hatred of evil; and from that, to your galling disappointment, you shall see that I can draw both energy and courage."

The features of the visitor began to undergo a wonderful and lovely change: they brightened and softened with a tender triumph; and, even as they brightened, faded and dislimned. But Markheim did not pause to watch or understand the transformation. He opened the door and went downstairs very slowly, thinking to himself. His past went soberly before him; he beheld it as it was, ugly and strenuous like a dream, random as chance medley—a scene of defeat. Life, as he thus reviewed it, tempted him no longer; but on the further side he perceived a quiet haven for his bark. He paused in the passage, and looked into the shop, where the candle still burned by the dead body. It was strangely silent. Thoughts of the dealer swarmed into his mind, as he stood gazing. And then the bell once more broke out into impatient clamour.

He confronted the maid upon the threshold with something like a smile.

"You had better go for the police," said he: "I have killed your master."

The Beach of Falesá

Being the Narrative of a South Sea Trader

CHAPTER 1

A South Sea Bridal

I SAW THAT ISLAND first when it was neither night nor morning. The moon was to the west, setting, but still broad and bright. To the east, and right amidships of the dawn, which was all pink, the daystar sparkled like a diamond. The land breeze blew in our faces, and smelt strong of wild lime and vanilla; other things besides, but these were the most plain; and the chill of it set me sneezing. I should say I had been for years on a low island near the line, living for the most part solitary among natives. Here was a fresh experience; even the tongue would be quite strange to me; and the look of these woods and mountains, and the rare smell of them, renewed my blood.

The captain blew out the binnacle lamp.

"There!" said he, "there goes a bit of smoke, Mr. Wiltshire, behind the break of the reef. That's Falesá, where your station is, the last village to the east; nobody lives to windward—I don't know why. Take my glass, and you can make the houses out."

I took the glass; and the shores leaped nearer, and I saw the tangle of the woods and the breach of the surf, and the brown roofs and the black insides of houses peeped among the trees.

"Do you catch a bit of white there to the east'ard?" the captain continued. "That's your house. Coral-built, stands high, verandah you could walk on three abreast; best station in the South Pacific. When old Adams saw it, he took and shook me by the hand. 'I've dropped into a soft thing here,' says he. 'So you have,' says I, 'and time too!' Poor Johnny! I never saw him again but the once, and then he had changed his tune—couldn't get on with the natives, or the whites, or something; and the next time we came round there, he was dead and buried. I took and put up a bit of a stick to him: 'John Adams, *obit* eighteen and sixty-eight. Go thou and do likewise.' I missed that man. I never could see much harm in Johnny."

"What did he die of?" I inquired.

"Some kind of sickness," says the captain. "It appears it took him sudden. Seems he got up in the night, and filled up on Pain Killer and Kennedy's Discovery. No go—he was booked beyond Kennedy. Then he had tried to open a case of gin. No go again—not strong enough. Then he must have turned to and run out on the verandah, and capsized over the rail. When they found him, the next day, he was clean crazy—carried on all the time about somebody watering his copra. Poor John!"

"Was it thought to be the island?" I asked.

"Well, it was thought to be the island, or the trouble, or something," he replied. "I never could hear but what it was a healthy place. Our last man, Vigours, never turned a hair. He left because of the beach—said he was afraid of Black Jack and Case and Whistling Jimmie, who was still alive at the time, but got drowned soon afterward when drunk. As for old Captain Randall, he's been here anytime since eighteen-forty, forty-five. I never could see much harm in Billy, nor much change. Seems as if he might live to be Old Kafoozleum. No, I guess it's healthy."

"There's a boat coming now," said I. "She's right in the pass; looks to be a sixteen-foot whale; two white men in the stern sheets."

"That's the boat that drowned Whistling Jimmie!" cried the captain; "let's see the glass. Yes, that's Case, sure enough, and the darkie. They've got a gallows bad reputation, but you know what a place the beach is for talking. My belief, that Whistling Jimmie was the worst of the trouble; and he's gone to glory, you see. What'll you bet they ain't after gin? Lay you five to two they take six cases."

When these two traders came aboard I was pleased with the looks of them at once, or, rather, with the looks of both, and the speech of one. I was sick for white neighbours after my four years at the line, which I always counted years of prison; getting tabooed, and going down to the Speak House to see and get it taken off; buying gin and going on a break, and then repenting; sitting in the house at night with the lamp for company; or walking on the beach and wondering what kind of a fool to call myself for being where I was. There were no other whites upon my island, and when I sailed to the next, rough customers made the most of the society. Now to see these two when they came aboard was a pleasure. One was a Negro, to be sure; but they were both rigged out smart in striped pyjamas and straw hats, and Case would have passed muster in a city. He was yellow and smallish, had a hawk's nose to his face, pale eyes, and his beard trimmed with scissors. No man knew his country, beyond he was of English speech; and it was clear he came of a good family and was splendidly educated. He was accomplished too; played the accordion first-rate; and give him a piece of a string or a cork or a pack of cards, and he could show you tricks equal to any professional. He could speak, when he chose, fit for a drawing room; and when he chose he could blaspheme worse than a Yankee boatswain, and talk smart to sicken a Kanaka. The way he thought would pay best at the moment, that was Case's way, and it always seemed to come natural, and like as if he was born to it. He had the courage of a lion and the cunning of a rat; and if he's not in hell today, there's no such place. I know but one good point to the man—that he was fond of his wife, and kind to her. She was a Samoa woman, and dyed her hair red—Samoa style; and when he came to die (as I have to tell of) they found one strange thing—that he had made a will, like a Christian, and the widow got the lot; all his, they said, and all Black Jack's, and the most of Billy Randall's in the bargain, for it was Case that kept the books. So she went off home in the schooner *Manu'a*, and does the lady to this day in her own place.

But of all this on the first morning I knew no more than a fly. Case used me like a gentleman and like a friend, made me welcome to Falesá, and put his services at my disposal, which was the more helpful from my ignorance of the natives. All the better part of the day we sat drinking better acquaintance in the cabin, and I never heard a man talk more to the point. There was no smarter trader, and none dodgier, in the islands. I thought Falesá seemed to be the right kind of a place; and the more I drank the lighter my heart. Our last trader had fled the place at half an hour's notice, taking a chance passage in a labour ship from up west. The captain, when he came, had found the station closed, the keys left with the native pastor, and a letter from the runaway, confessing he was fairly frightened of his life. Since then the firm had not been represented, and of course there was no cargo. The wind, besides, was fair, the captain hoped he could make his next island by dawn, with a good tide, and the business of landing my trade was gone about lively. There was no call for me to fool with it, Case said; nobody would touch my things, every-one was honest in Falesá, only about chickens or an odd knife or an odd stick of tobacco; and the best I could do was to sit quiet till the vessel left, then come straight to his house, see old Captain Randall, the father of the beach, take potluck, and go home to sleep when it got dark. So it was high noon, and the schooner was under way before I set my foot on shore at Falesá.

I had a glass or two on board; I was just off a long cruise, and the ground heaved under me like a ship's deck. The world was like all new-painted; my foot went along to music; Falesá might have been Fiddler's Green, if there is such a place, and more's the pity if there isn't! It was good to foot the grass, to look aloft at the green mountains, to see the men with their green wreaths and the women in their bright dresses, red and blue. On we went, in the strong sun and the cool shadow, liking both; and all the children in the town came trotting after with their shaven heads and their brown bodies, and raising a thin kind of a cheer in our wake, like crowing poultry.

"By the by," says Case, "we must get you a wife."

"That's so," said I; "I had forgotten."

There was a crowd of girls about us, and I pulled myself up and looked among them like a bashaw. They were all dressed out for the sake of the ship being in; and the women of Falesá are a handsome lot to see. If they have a fault, they are a trifle broad in the beam; and I was just thinking so when Case touched me.

"That's pretty," says he.

I saw one coming on the other side alone. She had been fishing; all she wore was a chemise, and it was wetted through. She was young and very slender for an island maid, with a long face, a high forehead, and a shy, strange, blindish look, between a cat's and a baby's.

"Who's she?" said I. "She'll do."

"That's Uma," said Case, and he called her up and spoke to her in the native. I didn't know what he said; but when he was in the midst she looked up at me quick and timid, like a child dodging a blow, then down again, and presently smiled. She had a wide mouth, the lips and chin cut like any statue's; and the smile came out for a moment and was gone. Then she stood with her head bent, and heard Case to an end, spoke back in the pretty Polynesian voice, looking him full in the face, heard him again in answer, and then with an obeisance started off. I had just a share of the bow, but never another shot of her eye, and there was no more word of smiling.

"I guess it's all right," said Case. "I guess you can have her. I'll make it square with the old lady. You can have your pick of the lot for a plug of tobacco," he added, sneering.

I suppose it was the smile that stuck in my memory, for I spoke back sharp. "She doesn't look that sort," I cried.

"I don't know that she is," said Case. "I believe she's as right as the mail. Keeps to herself, don't go round with the gang, and that. Oh, no, don't you misunderstand me—Uma's on the square." He spoke eager, I thought, and that surprised and pleased me. "Indeed," he went on, "I shouldn't make so sure of getting her, only she cottoned to the cut of your jib. All you have to do is to keep dark and let me work the mother my own way; and I'll bring the girl round to the captain's for the marriage."

I didn't care for the word marriage, and I said so.

"Oh, there's nothing to hurt in the marriage," says he. "Black Jack's the chaplain."

By this time we had come in view of the house of these three white men; for a Negro is counted a white man, and so is a Chinese! A strange idea, but common in the islands. It was a board house with a strip of rickety verandah. The store was to the front, with a counter, scales, and the finest possible display of trade: a case or two of tinned meats; a barrel of hard bread, a few bolts of cotton stuff, not to be compared with mine; the only thing well represented being the contraband firearms and liquor. "If these are my only rivals," thinks I, "I should do well in Falesá." Indeed, there was only the one way they could touch me, and that was with the guns and drink.

In the back room was old Captain Randall, squatting on the floor native-fashion, fat and pale, naked to the waist, grey as a badger, and his eyes set with drink. His body was covered with grey hair and crawled over by flies; one was in the corner of his eye—he never heeded; and the mosquitoes hummed about the man like bees. Any clean-minded man would have had the creature out at once and buried him; and to see him, and think he was seventy, and remember he had once commanded a ship, and come ashore in his smart togs, and talked big in bars and consulates, and sat in club verandahs, turned me sick and sober.

He tried to get up when I came in, but that was hopeless; so he reached me a hand instead, and stumbled out some salutation.

"Papa's[1] pretty full this morning," observed Case. "We've had an epidemic here; and Captain Randall takes gin for a prophylactic—don't you, Papa?"

"Never took such a thing in my life!" cried the captain, indignantly. "Take gin for my health's sake, Mr. What's-ever-your-name—'s a precautionary measure."

"That's all right, Papa," said Case. "But you'll have to brace up. There's going to be a marriage—Mr. Wiltshire here is going to get spliced."

[1]Please pronounce *pappa* throughout.

The old man asked to whom.

"To Uma," said Case.

"Uma!" cried the captain. "What's he want Uma for? 's he come here for his health, anyway? Wha' 'n hell's he want Uma for?"

"Dry up, Papa," said Case. " 'Tain't you that's to marry her. I guess you're not her godfather and godmother. I guess Mr. Wiltshire's going to please himself."

With that he made an excuse to me that he must move about the marriage, and left me alone with the poor wretch that was his partner and (to speak truth) his gull. Trade and station belonged both to Randall; Case and the Negro were parasites; they crawled and fed upon him like the flies, he none the wiser. Indeed, I have no harm to say of Billy Randall beyond the fact that my gorge rose at him, and the time I now passed in his company was like a nightmare.

The room was stifling hot and full of flies; for the house was dirty and low and small, and stood in a bad place, behind the village, in the borders of the bush, and sheltered from the trade. The three men's beds were on the floor, and a litter of pans and dishes. There was no standing furniture; Randall, when he was violent, tearing it to laths. There I sat and had a meal which was served us by Case's wife; and there I was entertained all day by that remains of man, his tongue stumbling among low old jokes and long old stories, and his own wheezy laughter always ready, so that he had no sense of my depression. He was nipping gin all the while. Sometimes he fell asleep, and awoke again, whimpering and shivering, and every now and again he would ask me why I wanted to marry Uma. "My friend," I was telling myself all day, "you must not come to be an old gentleman like this."

It might be four in the afternoon, perhaps, when the back door was thrust slowly open, and a strange old native woman crawled into the house almost on her belly. She was swathed in black stuff to her heels; her hair was grey in swatches; her face was tattooed, which was not the practice in that island; her eyes big and bright and crazy. These she fixed upon me with a rapt expression that I saw to be part acting. She said no plain word, but smacked and mumbled with her lips, and hummed aloud, like a child over its Christmas pudding. She came straight across the house, heading for me, and, as soon as she was alongside, caught up my hand and purred and crooned over it like a great cat. From this she slipped into a kind of song.

"Who the devil's this?" cried I, for the thing startled me.

"It's Fa'avao," says Randall; and I saw he had hitched along the floor into the farthest corner.

"You ain't afraid of her?" I cried.

"Me 'fraid!" cried the captain. "My dear friend, I defy her! I don't let her put her foot in here, only I suppose's different today for the marriage. 's Uma's mother."

"Well, suppose it is; what's she carrying on about?" I asked, more irritated, perhaps more frightened, than I cared to show; and the captain told me she was making up a quantity of poetry in my praise because I was to marry Uma. "All right, old lady," says I, with rather a failure of a laugh, "anything to oblige. But when you're done with my hand, you might let me know."

She did as though she understood; the song rose into a cry, and stopped; the woman crouched out of the house the same way that she came in, and must have plunged straight into the bush, for when I followed her to the door she had already vanished.

"These are rum manners," said I.

" 'S a rum crowd," said the captain, and, to my surprise, he made the sign of the cross on his bare bosom.

"Hillo!" says I, "are you a Papist?"

He repudiated the idea with contempt. "Hard-shell Baptis'," said he. "But, my dear friend, the Papists got some good ideas too; and that's one of 'em. You take my advice, and whenever you come across Uma or Fa'avao or Vigours, or any of that crowd, you take a leaf out o' the priests, and do what I do. Savvy?" says he, repeated the sign, and winked his dim eye at me. "No, *sir!*" he broke out again, "no Papists here!" and for a long time entertained me with his religious opinions.

I must have been taken with Uma from the first, or I should certainly have fled from that house, and got into the clean air, and the clean sea, or some convenient river—though, it's true, I was committed to Case; and, besides, I could never have held my head up in that island if I had run from a girl upon my wedding night.

The sun was down, the sky all on fire, and the lamp had been some time lighted, when Case came back with Uma and the Negro. She was dressed and scented; her kilt was of fine tapa, looking richer in the folds than any silk; her bust, which was of the colour of dark honey, she wore bare, only for some half a dozen necklaces of seeds and flowers; and behind her ears and in her hair she had the scarlet flowers of the hibiscus. She showed the best bearing for a bride conceivable, serious and still; and I thought shame to stand up with her in that mean house and before that grinning Negro. I thought shame, I say; for the mountebank was dressed with a big paper collar, the book he made believe to read from was an old volume of a novel, and the words of his service not fit to be set down. My conscience smote me when we joined hands; and when she got her certificate I was tempted to throw up the bargain and confess. Here is the document. It was Case that wrote it, signatures and all, in a leaf out of the ledger:

This is to certify that Uma, daughter of Fa'avao of Falesá, Island of——, is illegally married to Mr. John Wiltshire for one week, and Mr. John Wiltshire is at liberty to send her to hell when he pleases.

JOHN BLACKAMOAR,
Chaplain to the Hulks.

Extracted from the Register
by William T. Randall,
Master Mariner.

A nice paper to put in a girl's hand and see her hide away like gold. A man might easily feel cheap for less. But it was the practice in these parts, and (as I told myself) not the least the fault of us white men, but of the missionaries. If they let the natives be, I had never needed this deception, but taken all the wives I wished and left them when I pleased, with a clear conscience.

The more ashamed I was, the more hurry I was in to be gone; and our desires thus jumping together, I made the less remark of a change in the traders. Case had been all eagerness to keep me; now, as though he had attained a purpose, he seemed all eagerness to have me go. Uma, he said, could show me to my house, and the three bade us farewell indoors.

The night was nearly come; the village smelt of trees and flowers and the sea and breadfruit cooking; there came a fine roll of sea from the reef, and from a distance, among the woods and houses, many pretty sounds of men and children. It did me good to breathe free air; it did me good to be done with the captain, and see, instead, the creature at my side. I felt for all the world as though she were some girl at home in the Old Country, and forgetting myself for the minute, took her hand to walk with. Her fingers nestled into mine, I heard her breathe deep and quick, and all at once she caught my hand to her face and pressed it there. "You good!" she cried, and ran ahead of me, and stopped and looked back and smiled, and ran ahead of me again, thus guiding me through the edge of the bush, and by a quiet way to my own house.

The truth is, Case had done the courting for me in style—told her I was mad to have her, and cared nothing for the consequences; and the poor soul, knowing that which I was still ignorant of, believed it, every word, and had her head nigh turned with vanity and gratitude. Now, of all this I had no guess; I was one of those most opposed to any nonsense about native women, having seen so many whites eaten up by their wives' relatives, and made fools of into the bargain; and I told myself I must make a stand at once, and bring her to her bearings. But she looked so quaint and pretty as she ran away and then awaited me, and the thing was done so like a child or a kind dog, that the best I could do was just to follow her whenever she went on, to listen for the fall of her bare feet, and to watch in the dusk for the shining of her body. And there was another thought came in my head. She played kitten with me now when we were alone; but in the house she had carried it the way a countess might, so proud and humble. And what with her dress—for all there was so little of it, and that native enough—what with her fine tapa and fine scents, and her red flowers and seeds, that were quite as bright as jewels, only larger—it came over me she was a kind of countess really, dressed to hear great singers at a concert, and no even mate for a poor trader like myself.

She looked at me, not speaking, with eyes
that were eager and yet daunted.

She was the first in the house; and while I was still without I saw a match flash and the lamplight kindle in the windows. The station was a wonderful fine place, coral-built, with quite a wide verandah, and the main room high and wide. My chests and cases had been piled in, and made rather of a mess; and there, in the thick of the confusion, stood Uma by the table, awaiting me. Her shadow went all the way up behind her into the hollow of the iron roof; she stood against it bright, the lamplight shining on her skin. I stopped in the door, and she looked at me, not speaking, with eyes that were eager and yet daunted; then she touched herself on the bosom.

"Me—your wifie," she said. It had never taken me like that before; but the want of her took and shook all through me, like the wind in the luff of a sail.

I could not speak if I had wanted; and if I could, I would not. I was ashamed to be so much moved about a native, ashamed of the marriage too, and the certificate she had treasured in her kilt; and I turned aside and made believe to rummage among my cases. The first thing I lighted on was a case of gin, the only one that I had brought; and partly for the girl's sake and partly for horror of the recollections of old Randall, took a sudden resolve. I prised the lid off. One by one I drew the bottles with a pocket corkscrew, and sent Uma out to pour the stuff from the verandah.

She came back after the last, and looked at me puzzled-like.

"No good," said I, for I was now a little better master of my tongue. "Man he drink, he no good."

She agreed with this, but kept considering. "Why you bring him?" she asked presently. "Suppose you no want drink, you no bring him, I think."

"That's all right," said I. "One time I want drink too much; now no want. You see, I no savvy I get one little wifie. Suppose I drink gin, my little wifie be 'fraid."

To speak to her kindly was about more than I was fit for; I had made my vow I would never let on to weakness with a native, and I had nothing for it but to stop.

She stood looking gravely down at me where I sat by the open case. "I think you good man," she said. And suddenly she had fallen before me on the floor. "I belong you all-e-same pig!" she cried.

CHAPTER 2

The Ban

I CAME ON THE verandah just before the sun rose on the morrow. My house was the last on the east; there was a cape of woods and cliffs behind that hid the sunrise. To the west, a swift, cold river ran down, and beyond was the green of the village, dotted with cocoa palms and breadfruits and houses. The shutters were some of them down and some open; I saw the mosquito bars still stretched with shadows of people new-awakened sitting up inside; and all over the green others were stalking silent, wrapped in their many-coloured sleeping clothes, like Bedouins in Bible pictures. It was mortal still and solemn and chilly, and the light of the dawn on the lagoon was like the shining of a fire.

But the thing that troubled me was nearer hand. Some dozen young men and children made a piece of a half-circle, flanking my house: the river divided them, some were on the near side, some on the far, and one on a boulder in the midst; and they all sat silent, wrapped in their sheets, and stared at me and my house as straight as pointer dogs. I thought it strange as I went out. When I had bathed and come back again, and found them all there, and two or three more along with them, I thought it stranger still. What could they see to gaze at in my house, I wondered, and went in.

But the thought of these starers stuck in my mind, and presently I came out again. The sun was now up, but it was still behind the cape of woods. Say a quarter of an hour had come and gone. The crowd was greatly increased, the far bank of the river was lined for quite a way—perhaps thirty grown folk, and of children twice as many, some standing, some squatted on the ground, and all staring at my house. I have seen a house in a South Sea village thus surrounded, but then a trader was thrashing his wife inside, and she singing out. Here was nothing—the stove was alight, the smoke going up in a Christian

manner; all was shipshape and Bristol fashion. To be sure, there was a
stranger come, but they had a chance to see that stranger yesterday, and
took it quiet enough. What ailed them now? I leaned my arms on the
rail and stared back. Devil a wink they had in them! Now and then I
could see the children chatter, but they spoke so low not even the hum
of their speaking came my length. The rest were like graven images: they
stared at me, dumb and sorrowful, with their bright eyes; and it came
upon me things would look not much different if I were on the platform
of the gallows and these good folk had come to see me hanged.

I felt I was getting daunted, and began to be afraid I looked it, which
would never do. Up I stood, made believe to stretch myself, came down
the verandah stair, and strolled towards the river. There went a short
buzz from one to the other, like what you hear in theatres when the
curtain goes up; and some of the nearest gave back the matter of a pace.
I saw a girl lay one hand on a young man and make a gesture upward
with the other; at the same time she said something in the native with
a gasping voice. Three little boys sat beside my path, where I must pass
within three feet of them. Wrapped in their sheets with their shaved
heads and bits of topknots, and queer faces, they looked like figures on
a chimneypiece. A while they sat their ground, solemn as judges. I came
up hand over fist, doing my five knots, like a man that meant business;
and I thought I saw a sort of a wink and gulp in the three faces. Then
one jumped up (he was the farthest off) and ran for his mammy. The
other two, trying to follow suit, got foul, came to the ground together
bawling, wriggled right out of their sheets, and in a moment there were
all three of them scampering for their lives, and singing out like pigs.
The natives, who would never let a joke slip, even at a burial, laughed
and let up, as short as a dog's bark.

They say it scares a man to be alone. No such thing. What scares him
in the dark or the high bush is that he can't make sure, and there might
be an army at his elbow. What scares him worse is to be right in the
midst of a crowd, and have no guess of what they're driving at. When
that laugh stopped, I stopped too. The boys had not yet made their
offing; they were still on the full stretch going the one way, when I had
already gone about ship and was sheering off the other. Like a fool I had

come out, doing my five knots; like a fool I went back again. It must have been the funniest thing to see, and what knocked me silly, this time no one laughed; only one old woman gave a kind of pious moan, the way you have heard Dissenters in their chapels at the sermon.

"I never saw such fools of Kanakas as your people here," I said once to Uma, glancing out of the window at the starers.

"Savvy nothing," says Uma, with a kind of disgusted air that she was good at.

And that was all the talk we had upon the matter, for I was put out, and Uma took the thing so much as a matter of course that I was fairly ashamed.

All day, off and on, now fewer and now more, the fools sat about the west end of my house and across the river, waiting for the show, whatever that was—fire to come down from heaven, I suppose, and consume me, bones and baggage. But by evening, like real islanders, they had wearied of the business, and got away, and had a dance instead in the big house of the village, where I heard them singing and clapping hands till maybe ten at night, and the next day it seemed they had forgotten I existed. If fire had come down from heaven or the earth opened and swallowed me, there would have been nobody to see the sport or take the lesson, or whatever you like to call it. But I was to find they hadn't forgot either, and kept an eye lifting for phenomena over my way.

I was hard at it these days both getting my trade in order and taking stock of what Vigours had left. This was a job that made me pretty sick, and kept me from thinking on much else. Ben had taken stock the trip before—I knew I could trust Ben—but it was plain somebody had been making free in the meantime. I found I was out by what might easily cover six months' salary and profit, and I could have kicked myself all round the village to have been such a blamed ass, sitting boozing with that Case instead of attending to my own affairs and taking stock.

However, there's no use crying over spilt milk. It was done now, and couldn't be undone. All I could do was to get what was left of it, and my new stuff (my own choice) in order, to go round and get after the rats and cockroaches, and to fix up that store regular Sydney style. A fine show I made of it; and the third morning, when I had lit my pipe and stood in the doorway and looked in, and turned and looked far up the mountain and saw the cocoanuts waving and posted up the tons of copra, and over the village green and saw the island dandies and reckoned up the yards of print they wanted for their kilts and dresses, I felt as if I was in the right place to make a fortune, and go home again and start a public house. There was I, sitting in that verandah, in as handsome a piece of scenery as you could find, a splendid sun, and a fine, fresh, healthy trade that stirred up a man's blood like sea bathing; and the whole thing was clean gone from me, and I was dreaming England, which is, after all, a nasty, cold, muddy hole, with not enough light to see to read by; and dreaming the looks of my public, by a cant of a broad highroad like an avenue and with the sign on a green tree.

So much for the morning, but the day passed and the devil anyone looked near me, and from all I knew of the natives in other islands I thought this strange. People laughed a little at our firm and their fine stations, and at this station of Falesá in particular; all the copra in the district wouldn't pay for it (I heard them say) in fifty years, which I suppose was an exaggeration. But when the day went, and no business came at all, I began to get downhearted; and, about three in the afternoon, I went out for a stroll to cheer me up. On the green I saw a white man coming with a cassock on, by which and by the face of him I knew he was a priest. He was a good-natured old soul to look at, gone a little grizzled, and so dirty you could have written with him on a piece of paper.

"Good day, sir," said I.

He answered me eagerly in native.

"Don't you speak any English?" said I.

"French," says he.

"Well," said I, "I'm sorry, but I can't do anything there."

He tried me a while in the French, and then again in native, which he seemed to think was the best chance. I made out he was after more than passing the time of day with me, but had something to communicate, and I listened the harder. I heard the names of Adams and Case and of Randall—Randall the oftenest—and the word "poison," or something like it, and a native word that he said very often. I went home, repeating it to myself.

"What does fussy-ocky mean?" I asked of Uma, for that was as near as I could come to it.

"Make dead," said she.

"The devil it does!" says I. "Did ever you hear that Case had poisoned Johnny Adams?"

"Every man he savvy that," says Uma, scornful-like. "Give him white sand—bad sand. He got the bottle still. Suppose he give you gin, you no take him."

Now I had heard much the same sort of story in other islands, and the same white powder always to the front, which made me think the less of it. For all that, I went over to Randall's place to see what I could pick up, and found Case on the doorstep, cleaning a gun.

"Good shooting here?" says I.

"A 1," says he. "The bush is full of all kinds of birds. I wish copra was as plenty," says he—I thought, slyly—"but there don't seem anything doing."

I could see Black Jack in the store, serving a customer.

"That looks like business, though," said I.

"That's the first sale we've made in three weeks," said he.

"You don't tell me?" says I. "Three weeks? Well, well."

"If you don't believe me," he cries, a little hot, "you can go and look at the copra house. It's half-empty to this blessed hour."

"I shouldn't be much the better for that, you see," says I. "For all I can tell, it might have been whole empty yesterday."

"That's so," says he, with a bit of a laugh.

"By the by," I said, "what sort of a party is that priest? Seems rather a friendly sort."

At this Case laughed right out loud. "Ah!" says he, "I see what ails you now. Galuchet's been at you." *Father Galoshes* was the name he went by most, but Case always gave it the French quirk, which was another reason we had for thinking him above the common.

"Yes, I have seen him," I says. "I made out he didn't think much of your Captain Randall."

"That he don't!" says Case. "It was the trouble about poor Adams. The last day, when he lay dying, there was young Buncombe round. Ever met Buncombe?"

I told him no.

"He's a cure, is Buncombe!" laughs Case. "Well, Buncombe took it in his head that, as there was no other clergyman about, bar Kanaka pastors, we ought to call in Father Galuchet, and have the old man administered and take the sacrament. It was all the same to me, you may suppose; but I said I thought Adams was the fellow to consult. He was jawing away about watered copra and a sight of foolery. 'Look here,' I said, 'you're pretty sick. Would you like to see Galoshes?' He sat right up on his elbow. 'Get the priest,' says he, 'get the priest; don't let me die here like a dog!' He spoke kind of fierce and eager, but sensible enough. There was nothing to say against that, so we sent and asked Galuchet if he would come. You bet he would. He jumped in his dirty linen at the thought of it. But we had reckoned without Papa. He's a hard-shelled Baptist, is Papa; no Papists need apply. And he took and locked the door. Buncombe told him he was bigoted, and I thought he would have had a fit. 'Bigoted!' he says. 'Me bigoted? Have I lived to hear it from a jackanapes like you?' And he made for Buncombe, and I had to hold them apart; and there was Adams in the middle, gone luny again, and carrying on about copra like a born fool. It was good as the play, and I was about knocked out of time with laughing, when all of a sudden Adams sat up, clapped his hands to his chest, and went into the horrors. He died hard, did John Adams," says Case, with a kind of a sudden sternness.

"And what became of the priest?" I asked.

"The priest?" says Case. "Oh! he was hammering on the door outside, and crying on the natives to come and beat it in, and singing out it was a soul he wished to save, and that. He was a rare taking, was the priest. But what would you have? Johnny had slipped his cable; no more Johnny in the market; and the administration racket clean played out. Next thing, word came to Randall that the priest was praying upon Johnny's grave. Papa was pretty full, and got a club, and lit out straight for the place, and there was Galoshes on his knees, and a lot of natives looking on. You wouldn't think Papa cared that much about anything, unless it was liquor; but he and the priest stuck to it two hours, slanging each other in native, and every time Galoshes tried to kneel down Papa went for him with the club. There never were such larks in Falesá. The end of it was that Captain Randall knocked over with some kind of a fit or stroke, and the priest got in his goods after all. But he was the angriest priest you ever heard of, and complained to the chiefs about the outrage, as he called it. That was no account, for our chiefs are Protestant here; and, anyway, he had been making trouble about the drum for morning school, and they were glad to give him a wipe. Now he swears old Randall gave Adams poison or something, and when the two meet they grin at each other like baboons."

He told this story as natural as could be, and like a man that enjoyed the fun; though now I come to think of it after so long, it seems rather a sickening yarn. However, Case never set up to be soft, only to be square and hearty, and a man all round; and, to tell the truth, he puzzled me entirely.

I went home and asked Uma if she were a Popey, which I made out to be the native word for Catholics.

"*E le ai!*" says she. She always used the native when she meant "no" more than usually strong, and indeed, there's more of it. "No good Popey," she added.

Then I asked her about Adams and the priest, and she told me much the same yarn in her own way. So that I was left not much further on, but inclined, upon the whole, to think the bottom of the matter was the row about sacrament, and the poisoning only talk.

The next day was a Sunday, when there was no business to be looked for. Uma asked me in the morning if I was going to "pray"; I told her she bet not, and she stopped home herself, with no more words. I thought this seemed unlike a native, and a native woman, and a woman that had new clothes to show off; however, it suited me to the ground, and I made the less of it. The queer thing was that I came next door to going to church after all, a thing I'm little likely to forget. I had turned out for a stroll, and heard the hymn tune up. You know how it is. If you hear folk singing, it seems to draw you; and pretty soon I found myself alongside the church. It was a little, long, low place, coral-built, rounded off at both ends like a whaleboat, a big native roof on the top of it, windows without sashes and doorways without doors. I stuck my head into one of the windows, and the sight was so new to me—for things went quite different in the islands I was acquainted with—that I stayed and looked on. The congregation sat on the floor on mats, the women on one side, the men on the other, all rigged out to kill—the women with dresses and trade hats, the men in white jackets and shirts. The hymn was over; the pastor, a big buck Kanaka, was in the pulpit, preaching for his life; and by the way he wagged his head, and worked his voice, and made his points, and seemed to argue with the folks, I made out he was a gun at the business. Well, he looked up suddenly and caught my eye, and I give you my word he staggered in the pulpit; his eyes bulged out of his head, his hand rose and pointed at me like as if against his will, and the sermon stopped right there.

It isn't a fine thing to say for yourself, but I ran away; and if the same kind of shock was given me, I should run away again tomorrow. To see that palavering Kanaka struck all of a heap at the mere sight of me gave me a feeling as if the bottom had dropped out of the world. I went right home, and stayed there, and said nothing. You might think I would tell Uma, but that was against my system. You might have thought I would have gone over and consulted Case; but the truth was I was ashamed to speak of such a thing, I thought everyone would blurt out laughing in my face. So I held my tongue, and thought all the more; and the more I thought, the less I liked the business.

By Monday night I got it clearly in my head I must be tabooed. A new store to stand open two days in a village and not a man or woman come to see the trade, was past believing.

"Uma," said I, "I think I'm tabooed."

"I think so," said she.

I thought a while whether I should ask her more, but it's a bad idea to set natives up with any notion of consulting them, so I went to Case. It was dark, and he was sitting alone, as he did mostly, smoking on the the stairs.

"Case," said I, "here's a queer thing. I'm tabooed."

"Oh, fudge!" says he; " 'tain't the practice in these islands."

"That may be, or it mayn't," said I. "It's the practice where I was before. You can bet I know what it's like; and I tell it you for a fact, I'm tabooed."

"Well," said he, "what have you been doing?"

"That's what I want to find out," said I.

"Oh, you can't," said he; "it ain't possible. However, I'll tell you what I'll do. Just to put your mind at rest, I'll go round and find out for sure. Just you waltz in and talk to Papa."

"Thank you," I said, "I'd rather stay right out here on the verandah. Your house is so close."

"I'll call Papa out here, then," says he.

"My dear fellow," I says, "I wish you wouldn't. The fact is, I don't take to Mr. Randall."

Case laughed, took a lantern from the store, and set out into the village. He was gone perhaps a quarter of an hour, and he looked mighty serious when he came back.

"Well," said he, clapping down the lantern on the verandah steps, "I would never have believed it. I don't know where the impudence of these Kanakas'll go next; they seem to have lost all idea of respect for whites. What we want is a man of war—a German, if we could—they know how to manage Kanakas."

"I *am* tabooed then?" I cried.

"Something of the sort," said he. "It's the worst thing of the kind I've heard of yet. But I'll stand by you, Wiltshire, man to man. You come round here tomorrow about nine, and we'll have it out with the chiefs. They're afraid of me, or they used to be; but their heads are so big by now I don't know what to think. Understand me, Wiltshire; I don't count this your quarrel," he went on, with a great deal of resolution, "I count it all of our quarrel, I count it the White Man's Quarrel, and I'll stand to it through thick and thin, and there's my hand on it."

"Have you found out what's the reason?" I asked.

"Not yet," said Case. "But we'll fix them down tomorrow."

Altogether I was pretty well pleased with his attitude, and almost more the next day, when we met to go before the chiefs, to see him so stern and resolved. The chiefs awaited us in one of their big oval houses, which was marked out to us from a long way off by the crowd about the eaves, a hundred strong if there was one—men, women, and children. Many of the men were on their way to work and wore green wreaths, and it put me in thoughts of the first of May at home. This crowd opened and buzzed about the pair of us as we went in, with a sudden angry animation. Five chiefs were there; four mighty, stately men, the fifth old and puckered. They sat on mats in their white kilts and jackets; they had fans in their hands, like fine ladies; and two of the younger ones wore Catholic medals, which gave me matter of reflection. Our place was set, and the mats laid for us over against these grandees, on the near side of the house; the midst was empty; the crowd, close at our backs, murmured and craned and jostled to look on, and the shadows of them tossed in front of us on the clean pebbles on the floor. I was just a hair put out by the excitement of the commons, but the quiet civil appearance of the chiefs reassured me, all the more when their spokesman began and made a long speech in a low tone of voice, sometimes waving his hand towards Case, sometimes towards me, and sometimes knocking with his knuckles on the mat. One thing was clear: there was no sign of anger in the chiefs.

"What's he been saying?" I asked, when he had done.

"Oh, just that they're glad to see you, and they understand by me you wish to make some kind of complaint, and you're to fire away, and they'll do the square thing."

"It took a precious long time to say that," said I.

"Oh, the rest was sawder and *bonjour* and that," said Case. "You know what Kanakas are."

"Well, they don't get much *bonjour* out of me," said I. "You tell them who I am. I'm a white man, and a British subject, and no end of a big chief at home; and I've come here to do them good, and bring them civilisation; and no sooner have I got my trade sorted out than they go and taboo me, and no one dare come near my place! Tell them I don't mean to fly in the face of anything legal; and if what they want's a present, I'll do what's fair. I don't blame any man looking out for himself, tell them, for that's human nature; but if they think they're going to come any of their native ideas over me, they'll find themselves mistaken. And tell them plain that I demand the reason of this treatment as a white man and a British subject."

That was my speech. I knew how to deal with Kanakas: give them plain sense and fair dealing, and—I'll do them that much justice—they knuckle under every time. They haven't any real government or any real law, that's what you've got to knock into their heads; and even if they had, it would be a good joke if it was to apply to a white man. It would be a strange thing if we came all this way and couldn't do what we pleased. The mere idea has always put my monkey up, and I rapped my speech out pretty big. Then Case translated it—or made believe to, rather—and the first chief replied, and then a second, and a third, all in the same style—easy and genteel, but solemn underneath. Once a question was put to Case, and he answered it, and all hands (both chiefs and commons) laughed out aloud, and looked at me. Last of all, the puckered old fellow and the big young chief that spoke first started in to put Case through a kind of catechism. Sometimes I made out that Case was trying to fence, and they stuck to him like hounds, and the sweat ran down his face, which was no very pleasant sight to me, and at some of his answers the crowd moaned and murmured, which was a worse hearing. It's a cruel shame I knew no native, for (as I now believe) they were asking Case about my marriage, and he must have had a tough job of it to clear his feet. But leave Case alone; he had the brains to run a parliament.

"Well, is that all?" I asked, when a pause came.

"Come along," said he, mopping his face; "I'll tell you outside."

"Do you mean they won't take the taboo off?" I cried.

"It's something queer," said he. "I'll tell you outside. Better come away."

"I won't take it at their hands," cried I. "I ain't that kind of a man. You don't find me turn my back on a parcel of Kanakas."

"You'd better," said Case.

He looked at me with a signal in his eye; and the five chiefs looked at me civilly enough, but kind of pointed; and the people looked at me and craned and jostled. I remembered the folks that watched my house, and how the pastor had jumped in his pulpit at the bare sight of me; and the whole business seemed so out-of-the-way that I rose and followed Case. The crowd opened again to let us through, but wider than before, the children on the skirts running and singing out, and as we two white men walked away they all stood and watched us.

"And now," said I, "what is all this about?"

"The truth is I can't rightly make it out myself. They have a down on you," says Case.

"Taboo a man because they have a down on him!" I cried. "I never heard the like."

"It's worse than that, you see," said Case. "You ain't tabooed—I told you that couldn't be. The people won't go near you, Wiltshire, and there's where it is."

"They won't go near me? What do you mean by that? Why won't they go near me?" I cried.

Case hesitated. "Seems they're frightened," says he, in a low voice.

I stopped dead short. "Frightened?" I repeated. "Are you gone crazy, Case? What are they frightened of?"

"I wish I could make out," Case answered, shaking his head. "Appears like one of their tomfool superstitions. That's what I don't cotton to," he said. "It's like the business about Vigours."

"I'd like to know what you mean by that, and I'll trouble you to tell me," says I.

"Well, you know, Vigours lit out and left all standing," said he. "It was some superstition business—I never got the hang of it; but it began to look bad before the end."

"I've heard a different story about that," said I, "and I had better tell you so. I heard he ran away because of you."

"Oh! well, I suppose he was ashamed to tell the truth," says Case; "I guess he thought it silly. And it's a fact that I packed him off. 'What would you do, old man?' says he. 'Get,' says I, 'and not think twice about it.' I was the gladdest kind of man to see him clear away. It ain't my notion to turn my back on a mate when he's in a tight place, but there was that much trouble in the village that I couldn't see where it might likely end. I was a fool to be so much about with Vigours. They cast it up to me today. Didn't you hear Maea—that's the young chief, the big one—ripping out about 'Vika'? That was him they were after. They don't seem to forget it, somehow."

"This is all very well," said I, "but it don't tell me what's wrong; it don't tell me what they're afraid of—what their idea is."

"Well, I wish I knew," said Case. "I can't say fairer than that."

"You might have asked, I think," says I.

"And so I did," says he. "But you must have seen for yourself, unless you're blind, that the asking got the other way. I'll go as far as I dare for another white man; but when I find I'm in the scrape myself, I think first of my own bacon. The loss of me is I'm too good-natured. And I'll take the freedom of telling you you show a queer kind of gratitude to a man who's got into all this mess along of your affairs."

"There's a thing I'm thinking of," said I. "You were a fool to be so much about with Vigours. One comfort, you haven't been much about with me. I notice you've never been inside my house. Own up now; you had word of this before?"

"It's a fact I haven't been," said he. "It was an oversight, and I am sorry for it, Wiltshire. But about coming now, I'll be quite plain."

"You mean you won't?" I asked.

"Awfully sorry, old man, but that's the size of it," says Case.

"In short, you're afraid?" says I.

"In short, I'm afraid," says he.

"And I'm still to be tabooed for nothing?" I asked.

"I tell you you're not tabooed," said he. "The Kanakas won't go near you, that's all. And who's to make 'em? We traders have a lot of gall, I must say; we make these poor Kanakas take back their laws, and take up their taboos, and that, whenever it happens to suit us. But you don't mean to say you expect a law obliging people to deal in your store whether they want to or not? You don't mean to tell me you've got the gall for that? And if you had, it would be a queer thing to propose to me. I would just like to point out to you, Wiltshire, that I'm a trader myself."

"I don't think I would talk of gall if I was you," said I. "Here's about what it comes to, as well as I can make out: None of the people are to trade with me, and they're all to trade with you. You're to have the copra, and I'm to go to the devil and shake myself. And I don't know any native, and you're the only man here worth mention that speaks English, and you have the gall to up and hint to me my life's in danger, and all you've got to tell me is you don't know why!"

"Well, it *is* all I have to tell you," said he. "I don't know—I wish I did."

"And so you turn your back and leave me to myself! Is that the position?" says I.

"If you like to put it nasty," says he. "I don't put it so. I say merely, 'I'm going to keep clear of you; or, if I don't I'll get in danger for myself.'"

"Well," says I, "you're a nice kind of a white man!"

"Oh, I understand; you're riled," said he. "I would be myself. I can make excuses."

"All right," I said, "go and make excuses somewhere else. Here's my way, there's yours!"

With that we parted, and I went straight home in a hot temper and found Uma trying on a lot of trade goods like a baby.

"Here," I said, "you quit that foolery! Here's a pretty mess to have made, as if I wasn't bothered enough anyway! And I thought I told you to get dinner!"

And then I believe I gave her a bit of the rough side of my tongue, as she deserved. She stood up at once, like a sentry to his officer; and I must say she was always well brought up, and had a great respect for whites.

"And now," says I, "you belong round here, you're bound to understand this. What am I tabooed for, anyway? Or, if I ain't tabooed, what makes the folks afraid of me?"

She stood and looked at me with eyes like saucers.

"You no savvy?" she gasps at last.

"No," said I. "How would you expect me to? We don't have any such craziness where I come from."

"Ese no tell you?" she asked again.

(*Ese* was the name the natives had for Case; it may mean foreign, or extraordinary; or it might mean a mummy apple; but most-like it was only his own name misheard and put in a Kanaka spelling.)

"Not much," said I.

"Damn Ese!" she cried.

You might think it funny to hear this Kanaka girl come out with a big swear. No such thing. There was no swearing in her—no, nor anger; she was beyond anger, and meant the word simple and serious. She stood there straight as she said it. I cannot justly say that I ever saw a woman look like that before or after, and it struck me mum. Then she made a kind of an obeisance, but it was the proudest kind, and threw her hands out open.

"I 'shamed," she said. "I think you savvy. Ese he tell me you savvy, he tell me you no mind, tell me you love me too much. Taboo belong me," she said, touching herself on the bosom as she had done upon our wedding night. "Now I go 'way, taboo he go 'way too. Then you get too much copra. You like more better, I think. *Tofá, alii*," says she in the native—"Farewell, chief!"

"Hold on!" I cried. "Don't be in such a hurry."

She looked at me sidelong with a smile. "You see, you get copra," she said, the same as you might offer candies to a child.

"Uma," said I, "hear reason. I didn't know, and that's a fact; and Case seems to have played it pretty mean upon the pair of us. But I do know now, and I don't mind; I love you too much. You no go 'way, you no leave me, I too much sorry."

"You no love me," she cried, "you talk me bad words!" And she threw herself in a corner of the floor and began to cry.

Well, I'm no scholar, but I wasn't born yesterday, and I thought the worst of that trouble was over. However, there she lay—her back turned, her face to the wall—and shook with sobbing like a little child, so that her feet jumped with it. It's strange how it hits a man when he's in love; for there's no use mincing things—Kanaka and all, I was in love with her, or just as good. I tried to take her hand, but she would none of that. "Uma," I said, "there's no sense in carrying on like this. I want you stop here, I want my little wifie, I tell you true."

"No tell me true," she sobbed.

"All right," says I, "I'll wait till you're through with this." And I sat right down beside her on the floor, and set to smooth her hair with my hand. At first she wriggled away when I touched her; then she seemed to notice me no more; then her sobs grew gradually less, and presently stopped; and the next thing I knew, she raised her face to mine.

"You tell me true? You like me stop?" she asked.

"Uma," I said, "I would rather have you than all the copra in the South Seas," which was a very big expression, and the strangest thing was that I meant it.

She threw her arms about me, sprang close up, and pressed her face to mine, in the island way of kissing, so that I was all wetted with her tears, and my heart went out to her wholly. I never had anything so near me as this little brown bit of a girl. Many things went together, and all helped to turn my head. She was pretty enough to eat, it seemed she was my only friend in that queer place; I was ashamed that I had spoken rough to her: and she was a woman, and my wife, and a kind of a baby besides that I was sorry for; and the salt of her tears was in my mouth. And I forgot Case and the natives; and I forgot that I knew nothing of the story, or only remembered it to banish the remembrance; and I forgot that I was to get no copra, and so could make no livelihood; and I forgot my employers, and the strange kind of service I was doing them, when I preferred my fancy to their business; and I forgot even that Uma was no true wife of mine, but just a maid beguiled, and that in a pretty shabby style. But that is to look too far on. I will come to that part of it next.

It was late before we thought of getting dinner. The stove was out, and gone stone-cold; but we fired up after a while, and cooked each a dish, helping and hindering each other, and making a play of it like children. I was so greedy of her nearness that I sat down to dinner with my lass upon my knee, and made sure of her with one hand, and ate with the other. Ay, and more than that. She was the worst cook, I suppose, God made; the things she set her hand to it would have sickened an honest horse to eat of; yet I made my meal that day on Uma's cookery, and can never call to mind to have been better pleased.

I didn't pretend to myself, and I didn't pretend to her. I saw I was clean gone; and if she was to make a fool of me, she must. And I suppose it was this that set her talking, for now she made sure that we were friends. A lot she told me, sitting in my lap and eating my dish, as I ate hers from foolery—a lot about herself and her mother and Case, all which would be very tedious, and fill sheets if I set it down in Beach de Mar, but which I must give a hint of in plain English, and one thing about myself, which had a very big effect on my concerns, as you are soon to hear.

It seems she was born in one of the Line Islands; had been only two or three years in these parts, where she had come with a white man, who was married to her mother and then died; and only the one year in Falesá. Before that they had been a good deal on the move, trekking about after the white man, who was one of those rolling stones that keep going round after a soft job. They talk about looking for gold at the end of a rainbow; but if a man wants an employment that'll last him till he dies, let him start out on the soft-job hunt. There's meat and drink in it too, and beer and skittles, for you never hear of them starving, and rarely see them sober; and as for steady sport, cockfighting isn't in the same county with it. Anyway, this beachcomber carried the woman and her daughter all over the shop, but mostly to out-of-the-way islands, where there were no police, and he thought, perhaps, the soft job hung out. I've my own view of this old party; but I was just as glad he had kept Uma clear of Apia and Papeete and these flash towns. At last he struck Falealii on this island, got some trade—the Lord knows how!— muddled it all away in the usual style, and died worth next to nothing, bar a bit of land at Falesá that he had got for a bad debt, which was what put in the minds of the mother and daughter to come there and live. It seems Case encouraged them all he could, and helped to get their house built. He was very kind those days, and gave Uma trade, and there is no doubt he had his eye on her from the beginning. However, they had scarce settled, when up turned a young man, a native, and wanted to marry her. He was a small chief, and had some fine mats and old songs in his family, and was "very pretty," Uma said; and, altogether, it was an extraordinary match for a penniless girl and an out-islander.

At the first word of this I got downright sick with jealousy.

"And you mean to say you would have married him?" I cried.

"*Ioe*, yes," said she. "I like too much!"

"Well!" I said. "And suppose I had come round after?"

"I like you more better now," said she. "But suppose I marry Ioane, I one good wife. I no common Kanaka. Good girl!" says she.

Well, I had to be pleased with that; but I promise you I didn't care about the business one little bit. And I liked the end of that yarn no better than the beginning. For it seems this proposal of marriage was a start of all the trouble. It seems, before that, Uma and her mother had been looked down upon, of course, for kinless folk and out-islanders, but nothing to hurt; and, even when Ioane came forward, there was less trouble at first than might have been looked for. And then, all of a sudden, about six months before my coming, Ioane backed out and left that part of the island, and from that day to this Uma and her mother had found themselves alone. None called at their house—none spoke to them on the roads. If they went to church, the other women drew their mats away and left them in a clear place by themselves. It was a regular excommunication, like what you read of in the Middle Ages; and the cause or sense of it beyond guessing. It was some *talo pepelo*, Uma said, some lie, some calumny; and all she knew of it was that the girls who had been jealous of her luck with Ioane used to twit her with his desertion, and cry out, when they met her alone in the woods, that she would never be married. "They tell me no man he marry me. He too much 'fraid," she said.

The only soul that came about them after this desertion was Master Case. Even he was chary of showing himself, and turned up mostly by night; and pretty soon he began to table his cards and make up to Uma. I was still sore about Ioane, and when Case turned up in the same line of business I cut up downright rough.

"Well," I said, sneering, "and I suppose you thought Case 'very pretty' and 'liked too much'?"

"Now you talk silly," said she. "White man, he come here, I marry him all-e-same Kanaka; very well then, he marry me all-e-same white woman. Suppose he no marry, he go 'way, woman he stop. All-e-same thief, empty-handed, Tonga-heart—no can love! Now you come marry me. You big heart—you no 'shamed island-girl. That thing I love you far too much. I proud."

I don't know that ever I felt sicker all the days of my life. I laid down my fork, and I put away the "island-girl"; I didn't seem somehow to have any use for either, and I went and walked up and down in the house, and Uma followed me with her eyes, for she was troubled, and small wonder! But troubled was no word for it with me. I so wanted, and so feared, to make a clean breast of the sweep that I had been.

And just then there came a sound of singing out of the sea; it sprang up suddenly clear and near, as the boat turned the headland, and Uma, running to the window, cried out it was "Misi" come upon his rounds.

I thought it was a strange thing I should be glad to have a missionary; but if it was strange, it was still true.

"Uma," said I, "you stop here in this room, and don't budge a foot out of it till I come back."

CHAPTER 3

The Missionary

As I CAME OUT on the verandah, the mission boat was shooting for the mouth of the river. She was a long whaleboat painted white; a bit of an awning astern; a native pastor crouched on the wedge of the poop, steering; some four-and-twenty paddles flashing and dipping, true to the boat song; and the missionary under the awning, in his white clothes, reading in a book; and set him up! It was pretty to see and hear; there's no smarter sight in the islands than a missionary boat with a good crew and a good pipe to them; and I considered it for half a minute, with a bit of envy perhaps, and then strolled down towards the river.

From the opposite side there was another man aiming for the same place, but he ran and got there first. It was Case; doubtless his idea was to keep me apart from the missionary, who might serve me as interpreter; but my mind was upon other things. I was thinking how he had jockeyed us about the marriage, and tried his hand on Uma before; and at the sight of him rage flew into my nostrils.

"Get out of that, you low, swindling thief!" I cried.

"What's that you say?" says he.

I gave him the word again, and rammed it down with a good oath. "And if I ever catch you within six fathoms of my house," I cried, "I'll clap a bullet in your measly carcass."

"You must do as you like about your house," said he, "where I told you I have no thought of going; but this is a public place."

"It's a place where I have private business," said I. "I have no idea of a hound like you eavesdropping, and I give you notice to clear out."

"I don't take it, though," says Case.

"I'll show you then," said I.

"We'll have to see about that," said he.

He was quick with his hands, but he had neither the height nor the weight, being a flimsy creature alongside a man like me, and, besides, I was blazing to that height of wrath that I could have bit into a chisel. I gave him first the one then the other, so that I could hear his head rattle and crack, and he went down straight.

"Have you had enough?" cried I. But he only looked up white and blank, and the blood spread upon his face like wine upon a napkin. "Have you had enough?" I cried again. "Speak up and don't lie malingering there, or I'll take my feet to you."

He sat up at that, and held his head—by the look of him you could see it was spinning—and the blood poured on his pyjamas.

"I've had enough for this time," says he, and he got up staggering, and went off by the way that he had come.

The boat was close in; I saw the missionary had laid his book to one side, and I smiled to myself. "He'll know I'm a man, anyway," thinks I.

This was the first time, in all my years in the Pacific, I had ever exchanged two words with any missionary, let alone asked one for a favour. I didn't like the lot, no trader does; they look down upon us, and make no concealment; and, besides, they're partly Kanakaised, and suck up with natives instead of with other white men like themselves. I had on a rig of clean, striped pyjamas—for, of course, I had dressed decent to go before the chiefs; but when I saw the missionary step out of this boat in the regular uniform, white duck clothes, pith helmet, white shirt and tie, and yellow boots to his feet, I could have bunged stones at him. As he came nearer, queering me pretty curious (because of the fight, I suppose), I saw he looked mortal sick, for the truth was he had a fever on, and had just had a chill in the boat.

"Mr. Tarleton, I believe?" says I, for I had got his name.

"And you, I suppose, are the new trader?" says he.

"I want to tell you first that I don't hold with missions," I went on, "and that I think you and the likes of you do a sight of harm, filling up the natives with old wives' tales and bumptiousness."

"You are perfectly entitled to your opinions," says he, looking a bit ugly, "but I have no call to hear them."

"It so happens that you've got to hear them," I said. "I'm no missionary, nor missionary lover; I'm no Kanaka, nor favourer of Kanakas—I'm just a trader; I'm just a common low goddamned white man and British subject, the sort you would like to wipe your boots on. I hope that's plain!"

"Yes, my man," said he. "It's more plain than creditable. When you are sober, you'll be sorry for this."

He tried to pass on, but I stopped him with my hand. The Kanakas were beginning to growl. Guess they didn't like my tone, for I spoke to that man as I would to you.

"Now you can't say I've deceived you," said I, "and I can go on. I want a service—I want two services, in fact; and, if you care to give me them, I'll perhaps take more stock in what you call your Christianity."

He was silent for a moment. Then he smiled. "You are rather a strange sort of man," says he.

"I'm the sort of man God made me," says I. "I don't set up to be a gentleman," I said.

"I am not quite so sure," said he. "And what can I do for you, Mr.——?"

"Wiltshire," I says, "though I'm mostly called Welsher; but Wiltshire is the way it's spelt, if the people on the beach could only get their tongues about it. And what do I want? Well, I'll tell you the first thing.

I'm what you call a sinner—what I call a sweep—and I want you to help me to make it up to a person I've deceived."

He turned and spoke to his crew in the native. "And now I am at your service," said he, "but only for the time my crew are dining. I must be much farther down the coast before night. I was delayed at Papa-Malulu till this morning, and I have an engagement in Fale-alii tomorrow night."

I led the way to my house in silence, and rather pleased with myself for the way I had managed the talk, for I like a man to keep his self-respect.

"I was sorry to see you fighting," says he.

"Oh, that's part of the yarn I want to tell you," I said. "That's service number two. After you've heard it you'll let me know whether you're sorry or not."

We walked right in through the store, and I was surprised to find Uma had cleared away the dinner things. This was so unlike her ways that I saw she had done it out of gratitude, and liked her the better. She and Mr. Tarleton called each other by name, and he was very civil to her seemingly. But I thought little of that; they can always find civility for a Kanaka, it's us white men they lord it over. Besides, I didn't want much Tarleton just then. I was going to do my pitch.

"Uma," said I, "give us your marriage certificate." She looked put out. "Come," said I, "you can trust me. Hand it up."

She had it about her person, as usual; I believe she thought it was a pass to heaven, and if she died without having it handy she would go to hell. I couldn't see where she put it the first time, I couldn't see now where she took it from; it seemed to jump into her hand like that Blavatsky business in the papers. But it's the same way with all island women, and I guess they're taught it when young.

"Now," said I, with the certificate in my hand, "I was married to this girl by Black Jack, the Negro. The certificate was wrote by Case, and it's a dandy piece of literature, I promise you. Since then I've found that there's a kind of cry in the place against this wife of mine, and so long as I keep her I cannot trade. Now, what would any man do in my place, if he was a man?" I said. "The first thing he would do is this, I guess."

And I took and tore up the certificate and bunged the pieces on the floor.

"Aué!"[2] cried Uma, and began to clap her hands; but I caught one of them in mine.

"And the second thing that he would do," said I, "if he was what I would call a man and you would call a man, Mr. Tarleton, is to bring the girl right before you or any other missionary, and to up and say: 'I was wrong married to this wife of mine, but I think a heap of her, and now I want to be married to her right.' Fire away, Mr. Tarleton. And I guess you'd better do it in native; it'll please the old lady," I said, giving her the proper name of a man's wife upon the spot.

So we had in two of the crew for witnesses, and were spliced in our own house; and the parson prayed a good bit, I must say—but not so long as some—and shook hands with the pair of us.

"Mr. Wiltshire," he says, when he had made out the lines and packed off the witnesses, "I have to thank you for a very lively pleasure. I have rarely performed the marriage ceremony with more grateful emotions."

That was what you would call talking. He was going on, besides, with more of it, and I was ready for as much taffy as he had in stock, for I felt good. But Uma had been taken up with something half through the marriage, and cut straight in.

"How your hand he get hurt?" she asked.

"You ask Case's head, old lady," says I.

She jumped with joy, and sang out.

"You haven't made much of a Christian of this one," says I to Mr. Tarleton.

"We didn't think her one of our worst," says he, "when she was at Fale-alii; and if Uma bears malice I shall be tempted to fancy she has good cause."

"Well, there we are at service number two," said I. "I want to tell you our yarn, and see if you can let a little daylight in."

"Is it long?" he asked.

"Yes," I cried; "it's a goodish bit of a yarn!"

[2]Alas!

"Well, I'll give you all the time I can spare," says he, looking at his watch. "But I must tell you fairly, I haven't eaten since five this morning, and, unless you can let me have something, I am not likely to eat again before seven or eight tonight."

"By God, we'll give you dinner!" I cried.

I was a little caught up at my swearing, just when all was going straight; and so was the missionary, I suppose, but he made believe to look out of the window, and thanked us.

So we ran him up a bit of a meal. I was bound to let the old lady have a hand in it, to show off, so I deputised her to brew the tea. I don't think I ever met such tea as she turned out. But that was not the worst, for she got round with the saltbox, which she considered an extra European touch, and turned my stew into seawater. Altogether, Mr. Tarleton had a devil of a dinner of it; but he had plenty entertainment by the way, for all the while that we were cooking, and afterwards, when he was making believe to eat, I kept posting him up on Master Case and the beach of Falesá, and he putting questions that showed he was following close.

"Well," said he at last, "I am afraid you have a dangerous enemy. This man Case is very clever, and seems really wicked. I must tell you I have had my eye on him for nearly a year, and have rather had the worst of our encounters. About the time when the last representative of your firm ran so suddenly away, I had a letter from Namu, the native pastor, begging me to come to Falesá at my earliest convenience, as his flock were all 'adopting Catholic practices.' I had great confidence in Namu; I fear it only shows how easily we are deceived. No one could hear him preach and not be persuaded he was a man of extraordinary parts. All our islanders easily acquire a kind of eloquence, and can roll out and illustrate, with a great deal of vigour and fancy, secondhand sermons; but Namu's sermons are his own, and I cannot deny that I have found them means of grace. Moreover, he has a keen curiosity in secular things, does not fear work, is clever at carpentering, and has made himself so much respected among the neighbouring pastors that we call him, in a jest which is half-serious, the Bishop of the East. In short, I was proud of the man; all the more puzzled by his letter, and took an occasion to come this way. The morning before my arrival, Vigours had been sent on board the *Lion*, and Namu was perfectly at his ease, apparently ashamed of his letter, and quite unwilling to explain it. This, of course, I could not allow, and he ended by confessing that he had been much concerned to find his people using the sign of the cross, but since he had learned the explanation his mind was satisfied. For Vigours had the Evil Eye, a common thing in a country of Europe called Italy, where men were often struck dead by that kind of devil, and it appeared the sign of the cross was a charm against its power.

" 'And I explain it, Misi,' said Namu, 'in this way: the country in Europe is a Popey country, and the devil of the Evil Eye may be a Catholic devil, or, at least, used to Catholic ways. So then I reasoned thus: if this sign of the cross were used in a Popey manner it would be sinful, but when it is used only to protect men from a devil, which is a thing harmless in itself, the sign too must be harmless. For the sign is neither good nor bad, even as a bottle is neither good nor bad. But if the bottle be full of gin, the gin is bad; and if the sign made in idolatry be bad, so is the idolatry.' And, very like a native pastor, he had a text apposite about the casting out of devils.

" 'And who has been telling you about the Evil Eye?' I asked.

"He admitted it was Case. Now, I am afraid you will think me very narrow, Mr. Wiltshire, but I must tell you I was displeased, and cannot think a trader at all a good man to advise or have an influence upon my pastors. And, besides, there had been some flying talk in the country of old Adams and his being poisoned, to which I had paid no great heed; but it came back to me at the moment.

" 'And is this Case a man of a sanctified life?' I asked.

"He admitted he was not; for, though he did not drink, he was profligate with women, and had no religion.

" 'Then,' said I, 'I think the less you have to do with him the better.'

"But it is not easy to have the last word with a man like Namu. He was ready in a moment with an illustration. 'Misi,' said he, 'you have told me there were wise men, not pastors, not even holy, who knew many things useful to be taught—about trees, for instance, and beasts, and to print books, and about the stones that are burned to make knives of. Such men teach you in your college, and you learn from them, but take care not to learn to be unholy. Misi, Case is my college.'

"I knew not what to say. Mr. Vigours had evidently been driven out of Falesá by the machinations of Case and with something not very unlike the collusion of my pastor. I called to mind it was Namu who had reassured me about Adams and traced the rumour to the ill will of the priest. And I saw I must inform myself more thoroughly from an impartial source. There is an old rascal of a chief here, Faiaso, whom I daresay you saw today at the council; he has been all his life turbulent and sly, a great fomenter of rebellions, and a thorn in the side of the mission and the island. For all that he is very shrewd, and, except in politics or about his own misdemeanours, a teller of the truth. I went to his house, told him what I had heard, and besought him to be frank. I do not think I had ever a more painful interview. Perhaps you will understand me, Mr. Wiltshire, if I tell you that I am perfectly serious in these old wives' tales with which you reproached me, and as anxious to do well for these islands as you can be to please and to protect your pretty wife. And you are to remember that I thought Namu a paragon, and was proud of the man as one of the first ripe fruits of the mission. And now I was informed that he had fallen in a sort of dependence upon Case. The beginning of it was not corrupt; it began, doubtless, in fear and respect, produced by trickery and pretence; but I was shocked to find that another element had been lately added, that Namu helped himself in the store, and was believed to be deep in Case's debt. Whatever the trader said, that Namu believed with trembling. He was not alone in this; many in the village lived in a similar subjection; but Namu's case was the most influential, it was through Namu that Case had wrought most evil; and with a certain following among the chiefs, and the pastor in his pocket, the man was as good as master of the village. You know something of Vigours and Adams, but perhaps you have never heard of old Underhill, Adams's predecessor. He was a quiet, mild old fellow, I remember, and we were told he had died suddenly: white men die very suddenly in Falesá. The truth, as I now heard it, made my blood run cold. It seems he was struck with a general palsy, all of him dead but one eye, which he continually winked. Word was started that the helpless old man was now a devil, and this vile fellow Case worked upon the natives' fears, which he professed to share, and pretended he durst not go into the house alone. At last a grave was dug, and the living body buried at the far end of the village. Namu, my pastor, whom I had helped to educate, offered up a prayer at the hateful scene.

"I felt myself in a very difficult position. Perhaps it was my duty to have denounced Namu and had him deposed. Perhaps I think so now, but at the time it seemed less clear. He had a great influence, it might prove greater than mine. The natives are prone to superstition; perhaps by stirring them up I might but ingrain and spread these dangerous fancies. And Namu besides, apart from this novel and accursed influence, was a good pastor, an able man, and spiritually minded. Where should I look for a better? How was I to find as good? At that moment, with Namu's failure fresh in my view, the work of my life appeared a mockery; hope was dead in me. I would rather repair such tools as I had than go abroad in quest of others that must certainly prove worse; and a scandal is, at the best, a thing to be avoided when humanly possible. Right or wrong, then, I determined on a quiet course. All that night I denounced and reasoned with the erring pastor, twitted him with his ignorance and want of faith, twitted him with his wretched attitude, making clean the outside of the cup and platter, callously helping at a murder, childishly flying in excitement about a few childish, unnecessary, and inconvenient gestures; and long before day I had him on his knees and bathed in tears of what seemed a genuine repentance. On Sunday I took the pulpit in the morning, and preached from First Kings, nineteenth, on the fire, the earthquake, and the voice, distinguishing the true spiritual power, and referring with such plainness as I dared to recent events in Falesá. The effect produced was great, and it was much increased when Namu rose in his turn and confessed that he had been wanting in faith and conduct, and was convinced of sin. So far, then, all was well, but there was one unfortunate circumstance. It was nearing the time of our 'May' in the island, when the native contributions to the missions are received; it fell in my duty to make a notification on the subject, and this gave my enemy his chance, by which he was not slow to profit.

"News of the whole proceedings must have been carried to Case as soon as church was over, and the same afternoon he made an occasion to meet me in the midst of the village. He came up with so much intentness and animosity that I felt it would be damaging to avoid him.

" 'So,' says he, in native, 'here is the holy man. He has been preaching against me, but that was not in his heart. He has been preaching upon the love of God; but that was not in his heart, it was between his teeth. Will you know what was in his heart?' cries he. 'I will show it to you!' And, making a snatch at my head, he made believe to pluck out a dollar, and held it in the air.

"There went that rumour through the crowd with which Polynesians receive a prodigy. As for myself, I stood amazed. The thing was a common conjuring trick which I have seen performed at home a score of times; but how was I to convince the villagers of that? I wish I had learned legerdemain instead of Hebrew, that I might have paid the fellow out with his own coin. But there I was; I could not stand there silent, and the best I could find to say was weak.

" 'I will trouble you not to lay hands on me again,' said I.

" 'I have no such thought,' said he, 'nor will I deprive you of your dollar. Here it is,' he said, and flung it at my feet. I am told it lay where it fell three days."

"I must say it was well played," said I.

"Oh! he is clever," said Mr. Tarleton, "and you can now see for yourself how dangerous. He was a party to the horrid death of the paralytic; he is accused of poisoning Adams; he drove Vigours out of the place by lies that might have led to murder; and there is no question but he has now made up his mind to rid himself of you. How he means to try we have no guess; only be sure, it's something new. There is no end to his readiness and invention."

"He gives himself a sight of trouble," says I. "And, after all, what for?"

"Why, how many tons of copra may they make in this district?" asked the missionary.

"I daresay as much as sixty tons," says I.

"And what is the profit to the local trader?" he asked.

"You may call it three pounds," said I.

"Then you can reckon for yourself how much he does it for," said Mr. Tarleton. "But the more important thing is to defeat him. It is clear he spread some report against Uma, in order to isolate and have his wicked will of her. Failing of that, and seeing a new rival come upon the scene, he used her in a different way. Now, the first point to find out is about Namu.—Uma, when people began to leave you and your mother alone, what did Namu do?"

"Stop away all-e-same," says Uma.

"I fear the dog has returned to his vomit," said Mr. Tarleton. "And now what am I to do for you? I will speak to Namu, I will warn him he is observed; it will be strange if he allow anything to go amiss when he is put upon his guard. At the same time, this precaution may fail, and then you must turn elsewhere. You have two people at hand to whom you might apply. There is, first of all, the priest, who might protect you by the Catholic interest; they are a wretchedly small body, but they count two chiefs. And then there is old Faiaso. Ah! if it had been some years ago you would have needed no one else; but his influence is much reduced, it has gone into Maea's hands, and Maea, I fear, is one of Case's jackals. In fine, if the worst comes to the worst, you must send up or come yourself to Fale-alii, and, though I am not due at this end of the island for a month, I will just see what can be done."

So Mr. Tarleton said farewell; and half an hour later the crew were singing and the paddles flashing in the missionary boat.

CHAPTER 4

Devil Work

NEAR A MONTH went by without much doing. The same night of our marriage Galoshes called round, and made himself mighty civil, and got into a habit of dropping in about dark and smoking his pipe with the family. He could talk to Uma, of course, and started to teach me native and French at the same time. He was a kind old buffer, though the dirtiest you would wish to see, and he muddled me up with foreign languages worse than the Tower of Babel.

That was one employment we had, and it made me feel less lonesome; but there was no profit in the thing, for though the priest came and sat and yarned, none of his folks could be enticed into my store, and if it hadn't been for the other occupation I struck out, there wouldn't have been a pound of copra in the house. This was the idea: Fa'avao (Uma's mother) had a score of bearing trees. Of course we could get no labour, being all as good as tabooed, and the two women and I turned to and made copra with our own hands. It was copra to make your mouth water when it was done—I never understood how much the natives cheated me till I had made that four hundred pounds of my own hand—and it weighed so light I felt inclined to take and water it myself.

When we were at the job a good many Kanakas used to put in the best of the day looking on, and once that nigger turned up. He stood back with the natives and laughed and did the big don and the funny dog, till I began to get riled.

"Here, you nigger!" says I.

"I don't address myself to you, Sah," says the nigger. "Only speak to gen'le'um."

"I know," says I, "but it happens I was addressing myself to you, Mr. Black Jack. And all I want to know is just this: did you see Case's figurehead about a week ago?"

"No, Sah," says he.

"That's all right, then," says I; "for I'll show you the own brother to it, only black, in the outside of about two minutes."

And I began to walk towards him, quite slow, and my hands down; only there was trouble in my eye, if anybody took the pains to look.

"You're a low, obstropulous fellow, Sah," says he.

"You bet!" says I.

By that time he thought I was about as near as convenient, and lit out so it would have done your heart good to see him travel. And that was all I saw of that precious gang until what I am about to tell you.

It was one of my chief employments these days to go pot hunting in the woods, which I found (as Case had told me) very rich in game. I have spoken of the cape which shut up the village and my station from the east. A path went about the end of it, and led into the next bay. A strong wind blew here daily, and as the line of the barrier reef stopped at the end of the cape, a heavy surf ran on the shores of the bay. A little cliffy hill cut the valley in two parts, and stood close on the beach; and at high water the sea broke right on the face of it, so that all passage was stopped. Woody mountains hemmed the place all round; the barrier to the east was particularly steep and leafy, the lower parts of it, along the sea, falling in sheer black cliffs streaked with cinnabar; the upper part lumpy with the tops of the great trees. Some of the trees were bright green, and some red, and the sand of the beach as black as your shoes. Many birds hovered round the bay, some of them snow-white and the flying fox (or vampire) flew there in broad daylight, gnashing its teeth.

For a long while I came as far as the shooting, and went no farther. There was no sign of any path beyond, and the cocoa palms in the front of the foot of the valley were the last this way. For the whole "eye" of the island, as the natives called the windward end, lay desert. From Falesá round about to Papa-Malulu, there was neither house, nor man, nor planted fruit tree; and the reef being mostly absent, and the shore bluff, the sea beat direct among crags, and there was scarce a landing place.

I should tell you that after I began to go in the woods, although no one appeared to come near my store, I found people willing enough to pass the time of day with me where nobody would see them; and as I had begun to pick up native, and most of them had a word or two of English, I began to hold little odds and ends of conversation, not to much purpose, to be sure, but they took off the worst of the feeling, for it's a miserable thing to be made a leper of.

It chanced one day towards the end of the month that I was sitting in this bay in the edge of the bush, looking east, with a Kanaka. I had given him a fill of tobacco, and we were making out to talk as best we could; indeed, he had more English than most.

I asked him if there was no road going eastward.

"One time one road," said he. "Now he dead."

"Nobody he go there?" I asked.

"No good," said he. "Too much devil he stop there."

"Oho!" says I, "got-um plenty devil, that bush?"

"Man devil, woman devil; too much devil," said my friend. "Stop there all-e-time. Man he go there, no come back."

I thought if this fellow was so well posted on devils and spoke of them so free, which is not common, I had better fish for a little information about myself and Uma.

"You think me one devil?" I asked.

"No think devil," said he, soothingly. "Think all-e-same fool."

"Uma, she devil?" I asked again.

"No, no; no devil. Devil stop bush," said the young man.

I was looking in front of me across the bay, and I saw the hanging front of the woods pushed suddenly open, and Case, with a gun in his hand, step forth into the sunshine on the black beach. He was got up in light pyjamas, near-white, his gun sparkled, he looked mighty conspicuous; and the land crabs scuttled from all around him to their holes.

"Hullo, my friend!" says I, "you no talk all-e-same true. Ese he go, he come back."

"Ese no all-e-same; Ese *Tiapolo*," says my friend; and, with a "Goodbye," slunk off among the trees.

I watched Case all around the beach, where the tide was low; and let him pass me on the homeward way to Falesá. He was in deep thought, and the birds seemed to know it, trotting quite near him on the sand, or wheeling and calling in his ears. When he passed me I could see by the working of his lips that he was talking to himself, and what pleased me mightily, he had still my trademark on his brow. I tell you the plain truth: I had a mind to give him a gunful in his ugly mug, but I thought better of it.

All this time, and all the time I was following home, I kept repeating that native word, which I remembered by "Polly, put the kettle on and make us all some tea," tea-a-pollo.

"Uma," says I, when I got back, "what does *Tiapolo* mean?"

"Devil," says she.

"I thought *aitu* was the word for that," I said.

"*Aitu* 'nother kind of devil," said she; "stop bush, eat Kanaka. Tiapolo big chief devil, stop home; all-e-same Christian devil."

"Well, then," said I, "I'm no farther forward. How can Case be Tiapolo?"

"No all-e-same," said she. "Ese belong Tiapolo. Tiapolo too much like; Ese all-e-same his son. Suppose Ese he wish something, Tiapolo he make him?"

"That's mighty convenient for Ese," says I. "And what kind of things does he make for him?"

Well, out came a rigmarole of all sorts of stories, many of which (like the dollar he took from Mr. Tarleton's head) were plain enough to me, but others I could make nothing of; and the thing that most surprised the Kanakas was what surprised me least—namely, that he would go in the desert among all the *aitus*. Some of the boldest, however, had accompanied him, and had heard him speak with the dead and give them orders, and, safe in his protection, had returned unscathed. Some said he had a church there, where he worshipped Tiapolo, and Tiapolo appeared to him; others swore that there was no sorcery at all, that he performed his miracles by the power of prayer, and the church was no church, but a prison, in which he had confined a dangerous *aitu*. Namu had been in the bush with him once, and returned glorifying God for these wonders. Altogether, I began to have a glimmer of the man's position, and the means by which he had acquired it, and, though I saw he was a tough nut to crack, I was noways cast down.

"Very well," said I, "I'll have a look at Master Case's place of worship myself, and we'll see about the glorifying."

At this Uma fell in a terrible taking; if I went in the high bush I should never return; none could go there but by the protection of Tiapolo.

"I'll chance it on God's," said I. "I'm a good sort of a fellow, Uma, as fellows go, and I guess God'll con me through."

She was silent for a while. "I think," said she, mighty solemn—and then, presently—"Victoreea, he big chief?"

"You bet!" said I.

"He like you too much?" she asked again. I told her, with a grin, I believed the old lady was rather partial to me.

"All right," said she. "Victoreea he big chief, like you too much. No can help you here in Falesá; no can do—too far off. Maea he be small

And I saw Case, with a gun in his hand,
step forth into the sunshine.

chief—stop here. Suppose he like you—make you all right. All-e-same God and Tiapolo. God he big chief—got too much work. Tiapolo he small chief—he like too much make-see, work very hard."

"I'll have to hand you over to Mr. Tarleton," said I. "Your theology's out of its bearings, Uma."

However, we stuck to this business all the evening, and, with the stories she told me of the desert and its dangers, she came near frightening herself into a fit. I don't remember half a quarter of them, of course, for I paid little heed; but two come back to me kind of clear.

About six miles up the coast there is a sheltered cove they called *Fanga-anaana*—"the haven full of caves." I've seen it from the sea myself, as near as I could get my boys to venture in; and it's a little strip of yellow sand, black cliffs overhang it, full of the black mouths of caves; great trees overhang the cliffs, and dangle down lianas; and in one place, about the middle, a big brook pours over in a cascade. Well, there was a boat going by here, with six young men of Falesá, "all very pretty," Uma said, which was the loss of them. It blew strong, there was a heavy head sea, and by the time they opened Fanga-anaana, and saw the white cascade and the shady beach, they were all tired and thirsty, and their water had run out. One proposed to land and to get a drink, and, being reckless fellows they were all of the same mind except the youngest. Lotu was his name; he was a very good young gentleman, and very wise; and he held out that they were crazy, telling them the place was given over to spirits and devils and the dead, and there were no living folk nearer than six miles the one way, and maybe twelve the other. But they laughed at his words, and, being five to one, pulled in, beached the boat and landed. It was a wonderful pleasant place, Lotu said, and the water excellent. They walked round the beach, but could see nowhere any way to mount the cliffs, which made them easier in their mind; and at last they sat down to make a meal on the food they had brought with them. They were scarce set, when there came out of the mouth of one of the black caves six of the most beautiful ladies ever seen; they had flowers in their hair, and the most beautiful breasts, and necklaces of scarlet seeds; and began to jest with these young gentlemen, and the young gentlemen to jest back with them, all but Lotu. As for Lotu, he saw there would be no living woman in such a place, and ran, and flung himself in the bottom of the boat, and covered his face, and prayed. All the time the business lasted Lotu made one clean break of prayer, and that was all he knew of it, until his friends came back, and made him sit up, and they put to sea again out of the bay, which was now quite desert, and no word of the six ladies. But what frightened Lotu most, not one of the five remembered anything of what had passed, but they were all like drunken men, and sang and laughed in the boat, and skylarked. The wind freshened and came squally, and the sea rose extraordinarily high; it was such weather as any man in the islands would have turned his back to and fled home to Falesá; but these five were like crazy folk, and cracked on all sail and drove their boat into the seas. Lotu went to the bailing; none of the others thought to help him, but sang and skylarked and carried on, and spoke singular things beyond a man's comprehension, and laughed out loud when they said them. So the rest of the day Lotu bailed for his life in the bottom of the boat, and was all drenched with sweat and cold seawater; and none heeded him. Against all expectation, they came safe in a dreadful tempest to Papa-Malulu, where the palms were singing out, and the cocoanuts flying like cannonballs about the village green; and the same night the five young gentlemen sickened, and spoke never a reasonable word until they died.

"And do you mean to tell me you can swallow a yarn like that?" I asked.

She told me the thing was well known, and with handsome young men alone it was even common; but this was the only case where five had been slain the same day and in a company by the love of the women devils; and it had made a great stir in the island, and she would be crazy if she doubted.

"Well, anyway," says I, "you needn't be frightened about me. I've no use for the women devils. You're all the women I want, and all the devil too, old lady."

To this she answered there were other sorts, and she had seen one with her own eyes. She had gone one day alone to the next bay, and, perhaps, got too near the margin of the bad place. The boughs of the high bush overshadowed her from the cant of the hill, but she herself was outside on a flat place, very stony and growing full of young mummy apples four and five feet high. It was a dark day in the rainy season, and now there came squalls that tore off the leaves and sent them flying, and now it was all still as in a house. It was in one of these still times that a whole gang of birds and flying foxes came pegging out of the bush like creatures frightened. Presently after she heard a rustle nearer hand, and saw, coming out of the margin of the trees, among the mummy apples, the appearance of a lean grey old boar. It seemed to think as it came, like a person; and all of a sudden, as she looked at it coming, she was aware it was no boar, but a thing that was a man with a man's thoughts. At that she ran, and the pig after her, and as the pig ran it holla'd aloud, so that the place rang with it.

"I wish I had been there with my gun," said I. "I guess that pig would have holla'd so as to surprise himself."

But she told me a gun was of no use with the like of these, which were the spirits of the dead.

Well, this kind of talk put in the evening, which was the best of it; but of course it didn't change my notion, and the next day, with my gun and a good knife, I set off upon a voyage of discovery. I made, as near as I could, for the place where I had seen Case come out; for if it was true he had some kind of establishment in the bush I reckoned I should find a path. The beginning of the desert was marked off by a wall, to call it so, for it was more of a long mound of stones. They say it reaches right across the island, but how they know it is another question, for I doubt if anyone has made the journey in a hundred years, the natives sticking chiefly to the sea and their little colonies along the coast, and that part being mortal high and steep and full of cliffs. Up to the west side of the wall the ground has been cleared, and there are cocoa palms and mummy apples and guavas, and lots of sensitive. Just across, the bush begins outright; high bush at that, trees going up like the masts of ships, and ropes of liana hanging down like a ship's rigging, and nasty orchids growing in the forks like funguses. The ground where there was no underwood looked to be a heap of boulders. I saw many green pigeons which I might have shot, only I was there with a different idea. A number of butterflies flopped up and down along the ground like dead leaves; sometimes I would hear a bird calling, sometimes the wind overhead, and always the sea along the coast.

But the queerness of the place it's more difficult to tell of, unless to one who has been alone in the high bush himself. The brightest kind of a day it is always dim down there. A man can see to the end of nothing; whichever way he looks the wood shuts up, one bough folding with another like the fingers of your hand; and whenever he listens he hears always something new—men talking, children laughing, the strokes of an axe a far way ahead of him, and sometimes a sort of a quick, stealthy scurry near at hand that makes him jump and look to his weapons. It's all very well for him to tell himself that he's alone, bar trees and birds; he can't make out to believe it; whichever way he turns, the whole place seems to be alive and looking on. Don't think it was Uma's yarns that put me out; I don't value native talk a fourpenny-piece; it's a thing that's natural in the bush, and that's the end of it.

As I got near the top of the hill, for the ground of the wood goes up in this place steep as a ladder, the wind began to sound straight on, and the leaves to toss and switch open and let in the sun. This suited me better; it was the same noise all the time, and nothing to startle. Well, I had got to a place where there was an underwood of what they call wild cocoanut—mighty pretty with its scarlet fruit—when there came a sound of singing in the wind that I thought I had never heard the like of. It was all very fine to tell myself it was the branches; I knew better. It was all very fine to tell myself it was a bird; I knew never a bird that sang like that. It rose and swelled, and died away and swelled again; and now I thought it was like someone weeping, only prettier; and now I thought it was like harps; and there was one thing I made sure of, it was a sight too sweet to be wholesome in a place like that. You may laugh if you like; but I declare I called to mind the six young ladies that came, with their scarlet necklaces, out of the cave at Fanga-anaana, and wondered if they sang like that. We laugh at the natives and their superstitions; but see how many traders take them up, splendidly educated white men, that have been bookkeepers (some of them) and clerks in the old country. It's my belief a superstition grows up in a place like the different kinds of weeds; and as I stood there and listened to that wailing I twittered in my shoes.

You may call me a coward to be frightened; I thought myself brave enough to go on ahead. But I went mighty carefully, with my gun cocked, spying all about me like a hunter, fully expecting to see a handsome young woman sitting somewhere in the bush, and fully determined (if I did) to try her with a charge of duck shot. And sure enough, I had not gone far when I met with a queer thing. The wind came on the top of the wood in a strong puff, the leaves in front of me burst open, and I saw for a second something hanging in a tree. It was gone in a wink, the puff blowing by and the leaves closing. I tell you the truth: I had made up my mind to see an *aitu*; and if the thing had looked like a pig or a woman, it wouldn't have given me the same turn. The trouble was that it seemed kind of square, and the idea of a square thing that was alive and sang knocked me sick and silly. I must have stood quite a while; and I made pretty certain it was right out of the same tree that the singing came. Then I began to come to myself a bit.

"Well," says I, "if this is really so, if this is a place where there are square things that sing, I'm gone up anyway. Let's have my fun for my money."

But I thought I might as well take the off chance of a prayer being any good; so I jumped on my knees and prayed out loud; and all the time I was praying the strange sounds came out of the tree, and went up and down, and changed, for all the world like music, only you could see it wasn't human—there was nothing there that you could whistle.

As soon as I had made an end in proper style, I laid down my gun, stuck my knife between my teeth, walked right up to that tree and began to climb. I tell you my heart was like ice. But presently, as I went up, I caught another glimpse of the thing, and that relieved me, for I thought it seemed like a box; and when I had got right up to it I near fell out of the tree with laughing.

A box it was, sure enough, and a candle box at that, with the brand upon the side of it; and it had banjo-strings stretched so as to sound when the wind blew. I believe they call the thing a Tyrolean[3] harp, whatever that may mean.

"Well, Mr. Case," said I, "you frightened me once, but I defy you to

[3]Æolian.

179

frighten me again," I says, and slipped down the tree, and set out again to find my enemy's head office, which I guessed would not be far away.

The undergrowth was thick in this part; I couldn't see before my nose, and must burst my way through by main force and ply the knife as I went, slicing the cords of the lianas and slashing down whole trees at a blow. I call them trees for the bigness, but in truth they were just big weeds, and sappy to cut through like carrot. From all this crowd, and kind of vegetation, I was just thinking to myself, the place might have once been cleared, when I came on my nose over a pile of stones, and saw in a moment it was some kind of a work of man. The Lord knows when it was made or when deserted, for this part of the island has lain undisturbed since long before the whites came. A few steps beyond I hit into the path I had been always looking for. It was narrow, but well beaten, and I saw that Case had plenty of disciples. It seems, indeed it was, a piece of fashionable boldness to venture up here with the trader, and a young man scarce reckoned himself grown till he had got his breech tattooed, for one thing, and seen Case's devils for another. This is mighty like Kanakas: but, if you look at it another way, it's mighty like white folks too.

A bit along the path I was brought to a clear stand, and had to rub my eyes. There was a wall in front of me, the path passing it by a gap; it was tumbledown and plainly very old, but built of big stones very well laid; and there is no native alive today upon that island that could dream of such a piece of building! Along all the top of it was a line of queer figures, idols or scarecrows, or whatnot. They had carved and painted faces ugly to view, their eyes and teeth were of shell, their hair and their bright clothes blew in the wind, and some of them worked with the tugging. There are islands up west where they make these kind of figures till today; but if ever they were made in this island, the practice and the very recollection of it are now long forgotten. And the singular thing was that all these bogies were as fresh as toys out of a shop.

Then it came in my mind that Case had let out to me the first day that he was a good forger of island curiosities — a thing by which so many traders turn an honest penny. And with that I saw the whole business, and how this display served the man a double purpose; first of all, to season his curiosities, and then to frighten those that came to visit him.

But I should tell you (what made the thing more curious) that all the time the Tyrolean harps were harping round me in the trees, and even while I looked, a green-and-yellow bird (that, I suppose, was building) began to tear the hair off the head of one of the figures.

A little farther on I found the best curiosity of the museum. The first I saw of it was a longish mound of earth with a twist to it. Digging off the earth with my hands, I found underneath tarpaulin stretched on boards, so that this was plainly the roof of a cellar. It stood right on the top of the hill, and the entrance was on the far side, between two rocks, like the entrance to a cave. I went as far in as the bend, and, looking round the corner, saw a shining face. It was big and ugly, like a pantomime mask, and the brightness of it waxed and dwindled, and at times it smoked.

"Oho!" says I, "luminous paint!"

And I must say I rather admired the man's ingenuity. With a box of tools and a few mighty simple contrivances he had made out to have a devil of a temple. Any poor Kanaka brought up here in the dark, with the harps whining all round him, and shown that smoking face in the bottom of a hole, would make no kind of doubt but he had seen and heard enough devils for a lifetime. It's easy to find out what Kanakas think. Just go back to yourself anyway round from ten to fifteen years old, and there's an average Kanaka. There are some pious, just as there are pious boys; and the most of them, like the boys again, are middling honest and yet think it rather larks to steal, and are easy scared, and rather like to be so. I remember a boy I was at school with at home who played the Case business. He didn't know anything, that boy; he couldn't do anything; he had no luminous paint and no Tyrolean harps; he just boldly said he was a sorcerer, and frightened us out of our boots, and we loved it. And then it came in my mind how the master had once flogged that boy, and the surprise we were all in to see the sorcerer catch it and hum like anybody else. Thinks I to myself: "I must find some way of fixing it so for Master Case." And the next moment I had my idea.

I went back by the path, which, when once you had found it, was quite plain and easy walking; and when I stepped out on the black sands, who should I see but Master Case himself! I cocked my gun and held it handy, and we marched up and passed without a word, each keeping the tail of his eye on the other; and no sooner had we passed than we each wheeled round like fellows drilling, and stood face to face. We had each taken the same notion in his head, you see, that the other fellow might give him the load of his gun in the stern.

"You've shot nothing," says Case.

"I'm not on the shoot today," said I.

"Well, the devil go with you for me," says he.

"The same to you," says I.

But we stuck just the way we were; no fear of either of us moving.

Case laughed. "We can't stop here all day, though," said he.

"Don't let me detain you," says I.

He laughed again. "Look here, Wiltshire, do you think me a fool?" he asked.

"More of a knave, if you want to know," says I.

"Well, do you think it would better me to shoot you here, on this open beach?" said he. "Because I don't. Folks come fishing every day. There may be a score of them up the valley now, making copra; there might be a half a dozen on the hill behind you, after pigeons; they might be watching us this minute, and I shouldn't wonder. I give you my word I don't want to shoot you. Why should I? You don't hinder me any. You haven't got one pound of copra but what you made with your own hands, like a Negro slave. You're vegetating—that's what I call it—and I don't care where you vegetate, nor yet how long. Give me your word you don't mean to shoot me, and I'll give you a lead and walk away."

"Well," said I, "you're frank and pleasant, ain't you? And I'll be the same. I don't mean to shoot you today. Why should I? This business is beginning; it ain't done yet, Mr. Case. I've given you one turn already. I can see the marks of my knuckles on your head to this blooming hour, and I've more cooking for you. I'm not a paralee, like Underhill. My name ain't Adams, and it ain't Vigours; and I mean to show you that you've met your match."

"This is a silly way to talk," said he. "This is not the talk to make me move on with."

"All right," said I, "stay where you are. I ain't in any hurry, and you know it. I can put in a day on this beach and never mind. I ain't got any copra to bother with. I ain't got any luminous paint to see to."

I was sorry I said that last, but it whipped out before I knew. I could see it took the wind out of his sails, and he stood and stared at me with his brow drawn up. Then I suppose he made up his mind he must get to the bottom of this.

"I take you at your word," says he, and turned his back, and walked right into the devil's bush.

I let him go, of course, for I had passed my word. But I watched him as long as he was in sight, and after he was gone lit out for cover as lively as you would want to see, and went the rest of the way home under the bush, for I didn't trust him sixpence worth. One thing I saw, I had been ass enough to give him warning, and that which I meant to do I must do at once.

You would think I had had about enough excitement for one morning, but there was another turn waiting me. As soon as I got far enough round the Cape to see my house I made out there were strangers there; a little farther, and no doubt about it. There was a couple of armed sentinels squatting at my door. I could only suppose the trouble about Uma must have come to a head, and the station been seized. For aught I could think, Uma was taken up already, and these armed men were waiting to do the like with me.

However, as I came nearer, which I did at top speed, I saw there was a third native sitting on the verandah like a guest, and Uma was talking with him like a hostess. Nearer still I made out it was the big young chief, Maea, and that he was smiling away and smoking. And what was he smoking? None of your European cigarettes fit for a cat, not even the genuine big, knock-me-down native article that a fellow can really put in the time with if his pipe is broke—but a cigar, and one of my Mexicans at that, that I could swear to. At sight of this my heart started beating, and I took a wild hope in my head that the trouble was over, and Maea had come round.

Uma pointed me out to him as I came up, and he met me at the head of my own stairs like a thorough gentleman.

"Vilivili," said he, which was the best they could make of my name, "I pleased."

There is no doubt when an island chief wants to be civil he can do it. I saw the way things were from the word go. There was no call for Uma to say to me: "He no 'fraid Ese now, come bring copra." I tell you I shook hands with that Kanaka like as if he was the best white man in Europe.

The fact was, Case and he had got after the same girl, or Maea suspected it, and concluded to make hay of the trader on the chance. He had dressed himself up, got a couple of his retainers cleaned and armed to kind of make the thing more public, and, just waiting till Case was clear of the village, came round to put the whole of his business my way. He was rich as well as powerful. I suppose that man was worth fifty thousand nuts per annum. I gave him the price of the beach and a quarter cent better, and as for credit, I would have advanced him the inside of the store and the fittings besides, I was so pleased to see him. I must say he bought like a gentleman: rice and tins and biscuits enough for a week's feast, and stuffs by the bolt. He was agreeable besides; he had plenty fun to him; and we cracked jests together, mostly through the interpreter, because he had mighty little English, and my native was still off-colour. One thing I made out: he could never really have thought much harm of Uma; he could never have been really frightened, and must just have made believe from dodginess, and because he thought Case had a strong pull in the village and could help him on.

This set me thinking that both he and I were in a tightish place. What he had done was to fly in the face of the whole village, and the thing might cost him his authority. More than that, after my talk with Case on the beach, I thought it might very well cost me my life. Case had as good as said he would pot me if ever I got any copra; he would come home to find the best business in the village had changed hands, and the best thing I thought I could do was to get in first with the potting.

"See here, Uma," says I, "tell him I'm sorry I made him wait, but I was up looking at Case's Tiapolo store in the bush."

"He want savvy if you no 'fraid?" translated Uma.

I laughed out. "Not much!" says I. "Tell him the place is a blooming toy shop! Tell him, in England we give these things to the kids to play with."

"He want savvy if you hear devil sing?" she asked next.

"Look here," I said, "I can't do it now, because I've got no banjo strings in stock; but the next time the ship comes round I'll have one of these same contraptions right here in my verandah, and he can see for himself how much devil there is to it. Tell him, as soon as I can get the strings I'll make one for his pickaninnies. The name of the concern is a Tyrolean harp; and you can tell him the name means in English that nobody but damn fools give a cent for it."

This time he was so pleased he had to try his English again. "You talk true?" says he.

"Rather!" said I. "Talk all-e-same Bible. Bring out a Bible here, Uma, if you've got such a thing, and I'll kiss it. Or, I'll tell you what's better still," says I, taking a header, "ask him if he's afraid to go up there himself by day."

It appeared he wasn't; he could venture as far as that by day and in company.

"That's the ticket, then!" said I. "Tell him the man's a fraud and the place foolishness, and if he'll go up there tomorrow he'll see all that's left of it. But tell him this, Uma, and mind he understands it. If he gets talking it's bound to come to Case, and I'm a dead man! I'm playing his game, tell him, and if he says one word my blood will be at his door and be the damnation of him here and after."

She told him, and he shook hands with me up to the hilt, and, says he: "No talk. Go up tomollow. You my friend?"

"No, sir," says I, "no such foolishness. I've come here to trade, tell him, and not to make friends. But, as to Case, I'll send that man to glory!"

So off Maea went, pretty well pleased, as I could see.

CHAPTER 5

Night in the Bush

WELL, I WAS COMMITTED now; Tiapolo had to be smashed up before next day, and my hands were pretty full, not only with preparations, but with argument. My house was like a mechanics' debating society. Uma was so made up that I shouldn't go into the bush by night, or that, if I did, I was never to come back again. You know her style of arguing: you've had a specimen about Queen Victoria and the devil; and I leave you to fancy if I was tired of it before dark.

At last I had a good idea. "What was the use of casting my pearls before her?" I thought; some of her own chopped hay would be likelier to do the business.

"I'll tell you what, then," said I. "You fish out your Bible, and I'll take that up along with me. That'll make me right."

She swore a Bible was no use.

"That's just your Kanaka ignorance," said I. "Bring the Bible out."

She brought it, and I turned to the title page, where I thought there would likely be some English, and so there was. "There!" said I. "Look at that! *'London: Printed for the British Foreign Bible Society, Blackfriars,'* and the date, which I can't read, owing to its being in these X's. There's no devil in hell can look near the Bible Society, Blackfriars. Why, you silly," I said, "how do you suppose we get along with our own *aitus* at home? All Bible Society!"

"I think you no got any," said she. "White man, he tell me you no got."

"Sounds likely, don't it?" I asked. "Why would these islands all be chock-full of them and none in Europe?"

"Well, you no got breadfruit," said she.

I could have torn my hair. "Now, look here, old lady," said I, "you dry up, for I'm tired of you. I'll take the Bible, which'll put me as straight as the mail, and that's the last word I've got to say."

The night fell extraordinary dark, clouds coming up with sundown and overspreading all; not a star showed; there was only an end of a moon, and that not due before the small hours. Round the village, what with the lights and the fires in the open houses, and the torches of many fishers moving on the reef, it kept as gay as an illumination; but the sea and the mountains and woods were all clean gone. I suppose it might be eight o'clock when I took the road, laden like a donkey. First there was that Bible, a book as big as your head, which I had let myself in for by my tomfoolery. Then there was my gun, and knife, and lantern, and patent matches, all necessary. And then there was the real plant of the affair in hand, a mortal weight of gunpowder, a pair of dynamite fishing bombs, and two or three pieces of slow match that I had hauled out of the tin cases and spliced together the best way I could; for the match was only trade stuff, and a man would be crazy that trusted it. Altogether, you see, I had the materials of a pretty good blowup! Expense was nothing to me; I wanted that thing done right.

As long as I was in the open, and had the lamp in my house to steer by, I did well. But when I got to the path, it fell so dark I could make no headway, walking into trees and swearing there, like a man looking for the matches in his bedroom. I knew it was risky to light up, for my lantern would be visible all the way to the point of the cape, and as no one went there after dark, it would be talked about, and come to Case's ears. But what was I to do? I had either to give the business over and lose caste with Maea, or light up, take my chance, and get through the thing the smartest I was able.

As long as I was on the path I walked hard, but when I came to the black beach I had to run. For the tide was now nearly flowed; and to get through with my powder dry between the surf and the steep hill took all the quickness I possessed. As it was, even the wash caught me to the knees, and I came near falling on a stone. All this time the hurry I was in, and the free air and smell of the sea, kept my spirits lively; but when I was once in the bush and began to climb the path I took it easier. The fearsomeness of the wood had been a good bit rubbed off for me by Master Case's banjo strings and graven images, yet I thought it was a dreary walk, and guessed, when the disciples were up there, they must be badly scared. The light of the lantern, striking among all these trunks and forked branches and twisted rope ends of lianas, made the whole place, or all that you could see of it, a kind of a puzzle of turning shadows. They came to meet you, solid and quick like giants, and then spun off and vanished; they hove up over your head like clubs, and flew away into the night like birds. The floor of the bush glimmered with dead wood, the way the matchbox used to shine after you had struck a lucifer. Big, cold drops fell on me from the branches overhead like sweat. There was no wind to mention; only a little icy breath of a land breeze that stirred nothing; and the harps were silent.

The first landfall I made was when I got through the bush of wild cocoanuts, and came in view of the bogies on the wall. Mighty queer they looked by the shining of the lantern, with their painted faces and shell eyes, and their clothes, and their hair hanging. One after another I pulled them all up and piled them in a bundle on the cellar roof, so as they might go to glory with the rest. Then I chose a place behind one of the big stones at the entrance, buried my powder and the two shells, and arranged my match along the passage. And then I had a look at the smoking head, just for good-bye. It was doing fine.

"Cheer up," says I. "You're booked."

It was my first idea to light up and be getting homeward; for the darkness and the glimmer of the dead wood and the shadows of the lantern made me lonely. But I knew where one of the harps hung; it seemed a pity it shouldn't go with the rest; and at the same time I couldn't help letting on to myself that I was mortal tired of my employment, and would like best to be at home and have the door shut. I stepped out of the cellar and argued it fore and back. There was a sound of the sea far down below me on the coast; nearer hand not a leaf stirred; I might have been the only living creature this side of Cape Horn. Well, as I stood there thinking, it seemed the bush woke and became full of little noises. Little noises they were, and nothing to hurt; a bit of a crackle, a bit of a rush; but the breath jumped right out of me and my throat went as dry as a biscuit. It wasn't Case I was afraid of, which would have been common sense; I never thought of Case; what took me, as sharp as the colic, was the old wives' tales—the devil women and the man pigs. It was the toss of a penny whether I should run; but I got a purchase on myself, and stepped out, and held up the lantern (like a fool) and looked all around.

In the direction of the village and the path there was nothing to be seen; but when I turned inland it's a wonder to me I didn't drop. There, coming right up out of the desert and the bad bush—there, sure enough, was a devil woman, just as the way I had figured she would look. I saw the light shine on her bare arms and her bright eyes, and there went out of me a yell so big that I thought it was my death.

"Ah! No sing out!" says the devil woman, in a kind of a high whisper. "Why you talk big voice? Put out light! Ese he come."

"My God Almighty, Uma, is that you?" says I.

"*Ioe*," [4] says she. "I come quick. Ese here soon."

"You come alone?" I asked. "You no 'fraid?"

"Ah, too much 'fraid!" she whispered, clutching me. "I think die."

"Well," says I, with a kind of a weak grin, "I'm not the one to laugh at you, Mrs. Wiltshire, for I'm about the worst scared man in the South Pacific myself."

She told me in two words what brought her. I was scarce gone, it seems, when Fa'avao came in, and the old woman had met Black Jack running as hard as he was fit from our house to Case's. Uma neither spoke nor stopped, but lit right out to come and warn me. She was so close at my heels that the lantern was her guide across the beach, and afterwards, by the glimmer of it in the trees, she got her line uphill. It was only when I had got to the top or was in the cellar that she wandered—Lord knows where!—and lost a sight of precious time, afraid to call out lest Case was at the heels of her, and falling in the bush, so that she was all knocked and bruised. That must have been when she got too far to the southward, and how she came to take me in the flank at last and frighten me beyond what I've got the words to tell of.

Well, anything was better than a devil woman, but I thought her yarn serious enough. Black Jack had no call to be about my house, unless he was set there to watch; and it looked to me as if my tomfool word about the paint, and perhaps some chatter of Maea's, had got us all in a clove hitch. One thing was clear: Uma and I were here for the night; we daren't

[4]Yes.

try to go home before day, and even then it would be safer to strike round up the mountain and come in by the back of the village, or we might walk into an ambuscade. It was plain, too, that the mine should be sprung immediately, or Case might be in time to stop it.

I marched into the tunnel, Uma keeping tight hold of me, opened my lantern and lit the match. The first length of it burned like a spill of paper, and I stood stupid, watching it burn, and thinking we were going aloft with Tiapolo, which was none of my views. The second took to a better rate, though faster than I cared about; and at that I got my wits again, hauled Uma clear of the passage, blew out and dropped the lantern, and the pair of us groped our way into the bush until I thought it might be safe, and lay down together by a tree.

"Old lady," I said, "I won't forget this night. You're a trump, and that's what's wrong with you."

She bumped herself close up to me. She had run out the way she was, with nothing on her but her kilt; and she was all wet with the dews and the sea on the black beach, and shook straight on with cold and the terror of the dark and the devils.

"Too much 'fraid," was all she said.

The far side of Case's hill goes down near as steep as a precipice into the next valley. We were on the very edge of it, and I could see the dead wood shine and hear the sea sound far below. I didn't care about the position, which left me no retreat, but I was afraid to change. Then I saw I had made a worse mistake about the lantern, which I should have left lighted, so that I could have had a crack at Case when he stepped into the shine of it. And since I hadn't had the wit to do that, it seemed a senseless thing to leave the good lantern to blow up with the graven images. The thing belonged to me, after all, and was worth money, and might come in handy. If I could have trusted the match, I might have run in still and rescued it. But who was going to trust the match? You know what trade is. The stuff was good enough for Kanakas to go fishing with, where they've got to look lively anyway, and the most they risk is only to have their hand blown off. But for anyone that wanted to fool around a blowup like mine that match was rubbish.

Altogether the best I could do was to lie still, see my shotgun handy, and wait for the explosion. But it was a solemn kind of a business. The blackness of the night was like solid; the only thing you could see was the nasty bogy glimmer of the dead wood, and that showed you nothing but itself; and as for sounds, I stretched my ears till I thought I could have heard the match burn in the tunnel, and that bush was as silent as a coffin. Now and then there was a bit of a crack; but whether it was near or far, whether it was Case stubbing his toes within a few yards of me, or a tree breaking miles away, I knew no more than the babe unborn.

And then all of a sudden, Vesuvius went off. It was a long time coming; but when it came (though I say it that shouldn't) no man could ask to see a better. At first it was just a son of a gun of a row, and a spout of fire, and the wood lighted up so that you could see to read. And then the trouble began. Uma and I were half-buried under a wagonful of earth, and glad it was no worse, for one of the rocks at the entrance of the tunnel was fired clean into the air, fell within a couple of fathoms of where we lay, and bounded over the edge of the hill, and went pounding down into the next valley. I saw I had rather undercalculated our distance, or overdone the dynamite and powder, which you please.

And presently I saw I had made another slip. The noise of the thing began to die off, shaking the island; the dazzle was over; and yet the night didn't come back the way I expected. For the whole wood was scattered with red coals and brands from the explosion; they were all round me on the flat, some had fallen below in the valley, and some stuck and flared in the treetops. I had no fear of fire, for these forests are too wet to kindle. But the trouble was that the place was all lit up—not very bright, but good enough to get a shot by; and the way the coals were scattered, it was just as likely Case might have the advantage as myself. I looked all round for his white face, you may be sure; but there was not a sign of him. As for Uma, the life seemed to have been knocked right out of her by the bang and blaze of it.

There was one bad point in my game. One of the blessed graven images had come down all afire, hair and clothes and body, not four yards away from me. I cast a mighty noticing glance all round; there was still no Case, and I made up my mind I must get rid of that burning stick before he came, or I should be shot there like a dog.

It was my first idea to have crawled, and then I thought speed was the main thing, and stood half up to make a rush. The same moment, from somewhere between me and the sea, there came a flash and a report, and a rifle bullet screeched in my ear. I swung straight round and up with my gun, but the brute had a Winchester, and before I could as much as see him his second shot knocked me over like a ninepin. I seemed to fly in the air, then came down by the run and lay half a minute, silly; and then I found my hands empty and my gun had flown over my head as I fell. It makes a man mighty wide-awake to be in the kind of a box that I was in. I scarcely knew where I was hurt, or whether I was hurt or not, but turned right over on my face to crawl after my weapon. Unless you have tried to get about with a smashed leg you don't know what pain is, and I let out a howl like a bullock's.

This was the unluckiest noise that ever I made in my life. Up to then Uma had stuck to her tree like a sensible woman, knowing she would be only in the way; but as soon as she heard me sing out she ran forward. The Winchester cracked again, and down she went.

I had sat up, leg and all, to stop her; but when I saw her tumble I clapped down again where I was, lay still, and felt the handle of my knife. I had been scurried and put out before. No more of that for me. He had knocked over my girl, I had got to fix him for it; and I lay there and gritted my teeth, and footed up the chances. My leg was broke, my gun was gone. Case had still ten shots in his Winchester. It looked a kind of hopeless business. But I never despaired nor thought upon despairing: that man had got to go.

For a goodish bit not one of us let on. Then I heard Case begin to move nearer in the bush, but mighty careful. The image had burned out, there were only a few coals left here and there, and the wood was main dark, but had a kind of a low glow in it like a fire on its last legs. It was by this that I made out Case's head looking at me over a big tuft of ferns, and at the same time the brute saw me and shouldered his Winchester. I lay quite still, and as good as looked into the barrel; it was my last chance, but I thought my heart would come right out of its bearings. Then he fired. Lucky for me it was no shotgun, for the bullet struck within an inch of me and knocked the dirt in my eyes.

Just you try and see if you can lie quiet, and let a man take a sitting shot at you and miss you by a hair. But I did, and lucky, too. A while

I had rather undercalculated our distance,
or overdone the dynamite.

Case stood with the Winchester at the port arms; then he gave a little laugh to himself and stepped round the ferns.

"Laugh!" thought I. "If you had the wit of a louse you would be praying!"

I was all as taut as a ship's hawser or the spring of a watch, and as soon as he came within reach of me I had him by the ankle, plucked the feet right out from under him, laid him out, and was upon the top of him, broken leg and all, before he breathed. His Winchester had gone the same road as my shotgun; it was nothing to me—I defied him now. I'm a pretty strong man anyway, but I never knew what strength was till I got hold of Case. He was knocked out of time by the rattle he came down with, and threw up his hands together, more like a frightened woman, so that I caught both of them with my left. This wakened him up, and he fastened his teeth in my forearm like a weasel. Much I cared. My leg gave me all the pain I had any use for, and I drew my knife and got it in the place.

"Now," said I, "I've got you; and you're gone up, and a good job too! Do you feel the point of that? That's for Underhill! And there's for Adams! And now here's for Uma, and that's going to knock your blooming soul right out of you!"

With that I gave him the cold steel for all I was worth. His body kicked under me like a spring sofa; he gave a dreadful kind of a long moan, and lay still.

"I wonder if you're dead? I hope so!" I thought, for my head was swimming. But I wasn't going to take chances; I had his own example too close before me for that; and I tried to draw the knife out to give it him again. The blood came over my hands, I remember, hot as tea; and with that I fainted clean away, and fell with my head on the man's mouth.

When I came to myself it was pitch-dark; the cinders had burned out; there was nothing to be seen but the shine of the dead wood, and I couldn't remember where I was nor why I was in such pain, nor what I was all wetted with. Then it came back, and the first thing I attended to was to give him the knife again a half a dozen times up to the handle. I believe he was dead already, but it did him no harm and did me good.

"I bet you're dead now," I said, and then I called to Uma.

Nothing answered, and I made a move to go and grope for her, fouled my broken leg, and fainted again.

When I came to myself the second time the clouds had all cleared away, except a few that sailed there, white as cotton. The moon was up—a tropic moon. The moon at home turns a wood black, but even this old butt end of a one showed up that forest as green as by day. The night birds—or, rather, they're a kind of early morning bird—sang out with their long, falling notes like nightingales. And I could see the dead man, that I was still half-resting on, looking right up into the sky with his open eyes, no paler than when he was alive; and a little way off Uma tumbled on her side. I got over to her the best way I was able, and when I got there she was broad awake and crying, and sobbing to herself with no more noise than an insect. It appears she was afraid to cry out loud, because of the *aitus*. Altogether she was not much hurt, but scared beyond belief; she had come to her senses a long while ago, cried out to me, heard nothing in reply, made out we were both dead, and had lain there ever since, afraid to budge a finger. The ball had ploughed up her shoulder, and she had lost a main quantity of blood; but I soon had that tied up the way it ought to be with the tail of my shirt and a scarf I had on, got her head on my sound knee and my back against a trunk, and settled down to wait for morning. Uma was for neither use nor ornament, and could only clutch hold of me and shake and cry. I don't suppose there was ever anybody worse scared, and, to do her justice, she had had a lively night of it. As for me, I was in a good bit of pain and fever, but not so bad when I sat still; and every time I looked over to Case I could have sung and whistled. Talk about meat and drink! To see that man lying there dead as a herring filled me full.

The night birds stopped after a while; and then the light began to change, the east came orange, the whole wood began to whirr with singing like a musical box, and there was the broad day.

I didn't expect Maea for a long while yet; and, indeed, I thought there was an off chance he might go back on the whole idea and not come at all. I was the better pleased when, about an hour after daylight, I heard sticks smashing and a lot of Kanakas laughing and singing out to keep their courage up. Uma sat up quite brisk at the first word of it; and presently we saw a party come stringing out of the path, Maea in front, and behind him a white man in a pith helmet. It was Mr. Tarleton, who had turned up late last night in Falesá, having left his boat and walked the last stage with a lantern.

They buried Case upon the field of glory, right in the hole where he had kept the smoking head. I waited till the thing was done; and Mr. Tarleton prayed, which I thought tomfoolery, but I'm bound to say he gave a pretty sick view of the dear departed's prospects, and seemed to have his own ideas of hell. I had it out with him afterwards, told him he had scamped his duty, and what he had ought to have done was to up like a man and tell the Kanakas plainly Case was damned, and a good riddance; but I never could get him to see it my way. Then they made me a litter of poles and carried me down to the station. Mr. Tarleton set my leg, and made a regular missionary splice of it, so that I limp to this day. That done, he took down my evidence, and Uma's, and Maea's, wrote it all out fine, and had us sign it; and then he got the chiefs and marched over to Papa Randall's to seize Case's papers.

All they found was a bit of a diary, kept for a good many years, and all about the price of copra, and chickens being stolen, and that; and the books of the business and the will I told you of in the beginning, by both of which the whole thing (stock, lock, and barrel) appeared to belong to the Samoa woman. It was I that bought her out at a mighty reasonable figure, for she was in a hurry to get home. As for Randall and the black, they had to tramp; got into some kind of a station on the Papa-Malulu side; did very bad business, for the truth is neither of the pair was fit for it, and lived mostly on fish, which was the means of Randall's death. It seems there was a nice shoal in one day, and papa went after them with the dynamite; either the match burned too fast, or papa was full, or both, but the shell went off (in the usual way) before he threw it, and where was papa's hand? Well, there's nothing to hurt in that; the islands up north are full of one-handed men like the parties in the *Arabian Nights*; but either Randall was too old, or he drank too much, and the short and the long of it was that he died. Pretty soon after the nigger was turned out of the island for stealing from white men, and went off to the west, where he found men of his own colour, in case he liked that, and the men of his own colour took and ate him at some kind of a corroborree, and I'm sure I hope he was to their fancy!

So there was I, left alone in my glory at Falesá; and when the schooner came round I filled her up, and gave her a deck cargo half as high as the house. I must say Mr. Tarleton did the right thing by us; but he took a meanish kind of a revenge.

"Now, Mr. Wiltshire," said he, "I've put you all square with everybody here. It wasn't difficult to do, Case being gone; but I have done it, and given my pledge besides that you will deal fairly with the natives. I must ask you to keep my word."

Well, so I did. I used to be bothered about my balances, but I reasoned it out this way. We all have queerish balances, and the natives all know it and water their copra in a proportion so that it's fair all round; but the truth is, it did use to bother me, and, though I did well in Falesá, I was half-glad when the firm moved me on to another station, where I was under no kind of a pledge and could look my balances in the face.

As for the old lady, you know her as well as I do. She's only the one fault. If you don't keep your eye lifting she would give away the roof off the station. Well, it seems it's natural in Kanakas. She turned a powerful big woman now, and could throw a London bobby over her shoulder. But that's natural in Kanakas too, and there's no manner of doubt that she's an A 1 wife.

Mr. Tarleton's gone home, his trick being over. He was the best missionary I ever struck, and now, it seems, he's parsonising down Somerset way. Well, that's best for him; he'll have no Kanakas there to get luny over.

My public house? Not a bit of it, nor ever likely. I'm stuck here, I fancy. I don't like to leave the kids, you see: and—there's no use talking—they're better here than what they would be in a white man's country, though Ben took the eldest up to Auckland, where he's being schooled with the best. But what bothers me is the girls. They're only half-castes, of course; I know that as well as you do, and there's nobody thinks less of half-castes than I do; but they're mine, and about all I've got. I can't reconcile my mind to their taking up with Kanakas, and I'd like to know where I'm to find the whites?

Thrawn Janet

THE REVEREND Murdoch Soulis was long minister of the moorland parish of Balweary, in the vale of Dule. A severe, bleak-faced old man, dreadful to his hearers, he dwelt in the last years of his life, without relative or servant or any human company, in the small and lonely manse under the Hanging Shaw. In spite of the iron composure of his features, his eye was wild, scared, and uncertain; and when he dwelt, in private admonition, on the future of the impenitent, it seemed as if his eye pierced through the storms of time to the terrors of eternity. Many young persons, coming to prepare themselves against the season of the Holy Communion, were dreadfully affected by his talk. He had a sermon on 1st Peter, v. and 8th, "The devil as a roaring lion," on the Sunday after every seventeenth of August, and he was accustomed to surpass himself upon that text both by the appalling nature of the matter and the terror of his bearing in the pulpit. The children were frightened into fits, and the old looked more than usually oracular, and were, all that day, full of those hints that Hamlet deprecated. The manse itself, where it stood by the water of Dule among some thick trees, with the Shaw overhanging it on the one side, and on the other many cold, moorish hilltops rising towards the sky, had begun, at a very early period of Mr. Soulis's ministry, to be avoided in the dusk hours by all who valued themselves upon their prudence; and guidmen sitting at the clachan alehouse shook their heads together at the thought of passing late by that uncanny neighbourhood. There was one spot, to be more particular, which was regarded with especial awe. The manse stood between the highroad and the water of Dule, with a gable to each; its back was towards the kirktown of Balweary, nearly half a mile away; in front of it, a bare garden, hedged with thorn, occupied the land between the river and the road. The house was two storeys high, with two large rooms on each. It opened not directly on the garden, but on a causewayed path, or passage, giving on the road on the one hand, and closed on the other by the tall willows and elders that bordered on the stream. And it was this strip of causeway that enjoyed among the young parishioners of Balweary so infamous a reputation. The minister walked there often after dark, sometimes groaning aloud in the instancy of his unspoken prayers; and when he was from home, and the manse door was locked, the more daring schoolboys ventured, with beating hearts, to "follow my leader" across that legendary spot.

This atmosphere of terror, surrounding, as it did, a man of God of spotless character and orthodoxy, was a common cause of wonder and subject of inquiry among the few strangers who were led by chance or business into that unknown, outlying country. But many even of the people of the parish were ignorant of the strange events which had marked the first year of Mr. Soulis's ministrations; and among those who were better informed, some were naturally reticent, and others shy of that particular topic. Now and again, only, one of the older folk would warm into courage over his third tumbler, and recount the cause of the minister's strange looks and solitary life.

Fifty years syne, when Mr. Soulis cam' first into Ba'weary, he was still a young man—a callant, the folk said—fu' o' book-learnin' an' grand at the exposition, but, as was natural in sae young a man, wi' nae leevin' experience in religion. The younger sort were greatly taken wi' his gifts and his gab; but auld, concerned serious men and women were moved even to prayer for the young man, whom they took to be a self-deceiver, and the parish that was like to be sae ill supplied. It was before the days o' the moderates—weary fa' them; but ill things are like guid—they baith come bit by bit, a pickle at a time; and there were folk even then that said the Lord had left the college professors to their ain devices, an' the lads that went to study wi' them wad hae done mair an' better sittin' in a peat bog, like their forbears of the persecution, wi' a Bible under their oxter an' a speerit o' prayer in their heart. There was nae doubt onyway but that Mr. Soulis had been ower lang at the college. He was careful and troubled for mony things besides the ae thing needful. He had a feck o' books wi' him—mair than had ever been seen before in a' that presbytery; and a sair wark the carrier had wi' them, for they were a' like to have smoored in the De'il's Hag between this and Kilmackerlie. They were books o' divinity, to be sure, or so they ca'd them; but the serious were o' opinion there was little service for sae mony, when the hail o' God's Word would gang in the neuk o' a plaid. Then he wad sit half the day and half the nicht forbye, which was scant decent—writin', nae less; an' first they were feared he wad read his sermons; an' syne it proved he was writin' a book himsel', which was surely no' fittin' for ane o' his years an' sma' experience.

Onyway, it behoved him to get an auld, decent wife to keep the manse for him an' see to his bit denners; an' he was recommended to an auld limmer—Janet M'Clour, they ca'd her—an' sae far left to himsel' as to be ower persuaded. There was mony advised him to the contrar, for Janet was mair than suspeckit by the best folk in Ba'weary. Lang or that, she had had a wean to a dragoon; she hadna come forrit[1] for maybe thretty year; and bairns had seen her mumblin' to hersel' up on Key's Loan in the gloamin', whilk was an unco time an' place for a God-fearin' woman. Howsoever, it was the laird himsel' that had first tauld the minister o' Janet; an' in thae days he wad hae gane a far gate to pleesure the laird. When folk tauld him that Janet was sib to the de'il, it was a'

---

[1]"To come forrit"—to offer oneself as a communicant.

superstition by his way o' it; an' when they cast up the Bible to him an' the witch of Endor, he wad threep it doun their thrapples that th'ir days were a' gane by, an' the de'il was mercifully restrained.

Weel, when it got about the clachan that Janet M'Clour was to be servant at the manse, the folk were fair mad wi' her an' him thegither; an' some o' the guidwives had nae better to dae than get round her door cheeks and chairge her wi' a' that was ken't again' her, frae the sodger's bairn to John Tamson's twa kye. She was nae great speaker; folk usually let her gang her ain gate, an' she let them gang theirs, wi' neither Fair-guid-een nor Fair-guid-day; but when she buckled to, she had a tongue to deave the miller. Up she got, an' there wasna an auld story in Ba'weary but she gart somebody lowp for it that day; they couldna say ae thing but she could say twa to it; till, at the hinder end, the guidwives up an' claught haud of her, an' clawed the coats aff her back, and pu'd her doun the clachan to the water o' Dule, to see if she were a witch or no, soom or droun. The carline skirled till ye could hear her at the Hangin' Shaw, an' she focht like ten; there was mony a guidwife bure the mark o' her neist day an' mony a lang day after; an' just in the hettest o' the collieshangie, wha suld come up (for his sins) but the new minister!

"Women," said he (an' he had a grand voice), "I charge you in the Lord's name to let her go."

Janet ran to him—she was fair wud wi' terror—an' clang to him, an' prayed him, for Christ's sake, save her frae the cummers; an' they, for their pairt, tauld him a' that was ken't an' maybe mair.

"Woman," says he to Janet, "is this true?"

"As the Lord sees me," says she, "as the Lord made me, no' a word o't. Forbye the bairn," says she, "I've been a decent woman a' my days."

"Will you," says Mr. Soulis, "in the name of God, and before me, His unworthy minister, renounce the devil and his works?"

Weel, it wad appear that when he askit that, she gave a girn that fairly frichtit them that saw her, an' they could hear her teeth play dirl thegither in her chafts; but there was naething for it but the ae way or the ither; an' Janet lifted up her hand an' renounced the de'il before them a'.

"And now," says Mr. Soulis to the guidwives, "home with ye, one and all, and pray to God for His forgiveness."

An' he gied Janet his arm, though she had little on her but a sark, and took her up the clachan to her ain door like a leddy o' the land; an' her screighin' an' laughin' as was a scandal to be heard.

There were mony grave folk lang ower their prayers that nicht; but when the morn cam' there was sic a fear fell upon a' Ba'weary that the bairns hid theirsels, an' even the menfolk stood an' keekit frae their doors. For there was Janet comin' doun the clachan—her or her likeness, nane could tell—wi' her neck thrawn, an' her heid on ae side, like a body that has been hangit, an' a girn on her face like an unstreakit corp. By an' by they got used wi' it, an' even speered at her to ken what was wrang; but frae that day forther she couldna speak like a Christian woman, but slavered an' played click wi' her teeth like a pair o' shears; an' frae that day forth the name o' God cam' never on her lips. Whiles she wad try to say it, but it michtna be. Them that kenned best said least; but they never gied that Thing the name o' Janet M'Clour, for the auld Janet, by their way o't, was in muckle hell that day. But the minister was neither to haud nor to bind; he preached about naething but the folk's cruelty that had gi'en her a stroke of the palsy; he skelpit the bairns that meddled her; an' he had her up to the manse that same nicht, an' dwalled there a' his lane wi' her under the Hangin' Shaw.

Weel, time gaed by: and the idler sort commenced to think mair lichtly o' that black business. The minister was weel thocht o'; he was aye late at the writing, folk wad see his can'le doon by the Dule water after twal' at e'en; and he seemed pleased wi' himsel' an' upsitten as at first, though a' body could see that he was dwining. As for Janet, she cam' an' she gaed; if she didna speak muckle afore, it was reason she should speak less then; she meddled naebody; but she was an eldritch thing to see, an' nane wad hae mistrysted wi' her for Ba'weary glebe.

About the end o' July there cam' a spell o' weather, the like o't never was in that countryside; it was lown an' het an' heartless; the herds couldna win up the Black Hill, the bairns were ower weariet to play; an' yet it was gousty too, wi' claps o' het wund that rumm'led in the glens, and bits o' shouers that slockened naething. We aye thocht it büt to thun'er on the morn; but the morn cam', an' the morn's morning, an' it was aye the same uncanny weather, sair on folks and bestial. O' a' that were the waur, nane suffered like Mr. Soulis; he could neither sleep nor eat, he tauld his elders; an' when he wasna writin' at his weary book, he wad be stravaguin' ower a' the countryside like a man possessed, when a' body else was blithe to keep caller ben the house.

Abune Hangin' Shaw, in the bield o' the Black Hill, there's a bit enclosed grund wi' an iron yett; an' it seems in the auld days that was the kirkyaird o' Ba'weary, an' consecrated by the Papists before the blessed licht shone upon the kingdom. It was a great howff, o' Mr. Soulis's onyway; there he wad sit an' consider his sermons; an' indeed it's a bieldy bit. Weel, as he cam' ower the wast end o' the Black Hill, ae day, he saw first twa, an' syne fower, an' syne seeven corbie craws fleein' round an' round abune the auld kirkyaird. They flew laigh an' heavy, an' squawked to ither as they gaed; an' it was clear to Mr. Soulis that something had put them frae their ordinar. He wasna easy fleyed, an' gaed straucht up to the wa's; an' what suld he find there but a man, or the appearance o' a man, sittin' in the inside upon a grave. He was of a great stature, an' black as hell, and his e'en were singular to see.[2] Mr. Soulis had heard tell o' black men, mony's the time; but there was something unco about this black man that daunted him. Het as he was, he took a kind o' cauld grue in the marrow o' his banes; but up he spak for a' that; an' says he: "My friend, are you a stranger in this place?" The black man answered never a word; he got upon his feet, an' begoud on to hirsle to the wa' on the far side; but he aye lookit at the minister; an' the minister stood an' lookit back; till a' in a meenit the black man was ower the wa' an' rinnin' for the bield o' the trees. Mr. Soulis, he hardly kenned why, ran after him; but he was fair forjeskit wi' his walk an' the het, unhalesome weather; an' rin as he likit, he got nae mair than a glisk o' the black man amang the birks, till he won doun to the foot o' the hillside, an' there he saw him ance mair, gaun, hapstep-an'-lawp, ower Dule water to the manse.

Mr. Soulis wasna weel pleased that this fearsome gangrel suld mak' sae free wi' Ba'weary manse; an' he ran the harder, an', wet shoon, ower the burn, an' up the walk; but the de'il a black man was there to see. He

---

[2] It was a common belief in Scotland that the devil appeared as a black man. This appears in several witch trials and I think in Law's *Memorials,* that delightful storehouse of the quaint and grisly.

stepped out upon the road, but there was naebody there; he gaed a' ower
the gairden, but na, nae black man. At the hinder end, an' a bit feared
as was but natural, he lifted the hasp an' into the manse; and there was
Janet M'Clour before his e'en, wi' her thrawn craig, an' nane sae pleased
to see him. An' he aye minded sinsyne, when first he set his e'en upon
her, he had the same cauld and deidly grue.

"Janet," says he, "have you seen a black man?"

"A black man!" quo' she. "Save us a'! Ye're no wise, minister. There's
nae black man in a' Ba'weary."

But she didna speak plain, ye maun understand; but yam-yammered,
like a powney wi' the bit in its moo.

"Weel," says he, "Janet, if there was nae black man, I have spoken with
the Accuser of the Brethren."

An' he sat doun like ane wi' a fever, an' his teeth chittered in his heid.

"Hoots," says she, "think shame to yoursel', minister"; an' gied him
a drap brandy that she keepit aye by her.

Syne Mr. Soulis gaed into his study amang a' his books. It's a lang,
laigh, mirk chalmer, perishin' cauld in winter, an' no' very dry even in
the top o' the simmer, for the manse stands near the burn. Sae doun he
sat, and thocht of a' that had come an' gane since he was in Ba'weary,
an' his hame, an' the days when he was a bairn an' ran daffin' on the
braes; an' that black man aye ran in his heid like the owercome of a sang.
Aye the mair he thocht, the mair he thocht o' the black man. He tried
the prayer, an' the words wouldna come to him; an' he tried, they say,
to write at his book, but he couldna mak' nae mair o' that. There was
whiles he thocht the black man was at his oxter, an' the swat stood upon
him cauld as well water; and there was ither whiles, when he cam' to
himsel' like a christened bairn an' minded naething.

The upshot was that he gaed to the window an' stood glowrin' at Dule
water. The trees are unco thick, an' the water lies deep an' black under
the manse; an' there was Janet washin' the cla'es wi' her coats kilted. She
had her back to the minister, an' he, for his pairt, hardly kenned what
he was lookin' at. Syne she turned round, an' shawed her face; Mr. Soulis
had the same cauld grue as twice that day afore, an' it was borne in upon
him what folk said, that Janet was deid lang syne, an' this was a bogle

in her clay-cauld flesh. He drew back a pickle and he scanned her narrowly. She was tramp-trampin' in the cla'es croonin' to hersel'; and eh! Gude guide us, but it was a fearsome face. Whiles she sang louder, but there was nae man born o' woman that could tell the words o' her sang; an' whiles she lookit sidelang doun, but there was naething there for her to look at. There gaed a scunner through the flesh upon his banes; an' that was Heeven's advertisement. But Mr. Soulis just blamed himsel', he said, to think sae ill o' a puir, auld afflicted wife that hadna a freend forbye himsel'; an' he put up a bit prayer for him an' her, an' drank a little caller water—for his heart rose again' the meat—an' gaed up to his naked bed in the gloamin'.

That was a nicht that has never been forgotten in Ba'weary, the nicht o' the seeventeenth o' August, seeventeen hun'er' an' twal'. It had been het afore, as I hae said, but that nicht it was hetter than ever. The sun gaed doun amang unco-lookin' clouds; it fell as mirk as the pit; no' a star, no' a breath o' wund; ye couldna see your han' afore your face, an' even the auld folk cuist the covers frae their beds an' lay pechin' for their breath. Wi' a' that he had upon his mind, it was gey an' unlikely Mr. Soulis wad get muckle sleep. He lay an' he tummled; the gude, caller bed that he got into brunt his very banes; whiles he slept, an' whiles he waukened; whiles he heard the time o' nicht, an' whiles a tyke yowlin' up the muir, as if somebody was deid; while he thocht he heard bogles claverin' in his lug, an' whiles he saw spunkies in the room. He behoved, he judged, to be sick; an' sick he was—little he jaloosed the sickness.

At the hinder end, he got a clearness in his mind, sat up in his sark on the bedside, an' fell thinkin' ance mair o' the black man an' Janet. He couldna weel tell how—maybe it was the cauld to his feet—but it cam' in upon him wi' a spate that there was some connection between thir twa, an' that either or baith o' them were bogles. An' just at that moment, in Janet's room, which was neist to his, there cam' a stramp o' feet as if men were warslin', an' then a loud bang; an' then a wund gaed reishling round the fower quarters o' the house; an' then a' was ance mair as seelent as the grave.

Mr. Soulis was feared for neither man nor de'il. He got his tinderbox, an' lit a can'le, an' made three steps o't ower to Janet's door. It was on the hasp, an' he pushed it open, an' keeked bauldly in. It was a big room, as big as the minister's ain, an' plenished wi' grand, auld solid gear, for he had naething else. There was a fower-posted bed wi' auld tapestry; an' a braw cabinet o' aik, that was fu' o' the minister's divinity books, an' put there to be out o' the gate; an' a wheen duds o' Janet's lying here an' there about the floor. But nae Janet could Mr. Soulis see; nor ony sign o' a contention. In he gaed (an' there's few that wad hae followed him) an' lookit a' round, an' listened. But there was naething to be heard, neither inside the manse nor in a' Ba'weary parish, an' naething to be seen but the muckle shadows turnin' round the can'le. An' then, a' at aince, the minister's heart played dunt an' stood stockstill; an' a cauld wund blew amang the hairs o' his heid. Whaten a weary sicht was that for the puir man's e'en! For there was Janet hangin' frae a nail beside the auld aik cabinet: her heid aye lay on her shouther, her e'en were steekit, the tongue projected frae her mouth, an' her heels were twa feet clear abune the floor.

"God forgive us all!" thocht Mr. Soulis, "poor Janet's dead."

He cam' a step nearer to the corp; an' then his heart fair whammled in his inside. For by what cantrip it wad ill beseem a man to judge, she was hangin' frae a single nail an' by a single wursted thread for darnin' hose.

It's a awfu' thing to be your lane at nicht wi' siccan prodigies o' darkness; but Mr. Soulis was strong in the Lord. He turned an' gaed his ways oot o' that room, an' lockit the door ahint him; an' step by step, doun the stairs, as heavy as leed; and set doun the can'le on the table at the stairfoot. He couldna pray, he couldna think, he was dreepin' wi' caul' swat, an' naething could he hear but the dunt-dunt-duntin' o' his ain heart. He micht maybe hae stood there an hour, or maybe twa, he minded sae little; when a' o' a sudden, he heard a laigh, uncanny steer upstairs; a foot gaed to an' fro in the chalmer whaur the corp was hangin'; syne the door was opened, though he minded weel that he had lockit it; an' syne there was a step upon the landin', an' it seemed to him as if the corp was lookin' ower the rail and doun upon him whaur he stood.

He took up the can'le again (for he couldna want the licht), an' as saftly as ever he could, gaed straucht out o' the manse an' to the far end o' the causeway. It was aye pit-mirk; the flame o' the can'le when he set it on the grund, brunt steedy and clear as in a room; naething moved, but the Dule water seepin' and sabbin' doun the glen, an' yon unhaly footstep that cam' ploddin' doun the stairs inside the manse. He keened the foot ower weel, for it was Janet's; an' at ilka step that cam' a wee thing nearer, the cauld got deeper in his vitals. He commended his soul to Him, that made an' keepit him; "and, O Lord," said he, "give me strength this night to war against the powers of evil."

By this time the foot was comin' through the passage for the door; he could hear a hand skirt alang the wa', as if the fearsome thing was feelin' for its way. The ower the hills, the flame o' the can'le was blawn aboot; an' there stood the corp of Thrawn Janet, wi' her saughs tossed an' maned thegither, a long sigh cam' grogram goun an' her black mutch, wi' the heid aye upon the shouther, an' the girn still upon the face o't—leevin', ye wad hae said—deid, as Mr. Soulis weel keened—upon the threshold o' the manse.

It's a strange thing that the soul of man should be that thirled into his perishable body; but the minister saw that, an' his heart didna break.

She didna stand there lang; she began to move again an' cam' slowly towards Mr. Soulis whaur he stood under the saughs. A' the life o' his body, a' the strength o' his speerit, were glowerin' frae his e'en. It seemed she was gaun to speak, but wanted words, an' made a sign wi' the left hand. There cam' a clap' wund, like a cat's fuff; oot gaed the can'le, the saughs skreighed like folk; an' Mr. Soulis keened that, live or die, this was the end o't.

"Witch, beldame, devil!" he cried, "I charge you, by the power of God, begone—if you be dead, to the grave—if you be damned, to hell."

An' at that moment the Lord's ain hand out o' the Heevens struck the Horror whaur it stood; the auld, deid, desecrated corp o' the witch wife, sae lang keepit frae the grave and hirsled round by de'ils, lowed up like a brunstane spunk an' fell in ashes to the grund; the thunder followed, peal on dirling peal, the rairin' rain upon the back o' that; and Mr. Soulis lowped through the garden hedge, an' ran, wi' skelloch upon skelloch, for the clachan.

That same mornin', John Christie saw the Black Man pass the Muckle Cairn as it was chappin' six; before eicht, he gaed by the change house at Knockdow; an' no' lang after, Sandy M'Lellan saw him gaun linkin' doun the braes frae Kilmackerlie. There's little doubt but it was him that dwalled sae lang in Janet's body; but he was awa' at last; an' sinsyne the de'il has never fashed us in Ba'weary.

But it was a sair dispensation for the minister; lang, lang he lay ravin' in his bed; an' frae that hour to this, he was the man ye ken the day.

The Isle of Voices

K EOLA WAS MARRIED with Lehua, daughter of Kalamake, the wise man of Molokai, and he kept his dwelling with the father of his wife. There was no man more cunning than that prophet; he read the stars, he could divine by the bodies of the dead, and by the means of evil creatures: he could go alone into the highest parts of the mountain, into the region of the hobgoblins, and there he would lay snares to entrap the spirits of the ancient.

For this reason no man was more consulted in all the Kingdom of Hawaii. Prudent people bought, and sold, and married, and laid out their lives by his counsels; and the King had him twice to Kona to seek the treasures of Kamehameha. Neither was any man more feared; of his enemies, some had dwindled in sickness by the virtue of his incantations, and some had been spirited away, the life and the clay both, so that folk looked in vain for so much as a bone of their bodies. It was rumoured that he had the art or the gift of the old heroes. Men had seen him at night upon the mountains, stepping from one cliff to the next; they had seen him walking in the high forest, and his head and shoulders were above the trees.

This Kalamake was a strange man to see. He was come of the best blood in Molokai and Maui, of a pure descent; and yet he was more white to look upon than any foreigner; his hair the colour of dry grass, and his eyes red and very blind, so that "Blind as Kalamake that can see across tomorrow," was a byword in the islands.

Of all these doings of his father-in-law, Keola knew a little by the common repute, a little more he suspected, and the rest he ignored. But there was one thing troubled him. Kalamake was a man that spared for nothing, whether to eat or to drink, or to wear; and for all he paid in bright new dollars. "Bright as Kalamake's dollars," was another saying in the Eight Isles. Yet he neither sold, nor planted, nor took hire—only now and then from his sorceries—and there was no source conceivable for so much silver coin.

It chanced one day Keola's wife was gone upon a visit to Kaunakakai on the lee side of the island, and the men were forth at the sea fishing. But Keola was an idle dog, and he lay in the verandah and watched the surf beat on the shore and the birds fly about the cliff. It was a chief thought with him always—the thought of the bright dollars. When he lay down to bed he would be wondering why they were so many, and when he woke at morn he would be wondering why they were all new; and the thing was never absent from his mind. But this day of all days he made sure in his heart of some discovery. For it seems he had observed the place where Kalamake kept his treasure, which was a lock-fast desk against the parlour wall, under the print of Kamehameha the fifth, and a photograph of Queen Victoria with her crown; and it seems again that, no later than the night before, he found occasion to look in, and behold! the bag lay there empty. And this was the day of the steamer; he could see her smoke off Kalaupapa; and she must soon arrive with a month's goods, tinned salmon and gin, and all manner of rare luxuries for Kalamake.

"Now if he can pay for his goods today," Keola thought, "I shall know for certain that the man is a warlock, and the dollars come out of the devil's pocket."

While he was so thinking, there was his father-in-law behind him, looking vexed.

"Is that the steamer?" he asked.

"Yes," said Keola. "She has but to call at Pelekunu, and then she will be here."

"There is no help for it then," returned Kalamake, "and I must take you in my confidence, Keola, for the lack of anyone better. Come here within the house."

So they stepped together into the parlour, which was a very fine room, papered and hung with prints, and furnished with a rocking chair, and a table and a sofa in the European style. There was a shelf of books besides, and a family Bible in the midst of the table, and the lock-fast writing desk against the wall; so that anyone could see it was the house of a man of substance.

Kalamake made Keola close the shutters of the windows, while he himself locked all the doors and set open the lid of the desk. From this he brought forth a pair of necklaces hung with charms and shells, a bundle of dried herbs, and the dried leaves of trees, and a green branch of palm.

"What I am about," said he, "is a thing beyond wonder. The men of old were wise; they wrought marvels, and this among the rest; but that was at night, in the dark, under the fit stars and in the desert. The same will I do here in my own house, and under the plain eye of day." So saying, he put the Bible under the cushion of the sofa so that it was all covered, brought out from the same place a mat of a wonderfully fine texture, and heaped the herbs and leaves on sand in a tin pan. And then he and Keola put on the necklaces and took their stand upon the opposite corners of the mat.

"The time comes," said the warlock, "be not afraid."

With that he set flame to the herbs, and began to mutter and wave the branch of palm. At first the light was dim because of the closed shutters; but the herbs caught strongly afire, and the flames beat upon Keola, and the room glowed with the burning; and next the smoke rose and made his head swim and his eyes darken, and the sound of Kalamake muttering ran in his ears. And suddenly, to the mat on which they were standing came a snatch or twitch, that seemed to be more swift than lightning. In the same wink the room was gone, and the house, the breath all beaten from Keola's body. Volumes of sun rolled upon his eyes and head, and he found himself transported to a beach of the sea, under a strong sun, with a great surf roaring: he and the warlock standing there on the same mat, speechless, gasping and grasping at one another, and passing their hands before their eyes.

"What was this?" cried Keola, who came to himself the first, because he was the younger. "The pang of it was like death."

"It matters not," panted Kalamake. "It is now done."

"And, in the name of God, where are we?" cried Keola.

"That is not the question," replied the sorcerer. "Being here, we have matter in our hands, and that we must attend to. Go, while I recover my breath, into the borders of the wood, and bring me the leaves of such and such an herb, and such and such a tree, which you will find to grow there plentifully—three handfuls of each. And be speedy. We must be home again before the steamer comes; it would seem strange if we had disappeared." And he sat on the sand and panted.

Keola went up the beach, which was of shining sand and coral, strewn with singular shells; and he thought in his heart:

"How do I not know this beach? I will come here again and gather shells."

In front of him was a line of palms against the sky; not like the palms of the Eight Islands, but tall and fresh and beautiful and hanging out withered fans like gold among the green, and he thought in his heart:

"It is strange I should not have found this grove. I will come here again, when it is warm, to sleep." And he thought, "How warm it has grown suddenly!" For it was winter in Hawaii, and the day had been chill. And he thought also, "Where are the grey mountains? And where is the high cliff with the hanging forests and the wheeling birds?" And the more he considered, the less he might conceive in what quarter of the islands he was fallen.

In the border of the grove, where it met the beach, the herb was growing, but the tree farther back. Now, as Keola went towards the tree, he was aware of a young woman who had nothing on her body but a belt of leaves.

"Well!" thought Keola, "they are not very particular about their dress in this part of the country." And he paused, supposing she would observe him and escape; and seeing that she still looked before her, stood and hummed aloud. Up she leaped at the sound. Her face was ashen; she looked this way and that, and her mouth gaped with the terror of her soul. But it was a strange thing that her eyes did not rest upon Keola.

"Good day," said he. "You need not be so frightened, I will not eat you." And he had scarce opened his mouth before the young woman fled into the bush.

"These are strange manners," thought Keola, and, not thinking what he did, ran after her.

As she ran, the girl kept crying in some speech that was not practised in Hawaii, yet some of the words were the same, and he knew she kept calling and warning others. And presently he saw more people running—men, women, and children, one with another, all running and crying like people at a fire. And with that he began to grow afraid himself, and returned to Kalamake bringing the leaves. Him he told just what he had seen.

"You must pay no heed," said Kalamake. "All this is like a dream and shadows. All will disappear and be forgotten."

"It seemed none saw me," said Keola.

"And none did," replied the sorcerer. "We walk here in the broad sun invisible by reason of these charms. Yet they hear us; and therefore it is well to speak softly, as I do."

With that he made a circle round the mat with stones, and in the midst he set the leaves.

"It will be your part," said he, "to keep the leaves alight, and feed the fire slowly. While they blaze (which is but for a little moment) I must do my errand; and before the ashes blacken, the same power that brought us carries us away. Be ready now with the match; and do you call me in good time lest the flames burn out and I be left."

As soon as the leaves caught, the sorcerer leaped like a deer out of the circle, and began to race along the beach like a hound that has been bathing. As he ran, he kept stooping to snatch shells; and it seemed to Keola that they glittered as he took them. The leaves blazed with a clear flame that consumed them swiftly; and presently Keola had but a handful left, and the sorcerer was far off, running and stopping.

"Back!" cried Keola. "Back! The leaves are near done."

At that Kalamake turned, and if he had run before, now he flew. But fast as he ran, the leaves burned faster. The flame was ready to expire when, with a great leap, he bounded on the mat. The wind of his leaping blew it out; and with that the beach was gone, and the sun and the sea; and they stood once more in the dimness of the shuttered parlour, and were once more shaken and blinded; and on the mat betwixt them lay a pile of shining dollars. Keola ran to the shutters; and there was the steamer tossing in the swell close in.

The same night Kalamake took his son-in-law apart, and gave him five dollars in his hand.

"Keola," said he; "if you are a wise man (which I am doubtful of) you will think you slept this afternoon on the verandah, and dreamed as you were sleeping. I am a man of few words, and I have for my helpers people of short memories."

Never a word more said Kalamake, nor referred again to that affair. But it ran all the while in Keola's head—if he were lazy before, he would now do nothing.

"Why should I work," thought he, "when I have a father-in-law who makes dollars of seashells?"

Presently his share was spent. He spent it all upon fine clothes. And then he was sorry.

"For," thought he, "I had done better to have bought a concertina, with which I might have entertained myself all day long." And then he began to grow vexed with Kalamake.

"This man has the soul of a dog," thought he. "He can gather dollars when he pleases on the beach, and he leaves me to pine for a concertina! Let him beware: I am no child, I am as cunning as he, and hold his secret." With that he spoke to his wife Lehua, and complained of her father's manners.

"I would let my father be," said Lehua. "He is a dangerous man to cross."

"I care that for him!" cried Keola; and snapped his fingers. "I have him by the nose. I can make him do what I please." And he told Lehua the story.

But she shook her head.

"You may do what you like," said she; "but as sure as you thwart my father, you will be no more heard of. Think of this person, and that person; think of Hua, who was a noble of the House of Representatives, and went to Honolulu every year; and not a bone or a hair of him was found. Remember Kamau, and how he wasted to a thread, so that his wife lifted him with one hand. Keola, you are a baby in my father's hands; he will take you with his thumb and finger and eat you like a shrimp."

Now Keola was truly afraid of Kalamake, but he was vain too; and these words of his wife's incensed him.

"Very well," said he, "if that is what you think of me, I will show how much you are deceived." And he went straight to where his father-in-law was sitting in the parlour.

"Kalamake," said he, "I want a concertina."

"Do you, indeed?" said Kalamake.

"Yes," said he, "and I may as well tell you plainly, I mean to have it. A man who picks up dollars on the beach can certainly afford a concertina."

"I had no idea you had so much spirit," replied the sorcerer. "I thought you were a timid, useless lad, and I cannot describe how much pleased I am to find I was mistaken. Now I begin to think I may have found an assistant and successor in my difficult business. A concertina? You shall have the best in Honolulu. And tonight, as soon as it is dark, you and I will go and find the money."

"Shall we return to the beach?" asked Keola.

"No, no!" replied Kalamake; "you must begin to learn more of my secrets. Last time I taught you to pick shells; this time I shall teach you to catch fish. Are you strong enough to launch Pili's boat?"

"I think I am," returned Keola. "But why should we not take your own, which is afloat already?"

"I have a reason which you will understand thoroughly before tomorrow," said Kalamake. "Pili's boat is the better suited for my purpose.

So, if you please, let us meet there as soon as it is dark; and in the meanwhile, let us keep our own counsel, for there is no cause to let the family into our business."

Honey is not more sweet than was the voice of Kalamake, and Keola could scarce contain his satisfaction.

"I might have had my concertina weeks ago," thought he, "and there is nothing needed in this world but a little courage."

Presently after he spied Lehua weeping, and was half in a mind to tell her all was well.

"But no," thinks he; "I shall wait till I can show her the concertina; we shall see what the chit will do then. Perhaps she will understand in the future that her husband is a man of some intelligence."

As soon as it was dark father and son-in-law launched Pili's boat and set the sail. There was a great sea, and it blew strong from the leeward; but the boat was swift and light and dry, and skimmed the waves. The wizard had a lantern, which he lit and held with his finger through the ring; and the two sat in the stern and smoked cigars, of which Kalamake had always a provision, and spoke like friends of magic and the great sums of money which they could make by its exercise, and what they should buy first, and what second; and Kalamake talked like a father.

Presently he looked all about, and above him at the stars, and back at the island, which was already three parts sunk under the sea, and he seemed to consider ripely his position.

"Look!" says he, "there is Molokai already far behind us, and Maui like a cloud; and by the bearing of these three stars I know I am come to where I desire. This part of the sea is called the Sea of the Dead. It is in this place extraordinarily deep, and the floor is all covered with the bones of men, and in the holes of this part gods and goblins keep their habitation. The flow of the sea is to the north, stronger than a shark can swim, and any man who shall here be thrown out of a ship it bears away like a wild horse into the uttermost ocean. Presently he is spent and goes down, and his bones are scattered with the rest, and the gods devour his spirit."

Fear came on Keola at the words, and he looked, and by the light of the stars and the lantern, the warlock seemed to change.

"What ails you?" cried Keola, quick and sharp.

"It is not I who am ailing," said the wizard; "but there is one here very sick."

With that he changed his grasp upon the lantern, and, behold—as he drew his finger from the ring, the finger stuck and the ring was burst, and his hand was grown to be the bigness of three.

At that sight Keola screamed and covered his face.

But Kalamake held up the lantern. "Look rather at my face!" said he—and his head was huge as a barrel; and still he grew and grew as a cloud grows on a mountain, and Keola sat before him screaming, and the boat raced on the great seas.

"And now," said the wizard, "what do you think about that concertina? And are you sure you would not rather have a flute? No?" says he; "that is well, for I do not like my family to be changeable of purpose. But I begin to think I had better get out of this paltry boat, for my bulk swells to a very unusual degree, and if we are not the more careful she will presently be swamped."

With that he threw his legs over the side. Even as he did so, the greatness of the man grew thirtyfold and fortyfold as swift as sight or thinking, so that he stood in the deep sea to the armpits, and his head and shoulders rose like a high isle, and the swell beat and burst upon his bosom, as it beats and breaks against a cliff. The boat ran still to the north, but he reached out his hand, and took the gunwale by the finger and thumb, and broke the side like a biscuit, and Keola was spilled into the sea. And the pieces of the boat the sorcerer crushed in the hollow of his hand and flung miles away into the night.

"Excuse me taking the lantern," said he; "for I have a long wade before me, and the land is far, and the bottom of the sea uneven, and I feel the bones under my toes."

And he turned and went off walking with great strides; and as soon as Keola sank in the trough he could see him no longer; but as often as he was heaved upon the crest, there he was striding and dwindling, and he held the lamp high over his head, and the waves broke white about him as he went.

Since first the islands were fished out of the sea, there was never a man so terrified as this Keola. He swam indeed, but he swam as puppies swim when they are cast in to drown, and knew not wherefore. He could but think of the hugeness of the swelling of the warlock, of that face which was great as a mountain, of those shoulders that were broad as an isle, and of the seas that beat on them in vain. He thought, too, of the concertina, and shame took hold upon him; and of the dead men's bones, and fear shook him.

Of a sudden he was aware of something dark against the stars that tossed, and a light below, and a brightness of the cloven sea; and he heard speech of men. He cried out aloud and a voice answered; and in a twinkling the bows of a ship hung above him on a wave like a thing balanced, and swooped down. He caught with his two hands in the chains of her, and the next moment was buried in the rushing seas, and the next hauled on board by seamen.

They gave him gin and biscuit and dry clothes, and asked him how he came where they found him, and whether the light which they had seen was the lighthouse, Lae o Ka Laau. But Keola knew white men are like children and only believe their own stories; so about himself he told them what he pleased, and as for the light (which was Kalamake's lantern) he vowed he had seen none.

This ship was a schooner bound for Honolulu, and then to trade in the low islands; and by a very good chance for Keola she had lost a man off the bowsprit in a squall. It was no use talking. Keola durst not stay in the Eight Islands. Word goes so quickly, and all men are so fond to talk and carry news, that if he hid in the north end of Kauai or in the south end of Kaü, the wizard would have wind of it before a month, and he must perish. So he did what seemed the most prudent, and shipped sailor in the place of the man who had been drowned.

In some ways the ship was a good place. The food was extraordinarily rich and plenty, with biscuits and salt beef every day, and pea soup and puddings made of flour and suet twice a week, so that Keola grew fat. The captain also was a good man, and the crew no worse than other whites. The trouble was the mate, who was the most difficult man to please Keola had ever met with, and beat and cursed him daily, both for what he did and what he did not. The blows that he dealt were very sure,

He stood in the deep sea, and his head and
shoulders rose like a high isle.

for he was strong; and the words he used were very unpalatable, for Keola was come of a good family and accustomed to respect. And what was the worst of all, whenever Keola found a chance to sleep, there was the mate awake and stirring him up with a rope's end. Keola saw it would never do; and he made up his mind to run away.

They were about a month out from Honolulu when they made the land. It was a fine starry night, the sea was smooth as well as the sky fair; it blew a steady trade; and there was the island on their weather bow, a ribbon of palm trees lying flat along the sea. The captain and the mate looked at it with the night glass, and named the name of it, and talked of it, beside the wheel where Keola was steering. It seemed it was an isle where no traders came. By the captain's way, it was an isle besides where no man dwelt; but the mate thought otherwise.

"I don't give a cent for the directory," said he. "I've been past here one night in the schooner *Eugenie*: it was just such a night as this; they were fishing with torches, and the beach was thick with lights like a town."

"Well, well," says the captain, "it's steep-to, that's the great point; and there ain't any outlying dangers by the chart, so we'll just hug the lee side of it. Keep her ramping full, don't I tell you!" he cried to Keola, who was listening so hard that he forgot to steer.

And the mate cursed him, and swore that Kanaka was for no use in the world, and if he got started after him with a belaying pin, it would be a cold day for Keola.

And so the captain and mate lay down on the house together, and Keola was left to himself.

"This island will do very well for me," he thought; "if no traders deal there, the mate will never come. And as for Kalamake, it is not possible he can ever get as far as this."

With that he kept edging the schooner nearer in. He had to do this quietly, for it was the trouble with these white men, and above all with the mate, that you could never be sure of them; they would all be sleeping sound, or else pretending, and if a sail shook, they would jump to their feet and fall on you with a rope's end. So Keola edged her up little by little, and kept all drawing. And presently the land was so close on board, and the sound of the sea on the sides of it grew loud.

With that, the mate sat up suddenly upon the house.

"What are you doing?" he roars. "You'll have the ship ashore!"

And he made one bound for Keola, and Keola made another clean over the rail and plump into the starry sea. When he came up again, the schooner had payed off on her true course, and the mate stood by the wheel himself, and Keola heard him cursing. The sea was smooth under the lee of the island; it was warm besides, and Keola had his sailor's knife, so he had no fear of sharks. A little way before him the trees stopped; there was a break in the line of the land like the mouth of a harbour; and the tide, which was then flowing, took him up and carried him through. One minute he was without, and the next within, had floated there in a wide shallow water, bright with ten thousand stars, and all about him was the ring of the land with its string of palm trees. And he was amazed, because this was a kind of island he had never heard of.

The time of Keola in that place was in two periods—the period when he was alone, and the period when he was there with the tribe. At first he sought everywhere and found no man; only some houses standing in a hamlet, and the marks of fires. But the ashes of the fires were cold and the rains had washed them away; and the winds had blown, and some of the huts were overthrown. It was here he took his dwelling; and he made a fire drill, and a shell hook, and fished and cooked his fish, and climbed after green cocoanuts, the juice of which he drank, for in all the isle there was no water. The days were long to him, and the nights terrifying. He made a lamp of cocoa shell, and drew the oil off the ripe nuts, and made a wick of fibre; and when evening came he closed up his hut, and lit his lamp, and lay and trembled till morning. Many a time he thought in his heart he would have been better in the bottom of the sea, his bones rolling there with the others.

All this while he kept by the inside of the island, for the huts were on the shore of the lagoon, and it was there the palms grew best, and the lagoon itself abounded with good fish. And to the outer side he went once only, and he looked but once at the beach of the ocean, and came away shaking. For the look of it, with its bright sand, and strewn shells, and strong sun and surf, went sore against his inclination.

"It cannot be," he thought, "and yet it is very like. And how do I know? These white men, although they pretend to know where they are sailing, must take their chances like other people. So that after all we have sailed in a circle, and I may be quite near to Molokai, and this may be the very beach where my father-in-law gathers his dollars."

So after that he was prudent, and kept to the land side.

It was perhaps a month later, when the people of the place arrived— the fill of six great boats. They were a fine race of men, and spoke a tongue that sounded very different from the tongue of Hawaii, but so many of the words were the same that it was not difficult to understand. The men besides were very courteous, and the women very towardly; and they made Keola welcome, and built him a house, and gave him a wife; and what surprised him the most, he was never sent to work with the young men.

And now Keola had three periods. First he had a period of being very sad, and then he had a period when he was pretty merry. Last of all, came the third, when he was the most terrified man in the four oceans.

The cause of the first period was the girl he had to wife. He was in doubt about the island, and he might have been in doubt about the speech, of which he had heard so little when he came there with the wizard on the mat. But about his wife there was no mistake conceivable, for she was the same girl that ran from him crying in the wood. So he had sailed all this way, and might as well have stayed in Molokai; and had left home and wife and all his friends for no other cause but to escape his enemy, and the place he had come to was that wizard's hunting ground, and the place where he walked invisible. It was at this period when he kept the most close to the lagoon side, and, as far as he dared, abode in the cover of his hut.

The cause of the second period was talk he had heard from his wife and the chief islanders. Keola himself said little. He was never so sure of his new friends, for he judged they were too civil to be wholesome, and since he had grown better acquainted with his father-in-law the man had grown more cautious. So he told them nothing of himself, but only his name and descent, and that he came from the Eight Islands, and what fine islands they were; and about the king's palace in Honolulu, and how he was a chief friend of the king and the missionaries. But he put many questions and learned much. The island where he was was called the Isle of Voices; it belonged to the tribe, but they made their home upon another, three hours sail to the southward. There they lived and had their permanent houses, and it was a rich island, where were eggs and chickens and pigs, and ships came trading with rum and tobacco. It was there the schooner had gone after Keola deserted; there, too, the mate had died, like the fool of a white man as he was. It seems, when the ship came, it was the beginning of the sickly season in that isle, when the fish of the lagoon are poisonous, and all who eat of them swell up and die. The mate was told of it; he saw the boats preparing, because in that season the people leave that island and sail to the Isle of Voices; but he was a fool of a white man, who would believe no stories but his own, and he caught one of these fish, cooked it and ate it, and swelled up and died, which was good news to Keola. As for the Isle of Voices, it lay solitary the most part of the year, only now and then a boat's crew came for copra, and in the bad season, when the fish at the main isle were poisonous, the tribe dwelt there in a body. It had its name from a marvel, for it seemed the seaside of it was all beset with invisible devils; day and night you heard them talking with one another in strange tongues; day and night little fires blazed up and were extinguished on the beach; and what was the cause of these doings no man might conceive. Keola asked them if it were the same in their own island where they stayed, and they told him no, not there, nor yet in any other of some hundred isles that lay all about them in that sea; but it was a thing peculiar to the Isle of Voices. They told him also that these fires and voices were ever on the seaside and in the seaward fringes of the wood, and a man might dwell by the lagoon two thousand years (if he could live so long) and never be any way troubled; and even on the seaside the devils did no harm if let alone. Only once a chief had cast a spear at one of the voices, and the same night he fell out of a cocoanut palm and was killed.

Keola thought a good bit with himself. He saw he would be all right when the tribe returned to the main island, and right enough where he was, if he kept by the lagoon, yet he had a mind to make things righter if he could. So he told the high chief he had once been in an isle that was pestered the same way, and the folk had found a means to cure that trouble.

"There was a tree growing in the bush there," says he, "and it seems these devils came to get the leaves of it. So the people of the isle cut down the tree wherever it was found, and the devils came no more."

They asked what kind of a tree this was, and he showed them the tree of which Kalamake burned the leaves. They found it hard to believe, yet the idea tickled them. Night after night the old men debated it in their councils, but the high chief (though he was a brave man) was afraid of the matter, and reminded them daily of the chief who cast a spear against the voices and was killed, and the thought of that brought all to a stand again.

Though he could not yet bring about the destruction of the trees, Keola was well enough pleased, and began to look about him and take pleasure in his days; and, among other things, he was the kinder to his wife, so that the girl began to love him greatly. One day he came to the hut, and she lay on the ground lamenting.

"Why," said Keola, "what is wrong with you now?"

She declared it was nothing.

The same night she woke him. The lamp burned very low, but he saw by her face she was in sorrow.

"Keola," she said, "put your ear to my mouth that I may whisper, for no one must hear us. Two days before the boats begin to be got ready, go you to the seaside of the isle and lie in a thicket. We shall choose that place beforehand, you and I, and hide food; and every night I shall come nearby there singing. So when a night comes and you do not hear me, you shall know we are clean gone out of the island, and you may come forth again in safety."

The soul of Keola died within him.

"What is this?" he cried. "I cannot live among devils. I will not be left behind upon this isle. I am dying to leave it."

"You will never leave it alive, my poor Keola," said the girl; "for to tell you the truth, my people are eaters of men; but this they keep secret. And the reason they will kill you before we leave is because in our island ships come, and Donat-Rimarau comes and talks for the French, and there is a white trader there in a house with a verandah, and a catechist. Oh, that is a fine place indeed! The trader has barrels filled with flour; and a French warship once came in the lagoon and gave everybody wine and biscuit. Ah, my poor Keola, I wish I could take you there, for great is my love to you, and it is the finest place in the seas except Papeete."

So now Keola was the most terrified man in the four oceans. He had heard tell of eaters of men in the south islands, and the thing had always been a fear to him; and here it was knocking at his door. He had heard besides, by travellers, of their practices, and how when they are in a mind to eat a man, they cherish and fondle him like a mother with a favourite baby. And he saw this must be his own case; and that was why he had been housed, and fed, and wived, and liberated from all work; and why the old men and the chiefs discoursed with him like a person of weight. So he lay on his bed and railed upon his destiny; and the flesh curdled on his bones.

The next day the people of the tribe were very civil, as their way was. They were elegant speakers, and they made beautiful poetry, and jested at meals, so that a missionary must have died laughing. It was little enough Keola cared for their fine ways; all he saw was the white teeth shining in their mouths, and his gorge rose at the sight; and when they were done eating, he went and lay in the bush like a dead man.

The next day it was the same, and then his wife followed him.

"Keola," she said, "if you do not eat, I tell you plainly you will be killed and cooked tomorrow. Some of the old chiefs are murmuring already. They think you are fallen sick and must lose flesh."

With that Keola got to his feet, and anger burned in him.

"It is little I care one way or the other," said he. "I am between the devil and the deep sea. Since die I must, let me die the quickest way; and since I must be eaten at the best of it, let me rather be eaten by hobgoblins than by men. Farewell," said he, and he left her standing, and walked to the seaside of that island.

It was all bare in the strong sun; there was no sign of man, only the beach was trodden, and all about him as he went, the voices talked and whispered, and the little fires sprang up and burned down. All tongues of the earth were spoken there: the French, the Dutch, the Russian, the

Tamil, the Chinese. Whatever land knew sorcery, there were some of its people whispering in Keola's ear. That beach was thick as a cried fair, yet no man seen; and as he walked he saw the shells vanish before him, and no man to pick them up. I think the devil would have been afraid to be alone in such a company; but Keola was past fear and courted death. When the fires sprang up, he charged for them like a bull. Bodiless voices called to and fro; unseen hands poured sand upon the flames; and they were gone from the beach before he reached them.

"It is plain Kalamake is not here," he thought, "or I must have been killed long since."

With that he sat him down in the margin of the wood, for he was tired, and put his chin upon his hands. The business before his eyes continued; the beach babbled with voices, and the fires sprang up and sank, and the shells vanished and were renewed again even while he looked.

"It was a by-day when I was here before," he thought, "for it was nothing to this."

And his head was dizzy with the thought of these millions and millions of dollars, and all these hundreds and hundreds of persons culling them upon the beach, and flying in the air higher and swifter than eagles.

"And to think how they have fooled me with their talk of mints," says he, "and that money was made there, when it is clear that all the new coin in all the world is gathered on these sands! But I will know better the next time!" said he.

And at last, he knew not very well how or when, sleep fell on Keola, and he forgot the island and all his sorrows.

Early the next day, before the sun was yet up, a bustle woke him. He awoke in fear, for he thought the tribe had caught him napping; but it was no such matter. Only, on the beach in front of him, the bodiless voices called and shouted one upon another, and it seemed they all passed and swept beside him up the coast of the island.

"What is afoot now?" thinks Keola. And it was plain to him it was something beyond ordinary, for the fires were not lighted nor the shells taken, but the bodiless voices kept posting up the beach, and hailing and dying away; and others following, and by the sound of them these wizards should be angry.

"It is not me they are angry at," thought Keola, "for they pass me close."

As when hounds go by, or horses in a race, or city folk coursing to a fire, and all men join and follow after, so it was now with Keola; and he knew not what he did, nor why he did it, but there, lo and behold! he was running with the voices.

So he turned one point of the island, and this brought him in view of a second; and there he remembered the wizard trees to have been growing by the score together in a wood. From this point there went up a hubbub of men crying not to be described; and by the sound of them, those that he ran with shaped their course for the same quarter. A little nearer, and there began to mingle with the outcry the crash of many axes. And at this a thought came at last into his mind that the high chief had consented; that the men of the tribe had set to cutting down these trees; that word had gone about the isle from sorcerer to sorcerer, and these were all now assembling to defend their trees. Desire of strange things swept him on. He posted with the voices, crossed the beach, and came into the borders of the wood, and stood astonished. One tree had fallen, others were part hewed away. There was the tribe clustered. They were back to back, and bodies lay, and blood flowed among their feet. The hue of fear was on all their faces; their voices went up to heaven shrill as a weasel's cry.

Have you seen a child when he is all alone and has a wooden sword, and fights, leaping and hewing with the empty air? Even so the man-eaters huddled back to back and heaved up their axes and laid on, and screamed as they laid on, and behold! No man to contend with them! Only here and there Keola saw an axe swinging over against them without hands; and time and again a man of the tribe would fall before it, clove in twain or burst asunder, and his soul sped howling.

For a while Keola looked upon this prodigy like one that dreams, and then fear took him by the midst as sharp as death, that he should behold such doings. Even in that same flash the high chief of the clan espied him standing, and pointed and called out his name. Thereat the whole tribe saw him also, and their eyes flashed, and their teeth clashed.

"I am too long here," thought Keola, and ran farther out of the wood and down the beach, not caring whither.

"Keola!" said a voice close by upon the empty sand.

"Lehua! is that you?" he cried, and gasped, and looked in vain for her; but by the eyesight he was stark alone.

"I saw you pass before," the voice answered; "but you would not hear me. Quick! get the leaves and the herbs, and let us flee."

"You are there with the mat?" he asked.

"Here, at your side," said she. And he felt her arms about him. "Quick! The leaves and the herbs, before my father can get back!"

So Keola ran for his life, and fetched the wizard fuel; and Lehua guided him back, and set his feet upon the mat, and made the fire. All the time of its burning, the sound of the battle towered out of the wood; the wizards and the man-eaters hard at fight; the wizards, the viewless ones, roaring out aloud like bulls upon a mountain, and the men of the tribe replying shrill and savage out of the terror of their souls. And all the time of the burning, Keola stood there and listened, and shook, and watched how the unseen hands of Lehua poured the leaves. She poured them fast, and the flame burned high, and scorched Keola's hands; and she speeded and blew the burning with her breath. The last leaf was eaten, the flame fell, and the shock followed, and there were Keola and Lehua in the room at home.

Now, when Keola could see his wife at last he was mighty pleased, and he was mighty pleased to be home again in Molokai and sit down beside a bowl of poi — for they make no poi on board ships, and there was none in the Isle of Voices — and he was out of the body with pleasure to be clean escaped out of the hands of the eaters of men. But there was another matter not so clear, and Lehua and Keola talked of it all night and were troubled. There was Kalamake left upon the isle. If, by the blessing of God, he could but stick there, all were well; but should he escape and return to Molokai, it would be an ill day for his daughter and her husband. They spoke of his gift of swelling and whether he could wade that distance in the seas. But Keola knew by this time where that island was — and that is to say, in the Low or Dangerous Archipelago.

So they fetched the atlas and looked upon the distance in the map, and by what they could make of it, it seemed a far way for an old gentleman to walk. Still, it would not do to make too sure of a warlock like Kalamake, and they determined at last to take counsel of a white missionary.

So the first one that came by Keola told him everything. And the missionary was very sharp on him for taking the second wife in the low island; but for all the rest, he vowed he could make neither head nor tail of it.

"However," says he, "if you think this money of your father's ill-gotten, my advice to you would be to give some of it to the lepers and some to the missionary fund. And as for this extraordinary rigmarole, you cannot do better than keep it to yourselves."

But he warned the police at Honolulu that, by all he could make out, Kalamake and Keola had been coining false money, and it would not be amiss to watch them.

Keola and Lehua took his advice, and gave many dollars to the lepers and the fund. And no doubt the advice must have been good, for from that day to this, Kalamake has never more been heard of. But whether he was slain in the battle by the trees, or whether he is still kicking his heels upon the Isle of Voices, who shall say?

Will o' the Mill

The Plain and the Stars

THE MILL WHERE Will lived with his adopted parents stood in a falling valley between pinewoods and great mountains. Above, hill after hill soared upwards until they soared out of the depth of the hardiest timber, and stood naked against the sky. Some way up, a long grey village lay like a seam or a rag of vapour on a wooded hillside; and when the wind was favourable, the sound of the church bells would drop down, thin and silvery, to Will. Below, the valley grew ever steeper and steeper, and at the same time widened out on either hand; and from an eminence beside the mill it was possible to see its whole length and away beyond it over a wide plain, where the river turned and shone, and moved on from city to city on its voyage towards the sea. It chanced that over this valley there lay a pass into a neighbouring kingdom, so that, quiet and rural as it was, the road that ran along beside the river was a high thoroughfare between two splendid and powerful societies. All through the summer, travelling carriages came crawling up, or went plunging briskly downward past the mill; and as it happened that the other side was very much easier of ascent, the path was not much frequented, except by people going in one direction; and of all the carriages that Will saw go by, five-sixths were plunging briskly downwards and only one-sixth crawling up. Much more was this the case with foot passengers. All the light-footed tourists, all the pedlars laden with strange wares, were tending downward like the river that accompanied their path. Nor was this all; for when Will was yet a child a disastrous war arose over a great part of the world. The newspapers were full of defeats and victories, the earth rang with cavalry hoofs, and often for days together and for miles around the coil of battle terrified good people from their labours in the field. Of all this, nothing was heard for a long time in the valley; but at last one of the commanders pushed an army over the pass by forced marches, and for three days horse and foot, cannon and tumbril, drum and standard, kept pouring downward past the mill. All day the child stood and watched them on their passage— the rhythmical stride, the pale, unshaven faces tanned about the eyes, the discoloured regimentals and the tattered flags, filled him with a sense of weariness, pity, and wonder; and all night long, after he was in bed, he could hear the cannon pounding and the feet trampling, and the great armament sweeping onward and downward past the mill. No one in the valley ever heard the fate of the expedition, for they lay out of the way of gossip in those troublous times; but Will saw one thing plainly, that not a man returned. Whither had they all gone? Whither went all the tourists and pedlars with strange wares? Whither all the brisk barouches with servants in the dicky? Whither the water of the stream, ever coursing downward and ever renewed from above? Even the wind blew oftener down the valley, and carried the dead leaves along with it in the fall. It seemed like a great conspiracy of things animate and inanimate; they all went downward, fleetly and gaily downward, and only he, it seemed, remained behind, like a stock upon the wayside. It sometimes made him glad when he noticed how the fishes kept their heads upstream. They, at least, stood faithfully by him, while all else were posting downward to the unknown world.

One evening he asked the miller where the river went.

"It goes down the valley," answered he, "and turns a power of mills—six-score mills, they say, from here to Unterdeck—and is none the wearier after all. And then it goes out into the lowlands, and waters the great corn country, and runs through a sight of fine cities (so they say) where kings live all alone in great palaces, with a sentry walking up and down before the door. And it goes under bridges with stone men upon them, looking down and smiling so curious at the water, and living folks leaning their elbows on the wall and looking over too. And then it goes on and on, and down through marshes and sands, until at last it falls into the sea, where the ships are that bring parrots and tobacco from the Indies. Ay, it has a long trot before it as it goes singing over our weir, bless its heart!"

"And what is the sea?" asked Will.

"The sea!" cried the miller. "Lord help us all, it is the greatest thing God made! That is where all the water in the world runs down into a great salt lake. There it lies, as flat as my hand and as innocent-like as a child; but they do say when the wind blows it gets up into water-mountains bigger than any of ours, and swallows down great ships bigger than our mill, and makes such a roaring that you can hear it miles away upon the land. There are great fish in it five times bigger than a bull, and one old serpent as long as our river and as old as all the world, with whiskers like a man, and a crown of silver on her head."

Will thought he had never heard anything like this, and he kept on asking question after question about the world that lay away down the river, with all its perils and marvels, until the old miller became quite interested himself, and at last took him by the hand and led him to the hilltop that overlooks the valley and the plain. The sun was near setting, and hung low down in a cloudless sky. Everything was defined and glorified in golden light. Will had never seen so great an expanse of country in his life; he stood and gazed with all his eyes. He could see the cities, and the woods and fields, and the bright curves of the river, and far away to where the rim of the plain trenched along the shining heavens. An overmastering emotion seized upon the boy, soul and body; his heart beat so thickly that he could not breathe; the scene swam before his eyes; the sun seemed to wheel round and round, and throw off, as it turned, strange shapes which disappeared with the rapidity of thought, and were succeeded by others. Will covered his face with his hands, and burst into a violent fit of tears; and the poor miller, sadly disappointed and perplexed, saw nothing better for it than to take him up in his arms and carry him home in silence.

From that day forward Will was full of new hopes and longings. Something kept tugging at his heartstrings; the running water carried his desires along with it as he dreamed over its fleeting surface; the wind, as it ran over innumerable treetops, hailed him with encouraging words; branches beckoned downward; the open road, as it shouldered round the angles and went turning and vanishing faster and faster down the valley, tortured him with its solicitations. He spent long whiles on the eminence, looking down the river shed and abroad on the flat lowlands, and watched the clouds that travelled forth upon the sluggish wind and trailed their purple shadows on the plain; or he would linger by the wayside, and follow the carriages with his eyes as they rattled downward by the river. It did not matter what it was; everything that went that way, were it cloud or carriage, bird or brown water in the stream, he felt his heart flow out after it in an ecstasy of longing.

We are told by men of science that all the ventures of mariners on the sea, all that countermarching of tribes and races that confounds old history with its dust and rumour, sprang from nothing more abstruse than the laws of supply and demand, and a certain natural instinct for cheap rations. To anyone thinking deeply, this will seem a dull and pitiful explanation. The tribes that came swarming out of the North and East, if they were indeed pressed onward from behind by others, were drawn at the same time by the magnetic influence of the South and West. The fame of other lands had reached them; the name of the eternal city rang in their ears; they were not colonists, but pilgrims; they travelled towards wine and gold and sunshine, but their hearts were set on something higher. That divine unrest, that old stinging trouble of humanity that makes all high achievements and all miserable failure, the same that spread wings with Icarus, the same that sent Columbus into the desolate Atlantic, inspired and supported these barbarians on their perilous march. There is one legend which profoundly represents their spirit, of how a flying party of these wanderers encountered a very old man shod with iron. The old man asked them whither they were going; and they answered with one voice: "To the Eternal City!" He looked upon them gravely. "I have sought it," he said, "over the most part of the world. Three such pairs as I now carry on my feet have I worn out upon this pilgrimage, and now the fourth is growing slender underneath my steps. And all this while I have not found the city." And he turned and went his own way alone, leaving them astonished.

And yet this would scarcely parallel the intensity of Will's feeling for the plain. If he could only go far enough out there, he felt as if his eyesight would be purged and clarified, as if his hearing would grow more delicate, and his very breath would come and go with luxury. He was transplanted and withering where he was; he lay in a strange country and was sick for home. Bit by bit, he pieced together broken notions of the world below; of the river, ever moving and growing until it sailed forth into the majestic ocean; of the cities, full of brisk and beautiful people, playing fountains, bands of music and marble palaces, and lighted up at night from end to end with artificial stars of gold; of the great churches, wise universities, brave armies, and untold money lying stored in vaults; of the high-flying vice that moved in the sunshine, and the stealth and swiftness of midnight murder. I have said he was sick as if for home: the figure halts. He was like some one lying in twilit, formless pre-existence, and stretching out his hands lovingly towards many-coloured, many-sounding life. It was no wonder he was unhappy, he would go and tell the fish; they were made for their life, wished for no more than worms and running water, and a hole below a falling bank; but he was differently designed, full of desires and aspirations, itching at the fingers, lusting with the eyes, whom the whole variegated world could not satisfy with aspects. The true life, the true bright sunshine, lay far out upon the plain. And O! to see this sunlight once before he died! To move with a jocund spirit in a golden land! To hear the trained singers and sweet church bells, and see the holiday gardens! "And, O fish!" he would cry, "if you would only turn your noses downstream, you could swim so easily into the fabled waters and see the vast ships passing over your head like clouds, and hear the great water hills making music over you all day long!" But the fish kept looking patiently in their own direction, until Will hardly knew whether to laugh or cry.

Hitherto the traffic on the road had passed by Will, like something seen in a picture: he had perhaps exchanged salutations with a tourist, or caught sight of an old gentleman in a travelling cap at a carriage window; but for the most part it had been a mere symbol, which he contemplated from apart and with something of a superstitious feeling. A time came at last when this was to be changed. The miller, who was a greedy man in his way, and never forewent an opportunity of honest profit, turned the mill house into a little wayside inn, and, several pieces of good fortune falling in opportunely, built stables and got the position of postmaster on the road. It now became Will's duty to wait upon people, as they sat to break their fasts in the little arbour at the top of the mill garden; and you may be sure that he kept his ears open, and learned many new things about the outside world as he brought the omelette or the wine. Nay, he would often get into conversation with single guests, and by adroit questions and polite attention, not only gratify his own curiosity, but win the goodwill of the travellers. Many complimented the old couple on their serving boy; and a professor was eager to take him away with him, and have him properly educated in the plain. The miller and his wife were mightily astonished and even more pleased. They thought it a very good thing that they should have opened their inn. "You see," the old man would remark, "he has a kind of talent for a publican; he never would have made anything else!" And so life wagged on in the valley, with high satisfaction to all concerned but Will. Every carriage that left the inn door seemed to take a part of him away with it; and when people jestingly offered him a lift, he could with difficulty command his emotion. Night after night he would dream that he was awakened by flustered servants, and that a splendid equipage waited at the door to carry him down into the plain; night after night; until the dream, which had seemed all jollity to him at first, began to take on a colour of gravity, and the nocturnal summons and waiting equipage occupied a place in his mind as something to be both feared and hoped for.

One day, when Will was about sixteen, a fat young man arrived at sunset to pass the night. He was a contented-looking fellow, with a jolly eye, and carried a knapsack. While dinner was preparing, he sat in the arbour to read a book; but as soon as he had begun to observe Will, the book was laid aside; he was plainly one of those who prefer living people to people made of ink and paper. Will, on his part, although he had not been much interested in the stranger at first sight, soon began to take a great deal of pleasure in his talk, which was full of good nature and good sense, and at last conceived a great respect for his character and wisdom. They sat far into the night; and about two in the morning Will opened his heart to the young man, and told him how he longed to leave the valley and what bright hopes he had connected with the cities of the plain. The young man whistled, and then broke into a smile.

"My young friend," he remarked, "you are a very curious little fellow, to be sure, and wish a great many things which you will never get. Why, you would feel quite ashamed if you knew how the little fellows in these fairy cities of yours are all after the same sort of nonsense, and keep breaking their hearts to get up into the mountains. And let me tell you, those who go down into the plains are a very short while there before they wish themselves heartily back again. The air is not so light nor so pure; nor is the sun any brighter. As for the beautiful men and women, you would see many of them in rags and many of them deformed with horrible disorders; and a city is so hard a place for people who are poor and sensitive that many choose to die by their own hand."

"You must think me very simple," answered Will. "Although I have never been out of this valley, believe me, I have used my eyes. I know how one thing lives on another; for instance, how the fish hangs in the eddy to catch his fellows; and the shepherd, who makes so pretty a picture carrying home the lamb, is only carrying it home for dinner. I do not expect to find all things right in your cities. That is not what troubles me; it might have been that once upon a time; but although I have lived here always, I have asked many questions and learned a good deal in these last years, and certainly enough to cure me of my old fancies. But you would not have me die like a dog and not see all that is to be seen, and do all that a man can do, let it be good or evil? you would not have me spend all my days between this road here and the river, and not so much as make a motion to be up and live my life?—I would rather die out of hand," he cried, "than linger on as I am doing."

"Thousands of people," said the young man, "live and die like you, and are none the less happy."

"Ah!" said Will, "if there are thousands who would like, why should not one of them have my place?"

It was quite dark; there was a hanging lamp in the arbour which lit up the table and the faces of the speakers; and along the arch, the leaves upon the trellis stood out illuminated against the night sky, a pattern of transparent green upon a dusky purple. The fat young man rose, and, taking Will by the arm, led him out under the open heavens.

"Did you ever look at the stars?" he asked, pointing upwards.

"Often and often," answered Will.

"And do you know what they are?"

"I have fancied many things."

"They are worlds like ours," said the young man. "Some of them less; many of them a million times greater; and some of the least sparkles that you see are not only worlds, but whole clusters of worlds turning about each other in the midst of space. We do not know what there may be in any of them; perhaps the answer to all our difficulties or the cure of all our sufferings: and yet we can never reach them; not all the skill of the craftiest of men can fit out a ship for the nearest of these our neighbours, nor would the life of the most aged suffice for such a journey. When a great battle has been lost or a dear friend is dead, when we are hipped or in high spirits, there they are unweariedly shining overhead. We may stand here, a whole army of us together, and shout until we break our hearts, and not a whisper reaches them. We may climb the highest mountain, and we are no nearer them. All we can do is to stand down here in the garden and take off our hats; the starshine lights upon our heads, and where mine is a little bald, I daresay you can see it glisten in the darkness. The mountain and the mouse. That is like to be all we shall ever have to do with Arcturus or Aldebaran. Can you apply a parable?" he added, laying his hand upon Will's shoulder. "It is not the same thing as a reason, but usually vastly more convincing."

Will hung his head a little, and then raised it once more to heaven.

The stars seemed to expand and emit a sharper brilliancy; and as he kept turning his eyes higher and higher, they seemed to increase in multitude under his gaze.

"I see," he said, turning to the young man. "We are in a rattrap."

"Something of that size. Did you ever see a squirrel turning in a cage? and another squirrel sitting philosophically over his nuts? I needn't ask you which of them looked more of a fool."

The Parson's Marjory

AFTER SOME YEARS the old people died, both in one winter, very carefully tended by their adopted son, and very quietly mourned when they were gone. People who had heard of his roving fancies supposed he would hasten to sell his property, and go down the river to push his fortunes. But there was never any sign of such an intention on the part of Will. On the contrary, he had the inn set on a better footing, and hired a couple of servants to assist him in carrying it on; and there he settled down, a kind, talkative, inscrutable young man, six feet three in his stockings, with an iron constitution and a friendly voice. He soon began to take rank in the district as a bit of an oddity: it was not much to be wondered at from the first, for he was always full of notions, and kept calling the plainest common sense in question; but what most raised the report upon him was the odd circumstance of his courtship with the parson's Marjory.

The parson's Marjory was a lass about nineteen, when Will would be about thirty; well-enough-looking, and much better educated than any other girl in that part of the country, as became her parentage. She held her head very high, and had already refused several offers of marriage with a grand air, which had got her hard names among the neighbours. For all that she was a good girl, and one that would have made any man well contented.

Will had never seen much of her; for although the church and parsonage were only two miles from his own door, he was never known to go there but on Sundays. It chanced, however, that the parsonage fell into disrepair, and had to be dismantled; and the parson and his daughter took lodgings for a month or so, on very much reduced terms, at Will's inn. Now, what with the inn, and the mill, and the old miller's savings, our friend was a man of substance; and besides that, he had a name for good temper and shrewdness which make a capital portion in marriage; and so it was currently gossiped, among their ill-wishers, that the parson and his daughter had not chosen their temporary lodging with their eyes shut. Will was about the last man in the world to be cajoled or frightened into marriage. You had only to look into his eyes, limpid and still like pools of water, and yet with a sort of clear light that seemed to come from within, and you would understand at once that here was one who knew his own mind, and would stand to it immovably. Marjory herself was no weakling by her looks, with strong, steady eyes and a resolute and quiet bearing. It might be a question whether she was not Will's match in steadfastness, after all, or which of them would rule the roost in marriage. But Marjory had never given it a thought, and accompanied her father with the most unshaken innocence and unconcern.

The season was still so early that Will's customers were few and far between; but the lilacs were already flowering, and the weather was so mild that the party took dinner under the trellis, with the noise of the river in their ears and the woods ringing about them with the songs of birds. Will soon began to take particular pleasure in these dinners. The parson was rather a dull companion, with a habit of dozing at table; but nothing rude or cruel ever fell from his lips. And as for the parson's daughter, she suited her surroundings with the best grace imaginable; and whatever she said seemed so pat and pretty that Will conceived a great idea of her talents. He could see her face, as she leaned forward, against a background of rising pinewoods; her eyes shone peaceably; the light lay around her hair like a kerchief; something that was hardly a smile rippled her pale cheeks, and Will could not contain himself from gazing on her in an agreeable dismay. She looked, even in her quietest moments, so complete in herself, and so quick with life down to her fingertips and the very skirts of her dress, that the remainder of created things became no more than a blot by comparison; and if Will glanced away from her to her surroundings, the trees looked inanimate and senseless, the clouds hung in heaven like dead things, and even the mountaintops were disenchanted. The whole valley could not compare in looks with this one girl.

Will was always observant in the society of his fellow creatures; but his observation became almost painfully eager in the case of Marjory. He listened to all she uttered, and read her eyes, at the same time, for the unspoken commentary. Many kind, simple, and sincere speeches found an echo in his heart. He became conscious of a soul beautifully poised upon itself, nothing doubting, nothing desiring, clothed in peace. It was not possible to separate her thoughts from her appearance. The turn of her wrist, the still sound of her voice, the light in her eyes, the lines of her body, fell in tune with her grave and gentle words, like the accompaniment that sustains and harmonises the voice of the singer. Her influence was one thing, not to be divided or discussed, only to be felt with gratitude and joy. To Will, her presence recalled something of his childhood, and the thought of her took its place in his mind beside that of dawn, of running water, and of the earliest violets and lilacs. It is the property of things seen for the first time, or for the first time after long, like the flowers in spring, to reawaken in us the sharp edge of sense and that impression of mystic strangeness which otherwise passes out of life with the coming of years; but the sight of a loved face is what renews a man's character from the fountain upwards.

One day after dinner Will took a stroll among the firs; a grave beatitude possessed him from top to toe, and he kept smiling to himself and the landscape as he went. The river ran between the stepping-stones with a pretty wimple; a bird sang loudly in the wood; the hilltops looked immeasurably high, and, as he glanced at them from time to time, seemed to contemplate his movements with a beneficent but awful curiosity. His way took him to the eminence which overlooked the plain; and there he sat down upon a stone, and fell into deep and pleasant thought. The plain lay abroad with its cities and silver river; everything was asleep, except a great eddy of birds which kept rising and falling and going round and round in the blue air. He repeated Marjory's name aloud, and the sound of it gratified his ear. He shut his eyes, and her image sprang up before him, quietly luminous and attended with good thoughts. The river might run forever; the birds fly higher and higher till they touched the stars. He saw it was empty bustle after all; for here, without stirring a foot, waiting patiently in his own narrow valley, he also had attained the better sunlight.

The next day Will made a sort of declaration across the dinner table, while the parson was filling his pipe.

"Miss Marjory," he said, "I never knew anyone I liked so well as you. I am mostly a cold, unkindly sort of man; not from want of heart, but out of strangeness in my way of thinking; and people seem far away from me. 'Tis as if there were a circle round me, which kept everyone out but you; I can hear the others talking and laughing; but you come quite close.—Maybe this is disagreeable to you?" he asked.

Marjory made no answer.

"Speak up, girl," said the parson.

"Nay, now," returned Will, "I wouldn't press her, Parson. I feel tongue-tied myself, who am not used to it; and she's a woman, and little more than a child, when all is said. But for my part, as far as I can understand what people mean by it, I fancy I must be what they call in love. I do not wish to be held as committing myself; for I may be wrong; but that is how I believe things are with me. And if Miss Marjory should feel any otherwise on her part, mayhap she would be so kind as shake her head."

Marjory was silent, and gave no sign that she had heard.

"How is that, Parson?" asked Will.

"The girl must speak," replied the parson, laying down his pipe. "Here's our neighbour who says he loves you, Madge. Do you love him, ay or no?"

"I think I do," said Marjory, faintly.

"Well then, that's all that could be wished!" cried Will, heartily. And he took her hand across the table, and held it a moment in both of his with great satisfaction.

"You must marry," observed the parson, replacing his pipe in his mouth.

"Is that the right thing to do, think you?" demanded Will.

"It is indispensable," said the parson.

"Very well," replied the wooer.

Two or three days passed away with great delight to Will, although a bystander might scarce have found it out. He continued to take his meals opposite Marjory, and to talk with her and gaze upon her in her father's presence; but he made no attempt to see her alone, nor in any other way changed his conduct towards her from what it had been since the beginning. Perhaps the girl was a little disappointed, and perhaps not unjustly; and yet if it had been enough to be always in the thoughts of another person, and so pervade and alter his whole life, she might have been thoroughly contented. For she was never out of Will's mind for an instant. He sat over the stream, and watched the dust of the eddy, and the poised fish, and straining weeds; he wandered out alone into the purple even, with all the blackbirds piping round him in the wood; he rose early in the morning; and saw the sky turn from grey to gold, and the light leap upon the hilltops; and all the while he kept wondering if he had never seen such things before, or how it was that they should look so different now. The sound of his own mill wheel, or of the wind among the trees, confounded and charmed his heart. The most enchanting thoughts presented themselves unbidden in his mind. He was so happy that he could not sleep at night, and so restless that he could hardly sit still out of her company. And yet it seemed as if he avoided her rather than sought her out.

One day, as he was coming home from a ramble, Will found Marjory in the garden picking flowers, and as he came up with her, slackened his pace and continued walking by her side.

"You like flowers?" he said.

"Indeed I love them dearly," she replied. "Do you?"

"Why, no," said he, "not so much. They are a very small affair, when all is done. I can fancy people caring for them greatly, but not doing as you are just now."

"How?" she asked, pausing and looking up at him.

"Plucking them," said he. "They are a deal better off where they are, and look a deal prettier, if you go to that."

"I wish to have them for my own," she answered, "to carry them near my heart, and keep them in my room. They tempt me when they grow here; they seem to say, 'Come and do something with us'; but once I have cut them and put them by, the charm is laid, and I can look at them with quite an easy heart."

"You wish to possess them," replied Will, "in order to think no more about them. It's a bit like killing the goose with the golden eggs. It's a bit like what I wished to do when I was a boy. Because I had a fancy for looking out over the plain, I wished to go down there—where I couldn't look out over it any longer. Was not that fine reasoning? Dear, dear, if they only thought of it, all the world would do like me; and you would let your flowers alone, just as I stay up here in the mountains." Suddenly he broke off sharp. "By the Lord!" he cried. And when she asked him what was wrong, he turned the question off, and walked away into the house with rather a humorous expression of face.

He was silent at table; and after the night had fallen and the stars had come out overhead, he walked up and down for hours in the courtyard and garden with an uneven pace. There was still a light in the window of Marjory's room: one little oblong patch of orange in a world of dark blue hills and silver starlight. Will's mind ran a great deal on the window; but his thoughts were not very lover-like. "There she is in her room," he thought, "and there are the stars overhead:—a blessing upon both!" Both were good influences in his life; both soothed and braced him in his profound contentment with the world. And what more should he desire with either? The fat young man and his counsels were so present to his mind, that he threw back his head, and putting his hands before his mouth, shouted aloud to the populous heavens. Whether from the position of his head or the sudden strain of the exertion, he seemed to see a momentary shock among the stars, and a diffusion of frosty light pass from one to another along the sky. At the same instant, a corner of the blind was lifted up and lowered again at once. He laughed a loud ho-ho! "One and another!" thought Will. "The stars tremble, and the blind goes up. Why, before Heaven, what a great magician I must be!

Now if I were only a fool, should not I be in a pretty way?" And he went off to bed, chuckling to himself: "If I were only a fool!"

The next morning, pretty early, he saw her once more in the garden, and sought her out.

"I have been thinking about getting married," he began abruptly; "and after having turned it all over, I have made up my mind it's not worthwhile."

She turned upon him for a single moment; but his radiant, kindly appearance would, under the circumstances, have disconcerted an angel, and she looked down again upon the ground in silence. He could see her tremble.

"I hope you don't mind," he went on, a little taken aback. "You ought not. I have turned it all over, and upon my soul there's nothing in it. We should never be one whit nearer than we are just now, and, if I am a wise man, nothing like so happy."

"It is unnecessary to go round about with me," she said. "I very well remember that you refused to commit yourself; and now that I see you were mistaken, and in reality have never cared for me, I can only feel sad that I have been so far misled."

"I ask your pardon," said Will stoutly; "you do not understand my meaning. As to whether I have ever loved you or not, I must leave that to others. But for one thing, my feeling is not changed; and for another, you may make it your boast that you have made my whole life and character something different from what they were. I mean what I say; no less. I do not think getting married is worthwhile. I would rather you went on living with your father, so that I could walk over and see you once, or maybe twice a week, as people go to church, and then we should both be all the happier between whiles. That's my notion. But I'll marry you if you will," he added.

"Do you know that you are insulting me?" she broke out.

"Not I, Marjory," said he; "if there is anything in a clear conscience, not I. I offer all my heart's best affections; you can take it or want it, though I suspect it's beyond either your power or mine to change what has once been done, and set me fancy-free. I'll marry you, if you like; but I tell you again and again, it's not worthwhile, and we had best stay friends. Though I am a quiet man I have noticed a heap of things in my life. Trust in me, and take things as I propose; or, if you don't like that, say the word, and I'll marry you out of hand."

There was a considerable pause, and Will, who began to feel uneasy, began to grow angry in consequence.

"It seems you are too proud to say your mind," he said. "Believe me, that's a pity. A clean shrift makes simple living. Can a man be more downright or honourable to a woman than I have been? I have said my say, and given you your choice. Do you want me to marry you? Or will you take my friendship, as I think best? Or have you had enough of me for good? Speak out, for the dear God's sake! You know your father told you a girl should speak her mind in these affairs."

She seemed to recover herself at that, turned without a word, walked rapidly through the garden, and disappeared into the house, leaving Will in some confusion as to the result. He walked up and down the garden, whistling softly to himself. Sometimes he stopped and contemplated the sky and hilltops; sometimes he went down to the tail of the weir and sat there, looking foolishly in the water. All this dubiety and perturbation was so foreign to his nature and the life which he had resolutely chosen for himself that he began to regret Marjory's arrival. "After all," he thought, "I was as happy as a man need be. I could come down here and watch my fishes all day long if I wanted: I was as settled and contented as my old mill."

Marjory came down to dinner, looking very trim and quiet; and no sooner were all three at table than she made her father a speech, with her eyes fixed upon her plate, but showing no other sign of embarrassment or distress.

"Father," she began, "Mr. Will and I have been talking things over. We see that we have each made a mistake about our feelings, and he has agreed, at my request, to give up all idea of marriage, and be no more than my very good friend, as in the past. You see, there is no shadow of a quarrel, and indeed I hope we shall see a great deal of him in the future, for his visits will always be welcome in our house. Of course, Father, you will know best, but perhaps we should do better to leave Mr. Will's house for the present. I believe, after what has passed, we should hardly be agreeable inmates for some days."

Will, who had commanded himself with difficulty from the first, broke out upon this into an inarticulate noise, and raised one hand with an appearance of real dismay, as if he were about to interfere and contradict. But she checked him at once, looking up at him with a swift glance and an angry flush upon her cheek.

"You will perhaps have the good grace," she said, "to let me explain these matters for myself."

Will was put entirely out of countenance by her expression and the ring of her voice. He held his peace, concluding that there were some things about this girl beyond his comprehension—in which he was exactly right.

The poor parson was quite crestfallen. He tried to prove that this was no more than a true lovers' tiff, which would pass off before night; and when he was dislodged from that position, he went on to argue that where there was no quarrel there could be no call for a separation; for the good man liked both his entertainment and his host. It was curious to see how the girl managed them, saying little all the time, and that very quietly, and yet twisting them round her finger and insensibly leading them wherever she would by feminine tact and generalship. It scarcely seemed to have been her doing—it seemed as if things had merely so fallen out—that she and her father took their departure that same afternoon in a farm cart, and went farther down the valley, to wait, until their own house was ready for them, in another hamlet. But Will had been observing closely, and was well aware of her dexterity and resolution. When he found himself alone he had a great many curious matters to turn over in his mind. He was very sad and solitary, to begin with. All the interest had gone out of his life, and he might look up at the stars as long as he pleased, he somehow failed to find support or consolation. And then he was in such a turmoil of spirit about Marjory. He had been puzzled and irritated at her behaviour, and yet he could not keep himself from admiring it. He thought he recognized a fine, perverse angel in that still soul which he had never hitherto suspected; and though he saw it was an influence that would fit but ill with his own life of artificial calm, he could not keep himself from ardently desiring to possess it. Like a man who has lived among shadows and now meets the sun, he was both pained and delighted.

As the days went forward he passed from one extreme to another; now pluming himself on the strength of his determination, now despising his timid and silly caution. The former was, perhaps, the true thought of his heart, and represented the regular tenor of the man's reflections; but the latter burst forth from time to time with an unruly violence, and then he would forget all consideration, and go up and down his house and garden or walk among the fir woods like one who is beside himself with remorse. To equable, steady-minded Will this state of matters was intolerable; and he determined, at whatever cost, to bring it to an end. So, one warm summer afternoon he put on his best clothes, took a thorn switch in his hand, and set out down the valley by the river. As soon as he had taken his determination, he had regained at a bound his customary peace of heart, and he enjoyed the bright weather and the variety of the scene without any admixture of alarm or unpleasant eagerness. It was nearly the same to him how the matter turned out. If she accepted him he would have to marry her this time, which perhaps was all for the best. If she refused him, he would have done his utmost, and might follow his own way in the future with an untroubled conscience. He hoped, on the whole, she would refuse him; and then, again, as he saw the brown roof which sheltered her, peeping through some willows at an angle of the stream, he was half-inclined to reverse the wish, and more than half-ashamed of himself for this infirmity of purpose.

Marjory seemed glad to see him, and gave him her hand without affectation or delay.

"I have been thinking about this marriage," he began.

"So have I," she answered. "And I respect you more and more for a very wise man. You understood me better than I understood myself; and I am now quite certain that things are all for the best as they are."

"At the same time——" ventured Will.

"You must be tired," she interrupted. "Take a seat and let me fetch you a glass of wine. The afternoon is so warm; and I wish you not to be displeased with your visit. You must come quite often; once a week, if you can spare the time; I am always so glad to see my friends."

"Oh, very well," thought Will to himself. "It appears I was right after all." And he paid a very agreeable visit, walked home again in capital spirits, and gave himself no further concern about the matter.

For nearly three years Will and Marjory continued on these terms, seeing each other once or twice a week without any word of love between them; and for all that time I believe Will was nearly as happy as a man can be. He rather stinted himself the pleasure of seeing her; and he would often walk halfway over to the parsonage, and then back again, as if to whet his appetite. Indeed, there was one corner of the road whence he could see the church spire wedged into a crevice of the valley between sloping fir woods, with a triangular snatch of plain by way of background, which he greatly affected as a place to sit and moralise in before returning homewards; and the peasants got so much into the habit of finding him there in the twilight that they gave it the name of "Will o' the Mill's Corner."

At the end of the three years Marjory played him a sad trick by suddenly marrying somebody else. Will kept his countenance bravely, and merely remarked that, for as little as he knew of women, he had acted very prudently in not marrying her himself three years before. She plainly knew very little of her own mind, and, in spite of a deceptive manner, was as fickle and flighty as the rest of them. He had to congratulate himself on an escape, he said, and would take a higher opinion of his own wisdom in consequence. But at heart he was reasonably displeased, moped a good deal for a month or two, and fell away in flesh, to the astonishment of his serving lads.

It was perhaps a year after this marriage that Will was awakened late one night by the sound of a horse galloping on the road, followed by precipitate knocking at the inn door. He opened his window and saw a farm servant, mounted and holding a led horse by the bridle, who told him to make what haste he could and go along with him; for Marjory was dying, and had sent urgently to fetch him to her bedside. Will was no horseman, and made so little speed upon the way that the poor young wife was very near her end before he arrived. But they had some minutes' talk in private, and he was present and wept very bitterly while she breathed her last.

Death

YEAR AFTER YEAR went away into nothing, with great explosions and outcries in the cities on the plain: red revolt springing up and being suppressed in blood, battle swaying hither and thither, patient astronomers in observatory towers picking out and christening new stars, plays being performed in lighted theatres, people being carried into hospitals on stretchers, and all the usual turmoil and agitation of men's lives in crowded centres. Up in Will's valley only the wind and seasons made an epoch; the fish hung in the swift stream, the birds circled overhead, the pine tops rustled underneath the stars, the tall hills stood over all; and Will went to and fro, minding his wayside inn, until the snow began to thicken on his head. His heart was young and vigorous; and if his pulses kept a sober time, they still beat strong and steady in his wrists. He carried a ruddy stain on either cheek, like a ripe apple; he stooped a little, but his step was still firm; and his sinewy hands were reached out to all men with a friendly pressure. His face was covered with those wrinkles which are got in open air, and which, rightly looked at, are no more than a sort of permanent sunburning; such wrinkles heighten the stupidity of stupid faces; but to a person like Will, with his clear eyes and smiling mouth, only give another charm by testifying to a simple and easy life. His talk was full of wise sayings. He had a taste for other people; and other people had a taste for him. When the valley was full of tourists in the season, there were merry nights in Will's arbour; and his views, which seemed whimsical to his neighbours, were often enough admired by learned people out of towns and colleges. Indeed, he had a very noble old age, and grew daily better known; so that his fame was heard of in the cities of the plain; and young men who had been summer travellers spoke together in cafés of Will o' the Mill and his rough philosophy. Many and many an invitation, you may be sure, he had; but nothing could tempt him from his upland valley. He would shake his head and smile over his tobacco pipe with a deal of meaning. "You come too late," he would answer. "I am a dead man now: I have lived and died already. Fifty years ago you would have brought my heart

He grew less talkative towards the end, and
would listen to other people by the hour.

into my mouth; and now you do not even tempt me. But that is the object of long living, that man should cease to care about life." And again: "There is only one difference between a long life and a good dinner: that, in the dinner, the sweets come last." Or once more: "When I was a boy, I was a bit puzzled, and hardly knew whether it was myself or the world that was curious and worth looking into. Now I know it is myself, and stick to that."

He never showed any symptom of frailty, but kept stalwart and firm to the last; but they say he grew less talkative towards the end, and would listen to other people by the hour in an amused and sympathetic silence. Only, when he did speak, it was more to the point and more charged with old experience. He drank a bottle of wine gladly; above all, at sunset on the hilltop or quite late at night under the stars in the arbour. The sight of something attractive and unattainable seasoned his enjoyment, he would say; and he professed he had lived long enough to admire a candle all the more when he could compare it with a planet.

One night, in his seventy-second year, he awoke in bed in such uneasiness of body and mind that he arose and dressed himself and went out to meditate in the arbour. It was pitch-dark, without a star; the river was swollen, and the wet woods and meadows loaded the air with perfume. It had thundered during the day, and it promised more thunder for the morrow. A murky, stifling night for a man of seventy-two! Whether it was the weather or the wakefulness, or some little touch of fever in his old limbs, Will's mind was besieged by tumultuous and crying memories. His boyhood, the night with the fat young man, the death of his adopted parents, the summer days with Marjory, and many of those small circumstances, which seem nothing to another, and are yet the very gist of a man's own life to himself—things seen, words heard, books misconstrued—arose from their forgotten corners and usurped his attention. The dead themselves were with him, not merely taking part in this thin show of memory that defiled before his brain, but revisiting his bodily senses as they do in profound and vivid dreams. The fat young man leaned his elbows on the table opposite; Marjory came and went with an apronful of flowers between the garden and the arbour; he could hear the old parson knocking out his pipe or blowing his resonant nose. The tide of his consciousness ebbed and flowed; he was sometimes half-asleep and drowned in his recollections of the past; and sometimes he was broad awake, wondering at himself. But about the middle of the night he was startled by the voice of the dead miller calling to him out of the house as he used to do on the arrival of custom. The hallucination was so perfect that Will sprang from his seat and stood listening for the summons to be repeated; and as he listened he became conscious of another noise besides the brawling of the river and the ringing of his feverish ears. It was like the stir of the horses and the creaking of harness, as though a carriage with an impatient team had been brought up upon the road before the courtyard gate. At such an hour, upon this rough and dangerous pass, the supposition was no better than absurd; and Will dismissed it from his mind, and resumed his seat upon the arbour chair; and sleep closed over him again like running water. He was once again awakened by the dead miller's call, thinner and more spectral than before; and once again he heard the noise of an equipage upon the road. And so thrice and four times, the same dream, or the same fancy, presented itself to his senses: until at length, smiling to himself as when one humours a nervous child, he proceeded towards the gate to set his uncertainty at rest.

From the arbour to the gate was no great distance, and yet it took Will some time; it seemed as if the dead thickened around him in the court, and crossed his path at every step. For, first, he was suddenly surprised by an overpowering sweetness of heliotropes; it was as if his garden had been planted with this flower from end to end, and the hot, damp night had drawn forth all their perfumes in a breath. Now the heliotrope had been Marjory's favourite flower, and since her death not one of them had ever been planted in Will's ground.

"I must be going crazy," he thought. "Poor Marjory and her heliotropes!"

And with that he raised his eyes towards the window that had once been hers. If he had been bewildered before, he was now almost terrified; for there was a light in the room; the window was an orange oblong as of yore; and the corner of the blind was lifted and let fall as on the night when he stood and shouted to the stars in his perplexity. The illusion only endured an instant; but it left him somewhat unmanned, rubbing his eyes and staring at the outline of the house and the black night behind it. While he thus stood, and it seemed as if he must have stood there quite a long time, there came a renewal of the noises on the road: and he turned in time to meet a stranger, who was advancing to meet him across the court. There was something like the outline of a great carriage discernible on the road behind the stranger, and, above that, a few black pine tops, like so many plumes.

"Master Will?" asked the newcomer, in brief military fashion.

"That same, sir," answered Will. "Can I do anything to serve you?"

"I have heard you much spoken of, Master Will," returned the other; "much spoken of, and well. And though I have both hands full of business, I wish to drink a bottle of wine with you in your arbour. Before I go, I shall introduce myself."

Will led the way to the trellis, and got a lamp lighted and a bottle uncorked. He was not altogether unused to such complimentary interviews, and hoped little enough for this one, being schooled by many disappointments. A sort of cloud had settled on his wits and prevented him from remembering the strangeness of the hour. He moved like a person in his sleep; and it seemed as if the lamp caught fire and the bottle came uncorked with the facility of thought. Still, he had some curiosity about the appearance of his visitor, and tried in vain to turn the light into his face; either he handled the lamp clumsily, or there was a dimness over his eyes; but he could make out little more than a shadow at table with him. He stared and stared at this shadow, as he wiped out the glasses, and began to feel cold and strange about the heart. The silence weighed upon him, for he could hear nothing now, not even the river, but the drumming of his own arteries in his ears.

"Here's to you," said the stranger, roughly.

"Here is my service, sir," replied Will, sipping his wine, which somehow tasted oddly.

"I understand you are a very positive fellow," pursued the stranger.

Will made answer with a smile of some satisfaction and a little nod.

"So am I," continued the other; "and it is the delight of my heart to tramp on people's corns. I will have nobody positive but myself; not one.

I have crossed the whims, in my time, of kings and generals and great artists. And what would you say," he went on, "if I had come up here on purpose to cross yours?"

Will had it on his tongue to make a sharp rejoinder; but the politeness of an old innkeeper prevailed; and he held his peace and made answer with a civil gesture of the hand.

"I have," said the stranger. "And if I did not hold you in a particular esteem, I should make no words about the matter. It appears you pride yourself on staying where you are. You mean to stick by your inn. Now I mean you shall come for a turn with me in my barouche; and before this bottle's empty, so you shall."

"That would be an odd thing, to be sure," replied Will, with a chuckle. "Why, sir, I have grown here like an old oak tree; the devil himself could hardly root me up: and for all I perceive you are a very entertaining old gentleman, I would wager you another bottle you lose your pains with me."

The dimness of Will's eyesight had been increasing all this while; but he was somehow conscious of a sharp and chilling scrutiny which irritated and yet overmastered him.

"You need not think," he broke out suddenly, in an explosive, febrile manner that startled and alarmed himself, "that I am a stay-at-home, because I fear anything under God. God knows I am tired enough of it all; and when the time comes for a longer journey than ever you dream of, I reckon I shall find myself prepared."

The stranger emptied his glass and pushed it away from him. He looked down for a little, and then, leaning over the table, tapped Will three times upon the forearm with a single finger. "The time has come!" he said solemnly.

An ugly thrill spread from the spot he touched. The tones of his voice were dull and startling, and echoed strangely in Will's heart.

"I beg your pardon," he said, with some discomposure. "What do you mean?"

"Look at me, and you will find your eyesight swim. Raise your hand; it is dead-heavy. This is your last bottle of wine, Master Will, and your last night upon the earth."

"You are a doctor?" quavered Will.

"The best that ever was," replied the other; "for I cure both mind and body with the same prescription. I take away all pain and I forgive all sins; and where my patients have gone wrong in life, I smooth out all complications and set them free again upon their feet."

"I have no need of you," said Will.

"A time comes for all men, Master Will," replied the doctor, "when the helm is taken out of their hands. For you, because you were prudent and quiet, it has been long of coming, and you have had long to discipline yourself for its reception. You have seen what is to be seen about your mill; you have sat close all your days like a hare in its form; but now that is at an end; and," added the doctor, getting on his feet, "you must arise and come with me."

"You are a strange physician," said Will, looking steadfastly upon his guest.

"I am a natural law," he replied, "and people call me Death."

"Why did you not tell me so at first?" cried Will. "I have been waiting for you these many years. Give me your hand, and welcome."

"Lean upon my arm," said the stranger, "for already your strength abates. Lean on me heavily as you need; for though I am old, I am very strong. It is but three steps to my carriage, and there all your trouble ends. Why, Will," he added, "I have been yearning for you as if you were my own son; and of all the men that ever I came for in my long days, I have come for you most gladly. I am caustic, and sometimes offend people at first sight; but I am a good friend at heart to such as you."

"Since Marjory was taken," returned Will, "I declare before God you were the only friend I had to look for."

So the pair went arm-in-arm across the courtyard.

One of the servants awoke about this time and heard the noise of horses pawing before he dropped asleep again; all down the valley that night there was a rushing as of a smooth and steady wind descending towards the plain; and when the world rose next morning, sure enough, Will o' the Mill had gone at last upon his travels.

The Body Snatcher

E VERY NIGHT IN THE year, four of us sat in the small parlour of the George at Debenham—the undertaker, and the landlord, and Fettes, and myself. Sometimes there would be more; but blow high, blow low, come rain or snow or frost, we four would be each planted in his own particular armchair. Fettes was an old drunken Scotsman, a man of education, obviously, and a man of some property, since he lived in idleness. He had come to Debenham years ago, while still young, and by a mere continuance of living had grown to be an adopted townsman. His blue camlet cloak was a local antiquity, like the church spire. His place in the parlour at the George, his absence from church, his old, crapulous, disreputable vices, were all things of course in Debenham. He had some vague Radical opinions and some fleeting infidelities, which he would now and again set forth and emphasise with tottering slaps upon the table. He drank rum—five glasses regularly every evening; and for the greater portion of his nightly visit to the George sat, with his glass in his right hand, in a state of melancholy alcoholic saturation. We called him the Doctor, for he was supposed to have some special knowledge of medicine, and had been known, upon a pinch, to set a fracture or reduce a dislocation; but, beyond these slight particulars, we had no knowledge of his character and antecedents.

One dark winter night—it had struck nine some time before the landlord joined us—there was a sick man in the George, a great neighbouring proprietor suddenly struck down with apoplexy on his way to Parliament; and the great man's still greater London doctor had been telegraphed to his bedside. It was the first time that such a thing had happened in Debenham, for the railway was but newly open, and we were all proportionately moved by the occurrence.

"He's come," said the landlord, after he had filled and lighted his pipe.

"He?" said I. "Who?—not the doctor?"

"Himself," replied our host.

"What is his name?"

"Dr. Macfarlane," said the landlord.

Fettes was far through his third tumbler, stupidly fuddled, now nodding over, now staring mazily around him; but at the last word he seemed to awaken, and repeated the name "Macfarlane" twice, quietly enough the first time, but with sudden emotion at the second.

"Yes," said the landlord, "that's his name, Doctor Wolfe Macfarlane."

Fettes became instantly sober; his eyes awoke, his voice became clear, loud, and steady, his language forcible and earnest. We were all startled by the transformation, as if a man had risen from the dead.

"I beg your pardon," he said, "I am afraid I have not been paying much attention to your talk. Who is this Wolfe Macfarlane?" And then, when he had heard the landlord out, "It cannot be, it cannot be," he added; "and yet I would like well to see him face-to-face."

"Do you know him, Doctor?" asked the undertaker, with a gasp.

"God forbid!" was the reply. "And yet the name is a strange one; it were too much to fancy two. Tell me, landlord, is he old?"

"Well," said the host, "he's not a young man, to be sure, and his hair is white; but he looks younger than you."

"He is older, though; years older. But," with a slap upon the table, "it's the rum you see in my face — rum and sin. This man, perhaps, may have an easy conscience and a good digestion. Conscience! Hear me speak. You would think I was some good, old, decent Christian, would you not? But no, not I; I never canted. Voltaire might have canted if he'd stood in my shoes; but the brains" — with a rattling fillip on his bald head — "the brains were clear and active, and I saw and made no deductions."

"If you know this doctor," I ventured to remark, after a somewhat awful pause, "I should gather that you do not share the landlord's good opinion."

Fettes paid no regard to me.

"Yes," he said, with sudden decision, "I must see him face-to-face."

There was another pause, and then a door was closed rather sharply on the first floor, and a step was heard upon the stair.

"That's the doctor," cried the landlord. "Look sharp, and you can catch him."

It was but two steps from the small parlour to the door of the old George Inn; the wide oak staircase landed almost in the street; there was room for a Turkey rug and nothing more between the threshold and the last round of the descent; but this little space was every evening brilliantly lit up, not only by the light upon the stair and the great signal lamp below the sign, but by the warm radiance of the barroom window. The George thus brightly advertised itself to passersby in the cold street. Fettes walked steadily to the spot, and we, who were hanging behind, beheld the two men meet, as one of them had phrased it, face-to-face. Dr. Macfarlane was alert and vigorous. His white hair set off his pale and placid, although energetic, countenance. He was richly dressed in the finest of broadcloth and the whitest of linen, with a great gold watchchain, and studs and spectacles of the same precious material. He wore a broad-folded tie, white and speckled with lilac, and he carried on his arm a comfortable driving coat of fur. There was no doubt but he became his years, breathing, as he did, of wealth and consideration; and it was a surprising contrast to see our parlour sot — bald, dirty, pimpled, and robed in his old camlet cloak — confront him at the bottom of the stairs.

"Macfarlane!" he said somewhat loudly, more like a herald than a friend.

The great doctor pulled up short on the fourth step, as though the familiarity of the address surprised and somewhat shocked his dignity.

"Toddy Macfarlane!" repeated Fettes.

The London man almost staggered. He stared for the swiftest of seconds at the man before him, glanced behind him with a sort of scare, and then in a startled whisper, "Fettes!" he said, "you!"

"Ay," said the other, "me! Did you think I was dead too? We are not so easy shut of our acquaintance."

"Hush, hush!" exclaimed the doctor. "Hush, hush! This meeting is so unexpected—I can see you are unmanned. I hardly knew you, I confess, at first; but I am overjoyed—overjoyed to have this opportunity. For the present it must be howd'ye-do and good-bye in one, for my fly is waiting, and I must not fail the train; but you shall—let me see—yes—you shall give me your address, and you can count on early news of me. We must do something for you, Fettes. I fear you are out at elbows; but we must see to that for auld lang syne, as once we sang at suppers."

"Money!" cried Fettes; "money from you! The money that I had from you is lying where I cast it in the rain."

Dr. Macfarlane had talked himself into some measure of superiority and confidence, but the uncommon energy of this refusal cast him back into his first confusion.

A horrible, ugly look came and went across his almost venerable countenance. "My dear fellow," he said, "be it as you please; my last thought is to offend you. I would intrude on none. I will leave you my address, however——"

"I do not wish it—I do not wish to know the roof that shelters you," interrupted the other. "I heard your name; I feared it might be you; I wished to know if, after all, there were a God; I know now that there is none. Begone!"

He still stood in the middle of the rug, between the stair and the doorway; and the great London physician, in order to escape, would be forced to step to one side. It was plain that he hesitated before the thought of this humiliation. White as he was, there was a dangerous glitter in his spectacles; but while he still paused uncertain, he became aware that the driver of his fly was peering in from the street at this unusual scene and caught a glimpse at the same time of our little body from the parlour, huddled by the corner of the bar. The presence of so many witnesses decided him at once to flee. He crouched together, brushing on the wainscot, and made a dart like a serpent, striking for the door. But his tribulation was not yet entirely at an end, for even as he was passing Fettes clutched him by the arm and these words came in a whisper, and yet painfully distinct, "Have you seen it again?"

The great rich London doctor cried out aloud with a sharp, throttling cry; he dashed his questioner across the open space, and, with his hands over his head, fled out of the door like a detected thief. Before it had occurred to one of us to make a movement, the fly was already rattling towards the station. The scene was over like a dream, but the dream had left proofs and traces of its passage. Next day the servant found the fine gold spectacles broken on the threshold, and that very night we were all standing breathless by the barroom window, and Fettes at our side, sober, pale, and resolute in look.

"God protect us, Mr. Fettes!" said the landlord, coming first into possession of his customary senses. "What in the universe is all this? These are strange things you have been saying."

Fettes turned towards us; he looked us each in succession in the face. "See if you can hold your tongues," said he. "That man Macfarlane is not safe to cross; those that have done so already have repented it too late."

And then, without so much as finishing his third glass, far less waiting for the other two, he bade us good-bye and went forth, under the lamp of the hotel, into the black night.

We three turned to our places in the parlour, with the big red fire and four clear candles; and as we recapitulated what had passed, the first chill of our surprise soon changed into a glow of curiosity. We sat late; it was the latest session I have known in the old George. Each man, before we parted, had his theory that he was bound to prove; and none of us had any nearer business in this world than to track out the past of our condemned companion, and surprise the secret that he shared with the great London doctor. It is no great boast, but I believe I was a better hand at worming out a story than either of my fellows at the George;

and perhaps there is now no other man alive who could narrate to you the following foul and unnatural events.

In his young days Fettes studied medicine in the schools of Edinburgh. He had talent of a kind, the talent that picks up swiftly what it hears and readily retails it for its own. He worked little at home; but he was civil, attentive, and intelligent in the presence of his masters. They soon picked him out as a lad who listened closely and remembered well; nay, strange as it seemed to me when I first heard it, he was in those days well favoured, and pleased by his exterior. There was, at that period, a certain extramural teacher of anatomy, whom I shall here designate by the letter K. His name was subsequently too well known. The man who bore it skulked through the streets of Edinburgh in disguise, while the mob that applauded at the execution of Burke called loudly for the blood of his employer. But Mr. K—— was then at the top of his vogue; he enjoyed a popularity due partly to his own talent and address, partly to the incapacity of his rival, the university professor. The students, at least, swore by his name, and Fettes believed himself, and was believed by others, to have laid the foundations of success when he had acquired the favour of this meteorically famous man. Mr. K—— was a *bon vivant* as well as an accomplished teacher; he liked a sly allusion no less than a careful preparation. In both capacities Fettes enjoyed and deserved his notice, and by the second year of his attendance he held the half-regular position of second demonstrator or subassistant in his class.

In this capacity, the charge of the theatre and lecture room devolved in particular upon his shoulders. He had to answer for the cleanliness of the premises and the conduct of the other students, and it was a part of his duty to supply, receive, and divide the various subjects. It was with a view to this last—at that time very delicate—affair that he was lodged by Mr. K—— in the same wynd, and at last in the same building, with the dissecting rooms. Here, after a night of turbulent pleasures, his hand still tottering, his sight still misty and confused, he would be called out of bed in the black hours before the winter dawn by the unclean and desperate interlopers who supplied the table. He would open the door to these men, since infamous throughout the land. He would help them with their tragic burthen, pay them their sordid price, and remain alone, when they were gone, with the unfriendly relics of humanity. From such a scene he would return to snatch another hour or two of slumber, to repair the abuses of the night, and refresh himself for the labours of the day.

Few lads could have been more insensible to the impressions of a life thus passed among the ensigns of mortality. His mind was closed against all general considerations. He was incapable of interest in the fate and fortunes of another, the slave of his own desires and low ambitions. Cold, light, and selfish in the last resort, he had that modicum of prudence, miscalled morality, which keeps a man from inconvenient drunkenness or punishable theft. He coveted, besides, a measure of consideration from his masters and his fellow pupils, and he had no desire to fail conspicuously in the external parts of life. Thus he made it his pleasure to gain some distinction in his studies, and day after day rendered unimpeachable eye service to his employer, Mr. K——. For his day of work he indemnified himself by nights of roaring, blackguardly enjoyment; and when that balance had been struck, the organ that he called his conscience declared itself content.

The supply of subjects was a continual trouble to him as well as to his master. In that large and busy class, the raw material of the anatomists kept perpetually running out; and the business thus rendered necessary was not only unpleasant in itself, but threatened dangerous consequences to all who were concerned. It was the policy of Mr. K—— to ask no questions in his dealings with the trade. "They bring the body, and we pay the price," he used to say, dwelling on the alliteration—"*quid pro quo.*" And, again, and somewhat profanely, "Ask no questions," he would tell his assistants, "for conscience's sake." There was no understanding that the subjects were provided by the crime of murder. Had that idea been broached to him in words, he would have recoiled in horror; but the lightness of his speech upon so grave a matter was in itself an offence against good manners, and a temptation to the men with whom he dealt. Fettes, for instance, had often remarked to himself upon the singular freshness of the bodies. He had been struck again and again by the hangdog, abominable looks of the ruffians who came to him before the dawn; and, putting things together clearly in his private thoughts, he perhaps attributed a meaning too immoral and too categorical to the unguarded counsels of his master. He understood his duty, in short, to have three branches: to take what was brought, to pay the price, and to avert the eye from any evidence of crime.

One November morning this policy of silence was put sharply to the test. He had been awake all night with a racking toothache—pacing his room like a caged beast or throwing himself in fury on his bed—and had fallen at last into that profound, uneasy slumber that so often follows on a night of pain, when he was awakened by the third or fourth angry repetition of the concerted signal. There was a thin, bright moonshine: it was bitter cold, windy, and frosty; the town had not yet awakened, but an indefinable stir already preluded the noise and business of the day. The ghouls had come later than usual, and they seemed more than usually eager to be gone. Fettes, sick with sleep, lighted them upstairs. He heard their grumbling Irish voices through a dream; and as they stripped the sack from their sad merchandise he leaned dozing, with his shoulder propped against the wall; he had to shake himself to find the men their money. As he did so, his eyes lighted on the dead face. He started; he took two steps nearer, with the candle raised.

"God Almighty!" he cried. "That is Jane Galbraith!"

The men answered nothing, but they shuffled nearer the door.

"I know her, I tell you," he continued. "She was alive and hearty yesterday. It's impossible she can be dead; it's impossible you should have got this body fairly."

"Sure, sir, you're mistaken entirely," said one of the men.

But the other looked Fettes darkly in the eyes, and demanded the money on the spot.

It was impossible to misconceive the threat or to exaggerate the danger. The lad's heart failed him. He stammered some excuses, counted out the sum, and saw his hateful visitors depart. No sooner were they gone than he hastened to confirm his doubts. By a dozen unquestionable marks he identified the girl he had jested with the day before. He saw, with horror, marks upon her body that might well betoken violence. A panic seized him, and he took refuge in his room. There he reflected at length over the discovery that he had made; considered soberly the bearing of Mr. K——'s instructions and the danger to himself of interference in so serious a business, and at last, in sore perplexity, determined to wait for the advice of his immediate superior, the class assistant.

This was a young doctor, Wolfe Macfarlane, a high favourite among all the reckless students, clever, dissipated, and unscrupulous to the last degree. He had travelled and studied abroad. His manners were agreeable and a little forward. He was an authority on the stage, skilful on the ice or the links with skate or golf club; he dressed with nice audacity, and, to put the finishing touch upon his glory, he kept a gig and a strong trotting horse. With Fettes he was on terms of intimacy; indeed, their relative positions called for some community of life; and when subjects were scarce the pair would drive far into the country in Macfarlane's gig, visit and desecrate some lonely graveyard, and return before dawn with their booty to the door of the dissecting room.

On that particular morning Macfarlane arrived somewhat earlier than his wont. Fettes heard him, and met him on the stairs, told him his story, and showed him the cause of his alarm. Macfarlane examined the marks on her body.

"Yes," he said with a nod, "it looks fishy."

"Well, what should I do?" asked Fettes.

"Do?" repeated the other. "Do you want to do anything? Least said soonest mended, I should say."

"Someone else might recognise her," objected Fettes. "She was as well known as the Castle Rock."

"We'll hope not," said Macfarlane, "and if anybody does—well, you didn't, don't you see, and there's an end. The fact is, this has been going on too long. Stir up the mud, and you'll get K—— into the most unholy trouble; you'll be in a shocking box yourself. So will I, if you come to that. I should like to know how any one of us would look, or what the devil we should have to say for ourselves, in any Christian witness box. For me, you know there's one thing certain—that, practically speaking, all our subjects have been murdered."

"Macfarlane!" cried Fettes.

"Come now!" sneered the other. "As if you hadn't suspected it yourself!"

"Suspecting is one thing——"

"And proof another. Yes, I know; and I'm as sorry as you are this should have come here," tapping the body with his cane. "The next best thing for me is not to recognise it; and," he added coolly, "I don't. You may, if you please. I don't dictate, but I think a man of the world would do as I do; and I may add, I fancy that is what K—— would look for at our hands. The question is, Why did he choose us for his assistants? And I answer, because he didn't want old wives."

This was the tone of all others to affect the mind of a lad like Fettes. He agreed to imitate Macfarlane. The body of the unfortunate girl was duly dissected, and no one remarked or appeared to recognise her.

One afternoon, when his day's work was over, Fettes dropped into a popular tavern and found Macfarlane sitting with a stranger. This was a small man, very pale and dark, with coal-black eyes. The cut of his features gave a promise of intellect and refinement which was but feebly realised in his manners, for he proved, upon a nearer acquaintance, coarse, vulgar, and stupid. He exercised, however, a very remarkable control over Macfarlane; issued orders like the Great Bashaw; became inflamed at the least discussion or delay, and commented rudely on the servility with which he was obeyed. This most offensive person took a fancy to Fettes on the spot, plied him with drinks, and honoured him with unusual confidences on his past career. If a tenth part of what he confessed were true, he was a very loathsome rogue; and the lad's vanity was tickled by the attention of so experienced a man.

"I'm a pretty bad fellow myself," the stranger remarked, "but Macfarlane is the boy—Toddy Macfarlane I call him. Toddy, order your friend another glass." Or it might be, "Toddy, you jump up and shut the door." "Toddy hates me," he said again. "Oh, yes, Toddy, you do!"

"Don't you call me that confounded name," growled Macfarlane.

"Hear him! Did you ever see the lads play knife? He would like to do that all over my body," remarked the stranger.

"We medicals have a better way than that," said Fettes. "When we dislike a dead friend of ours, we dissect him."

Macfarlane looked up sharply, as though this jest was scarcely to his mind.

The afternoon passed. Gray, for that was the stranger's name, invited Fettes to join them at dinner, ordered a feast so sumptuous that the tavern was thrown in commotion, and when all was done commanded Macfarlane to settle the bill. It was late before they separated; the man Gray was incapably drunk. Macfarlane, sobered by his fury, chewed the cud of the money he had been forced to squander and the slights he had been obliged to swallow. Fettes, with various liquors singing in his head, returned home with devious footsteps and a mind entirely in abeyance. Next day Macfarlane was absent from the class, and Fettes smiled to himself as he imagined him still squiring the intolerable Gray from tavern to tavern. As soon as the hour of liberty had struck he posted from place to place in quest of his last night's companions. He could find them, however, nowhere; so returned early to his rooms, went early to bed, and slept the sleep of the just.

At four in the morning he was awakened by the well-known signal. Descending to the door, he was filled with astonishment to find Macfarlane with his gig, and in the gig one of those long and ghastly packages with which he was so well acquainted.

"What?" he cried. "Have you been out alone? How did you manage?"

But Macfarlane silenced him roughly, bidding him turn to business. When they had got the body upstairs and laid it on the table, Macfarlane made at first as if he were going away. Then he paused and seemed to hesitate; and then, "You had better look at the face," said he, in tones of some constraint. "You had better," he repeated, as Fettes only stared at him in wonder.

"But where, and how, and when did you come by it?" cried the other.

"Look at the face," was the only answer.

Fettes was staggered; strange doubts assailed him. He looked from the young doctor to the body, and then back again. At last, with a start, he did as he was bidden. He had almost expected the sight that met his eyes, and yet the shock was cruel. To see, fixed in the rigidity of death and naked on that coarse layer of sackcloth, the man whom he left well-clad and full of meat and sin upon the threshold of a tavern, awoke,

271

even in the thoughtless Fettes, some of the terrors of the conscience. It was a *cras tibi* which reëchoed in his soul, that two whom he had known should have come to lie upon these icy tables. Yet these were only secondary thoughts. His first concern regarded Wolfe. Unprepared for a challenge so momentous, he knew not how to look his comrade in the face. He durst not meet his eye, and he had neither word nor voice at his command.

It was Macfarlane himself who made the first advance. He came up quietly behind and laid his hand gently but firmly on the other's shoulder.

"Richardson," said he, "may have the head."

Now Richardson was a student who had long been anxious for that portion of the human subject to dissect. There was no answer, and the murderer resumed: "Talking of business, you must pay me; your accounts, you see, must tally."

Fettes found a voice, the ghost of his own: "Pay you!" he cried. "Pay you for that?"

"Why, yes, of course you must. By all means and on every possible account, you must," returned the other. "I dare not give it for nothing, you dare not take it for nothing; it would compromise us both. This is another case like Jane Galbraith's. The more things are wrong the more we must act as if all were right. Where does old K—— keep his money?"

"There," answered Fettes hoarsely, pointing to a cupboard in the corner.

"Give me the key, then," said the other, calmly, holding out his hand.

There was an instant's hesitation, and the die was cast. Macfarlane could not suppress a nervous twitch, the infinitesimal mark of an immense relief, as he felt the key between his fingers. He opened the cupboard, brought out pen and ink and a paper book that stood in one compartment, and separated from the funds in a drawer a sum suitable to the occasion.

"Now, look here," he said, "there is the payment made—first proof of your good faith: first step to your security. You have now to clinch it by a second. Enter the payment in your book, and then you for your part may defy the devil."

The next few seconds were for Fettes an agony of thought; but in balancing his terrors it was the most immediate that triumphed. Any future difficulty seemed almost welcome if he could avoid a present quarrel with Macfarlane. He set down the candle which he had been carrying all the time, and with a steady hand entered the date, the nature, and the amount of the transaction.

"And now," said Macfarlane, "it's only fair that you should pocket the lucre. I've had my share already. By the bye, when a man of the world falls into a bit of luck, has a few shillings extra in his pocket—I'm ashamed to speak of it, but there's a rule of conduct in the case. No treating, no purchase of expensive class books, no squaring of old debts; borrow, don't lend."

"Macfarlane," began Fettes, still somewhat hoarsely, "I have put my neck in a halter to oblige you."

"To oblige me?" cried Wolfe. "Oh, come! You did, as near as I can see the matter, what you downright had to do in self-defence. Suppose I got into trouble, where would you be? This second little matter flows clearly from the first. Mr. Gray is the continuation of Miss Galbraith. You can't begin and then stop. If you begin, you must keep on beginning; that's the truth. No rest for the wicked."

A horrible sense of blackness and the treachery of fate seized hold upon the soul of the unhappy student.

"My God!" he cried, "but what have I done? And when did I begin? To be made a class assistant—in the name of reason, where's the harm in that? Service wanted the position; Service might have got it. Would *he* have been where *I* am now?"

"My dear fellow," said Macfarlane, "what a boy you are! What harm *has* come to you? What harm *can* come to you if you hold your tongue? Why, man, do you know what this life is? There are two squads of us—the lions and the lambs. If you're a lamb, you'll come to lie upon these tables like Gray or Jane Galbraith; if you're a lion, you'll live and drive a horse like me, like K——, like all the world with any wit or courage. You're staggered at the first. But look at K——! My dear fellow, you're clever, you have pluck. I like you, and K—— likes you. You were born to lead the hunt; and I tell you, on my honour and my experience of life, three days from now you'll laugh at all these scarecrows like a high-school boy at a farce."

And with that Macfarlane took his departure and drove off up the wynd in his gig to get under cover before daylight. Fettes was thus left alone with his regrets. He saw the miserable peril in which he stood involved. He saw, with inexpressible dismay, that there was no limit to his weakness, and that, from concession to concession, he had fallen from the arbiter of Macfarlane's destiny to his paid and helpless accomplice. He would have given the world to have been a little braver at the time, but it did not occur to him that he might still be brave. The secret of Jane Galbraith and the cursed entry in the daybook closed his mouth.

Hours passed; the class began to arrive; the members of the unhappy Gray were dealt out to one and to another, and received without remark. Richardson was made happy with the head; and before the hour of freedom rang Fettes trembled with exultation to perceive how far they had already gone towards safety.

For two days he continued to watch, with increasing joy, the dreadful process of disguise.

On the third day Macfarlane made his appearance. He had been ill, he said; but he made up for lost time by the energy with which he directed the students. To Richardson in particular he extended the most valuable assistance and advice, and that student, encouraged by the praise of the demonstrator, burned high with ambitious hopes, and saw the medal already in his grasp.

Before the week was out Macfarlane's prophecy had been fulfilled. Fettes had outlived his terrors and had forgotten his baseness. He began to plume himself upon his courage, and had so arranged the story in his mind that he could look back on these events with an unhealthy pride. Of his accomplice he saw but little. They met, of course, in the business of the class; they received their orders together from Mr. K——. At times they had a word or two in private, and Macfarlane was from first to last particularly kind and jovial. But it was plain that he avoided any reference to their common secret; and even when Fettes whispered to him that he had cast in his lot with the lions and foresworn the lambs, he only signed to him smilingly to hold his peace.

At length an occasion arose which threw the pair once more into a closer union. Mr. K——was again short of subjects; pupils were eager, and it was a part of this teacher's pretensions to be always well supplied. At the same time there came the news of a burial in the rustic graveyard of Glencorse. Time has little changed the place in question. It stood then, as now, upon a crossroad, out of call of human habitations, and buried fathom deep in the foliage of six cedar trees. The cries of the sheep upon the neighbouring hills, the streamlets upon either hand, one loudly singing among pebbles, the other dripping furtively from pond to pond, the stir of the wind in mountainous old flowering chestnuts, and once in seven days the voice of the bell and the old tunes of the precentor were the only sounds that disturbed the silence around the rural church. The Resurrection Man—to use a byname of the period—was not to be deterred by any of the sanctities of customary piety. It was part of his trade to despise and desecrate the scrolls and trumpets of old tombs, the paths worn by the feet of worshippers and mourners, and the offerings and the inscriptions of bereaved affection. To rustic neighbourhoods, where love is more than commonly tenacious, and where some bonds of blood or fellowship unite the entire society of a parish, the body snatcher, far from being repelled by natural respect, was attracted by the ease and safety of the task. To bodies that had been laid in earth, in joyful expectation of a far different awakening, there came that hasty, lamplit, terror-haunted resurrection of the spade and mattock. The coffin was forced, the cerements torn, and the melancholy relics, clad in sackcloth, after being rattled for hours on moonless byways, were at length exposed to uttermost indignities before a class of gaping boys.

Somewhat as two vultures may swoop upon a dying lamb, Fettes and Macfarlane were to be let loose upon a grave in that green and quiet resting place. The wife of a farmer, a woman who had lived for sixty years, and been known for nothing but good butter and a godly conversation, was to be rooted from her grave at midnight and carried, dead and naked, to that faraway city that she had always honoured with her Sunday best; the place beside her family was to be empty till the crack of doom; her innocent and almost venerable members to be exposed to that last curiosity of the anatomist.

Late one afternoon the pair set forth, well wrapped in cloaks and furnished with a formidable bottle. It rained without remission — a cold, dense, lashing rain. Now and again there blew a puff of wind, but these sheets of falling water kept it down. Bottle and all, it was a sad and silent drive as far as Penicuik, where they were to spend the evening. They stopped once to hide their implements in a thick bush not far from the churchyard, and once again at the Fisher's Tryst, to have a toast before the kitchen fire and vary their nips of whiskey with a glass of ale. When they reached their journey's end the gig was housed, the horse was fed and comforted, and the two young doctors in a private room sat down to the best dinner and the best wine the house afforded. The lights, the fire, the beating rain upon the window, the cold, incongruous work that lay before them, added zest to their enjoyment of the meal. With every glass their cordiality increased. Soon Macfarlane handed a little pile of gold to his companion.

"A compliment," he said. "Between friends these little d——d accommodations ought to fly like pipe lights."

Fettes pocketed the money, and applauded the sentiment to the echo. "You are a philosopher," he cried. "I was an ass till I knew you. You and K—— between you, by the Lord Harry! but you'll make a man of me."

"Of course we shall," applauded Macfarlane. "A man? I tell you, it required a man to back me up the other morning. There are some big, sprawling, forty-year-old cowards who would have turned sick at the look of the d——d thing; but not you — you kept your head. I watched you."

"Well, and why not?" Fettes thus vaunted himself. "It was no affair of mine. There was nothing to gain on the one side but disturbance, and on the other I could count on your gratitude, don't you see?" And he slapped his pocket till the gold pieces rang.

Macfarlane somehow felt a certain touch of alarm at these unpleasant words. He may have regretted that he had taught his young companion so successfully, but he had no time to interfere, for the other noisily continued in this boastful strain:

"The great thing is not to be afraid. Now, between you and me, I don't want to hang—that's practical; but for all cant, Macfarlane, I was born with a contempt. Hell, God, Devil, right, wrong, sin, crime, and all the old gallery of curiosities—they may frighten boys, but men of the world, like you and me, despise them. Here's to the memory of Gray!"

It was by this time growing somewhat late. The gig, according to order, was brought round to the door with both lamps brightly shining, and the young men had to pay their bill and take the road. They announced that they were bound for Peebles, and drove in that direction till they were clear of the last houses of the town; then, extinguishing the lamps, returned upon their course, and followed a byroad towards Glencorse. There was no sound but that of their own passage, and the incessant, strident pouring of the rain. It was pitch-dark; here and there a white gate or a white stone in the wall guided them for a short space across the night; but for the most part it was at a foot pace, and almost groping, that they picked their way through that resonant blackness to their solemn and isolated destination. In the sunken woods that traverse the neighbourhood of the burying ground the last glimmer failed them, and it became necessary to kindle a match and re-illumine one of the lanterns of the gig. Thus, under the dripping trees, and environed by huge and moving shadows, they reached the scene of their unhallowed labours.

They were both experienced in such affairs, and powerful with the spade; and they had scarce been twenty minutes at their task before they were rewarded by a dull rattle on the coffin lid. At the same moment Macfarlane, having hurt his hand upon a stone, flung it carelessly above his head. The grave, in which they now stood almost to the shoulders, was close to the edge of the plateau of the graveyard; and the gig lamp had been propped, the better to illuminate their labours, against a tree, and on the immediate verge of the steep bank descending to the stream. Chance had taken a sure aim with the stone. Then came a clang of broken glass; night fell upon them; sounds alternately dull and ringing announced the bounding of the lantern down the bank, and its occasional collision with the trees. A stone or two, which it had dislodged in its descent, rattled behind it into the profundities of the glen; and then silence, like night, resumed its sway; and they might bend their hearing to its utmost pitch, but naught was to be heard except the rain, now marching to the wind, now steadily falling over miles of open country.

They were so nearly at an end of their abhorred task that they judged it wisest to complete it in the dark. The coffin was exhumed and broken open; the body inserted in the dripping sack and carried between them to the gig; one mounted to keep it in its place, and the other, taking the horse by the mouth, groped along by wall and bush until they reached the wider road by the Fisher's Tryst. Here was a faint, diffused radiancy, which they hailed like daylight; by that they pushed the horse to a good pace and began to rattle along merrily in the direction of the town.

They had both been wetted to the skin during their operations, and now, as the gig jumped among the deep ruts, the thing that stood propped between them fell now upon one and now upon the other. At every repetition of the horrid contact each instinctively repelled it with greater haste; and the process, natural although it was, began to tell upon the nerves of the companions. Macfarlane made some ill-favoured jest about the farmer's wife, but it came hollowly from his lips, and was allowed to drop in silence. Still their unnatural burthen bumped from side to side; and now the head would be laid, as if in confidence, upon their shoulders, and now the drenching sackcloth would flap icily about their faces. A creeping chill began to possess the soul of Fettes. He peered at the bundle, and it seemed somehow larger than at first. All over the countryside, and from every degree of distance, the farm dogs accompanied their passage with tragic ululations; and it grew and grew upon his mind that some unnatural miracle had been accomplished, that some nameless change had befallen the dead body, and that it was in fear of their unholy burden that the dogs were howling.

"For God's sake," said he, making a great effort to arrive at speech, "for God's sake, let's have a light!"

Seemingly Macfarlane was affected in the same direction; for though he made no reply, he stopped the horse, passed the reins to his companion, got down, and proceeded to kindle the remaining lamp.

The coffin was exhumed and broken open.

They had by that time got no farther than the crossroad down to Auchendinny. The rain still poured as though the deluge were returning, and it was no easy matter to make a light in such a world of wet and darkness. When at last the flickering blue flame had been transferred to the wick and began to expand and clarify, and shed a wide circle of misty brightness round the gig, it became possible for the two young men to see each other and the thing they had along with them. The rain had moulded the rough sacking to the outlines of the body underneath; the head was distinct from the trunk, the shoulders plainly modelled; something at once spectral and human riveted their eyes upon the ghastly comrade of their drive.

For some time Macfarlane stood motionless, holding up the lamp. A nameless dread was swathed, like a wet sheet, about the body, and tightened the white skin upon the face of Fettes; a fear that was meaningless, a horror of what could not be, kept mounting to his brain. Another beat of the watch, and he had spoken. But his comrade forestalled him.

"That is not a woman," said Macfarlane, in a hushed voice.

"It was a woman when we put her in," whispered Fettes.

"Hold that lamp," said the other. "I must see her face."

And as Fettes took the lamp his companion untied the fastenings of the sack and drew down the cover from the head. The light fell very clear upon the dark, well-moulded features and smooth-shaven cheeks of a too-familiar countenance, often beheld in dreams of both of these young men. A wild yell rang up into the night; each leaped from his own side into the roadway; the lamp fell, broke, and was extinguished; and the horse, terrified by this unusual commotion, bounded and went off towards Edinburgh at a gallop, bearing along with it, sole occupant of the gig, the body of the dead and long-dissected Gray.

Providence and the Guitar

CHAPTER 1

ONSIEUR LÉON BERTHELINI had a great care of his appearance, and sedulously suited his deportment to the costume of the hour. He affected something Spanish in his air, and something of the bandit, with a flavour of Rembrandt at home. In person he was decidedly small and inclined to be stout; his face was the picture of good humour; his dark eyes, which were very expressive, told of a kind heart, a brisk, merry nature, and the most indefatigable spirits. If he had worn the clothes of the period you would have set him down for a hitherto undiscovered hybrid between the barber, the innkeeper, and the affable dispensing chemist. But in the outrageous bravery of velvet jacket and flapped hat, with trousers that were more accurately described as fleshings, a white handkerchief cavalierly knotted at his neck, a shock of Olympian curls upon his brow, and his feet shod through all weathers in the slenderest of Molière shoes — you had but to look at him and you knew you were in the presence of a Great Creature. When he

283

wore an overcoat he scorned to pass the sleeves; a single button held it round his shoulders; it was tossed backwards after the manner of a cloak, and carried with it the gait and presence of an Almaviva. I am of opinion that M. Berthelini was nearing forty. But he had a boy's heart, gloried in his finery, and walked through life like a child in a perpetual dramatic performance. If he were not Almaviva after all, it was not for lack of making believe. And he enjoyed the artist's compensation. If he were not really Almaviva, he was sometimes just as happy as though he were.

I have seen him, at moments when he has fancied himself alone with his Maker, adopt so gay and chivalrous a bearing, and represent his own part with so much warmth and conscience, that the illusion became catching, and I believed implicitly in the Great Creature's pose.

But, alas! life cannot be entirely conducted on these principles; man cannot live by Almavivery alone; and the Great Creature, having failed upon several theatres, was obliged to step down every evening from his heights, and sing from half a dozen to a dozen comic songs, twang a guitar, keep a country audience in good humour, and preside finally over the mysteries of a tombola.

Madame Berthelini, who was art and part with him in these undignified labours, had perhaps a higher position in the scale of beings, and enjoyed a natural dignity of her own. But her heart was not any more rightly placed, for that would have been impossible; and she had acquired a little air of melancholy, attractive enough in its way, but not good to see like the wholesome, skyscraping, boyish spirits of her lord.

He, indeed, swam like a kite on a fair wind, high above earthly troubles. Detonations of temper were not unfrequent in the zones he travelled; but sulky fogs and tearful depressions were there alike unknown. A well-delivered blow upon a table, or a noble attitude, imitated from Mélingue or Frédéric, relieved his irritation like a vengeance. Though the heaven had fallen, if he had played his part with propriety, Berthelini had been content! And the man's atmosphere, if not his example, reacted on his wife; for the couple doated on each other, and although you would have thought they walked in different worlds, yet continued to walk hand in hand.

It chanced one day that Monsieur and Madame Berthelini descended with two boxes and a guitar in a fat case at the station of the little town of Castel-le-Gâchis, and the omnibus carried them with their effects to the Hotel of the Black Head. This was a dismal, conventual building in a narrow street, capable of standing siege when once the gates were shut, and smelling strangely in the interior of straw and chocolate and old feminine apparel. Berthelini paused upon the threshold with a painful premonition. In some former state, it seemed to him, he had visited a hostelry that smelt not otherwise, and been ill received.

The landlord, a tragic person in a large felt hat, rose from a business table under the key rack, and came forward, removing his hat with both hands as he did so.

"Sir, I salute you. May I inquire what is your charge for artists?" inquired Berthelini, with a courtesy at once splendid and insinuating.

"For artists?" said the landlord. His countenance fell and the smile of welcome disappeared. "Oh, artists!" he added brutally; "four francs a day." And he turned his back upon these inconsiderable customers.

A commercial traveller is received, he also, upon a reduction — yet is he welcome, yet can he command the fatted calf; but an artist, had he the manners of an Almaviva, were he dressed like Solomon in all his glory, is received like a dog and served like a timid lady travelling alone.

Accustomed as he was to the rubs of his profession, Berthelini was unpleasantly affected by the landlord's manner.

"Elvira," said he to his wife, "mark my words: Castel-le-Gâchis is a tragic folly."

"Wait till we see what we take," replied Elvira.

"We shall take nothing," returned Berthelini; "we shall feed upon insults. I have an eye, Elvira: I have a spirit of divination; and this place is accursed. The landlord has been discourteous, the Commissary will be brutal, the audience will be sordid and uproarious, and you will take a cold upon your throat. We have been besotted enough to come; the die is cast — it will be a second Sedan."

Sedan was a town hateful to the Berthelinis, not only from patriotism (for they were French, and answered after the flesh to the somewhat homely name of Duval), but because it had been the scene of their most sad reverses. In that place they had lain three weeks in pawn for their hotel bill, and had it not been for a surprising stroke of fortune they might have been lying there in pawn until this day. To mention the name of Sedan was for the Berthelinis to dip the brush in earthquake and eclipse. Count Almaviva slouched his hat with a gesture expressive of despair, and even Elvira felt as if ill fortune had been personally invoked.

"Let us ask for breakfast," said she, with a woman's tact.

The Commissary of Police of Castel-le-Gâchis was a large red Commissary, pimpled, and subject to a strong cutaneous transpiration. I have repeated the name of his office because he was so very much more a Commissary than a man. The spirit of his dignity had entered into him. He carried his corporation as if it were something official. Whenever he insulted a common citizen it seemed to him as if he were adroitly flattering the Government by a side wind; in default of dignity he was brutal from an overweening sense of duty. His office was a den, whence passersby could hear rude accents laying down, not the law, but the good pleasure of the Commissary.

Six several times in the course of the day did M. Berthelini hurry thither in quest of the requisite permission for his evening's entertainment; six several times he found the official was abroad. Léon Berthelini began to grow quite a familiar figure in the streets of Castel-le-Gâchis; he became a local celebrity, and was pointed out as "the man who was looking for the Commissary." Idle children attached themselves to his footsteps, and trotted after him back and forward between the hotel and the office. Léon might try as he liked; he might roll cigarettes, he might straddle, he might cock his hat at a dozen different jaunty inclinations— the part of Almaviva was, under the circumstances, difficult to play.

As he passed the marketplace upon the seventh excursion the Commissary was pointed out to him, where he stood, with his waistcoat unbuttoned and his hands behind his back, to superintend the sale and measurement of butter. Berthelini threaded his way through the market stalls and baskets, and accosted the dignitary with a bow which was a triumph of the histrionic art.

"I have the honour," he asked, "of meeting M. le Commissaire?"

The Commissary was affected by the nobility of his address. He excelled Léon in the depth if not in the airy grace of his salutation.

"The honour," said he, "is mine!"

"I am," continued the strolling player, "I am, sir, an artist, and I have permitted myself to interrupt you on an affair of business. Tonight I give a trifling musical entertainment at the Café of the Triumphs of the Plough—permit me to offer you this programme—and I have come to ask you for the necessary authorisation."

At the word "artist," the Commissary had replaced his hat with the air of a person who, having condescended too far, should suddenly remember the duties of his rank.

"Go, go," said he, "I am busy—I am measuring butter."

"Heathen Jew!" thought Léon. "Permit me, sir," he resumed aloud. "I have gone six times already——"

"Put up your bills if you choose," interrupted the Commissary. "In an hour or so I will examine your papers at the office. But now go; I am busy."

"Measuring butter!" thought Berthelini. "Oh, France, and it is for this that we made '93!"

The preparations were soon made; the bills posted, programmes laid on the dinner table of every hotel in the town, and a stage erected at one end of the Café of the Triumphs of the Plough; but when Léon returned to the office, the Commissary was once more abroad.

"He is like Madame Benoîton," thought Léon, "Fichu Commissaire!"

And just then he met the man face-to-face.

"Here, sir," said he, "are my papers. Will you be pleased to verify?"

But the Commissary was now intent upon dinner.

"No use," he replied, "no use; I am busy; I am quite satisfied. Give your entertainment."

And he hurried on.

"Fichu Commissaire!" thought Léon.

CHAPTER 2

THE AUDIENCE WAS pretty large; and the proprietor of the café made a good thing of it in beer. But the Berthelinis exerted themselves in vain.

Léon was radiant in velveteen; he had a rakish way of smoking a cigarette between his songs that was worth money in itself; he underlined his comic points, so that the dullest numskull in Castel-le-Gâchis had a notion when to laugh; and he handled his guitar in a manner worthy of himself. Indeed his play with that instrument was as good as a whole romantic drama; it was so dashing, so florid, and so cavalier.

Elvira, on the other hand, sang her patriotic and romantic songs with more than usual expression; her voice had charm and plangency; and as Léon looked at her, in her low-bodiced maroon dress, with her arms bare to the shoulder, and a red flower set provocatively in her corset, he repeated to himself for the many hundredth time that she was one of the loveliest creatures in the world of women.

Alas! when she went round with the tambourine, the golden youth of Castel-le-Gâchis turned from her coldly. Here and there a single halfpenny was forthcoming; the net result of the collection never resulted in half a franc; and the Maire himself, after seven different applications, had contributed exactly twopence. A certain chill began to settle upon the artists themselves; it seemed as if they were singing to slugs; Apollo himself might have lost heart with such an audience. The Berthelinis struggled against the impression; they put their back into their work, they sang loud and louder, the guitar twanged like a living thing; and at last Léon arose in his might, and burst with inimitable conviction into his great song, "Y a des honnêtes gens partout!" Never had he given more proof of his artistic mastery; it was his intimate, indefeasible conviction that Castel-le-Gâchis formed an exception to the law he was now lyrically proclaiming, and was peopled exclusively by thieves and bullies; and yet, as I say, he flung it down like a challenge, he trolled it forth like an article of faith; and his face so

288

beamed the while that you would have thought he must make converts of the benches.

He was at the top of his register, with his head thrown back and his mouth open, when the door was thrown violently open, and a pair of newcomers marched noisily into the café. It was the Commissary, followed by the Garde Champêtre.

The undaunted Berthelini still continued to proclaim, "Y a des honnêtes gens partout!" But now the sentiment produced an audible titter among the audience. Berthelini wondered why; he did not know the antecedents of the Garde Champêtre; he had never heard of a little story about postage stamps. But the public knew all about the postage stamps and enjoyed the coincidence hugely.

The Commissary planted himself upon a vacant chair with somewhat the air of Cromwell visiting the Rump, and spoke in occasional whispers to the Garde Champêtre, who remained respectfully standing at his back. The eyes of both were directed upon Berthelini, who persisted in his statement.

"Y a des honnêtes gens partout," he was just chanting for the twentieth time; when up got the Commissary upon his feet and waved brutally to the singer with his cane.

"Is it me you want?" inquired Léon, stopping in his song.

"It is you," replied the potentate.

"Fichu Commissaire!" thought Léon, and he descended from the stage and made his way to the functionary.

"How does it happen, sir," said the Commissary, swelling in person, "that I find you mountebanking in a public café without my permission?"

"Without?" cried the indignant Léon. "Permit me to remind you —"

"Come, come, sir!" said the Commissary, "I desire no explanations."

"I care nothing about what you desire," returned the singer. "I choose to give them, and I will not be gagged. I am an artist, sir, a distinction that you cannot comprehend. I received your permission and stand here upon the strength of it; interfere with me who dare."

"You have not got my signature, I tell you," cried the Commissary. "Show me my signature! Where is my signature?"

That was just the question; where was his signature? Léon recognised that he was in a hole; but his spirit rose with the occasion, and he blustered nobly, tossing back his curls. The Commissary played up to him in the character of tyrant; and as the one leaned farther forward, the other leaned farther back—majesty confronting fury. The audience had transferred their attention to this new performance, and listened with that silent gravity common to all Frenchmen in the neighbourhood of the Police. Elvira had sat down, she was used to these distractions, and it was rather melancholy than fear that now oppressed her.

"Another word," cried the Commissary, "and I arrest you."

"Arrest me?" shouted Léon. "I defy you!"

"I am the Commissary of Police," said the official.

Léon commanded his feelings, and he replied, with great delicacy of innuendo:

"So it would appear."

The point was too refined for Castel-le-Gâchis; it did not raise a smile; and as for the Commissary, he simply bade the singer follow him to his office, and directed his proud footsteps towards the door. There was nothing for it but to obey. Léon did so with a proper pantomime of indifference, but it was a leek to eat, and there was no denying it.

The Maire had slipped out and was already waiting at the Commissary's door. Now the Maire, in France, is the refuge of the oppressed. He stands between his people and the boisterous rigours of the Police. He can sometimes understand what is said to him; he is not always puffed up beyond measure by his dignity. 'Tis a thing worth the knowledge of travellers. When all seems over, and a man has made up his mind to injustice, he has still, like the heroes of romance, a little bugle at his belt whereon to blow; and the Maire, a comfortable *deus ex machina*, may still descend to deliver him from the minions of the law. The Maire of Castel-le-Gâchis, although inaccessible to the charms of music as retailed by the Berthelinis, had no hesitation whatever as to the rights of the matter. He instantly fell foul of the Commissary in very high terms, and the Commissary, pricked by this humiliation, accepted battle on the point of fact. The argument lasted some little while with varying success, until at length victory inclined so plainly to the Commissary's side that the Maire was fain to reassert himself by an exercise of authority. He had been out-argued, but he was still the Maire. And so, turning from his interlocutor, he briefly but kindly recommended Léon to get back to his concert.

"It is already growing late," he added.

Léon did not wait to be told twice. He returned to the Café of the Triumphs of the Plough with all expedition. Alas! the audience had melted away during his absence; Elvira was sitting in a very disconsolate attitude on the guitar box; she had watched the company dispersing by twos and threes, and the prolonged spectacle had somewhat overwhelmed her spirits. Each man, she reflected, retired with a certain proportion of her earnings in his pocket, and she saw tonight's board and tomorrow's railway expenses, and finally even tomorrow's dinner, walk one after another out of the café door and disappear into the night.

"What was it?" she asked languidly.

But Léon did not answer. He was looking round him on the scene of defeat. Scarce a score of listeners remained, and these of the least promising sort. The minute hand of the clock was already climbing upward towards eleven.

"It's a lost battle," said he, and then taking up the money box, he turned it out. "Three francs seventy-five!" he cried, "as against four of board and six of railway fares and no time for the tombola. Elvira, this is Waterloo." And he sat down and passed both hands desperately among his curls. "O Fichu Commissaire!" he cried, "Fichu Commissaire!"

"Let us get the things together and be off," returned Elvira. "We might try another song, but there is not six halfpence in the room."

"Six halfpence?" cried Léon, "six hundred thousand devils. There is not a human creature in the town—nothing but pigs and dogs and commissaires! Pray heaven, we get safe to bed."

"Don't imagine things!" exclaimed Elvira, with a shudder.

And with that they set to work on their preparations. The tobacco jar, the cigarette holder, the three papers of shirt studs which were to have been the prizes of the tombola, had the tombola come off, were made into a bundle with the music; the guitar was stowed into the fat guitar case; and Elvira having thrown a thin shawl about her neck and shoulders, the pair issued from the café and set off for the Black Head.

As they crossed the marketplace the church bell rang out eleven. It was a dark, mild night, and there was no one in the streets.

"It is all very fine," said Léon; "but I have a presentiment. The night is not yet done."

CHAPTER 3

T HE BLACK HEAD presented not a single chink of light upon the street, and the carriage gate was closed.

"This is unprecedented," observed Léon. "An inn closed by five minutes after eleven! And there were several commercial travellers in the café up to a late hour. Elvira, my heart misgives me. Let us ring the bell."

The bell had a potent note; and being swung under the arch it filled the house from top to bottom with surly, clanging reverberations. The sound accentuated the conventual appearance of the building; a wintry sentiment, a thought of prayer and mortification, took hold upon Elvira's mind; and, as for Léon, he seemed to be reading the stage direction for a lugubrious fifth act.

"This is your fault," said Elvira, "this is what comes of fancying things!"

Again Léon pulled the bellrope; again the solemn tocsin awoke the echoes of the inn; and ere they had died away, a light glimmered in the carriage entrance, and a powerful voice was heard upraised and tremulous with wrath.

"What's all this?" cried the tragic host through the spars of the gate. "Hard upon twelve, and you come clamouring like Prussians at the door of a respectable hotel? Oh!" he cried, "I know you now! Common singers! People in trouble with the police! And you present yourselves at midnight like lords and ladies? Be off with you!"

"You will permit me to remind you," replied Léon, in thrilling tones, "that I am a guest in your house, that I am properly inscribed, and that I have deposited baggage to the value of four hundred francs."

"You cannot get in at this hour," returned the man. "This is no thieves' tavern, for mohocks and night rakes and organ-grinders."

"Brute!" cried Elvira, for the organ-grinders touched her home.

"Then I demand my baggage," said Léon, with unabated dignity.

"I know nothing of your baggage," replied the landlord.

"You detain my baggage? You dare to detain my baggage?" cried the singer.

"Who are you?" returned the landlord. "It is dark—I cannot recognise you."

"Very well, then—you detain my baggage," concluded Léon. "You shall smart for this. I will weary out your life with prosecutions; I will drag you from court to court; if there is justice to be had in France, it shall be rendered between you and me. And I will make you a byword—I will put you in a song—a scurrilous song—an indecent song—a popular song—which the boys shall sing to you in the street, and come and howl through these spars at midnight!"

He had gone on raising his voice at every phrase, for all the while the landlord was very placidly retiring; and now, when the last glimmer of light had vanished from the arch, and the last footstep died away in the interior, Léon turned to his wife with an heroic countenance.

"Elvira," said he, "I have now a duty in life. I shall destroy that man as Eugène Sue destroyed the concierge. Let us come at once to the Gendarmerie and begin our vengeance."

He picked up the guitar case, which had been propped against the wall, and they set forth through the silent and ill-lighted town with burning hearts.

The Gendarmerie was concealed beside the telegraph office at the bottom of a vast court, which was partly laid out in gardens; and here all the shepherds of the public lay locked in grateful sleep. It took a great deal of knocking to waken one; and he, when he came at last to the door, could find no other remark but that "it was none of his business." Léon reasoned with him, threatened him, besought him; here, he said, was Madame Berthelini in evening dress—a delicate woman—in an interesting condition—the last was thrown in, I fancy, for effect; and to all this the man-at-arms made the same answer:

"It is none of my business," said he.

"Very well," said Léon, "then we shall go to the Commissary." Thither they went; the office was closed and dark; but the house was close by, and Léon was soon swinging the bell like a madman. The Commissary's wife appeared at a window. She was a threadpaper creature, and informed them that the Commissary had not yet come home.

"Is he at the Maire's?" demanded Léon.

She thought that was not unlikely.

"Where is the Maire's house?" he asked.

And she gave him some rather vague information on that point.

"Stay you here, Elvira," said Léon, "lest I should miss him by the way. If, when I return, I find you here no longer, I shall follow at once to the Black Head."

And he set out to find the Maire's. It took him some ten minutes wandering among blind lanes, and when he arrived it was already half an hour past midnight. A long white garden wall, overhung by some thick chestnuts, a door with a letterbox, and an iron bellpull, that was all that could be seen of the Maire's domicile. Léon took the bellpull in both hands, and danced furiously upon the sidewalk. The bell itself was just upon the other side of the wall, it responded to his activity, and scattered an alarming clangour far and wide into the night.

A window was thrown open in a house across the street, and a voice inquired the cause of this untimely uproar.

"I wish the Maire," said Léon.

"He has been in bed this hour," returned the voice.

"He must get up again," returned Léon, and he was for tackling the bellpull once more.

"You will never make him hear," responded the voice. "The garden is of great extent, the house is at the farther end, and both the Maire and his housekeeper are deaf."

"Aha!" said Léon, pausing. "The Maire is deaf, is he? That explains." And he thought of the evening's concert with a momentary feeling of relief. "Ah!" he continued, "and so the Maire is deaf, and the garden vast, and the house at the far end?"

"And you might ring all night," added the voice, "and be none the better for it. You would only keep me awake."

"Thank you, neighbour," replied the singer. "You shall sleep."

And he made off again at his best pace for the Commissary's. Elvira was still walking to and fro before the door.

"He has not come?" asked Léon.

"Not he," she replied.

"Good," returned Léon. "I am sure our man's inside. Let me see the guitar case. I shall lay this siege in form, Elvira; I am angry; I am indignant; I am truculently inclined; but I thank my Maker I have still a sense of fun. The unjust judge shall be importuned in a serenade, Elvira. Set him up—and set him up."

He had the case opened by this time, struck a few chords, and fell into an attitude which was irresistibly Spanish.

"Now," he continued, "feel your voice. Are you ready? Follow me!"

The guitar twanged, and the two voices upraised, in harmony and with a startling loudness, the chorus of a song of old Béranger's:

> "*Commissaire! Commissaire!*
> *Colin bat sa ménagère.*"

The stones of Castel-le-Gâchis thrilled at this audacious innovation. Hitherto had the night been sacred to repose and nightcaps; and now what was this? Window after window was opened; matches scratched, and candles began to flicker; swollen, sleepy faces peered forth into the starlight. There were the two figures before the Commissary's house, each bolt upright, with head thrown back and eyes interrogating the starry heavens; the guitar wailed, shouted, and reverberated like half an orchestra; and the voices, with a crisp and spirited delivery, hurled the appropriate burden at the Commissary's window. All the echoes repeated the functionary's name. It was more like an entr'acte in a farce of Molière's than a passage of real life in Castel-le-Gâchis.

The Commissary, if he was not the first, was not the last of the neighbours to yield to the influence of music, and furiously throw open the window of his bedroom. He was beside himself with rage. He leaned far over the windowsill, raving and gesticulating; the tassel of his white nightcap danced like a thing of life: he opened his mouth to dimensions hitherto unprecedented, and yet his voice, instead of escaping from it in a roar, came forth shrill and choked and tottering. A little more serenading, and it was clear he would be better acquainted with the apoplexy.

I scorn to reproduce his language; he touched upon too many serious topics by the way for a quiet storyteller. Although he was known for a man who was prompt with his tongue, and had a power of strong expression at his command, he excelled himself so remarkably this night that one maiden lady, who had got out of bed like the rest to hear the serenade, was obliged to shut her window at the second clause. Even what she had heard disquieted her conscience; and next day she said she scarcely reckoned as a maiden lady any longer.

Léon tried to explain his predicament, but he received nothing but threats of arrest by way of answer.

"If I come down to you!" cried the Commissary.

"Ay," said Léon, "do!"

"I will not!" cried the Commissary.

"You dare not!" answered Léon.

At that the Commissary closed his window.

"All is over," said the singer. "The serenade was perhaps ill-judged. These boors have no sense of humour."

"Let us get away from here," said Elvira, with a shiver. "All these people looking—it is so rude and so brutal." And then giving way once more to passion—"Brutes!" she cried aloud to the candlelit spectators—"brutes! brutes! brutes!"

"*Sauve qui peut*," said Léon. "You have done it now!"

And taking the guitar in one hand and the case in the other, he led the way with something too precipitate to be merely called precipitation from the scene of this absurd adventure.

CHAPTER 4

To THE WEST OF Castel-le-Gâchis four rows of venerable lime trees formed, in this starry night, a twilit avenue with two side aisles of pitch darkness. Here and there stone benches were disposed between the trunks. There was not a breath of wind; a heavy atmosphere of perfume hung about the alleys; and every leaf stood stockstill upon its twig. Hither, after vainly knocking at an inn or two, the Berthelinis came at length to pass the night. After an amiable contention, Léon insisted on giving his coat to Elvira, and they sat down together on the first bench in silence. Léon made a cigarette, which he smoked to an end, looking up into the trees, and, beyond them, at the constellations, of which he tried vainly to recall the names. The silence was broken by the church bell; it rang the four quarters on a light and tinkling measure; then followed a single deep stroke that died slowly away with a thrill; and stillness resumed its empire.

"One," said Léon. "Four hours till daylight. It is warm; it is starry; I have matches and tobacco. Do not let us exaggerate, Elvira—the experience is positively charming. I feel a glow within me; I am born again. This is the poetry of life. Think of Cooper's novels, my dear."

"Léon," she said fiercely, "how can you talk such wicked, infamous nonsense? To pass all night out-of-doors—it is like a nightmare! We shall die."

"You suffer yourself to be led away," he replied soothingly. "It is not unpleasant here; only you brood. Come, now, let us repeat a scene. Shall we try 'Alceste and Célimène'? No? Or a passage from the 'Two Orphans'? Come, now, it will occupy your mind; I will play up to you as I never have played before; I feel art moving in my bones."

"Hold your tongue," she cried, "or you will drive me mad! Will nothing solemnise you—not even this hideous situation?"

"Oh, hideous!" objected Léon. "Hideous is not the word. Why, where would you be? 'Dites, la jeune belle, ou voulez-vous aller?' " he carolled. "Well, now," he went on, opening the guitar case, "there's another idea for you—sing. Sing 'Dites, la jeune belle!' It will compose your spirits, Elvira, I am sure."

And without waiting an answer he began to strum the symphony. The first chords awoke a young man who was lying asleep upon a neighbouring bench.

"Hullo!" cried the young man, "who are you?"

"Under which king, Bezonian?" declaimed the artist. "Speak or die!"

Or if it was not exactly that, it was something to much the same purpose from a French tragedy.

The young man drew near in the twilight. He was a tall, powerful, gentlemanly fellow, with a somewhat puffy face, dressed in a grey tweed suit, with a deerstalker hat of the same material; and as he now came forward he carried a knapsack slung upon one arm.

"Are you camping out here, too?" he asked, with a strong English accent. "I'm not sorry for company."

Léon explained their misadventure; and the other told them that he was a Cambridge undergraduate on a walking tour, that he had run short of money, could no longer pay for his night's lodging, had already been camping out for two nights, and feared he should require to continue the same manoeuvre for at least two nights more.

"Luckily, it's jolly weather," he concluded.

"You hear that, Elvira," said Léon. "Madame Berthelini," he went on, "is ridiculously affected by this trifling occurrence. For my part, I find it romantic and far from uncomfortable; or at least," he added, shifting on the stone bench, "not quite so uncomfortable as might have been expected. But pray be seated."

"Yes," returned the undergraduate, sitting down, "it's rather nice than otherwise when once you're used to it; only it's devilish difficult to get washed. I like the fresh air and these stars and things."

"Aha!" said Léon, "Monsieur is an artist."

"An artist?" returned the other with a blank stare. "Not if I know it!"

"Pardon me," said the actor. "What you said this moment about the orbs of heaven——"

"Oh, nonsense!" cried the Englishman. "A fellow may admire the stars and be anything he likes."

"You have an artist's nature, However, Mr.——I beg your pardon; may I, without indiscretion, inquire your name?" asked Léon.

"My name is Stubbs," replied the Englishman.

"I thank you," returned Léon. "Mine is Berthelini—Léon Berthelini, ex-artist of the theatres of Montrouge, Belleville, and Montmartre. Humble as you see me, I have created with applause more than one important rôle. The Press were unanimous in praise of my Howling Devil of the Mountains, in the piece of the same name. Madame, whom I now present to you, is herself an artist, and I must not omit to state, a better artist than her husband. She also is a creator; she created nearly twenty successful songs at one of the principal Parisian music halls. But, to continue, I was saying you had an artist's nature, Monsieur Stubbs, and you must permit me to be a judge in such a question. I trust you will not falsify your instincts; let me beseech you to follow the career of an artist."

"Thank you," returned Stubbs, with a chuckle. "I'm going to be a banker."

"No," said Léon, "do not say so. Not that. A man with such a nature as yours should not derogate so far. What are a few privations here and there, so long as you are working for a high and noble goal?"

"This fellow's mad," thought Stubbs; "but the woman's rather pretty, and he's not bad fun himself, if you come to that." What he said was different. "I thought you said you were an actor?"

"I certainly did so," replied Léon. "I am one, or, alas! I was."

"And so you want me to be an actor, do you?" continued the undergraduate. "Why, man, I could never so much as learn the stuff; my memory's like a sieve; and as for acting, I've no more idea than a cat."

"The stage is not the only course," said Léon. "Be a sculptor, be a dancer, be a poet or a novelist; follow your heart, in short, and do some thorough work before you die."

"And do you call all these things art?" inquired Stubbs.

"Why, certainly!" returned Léon. "Are they not all branches?"

"Oh! I didn't know," replied the Englishman. "I thought an artist meant a fellow who painted."

The singer stared at him in some surprise.

"It is the difference of language," he said at last. "This Tower of Babel, when shall we have paid for it? If I could speak English you would follow me more readily."

"Between you and me, I don't believe I should," replied the other. "You seem to have thought a devil of a lot about this business. For my part, I admire the stars, and like to have them shining — it's so cheery — but hang me if I had an idea it had anything to do with art! It's not in my line, you see. I'm not intellectual; I have no end of trouble to scrape through my exams, I can tell you! But I'm not a bad sort at bottom," he added, seeing his interlocutor looked distressed even in the dim starshine, "and I rather like the play, and music, and guitars, and things."

Léon had a perception that the understanding was incomplete. He changed the subject.

"And so you travel on foot?" he continued. "How romantic! How courageous! And how are you pleased with my land? How does the scenery affect you among these wild hills of ours?"

"Well, the fact is," began Stubbs — he was about to say that he didn't care for scenery, which was not at all true, being, on the contrary, only an athletic undergraduate pretension; but he had begun to suspect that Berthelini liked a different sort of meat, and substituted something else — "The fact is, I think it jolly. They told me it was no good up here; even the guidebook said so; but I don't know what they meant. I think it is deuced pretty — upon my word, I do."

At this moment, in the most unexpected manner, Elvira burst into tears.

"My voice!" she cried. "Léon, if I stay here any longer I shall lose my voice!"

"You shall not stay another moment," cried the actor. "If I have to beat in a door, if I have to burn the town, I shall find you shelter."

With that he replaced the guitar, and comforting her with some caresses, drew her arm through his.

"Monsieur Stubbs," said he, taking off his hat, "the reception I offer you is rather problematical; but let me beseech you to give us the pleasure of your society. You are a little embarrassed for the moment; you must, indeed, permit me to advance what may be necessary. I ask it as a favour; we must not part so soon after having met so strangely."

"Oh, come, you know," said Stubbs, "I can't let a fellow like you—"

"I have it," cried Léon. And he
broke forth into a song.

And there he paused, feeling somehow or other on a wrong tack.

"I do not wish to employ menaces," continued Léon, with a smile, "but if you refuse, indeed, I shall not take it kindly."

"I don't quite see my way out of it," thought the undergraduate; and then, after a pause, he said, aloud and ungraciously enough, "All right. I—I'm very much obliged, of course." And he proceeded to follow them, thinking in his heart, "But it's bad form, all the same, to force an obligation on a fellow."

CHAPTER 5

LÉON STRODE AHEAD as if he knew exactly where he was going; the sobs of Madame were still faintly audible, and no one uttered a word. A dog barked furiously in a courtyard as they went by; then the church clock struck two, and many domestic clocks followed or preceded it in piping tones. And just then Berthelini spied a light. It burned in a small house on the outskirts of the town, and thither the party now directed their steps.

"It is always a chance," said Léon.

The house in question stood back from the street behind an open space, part garden, part turnip field; and several outhouses stood forward from either wing at right angles to the front. One of these had recently undergone some change. An enormous window, looking towards the north, had been effected in the wall and roof, and Léon began to hope it was a studio.

"If it's only a painter," he said with a chuckle, "ten to one we get as good a welcome as we want."

"I thought painters were principally poor," said Stubbs.

"Ah!" cried Léon, "you do not know the world as I do. The poorer the better for us!"

And the trio advanced into the turnip field.

The light was in the ground floor; as one window was brightly illuminated and two others more faintly, it might be supposed that there was a single lamp in one corner of a large apartment; and a certain tremulousness and temporary dwindling showed that a live fire contributed to the effect. The sound of a voice now became audible; and the trespassers paused to listen. It was pitched in a high, angry key, but had still a good, full, and masculine note in it. The utterance was voluble, too voluble even to be quite distinct; a stream of words, rising and falling, with ever and again a phrase thrown out by itself, as if the speaker reckoned on its virtue.

Suddenly another voice joined in. This time it was a woman's; and if the man were angry, the woman was incensed to the degree of fury. There was that absolutely blank composure known to suffering males; that colourless unnatural speech which shows a spirit accurately balanced between homicide and hysterics; the tone in which the best of women sometimes utter words worse than death to those most dear to them. If Abstract Bones-and-Sepulchre were to be endowed with the gift of speech, thus, and not otherwise, would it discourse. Léon was a brave man, and I fear he was somewhat sceptically given (he had been educated in a Papistical country), but the habit of childhood prevailed, and he crossed himself devoutly. He had met several women in his career. It was obvious that his instinct had not deceived him, for the male voice broke forth instantly in a towering passion.

The undergraduate, who had not understood the significance of the woman's contribution, pricked up his ears at the change upon the man.

"There's going to be a free fight," he opined.

There was another retort from the woman, still calm but a little higher.

"Hysterics?" asked Léon of his wife. "Is that the stage direction?"

"How should I know?" returned Elvira, somewhat tartly.

"Oh, woman, woman!" said Léon, beginning to open the guitar case. "It is one of the burdens of my life, Monsieur Stubbs; they support each other; they always pretend there is no system; they say it's nature. Even Madame Berthelini, who is a dramatic artist!"

"You are heartless, Léon," said Elvira; "that woman is in trouble."

"And the man, my angel?" inquired Berthelini, passing the ribbon of his guitar. "And the man, *m'amour?*"

"He is a man," she answered.

"You hear that?" said Léon to Stubbs. "It is not too late for you. Mark the intonation. And now," he continued, "what are we to give them?"

"Are you going to sing?" asked Stubbs.

"I am a troubadour," replied Léon. "I claim a welcome by and for my art. If I were a banker could I do as much?"

"Well, you wouldn't need, you know," answered the undergraduate.

"Egad," said Léon, "but that's true. Elvira, that is true."

"Of course it is," she replied. "Did you not know it?"

"My dear," answered Léon impressively, "I know nothing but what is agreeable. Even my knowledge of life is a work of art superiorly composed. But what are we to give them? It should be something appropriate."

Visions of "Let dogs delight" passed through the undergraduate's mind; but it occurred to him that the poetry was English and that he did not know the air. Hence he contributed no suggestion.

"Something about our houselessness," said Elvira.

"I have it," cried Léon. And he broke forth into a song of Pierre Dupont's:

> "Savez-vous ou gite
> Mai, ce joli mois?"

Elvira joined in; so did Stubbs, with a good ear and voice, but an imperfect acquaintance with the music. Léon and the guitar were equal to the situation. The actor dispensed his throat notes with prodigality and enthusiasm; and, as he looked up to heaven in his heroic way, tossing the black ringlets, it seemed to him that the very stars contributed a dumb applause to his efforts, and the universe lent him its silence for a chorus. That is one of the best features of the heavenly bodies, that they belong to everybody in particular; and a man like Léon, a chronic Endymion who managed to get along without encouragement, is always the world's centre for himself.

He alone—and it is to be noted, he was the worst singer of the three—took the music seriously to heart, and judged the serenade from a high artistic point of view. Elvira, on the other hand, was preoccupied about their reception; and, as for Stubbs, he considered the whole affair in the light of a broad joke.

"Know you the lair of May, the lovely month?" went the three voices in the turnip field.

The inhabitants were plainly fluttered; the light moved to and fro, strengthening in one window, paling in another; and then the door was thrown open, and a man in a blouse appeared on the threshold carrying a lamp. He was a powerful young fellow, with bewildered hair and beard, wearing his neck open; his blouse was stained with oil colours in a harlequinesque disorder; and there was something rural in the droop and bagginess of his belted trousers.

From immediately behind him, and indeed over his shoulder, a woman's face looked out into the darkness; it was pale and a little weary, although still young; it wore a dwindling, disappearing prettiness, soon to be quite gone, and the expression was both gentle and sour, and reminded one faintly of the taste of certain drugs. For all that, it was not a face to dislike; when the prettiness had vanished, it seemed as if a certain pale beauty might step in to take its place; and as both the mildness and the asperity were characters of youth, it might be hoped that, with years, both would merge into a constant, brave, and not unkindly temper.

"What is all this?" cried the man.

CHAPTER 6

LÉON HAD HIS hat in his hand at once. He came forward with his customary grace; it was a moment which would have earned him a round of cheering on the stage. Elvira and Stubbs advanced behind him, like a couple of Admetus's sheep following the god Apollo.

"Sir," said Léon, "the hour is unpardonably late, and our little serenade has the air of an impertinence. Believe me, sir, it is an appeal. Monsieur is an artist, I perceive. We are here three artists benighted and without shelter, one a woman—a delicate woman—in evening dress— in an interesting situation. This will not fail to touch the woman's heart of Madame, whom I perceive indistinctly behind Monsieur her husband, and whose face speaks eloquently of a well-regulated mind. Ah! Monsieur, Madame—one generous movement, and you make three people happy! Two or three hours beside your fire—I ask it Monsieur in the name of Art—I ask it of Madame by the sanctity of womanhood."

The two, as by a tacit consent, drew back from the door.

"Come in," said the man.

"*Entrez, Madame*," said the woman.

The door opened directly upon the kitchen of the house, which was to all appearance the only sitting room. The furniture was both plain and scanty; but there were one or two landscapes on the wall handsomely framed, as if they had already visited the committee rooms of an exhibition and been thence extruded. Léon walked up to the pictures and represented the part of a connoisseur before each in turn, with his usual dramatic insight and force. The master of the house, as if irresistibly attracted, followed him from canvas to canvas with the lamp. Elvira was led directly to the fire, where she proceeded to warm herself, while Stubbs stood in the middle of the floor and followed the proceedings of Léon with mild astonishment in his eyes.

"You should see them by daylight," said the artist.

"I promise myself that pleasure," said Léon. "You possess, sir, if you will permit me an observation, the art of composition to a T."

"You are very good," returned the other. "But should you not draw nearer to the fire?"

"With all my heart," said Léon.

And the whole party was soon gathered at the table over a hasty and not an elegant cold supper, washed down with the least of small wines. Nobody liked the meal, but nobody complained; they put a good face upon it, one and all, and made a great clattering of knives and forks. To see Léon eating a single cold sausage was to see a triumph; by the time he had done he had got through as much pantomine as would have sufficed for a baron of beef, and he had the relaxed expression of the overeaten.

As Elvira had naturally taken a place by the side of Léon, and Stubbs as naturally, although I believe unconsciously, by the side of Elvira, the host and hostess were left together. Yet it was to be noted that they never addressed a word to each other, nor so much as suffered their eyes to meet. The interrupted skirmish still survived in ill feeling; and the instant the guests departed it would break forth again as bitterly as ever. The talk wandered from this to that subject—for with one accord the party had declared it was too late to go to bed; but those two never relaxed towards each other; Goneril and Regan in a sisterly tiff were not more bent on enmity.

It chanced that Elvira was so much tried by all the little excitements of the night, that for once she laid aside her company manners, which were both easy and correct, and in the most natural manner in the world leaned her head on Léon's shoulder. At the same time, fatigue suggesting tenderness, she locked the fingers of her right hand into those of her husband's left; and, half-closing her eyes, dozed off into a golden borderland between sleep and waking. But all the time she was not unaware of what was passing, and saw the painter's wife studying her with looks between contempt and envy.

It occurred to Léon that his constitution demanded the use of some tobacco; and he undid his fingers from Elvira's in order to roll a cigarette. It was gently done, and he took care that his indulgence should in no way disturb his wife's position. But it seemed to catch the eye of the painter's wife with a special significancy. She looked straight before her for an instant, and then, with a swift and stealthy movement, took hold of her husband's hand below the table. Alas! she might have spared herself the dexterity. For the poor fellow was so overcome by this caress that he stopped with his mouth open in the middle of a word, and by the expression of his face plainly declared to all the company that his thoughts had been diverted into softer channels.

If it had not been rather amiable, it would have been absurdly droll. His wife at once withdrew her touch; but it was plain she had to exert some force. Thereupon the young man coloured and looked for a moment beautiful.

Léon and Elvira both observed the byplay, and a shock passed from one to the other; for they were inveterate matchmakers, especially between those who were already married.

"I beg your pardon," said Léon suddenly. "I see no use in pretending. Before we came in here we heard sounds indicating—if I may so express myself—an imperfect harmony."

"Sir—" began the man.

But the woman was beforehand.

"It is quite true," she said. "I see no cause to be ashamed. If my husband is mad I shall at least do my utmost to prevent the consequences. Picture to yourself, Monsieur and Madame," she went on, for she passed Stubbs over, "that this wretched person—a dauber, an incompetent, not fit to be a sign painter—receives this morning an admirable offer from an uncle—an uncle of my own, my mother's brother, and tenderly beloved—of a clerkship with nearly a hundred and fifty pounds a year, and that he—picture to yourself!—he refuses it! Why? For the sake of Art, he says. Look at his art, I say—look at it! Is it fit to be seen? Ask him—is it fit to be sold? And it is for this, Monsieur and Madame, that he condemns me to the most deplorable existence, without luxuries, without comforts, in a vile suburb of a country town. O non!" she cried, "non—je ne me tairai pas—c'est plus fort que moi! I take these gentlemen and this lady for judges—is this kind? Is it decent? Is it manly? Do I not deserve better at his hands after having married him and"—a visible hitch—"done everything in the world to please him?"

I doubt if there were ever a more embarrassed company at a table; everyone looked like a fool; and the husband like the biggest.

"The art of Monsieur, however," said Elvira, breaking the silence, "is not wanting in distinction."

"It has this distinction," said the wife, "that nobody will buy it."

"I should have supposed a clerkship—" began Stubbs.

"Art is Art," swept in Léon. "I salute Art. It is the beautiful, the divine; it is the spirit of the world, and the pride of life. But—" And the actor paused.

"A clerk—" began Stubbs.

"I'll tell you what it is," said the painter. "I am an artist, and as this gentleman says, Art is this and the other; but of course, if my wife is going to make my life a piece of perdition all day long, I prefer to go and drown myself out of hand."

"Go!" said his wife. "I should like to see you!"

"I was going to say," resumed Stubbs, "that a fellow may be a clerk and paint almost as much as he likes. I know a fellow in a bank who makes capital water-colour sketches; he even sold one for seven-and-six."

To both the women this seemed a plank of safety; each hopefully interrogated the countenance of her lord; even Elvira, an artist herself!—but indeed there must be something permanently mercantile in the female nature. The two men exchanged a glance; it was tragic; not otherwise might two philosophers salute, as at the end of a laborious life each recognised that he was still a mystery to his disciples.

Léon arose.

"Art is Art," he repeated sadly. "It is not water-colour sketches, nor practicing on a piano. It is a life to be lived."

"And in the meantime people starve!" observed the woman of the house. "If that's a life, it is not one for me."

"I'll tell you what," burst forth Léon; "you, Madame, go into another room and talk it over with my wife; and I'll stay here and talk it over with your husband. It may come to nothing, but let's try."

"I am very willing," replied the young woman; and she proceeded to light a candle. "This way, if you please." And she led Elvira upstairs into a bedroom. "The fact is," said she, sitting down, "that my husband cannot paint."

"No more can mine act," replied Elvira.

"I should have thought he could," returned the other; "he seems clever."

"He is so, and the best of men besides," said Elvira; "but he cannot act."

"At least he is not a sheer humbug like mine; he can at least sing."

"You mistake Léon," returned his wife warmly. "He does not pretend to sing; he has too fine a taste; he does so for a living. And, believe me, neither of the men are humbugs. They are people with a mission—which they cannot carry out."

"Humbug or not," replied the other, "you came very near passing the night in the fields; and, for my part, I live in terror of starvation. I should think it was a man's mission to think twice about his wife. But it appears not. Nothing is their mission but to play the fool. Oh!" she broke out, "is it not something dreary to think of that man of mine? If he could only do it, who would care? But no—not he—no more than I can!"

"Have you any children?" asked Elvira.

"No; but then I may."

"Children change so much," said Elvira, with a sigh.

And just then from the room below there flew up a sudden snapping chord on the guitar; one followed after another; then the voice of Léon joined in; and there was an air being played and sung that stopped the speech of the two women. The wife of the painter stood like a person transfixed; Elvira, looking into her eyes, could see all manner of beautiful memories and kind thoughts that were passing in and out of her soul with every note; it was a piece of her youth that went before her; a green French plain, the smell of apple flowers, the far and shining ringlets of a river, and the words and presence of love.

"Léon has hit the nail," thought Elvira to herself. "I wonder how."

The how was plain enough. Léon had asked the painter if there were no air connected with courtship and pleasant times; and having learnt what he wished, and allowed an interval to pass, he had soared forth into

"O mon amante,
O mon désir,
Sachons cueillir
L'heure charmante!"

"Pardon me, Madame," said the painter's wife, "your husband sings admirably well."

"He sings that with some feeling," replied Elvira, critically, although she was a little moved herself, for the song cut both ways in the upper chamber; "but it is as an actor and not a musician."

"Life is very sad," said the other; "it so wastes away under one's fingers."

"I have not found it so," replied Elvira. "I think the good parts of it last and grow greater every day."

311

"Frankly, how would you advise me?"

"Frankly, I would let my husband do what he wished. He is obviously a very loving painter; you have not yet tried him as a clerk. And you know—if it were only as the possible father of your children—it is as well to keep him at his best."

"He is an excellent fellow," said the wife.

They kept it up till sunrise with music and all manner of good fellowship; and at sunrise, while the sky was still temperate and clear, they separated on the threshold with a thousand excellent wishes for each other's welfare. Castel-le-Gâchis was beginning to send up its smoke against the golden East; and the church bell was ringing six.

"My guitar is a familiar spirit," said Léon, as he and Elvira took the nearest way towards the inn, "it resuscitated a Commissary, created an English tourist, and reconciled a man and wife."

Stubbs, on his part, went off into the morning with reflections of his own.

"They are all mad," thought he, "all mad—but wonderfully decent."

The Enchantress

MY LAST REMAINING articles, a gold watch and a light summer overcoat, I had pawned that morning at Clermont. The proceeds had supplied me with a noonday meal at the restaurant of the casino; and thanks to some varieties of fortune, enabled me to remain at play throughout the afternoon. Between six and seven I stepped forth into the evening penniless. It was the hour of dinner; but there was no dinner for me, nor any supper, nor the least prospect of a bed. I sat on a bench in the grounds and considered my position gravely. Stranded in a foreign place, where I could not flatter myself I was at all believed, even by my one or two acquaintances, for in these last days of evil fortune I had not displayed my character in the most amiable light; hundreds of miles from any of my relations, who all detested me and whom I myself detested; destitute of any art whether of use or pleasing; destitute of luggage; bankrupt of self-reliance; with no other advantages than what is called a gentlemanly exterior and a suit of excellent clothes:

in what direction (I asked myself anxiously) can such a person turn? I could not dig; for I had no spade and nothing to dig in if I had. I was not in the least ashamed to beg: but where was the use of it? I knew my fellow creatures: even to the most clamant cases of distress (admitting mine to be one of the most clamant) they would be little likely to exceed a franc; and for francs, I had no use, my daily expenses being calculated in pounds sterling. For crime I had little fancy, and no talent. I might indeed join the Church of Rome, as an interesting convert; but my conversion would have to be something of the suddenest, or I might die ere my reception.

As I thus helplessly revolved my predicament, the brutes who had been feeding began to tramp out of their various hotels. The band struck up, the idle evening life of Royat had begun again; and here was I condemned to rove upon the outskirts of my customary haunts, and draw in the buckle of my trousers as the hours proceeded. It came upon me in a flash that I must gain time. Beggary, if it did not promise me a permanent livelihood, held forth some hopes of supper. With my address and the cut of my tailor it would be strange if I could not beg to some advantage. I saw too that the first time a man begged he would be likely to do the thing well, but that the performance must infallibly decline upon a repetition. If I chose the person wisely and nicely adjusted my bearing, I might possibly fly as high as a Napoleon. The person; the address—here were my two points, and it was clear the second depended altogether on the first. With one, romantic falsehood would be found enticing, with another the blunt truth. Upon the person, then, I fixed my attention singly. Being a man, I should certainly be a great ass if I did not choose a woman: upon that I did not hesitate an instant. But whether that woman should be fair or homely, young or old, was a matter not at all as obvious; indeed, I found such specious considerations in favour of each that I could by no manner of means arrive at a conclusion, and it was (as you are now to hear) an accident that finally decided me.

It had grown late, the night was very dark, many of the brutes had gone home, when, as I hurried in the dark path between the two casinos, I was aware of a young lady drawing near. Distant and broken lights from open doors and windows fell upon and left her as she came. These showed me she was dressed for the evening, and as she approached I was even able to recognise her face and to recall her name, which I had casually overheard. She was a Miss Croft; an orphan of wealth and beauty, resident here in Royat in the care of her guardian, a Mr. Hussey Ramley, with whom I had been several hours thus in contact at the card table. Mr. Ramley was a famous financier in those days, and a great and daring card player; nor will the reader have forgot the singular scandal with which, some ten years later, he collapsed and, like Samson, involved thousands in his fate. I had no sooner recognized Miss Croft, and the propitiousness of all the circumstances: of time, of darkness to conceal my blushes, and of solitude sufficient to protect me against interruption and yet not so great as to alarm the lady; than my mind was instantly made up. I took off my hat and advanced.

"Miss Croft, if I am not mistaken?" said I.

She paused and looked at me with some curiosity. "To whom have I the pleasure . . .?" she asked.

"Madam," said I, "I beg the favour of a few minutes' conversation. I will not detain you beyond the corner of the main street. I should have told you perhaps at first that I am a gentleman, and perfectly unaccustomed—indeed until tonight I should have thought myself equally incapable—you have no cause for alarm," I added.

"I see no reason for alarm," replied Miss Croft. "Whether in my case—or in yours." She said this very quietly, and it so much increased my confusion that I remained silent. "Well?" she added after a little.

"I am really so unaccustomed—" I began, and paused once more.

"To public speaking?" she suggested, with the slightest touch of entertainment in her tone.

"I cannot do it—I have made a mistake," said I. "I never looked at you before, or I would never have tried it. I can only beg pardon for this intrusion, and thank you for the patience with which you have heard me. Good evening, Miss Croft."

"O, no," she returned. "My patience is now quite at an end, and my curiosity thoroughly aroused. I have walked with you as far as to the corner. You will now walk with me as far at least as the Hôtel de Lyon."

"I cannot imagine," I began.

"I am pleased with your conversation," she returned.

"It must be the quality of my silence," said I.

"You came to tell me something, to propose something, to ask me something," she said. "After a prolonged covert study of my face, you judge me unfit to be your confidant. And yet I think you were right at first, and are now wrong. I think myself very fit to hear what you have to say; in all Royat there is no one more so; and fit or unfit, I have perfectly made up my mind that I shall hear it. Come, what is that to which you are unaccustomed, of which you once proudly thought yourself incapable of attempting, and which you now find yourself incapable of bringing to an end—at least with me."

"Miss Croft," said I, "I have told you, I cannot."

"Give me your arm," said she. "Is not your name Hatfield?"

"I cannot conceive how you should know it," I replied.

"Have you not met my guardian, Mr. Ramley, at the casino? Have you not been playing a good deal? And—losing a good deal? And did you not come to me tonight with some idea of negotiating a small advance?"

"Miss Croft, I—I had never looked at you. I would never have dreamed of such a thing if I had. You are far too pretty and too clever," I blurted out these silly speeches one upon the other's heels.

"It appears you thought me ugly and stupid?" said she. "But that is better than to fancy me ingenuous."

"Upon my word, I am not such a fool as I appear," I cried. "My position—"

"Yes," said she, "that is the point. How much do you want, Mr. Hatfield? Let me be your banker and"—with a shade of asperity that called the blood to my face—"do not let us have the spectacle of an English gentleman begging at large about a foreign country."

"Miss Croft," I broke out, "let us have no talk of lending; it is no loan, for I could never repay it. I have no money, no hopes, no friends, no honest trade; I am a common beggar, and that is the miserable truth."

"How on earth have you got to such a pitch?" she asked.

I told her at some length my miserable story; and though I was myself appalled by its unbroken silliness, I told it honestly. "You can judge for yourself," I added, "if it be worthwhile to help a creature so incompetent."

"I want to think," she answered softly. We walked on in silence up the hill road; as we went, the moon began to peer at intervals out of rifts among the clouds, and to shed flying glimpses on the Limagne and the towered city of Clermont at our feet. Presently she came to a wider island of clear sky, and her light fell now steadily around us.

"Let me see you," said Miss Croft.

I stopped and turned towards the light, and she looked for some little while intently in my face. Then she smiled. "I believe I have found a use for you," said she.

"A use?" I repeated blankly.

She held out her hand. "You are a gentleman?" she asked. "Put your hand in mine and promise you will obey me implicitly. You hesitate?"

"It is rather a large order," said I. But her smile, as she looked at me, was so alluring and so enigmatical, her blue eyes caught so soft and yet so merry a sparkle from the moon, her hand, as it awaited mine, was of so fine a design and of so fair a colour, that my resolution suddenly melted. "I cannot refuse your hand," said I, "cost what it may." And I not only took it in mine, I stooped and kissed it. "I will go where this hand leads me," said I.

"Is it the hand—or what is in it?" she inquired.

"Ah," said I, "you remind me that I am a beggar, and yet I was never a beggar till today."

"Your face is not a beggar's," she said, "or you should never have touched me; I do not give my hand without liking."

"Ah," said I bitterly, "it is impossible there should be any liking where there is no respect."

"They say so," she replied, "but I believe it is mere cant. At least Mr. Hatfield, I like *you* and to a certain point (as you shall find) I trust you." She took her purse from her pocket. "There should be something like a thousand francs in that," she continued. "It is yours without condition. If you wish to see no more of me, the world is before you; but"—and here her voice became a little softer— "if you do not regret your promise of obedience, if you wish to see more of one who may possibly become your friend, arrive tomorrow night in Paris, meet me on the platform, come up, address me by my name, and offer me your help. It will be found we are going to the same house, the Hôtel de Lille et d'Albion, and that we are both to cross on the next day by Calais. What more natural, Mr. Hatfield, than that we should continue the journey together? And if my maid disapproves, she must disapprove. Not a word just now. I wish you to have time for thought. Do not speak to me and do not follow me. Good night."

With that she was gone down the hill again, and I was left alone in the darkness, for the moon was again hid. I had no thought of the purse in my hand, no thought of the meal to which I had so long looked forward. The smile, the eyes, the touch, the voice so soft and yet significant, the gait and figure so express and dainty, of this exquisite being had completely robbed me of the remembrance of my own concerns; my mind ran upon nothing but Miss Croft. I sat there in the grass of the roadside, and rehearsed and hugged a thousand memories of our interview. I could not sufficiently wonder at that indifference with which I had so often seen without remarking her, or at that sudden overwhelming partiality that had now brought me to her feet. She had given me a place for penitence; I never so much as thought of profiting by that. The promise I had given was very sweeping; but it was given to her of the smile and the blue eyes, and that was enough for me. And indeed for a man in such a pickle as I had found myself in that afternoon no prospect could seem very alarming: I might be better indeed, it was hard to suppose I could be worse.

2

THE NEXT NIGHT WE met as if by accident and drove in the same vehicle to the hotel, where I had the honour of sitting down to the same table with her in the public room. The maid had made a third until that moment, and our communications in consequence had been conventional and those of mere acquaintances upon an ordinary footing.

But now, save for the presence of a waiter partially ignorant of every tongue in Europe, we felt ourselves at ease.

"And so," said she, "you have not thought better of your promise. Thank you!"

"I have thought better of it and much better," I replied, "I thought of it all night, Miss Croft; and will you let me tell you the burthen of my thinking? It seemed to me that I had promised much, and yet given nothing. It seemed to me that you had found me when I had lost all, even my self-respect, that you had picked me out of the gutter, that you had given me kind words and (what I value more) kind looks; and that I was quite empty-handed to repay. Even you must tell yourself stories, Miss Croft?"

"O, yes," she said, "and strange ones too."

"Well, in a man's stories, it is always he who gives," I continued, "and I find myself in the position of the taker. You will say I sought it; I deny the charge. I meant to hold out my hand before a stranger, close it on a piece of money, and escape. What would have been changed? There would have been one stranger in the world, whom I should have tried to avoid—for such is gratitude. But you have chosen otherwise; you would not remain a stranger; I am in a position to which I never dreamed of stooping; you are the man in this story, I the woman. And what can I say but *Be it so*! You have picked up a tool, Miss Croft; what do you propose to do with it? You have bought a slave; I hope you like him."

"Tool?" she repeated. "I do not like the word. Let me put it otherwise. You say you have nothing to give; but I think you will find in the long run you give more than I. I warn you of that from the beginning: for I know myself. I ask knightly service," she cried, with a certain enthusiasm. "How I shall be able to repay it, who can tell? Can it ever be repaid? Give? What can I give? Money—if you care for that; gratitude—if you believe in it, and you have said already that you do not. And from you—what do I ask?"

"It is what I wish I knew," I said.

"You say I picked you up," she continued. "You read in tales of magicians who pick up strays like you in the slums of mediaeval cities, and what is it they buy from them?—their wind, their appetite, their soul. You will begin to think me greedy, for I want a little of all that." She broke off with her smile. "I hope I frighten you," she said.

"You charm me," said I.

She looked at me in a manner too peculiar to be told, so much of doubt, of interest, of animation as that glance contained. "I did not say I wished your love," she said; and so turned the talk that until we separated for the night (which was soon after), nothing passed between us to diminish the effect of that ambiguous remark.

The next day we passed the channel. Except upon the steamer I had little talk with her; never in what she said was there anything to help me to the least decision. Had the accent been on love? Had it been upon the say? "I did not *say* I wished your love, I did not say I wished your *love*." I tried it over and over to myself; but the stress had been so evenly divided, that either reading in turn appeared to me to be the true one. Only the fact that she had used the word at all, only the look with which she had accompanied and emphasised it, remained to console and to inspirit me. She would not have so looked upon one quite indifferent, to one who had captured no interest in her mind, she would not have touched upon the thought. "No," was my conclusion, "she is either making an egregious ass of me, or I am the man."

The next day I was to call before ten, which seemed a very early hour, at the home of Mr. Ramley. That gentleman had remained behind at Royat to complete his cure and perfect his experience of baccarat; and it was in his study that I found Miss Croft surrounded by a great mass of business papers. She came forward and gave me her hand, with a charming rise of colour in her cheek, a still more charming kind of hesitation in her manner.

"This is to be a decisive interview, Mr. Hatfield," said she. "Sit down over there; no, further away, please—and look out of the window, not at me. You offered me your word as a gentleman; I have not yet taken it and you are still free. I have not yet taken it, because I do not know what it is worth, and I do not care for worthless gifts or purchases. Do not begin to be angry. I have been watching you closely, and I begin to think you are what you appear; I begin to think you are a gentleman— a gentleman indeed—a man who sets weight upon his word—even to a woman—even to a woman who puts herself into his power?"

"Try me," said I, dryly.

"I have something to say first," she resumed; "something to ask you; and it is this. Have you any claim upon me? Do I owe you anything? Whatever I do for you (if I shall do anything) will it not be given out of pure grace?"

"Out of pure grace, Miss Croft," I said.

"I want you to remember that admission; I bind you to it," she continued with emphasis. "So if I ever chance to give you anything, you shall not make it a foundation for exacting more."

"Miss Croft," I said, a little ruffled, "I did once ask you—to my shame—for money; I am now asking nothing, except that you believe me."

"Now!" she said—"yes!—But let us speak no more of this. I am going to my lawyer's, dear me—" looking at her watch, "it is already the time of my appointment: oblige me, by glancing over the rest of these papers; make a note of all the companies on which Mr. Ramley's name figures as director; and as soon as you have the list completed, take a hansom and follow me to my lawyer's office. Here is the address. Send the list in, and then wait for me; I shall not keep you long." She turned as she went from the room and turning to me with one of her most radiant smiles, "And now," said she, "I suppose you think I have been jesting. Not at all! I was never more serious, Mr. Hatfield, in my life; and perhaps, before the afternoon is over, you will see cause to believe me."

The strange task which she had left me to accomplish did not delay me very long. More than half of the great bulk of prospectuses had been already examined by herself and the results transferred in her own hand (which was as charming as her person) to a sheet of foolscap paper. Ere I had got to the end of the business, the third side of this sheet was very full; and I could not but wonder, as I drove to the lawyer's office, at the multiplicity and variety of Mr. Ramley's interests.

The list was sent in duly to where the lawyer was closeted with his fair client; and I had an opportunity for close upon three hours of studying the directory in the waiting room. At the end of that time, Miss Croft made her appearance in company with a tall and venerable gentleman.

"I am so sorry I kept you so long," said she. "It is all the fault of Mr. Venables."

"Is this the young gentleman?" inquired Mr. Venables. "Pleased to meet you, Mr. Hatfield," and methought he looked and smiled upon me somewhat strangely. But the fact of this respectable personage being in any way privy to the designs of my enchantress mightily relieved some private and perhaps fanciful anxieties which had tormented me till then. She could not mean to set me in a murder.

"I am dying of hunger," she cried gaily. "I declare nothing agrees with me like business. Mr. Hatfield, give me your arm, take me to Verrey's, and order me the best luncheon in London. Mr. Venables, good-bye!"

I cannot describe to you the winning graces to which she treated me upon the way and with which she continued to ravish me throughout the meal; she was sportive, she was aggressive, she teased, she tripped me up, she quizzed me; and through it all, I knew not what radiancy of tenderness beamed upon and sunned my heart. Such a pretty familiarity, as with a brother; such sudden looks, and lookings away; such pleasant speech, such pleasant silences; such an atmosphere of favour, of partiality, of confidence, of love—dared I call it love? Or if I dared not, what else was I to call it?

It was past three of the afternoon, before we had come to the dessert. The large room at Verrey's was nearly empty; yet every here and there belated lunchers were like ourselves trifling with their coffee. She glanced at me suddenly, "What is your first name?" said she.

I told her it was Edward.

"I have brought you on purpose to this public place," she continued, "for I wished to prevent the probability of anything like a scene, which I detest above everything. At the same time, just oblige by taking up some sort of countenance that you can keep. Pare some fruit or do what you like—Edward," said she. "There," she broke out, "I cannot even call you by your Christian name, but you change faces like a schoolgirl! Come—pare your pretty fruit. There is a good little fellow. So—that is better. Edward, I want to ask you a favour. My name is Emmeline. Will you grant me a favour, I wonder?"

"I have promised you implicit obedience," said I; "—we have spoken a great deal of payment, let me call you Emmeline, and what more should I dare to ask?"

"We shall see about that presently," she returned. "But do not mistake: the date of implicit obedience has not begun: that shall be after, this is before; if you reprove my favour, the whole thing is at an end."

"You may be very sure that I will grant it then," I cried.

"May I?" she said. "Let me finish. If you shall not choose to grant me what I ask, my lawyer has directions to set you up in some respectable business; you shall see me no more, you shall not want again. I will starve no man into consent."

"I am still to ask you what the favour is," said I, a trifle doggedly, for I was hurt.

"Must you ask? Must I tell you? Edward!" she said.

I would take no bait. "I am perhaps dull," I replied.

"And perhaps proud," said she.

"That also, possibly," was my return. "Even a beggar has pride."

"Very well," said she. "I remind you again this is a public place, and I wish no scenes. Answer me quietly and to the point; it is only yes or no. Will you marry me? O, these names are surely quite needless: all these days, you must have seen where I was coming," she cried, petulantly. "Have you trifled"—and here she was suddenly seized with laughter—"have you trifled with my affections?"

"Do you mean to say you like me?" I asked.

"I never said any such thing," replied she; "and the question is usually, on the man's side, prefaced with some assurances. But since we have got this thing so very much upside down, we may as well go on as we began; and I can honestly say, I never saw a man I liked so well. Do you like me?"

"I love you," said I.

"You do?" she asked. "Truly?"

"From my soul, I love you."

"I think that is rather a pity," she said. "I am not highly emotional myself. Look here: I must be yet more frank. If you say 'no' and go your own way, you are to want for nothing. If you say 'yes' and marry me, understand precisely what you do. First of all, you will get less in money: you will have to sign a marriage contract—you never saw the like of it for stiffness; after what you have done with your own I will not give you the chance to make hay of mine. It will be a loss in money. As for position, you have pledged me your word; you know what to expect: I marry you—not you me."

"Miss Croft," said I, "one would think you were trying to buy me off."

"It sounds like it," said she; "and I have already so far succeeded that you drop my Christian name. And yet, Mr. Hatfield, I do assure you, I make you this offer in all seriousness; and it will be a favour to me if you will deign to accept me. I have made your acquaintance, picked you up, I think were your own words—certainly I have laid by all reserve to make us better friends; I do not think you have had to complain of me; and you can now choose, with a free conscience, whether you prefer to be my husband or my pensioner."

"I think, madam," said I, "that I prefer upon the whole to go and sweep a crossing."

"Very well," said she. "Pay the bill and let us leave this hateful place."

I called the waiter and with her money, which I loathed to have in my hands, I paid the amount in which we were indebted. As I waited for the change, my eyes irresistibly wandered to her face; I beheld her undeniably moved, our looks crossed, in hers I read reproach and appeal; and my heart smote me, and then leaped.

"Emmeline," said I. "I told you that I loved you; it is the truth; do with me what you will. I am your chattel. I only wish to God it was worth more; but do with it what you please."

I spoke low, but my voice came from me with the note of a sincere emotion; and as I spoke, I leaned across the table, and offered her my hand.

She shook her head, and as she did so, a tear ran upon her cheek. "I have made a mistake," said she. "I never looked at you before or I would never have tried it."

"Those words were mine," I cried.

"And now they are mine," said she. "You will never understand."

"It is not necessary I should understand," I replied. "Let me obey; that is enough."

"I own," she said with a sudden smile, "I never heard of a young man so backward to receive a lady's hand. Take it, then; take me — as I am and as I choose; and swear as you are a gentleman, you will never seek to disobey, and will never be tempted to reproach me for what is your own free and considerate act."

She looked at me earnestly. A thousand suspicions flashed through my mind; I think I became as white as the tablecloth. I gave her my hand in silence. She looked at me with the same serious face. "Well," said she. "For better, for worse. And anyway, you would now be starving. You are to have three hundred a year now."

"O!" I cried, bounding from my seat, "spare me more of this. You have made me love you; I long to give myself, spare me the figure of my price."

"And yet you would now be starving," said she. "Don't let heroics blind you to the fact. There lies the way to the beginning of ingratitude."

"Emmeline," I cried, "I am a thousand miles beyond gratitude."

"And some of these days," said she, "you will be a thousand miles behind it. But when that temptation comes, tell yourself this. 'There was a girl who was not in the least a bad girl and far less a stupid one. I came before her in the most unfavourable light—with my hand stretched forth at the ditchside; and yet she judged me a gentleman, and put a trust in me that she would have put in not one out of ten thousand.' For that is the ungilded truth, Edward. You are prouder than I thought you were; in all the rest I have not been disappointed; and my confidence in the one gentleman I ever met is stronger than ever." She gave me her hand again, regardless of the waiter who had returned with the change upon a tray; and this was visible in her face, a genuine enthusiasm that swept away the last of my scruples. "You go to Edinburgh tonight; we shall be married in Scotland—for a thousand reasons; stay in the Caledonian Hotel, where my lawyer will communicate with you. I shall be with some friends close by, at a place called Garneside, where you must seek neither to see nor to write to me: all our communication must be through Mr. Venables; and when the legal delay is over, we can be married quietly. After that"—and here she paused.

3

THE CONTRACT WAS a very tight piece of drafting; you could not get a finger in any corner: there was an allowance of £300 a year for me payable quarterly; all the rest was put in trust for my wife's single benefit in the hands of their very reputable city men, with whom I confess it was a kind of pride to me to be connected even in this left-handed manner. In a last fling of self-respect I refused the allowance; but Mr. Venables assured me it was a condition *sine qua non*, and the match would be off if I insisted. The fact that I attempted even so much resistance shows my mind to have been still divided; and indeed the memory of our strange interview at Verrey's troubled me by day and night, as I tossed in my bed, as I paced around the Calton Hill which I made at that time my continual resort, and as I sat brooding in my little upstairs chamber in the inn. I need not trouble you with my suspicions and concerns; they passed so quickly in the way that I now can genuinely blush to recollect them. Enough that I was deeply unhappy; and that if I did not draw back from my engagement, it was from these unlikely but very urgent reasons: I thought she had taught me; I could not bear to disaffect the trust which she had so eloquently declared; and the light in her blue eyes led me continually forward.

When we had been proclaimed the due number of times, I met her at the Caledonian Station, and we went together to the home of a clergyman in a street which I think they call Great King Street. She took my arm on the way, but she did not look at me and said but little. Methought she was cruelly embarrassed; and I wondered to find my heart quite full of pity for her situation. "I will not trouble you with words," was all I said. "You shall never repent the trust that you have put in me." She pressed my arm. "I am sure of it," she said.

The clergyman, an elderly person in a wig, had in his wife and servants, before whom, in the front drawing room, we were properly united in the Scottish forms; a little wine and biscuits concluded the ceremony; and we came forth in the street again about five of a bright autumn afternoon, man and wife.

At the corner of the street, she paused.

"We are going to say good-bye," said she, in tones that scarcely rose above a whisper.

"Good-bye!" I cried.

"I must return to my friends," she returned, a little wildly. "I have to. I cannot help myself. Is this your obedience? I do not know what you will think of me; and indeed—indeed, I do not wish you to think badly."

Once more a great pity sealed my lips.

"Emmeline," said I, "you shall do exactly what you wish, and I likewise. When shall I hear from you, and where?"

"Stay in the same hotel," said she. "You shall hear soon. I place my trust in you—my trust."

And she was gone!

Two days later I received a letter from Mr. Venables, very politely and prettily expressed; in which he informed me, that after what had passed—these were his *ipsissima verba*—I must feel it was better for all parties that Mrs. Hatfield and I should meet no longer; that my wife had gone abroad; and that if I had any interest in the continent of America, he had his orders and would take a pleasure in forwarding my views

The next day I burst into his office.

"Ah, Mr. Hatfield," said he. "I—I rather anticipated this pleasure. What can I do to serve you?"

"What sort of a woman is my wife?" I cried.

"A very estimable young lady—somewhat independent—a very clear—O, a very clear business head. Quite a remarkable capacity, I should say."

"Well, and why did she marry me?" I cried.

"Hmm?" said the lawyer. "Ever see the will of the late Mr. Croft? No." He rang a bell, and a copy of that document was laid before me. I read it through.

"I see nothing here," said I.

"Well, sir," said he, "you will observe that after twenty-one she is quite free to marry. Mrs. Hatfield attained her majority two months ago."

"She lost no time," said I. "Flattery for me! But still, I am in the dark."

"You will observe further," said Mr. Venables, "that until her marriage, the whole property remains under the sole management of Mr. Richard Hussey Ramley. No way out of that except by marriage. Do you see now?"

"Not even now," said I.

"Well," said Mr. Venables, "she—she didn't think Mr. Ramley a sound man of business. She doubted—this is in the strictest confidence of course—she doubted his solvency and even his, well—his delicacy. I would not go as far as that myself, but his operations are to my old-fashioned eyes a little wild. O, I think Mrs. Hatfield fully justified."

"I have no doubt of that," said I; and then immediately, "and I suppose nothing can be done for me."

"Well," returned Mr. Venables. "You can go to law."

"I will never do that," cried I.

"I believe she rather figured on it in that way," returned the lawyer.

"She can go on figuring upon it in that way till Hell is cold, for me," I said, getting my hat.

"That was just as she expected; she had a great esteem for your character, Mr. Hatfield."

"And why were we married in Scotland?" I asked, pausing in the door.

"Well, it's quiet," replied Mr. Venables, "and then there are great facilities for divorce."

Afterword

Reflecting on the origins of *The Strange Case of Dr. Jekyll and Mr. Hyde,* Robert Louis Stevenson explained that "I had long been trying to write a story on this subject, to find a body, a vehicle, for that strong sense of man's double being which must at times come in upon and overwhelm the mind of every thinking creature." He found so effective a vehicle that his slim novel soon made him famous throughout the English-speaking world, inspiring plays and parodies, editorials and sermons. The numerous film versions in our own century testify to the lasting power of the work. The twin names of Jekyll and Hyde have entered our language, becoming tokens for a dangerous and painful division within a personality. What is the nature of that division, that doubleness, and how is it dramatized in the novel?

From the outset, many readers have answered the question in moral terms, interpreting the division as one between good and evil. Soon after the sensational novel was published in January 1886, ministers on both sides of the Atlantic began using it as a text for their Sunday sermons. The downfall of the doctor seemed to illustrate vividly the dangers of yielding to one's wicked impulses. The flavor of those sermons may be gathered from a review entitled "Secret Sin," which appeared in a Church of England journal: "It is a result of the Fall of Man that we have ever present a lower nature struggling to get the mastery." When Jekyll begins to change spontaneously into Hyde, according to the reviewer, "the appalling truth bursts on the victim that the will, which once was so powerful, has lost its strength, and that the lower nature, which everyone should seek to bring into subjection, has gained the ascendancy." These reflections led the reviewer to a pious conclusion: "God grant that this book may be a warning to many who are trifling with sin, unconscious of its awful power to drag them down to the lowest depths of hell."

But although the history of Stevenson's book lends itself to such a moralistic reading, we would probably not still be reading the novel today, a century after its publication, if it were only a didactic fable about the struggle between virtue and sin. More is going on here than meets the pious eye. Stevenson hinted as much in a letter to the English poet John Aldington Symonds: "*Jekyll* is a dreadful thing, I own; but the only thing I feel dreadful about is that damned old business of the war in the members. This time it came out; I hope it will stay in, in future." Those do not sound like the sentiments of a man who had written a simple moral tale.

In his letter Stevenson was echoing a phrase from the last chapter of the novel, where Henry Jekyll, in his own letter of confession, laments "the perennial war among my members". The doctor describes himself as having been "committed to a profound duplicity of life" from an early age. An "impatient gaiety of disposition" led him to indulge in secret pleasures, while in public he wore a "more than commonly grave countenance". Those pleasures are never specified, yet they could not have been too wicked, for the doctor claims that "many a man would have even blazoned such irregularities as I was guilty of; but from the high views that I had set before me, I regarded and hid them with an almost morbid sense of shame". Here the doubleness appears, not as the conflict between some absolute evil and good, but as the age-old conflict between what the heart desires and what society approves. The twin doors of Jekyll's house reflect the same divison, for he passes out by day through the respectable front door as the grave public man, and by night through the stained and blistered rear door as the secret Mr. Hyde. The London of the novel likewise appears divided between wide thorough-fares and hidden alleys, between the gleaming neighbourhoods of the wealthy and the dingy neighbourhoods of the poor.

The "high views" under which the doctor labours are the repressive social conventions of Victorian Britain, which would have permitted a wealthy older bachelor such as Henry Jekyll precious few outlets for gaiety or sensuality. He is "the very pink of the proprieties", in Mr. Enfield's words, and in the eyes of his friends he is the perfect gentleman—refined, devout, and charitable. Held to such high standards, the doctor suffers in extreme form the tug-of-war we all feel, between public codes and private urges, between society's thou-shalt-not's and the self's cravings.

Sigmund Freud, the father of psychoanalysis, spoke of that internal war as a struggle between the superego and the id, the former referring to the portion of the mind that exercises a prohibiting and chastising role derived from society, the latter referring to "the untamed passions", the source of instincts, appetites, desires. Governed entirely by the search for pleasure, the id "knows no judgments of value: no good and evil, no morality". According to Freud, the ego — our ordinary, everyday consciousness—must constantly negotiate between the amoral demands of the id and the fierce restrictions of the superego. The ego sometimes fails, and then "human beings fall ill of a conflict between the claims of instinctual life and the resistance which arises within them against it". In the most severe cases, that conflict can lead to a split personality. Whether or not we use Freud's labels—whether we call Jekyll's judgmental aspect the superego and his rebellious aspect the id—it is clear that Hyde represents "the claims of instinctual life".

Accounts of split personalities were published widely in Stevenson's day. One case he knew especially well was that of William Brodie, a prominent citizen of Edinburgh who led a double life for twenty years. During the day Brodie was a proper bachelor, successful businessman, and dignified city councilman; at night he was a brawling drunkard who gambled at dice and cards and cockfights, visited his two mistresses and five illegitimate children, led a gang of thieves, and committed robberies all over the city, usually in the homes and offices of friends. To mark the transformation, he dressed in white during the day and in black at night. Stevenson's childhood bedroom contained a chest built by Brodie, and his nanny primed him with stories about the duplicitous gentleman. As a youth, Stevenson made a point of frequenting the seedy parts of town where Brodie had performed his nightly mischief, and he wrote an early play about him, so it is likely that he thought of the two-sided councillor while imagining the two-sided doctor.

Brodie's dark side released not only aggression and violence, but also sexuality. What do we learn of Jekyll's dark side? We are told that Mr. Hyde tramples a girl and clubs an old man to death, both events occurring at night, both recounted secondhand by Richard Enfield and a maidservant. The deeds are brutal enough. Yet they are rendered so sketchily, by observers of such doubtful reliability, with so little sense of context or motives, that we may doubt whether these deeds alone can account for the universal condemnation of Edward Hyde. Everyone finds him loathsome, but no one can say precisely why. Enfield's response is typical: "There is something wrong with his appearance; something displeasing, something downright detestable. I never saw a man I so disliked, and yet I scarce know why. He must be deformed somewhere." Dr. Lanyon concludes that "there was something abnormal and misbegotten in the very essence of the creature." The straitlaced Mr. Utterson adds religious heat to these descriptions, but little light, when he thinks of Hyde as a "fiend", one who wears "Satan's signature". Everyone who encounters him is struck by a "haunting sense of unexpressed deformity". Indeed, much of Hyde's character and history remain unexpressed, implied but not disclosed. During the investigation after the murder, "tales came out of the man's cruelty, at once so callous and violent; of his vile life, of his strange associates, of the hatred that seemed to have surrounded his career." But we never hear those tales, we never learn any details of his "vile life". Jekyll refers to Hyde's pleasures as depraved, "undignified", and "monstrous", without revealing a single shady episode.

A modern reader cannot help wondering if those pleasures were not at least partly sexual. Even without the benefit of Freud, who would begin publishing his theories a few years after the publication of *The Strange Case of Dr. Jekyll and Mr. Hyde,* some of Stevenson's early readers saw the novel as a tale about sexual repression. In the stage versions and parodies that soon appeared, and in the film versions that appeared decades later, Hyde's nocturnal rambles are depicted as journeys of lust. Stevenson briskly defended his novel against such a reading. In a letter to the *New York Sun,* he protested that Hyde was not "a mere voluptuary . . . but people are so filled full of folly and inverted lust, that they can think of nothing but sexuality". Even had he chosen to deal openly with sex, Stevenson would have been prevented from doing so by Victorian conventions. His stepson, Lloyd Osbourne, recorded him as complaining, "How the French misuse their freedom; see nothing worth writing about save the eternal triangle; while we are muzzled like dogs . . . condemned to avoid half the life that passes us by. What books Dickens could have written had he been permitted! Think of Thackeray as unfettered as Flaubert or Balzac! What books I might have written myself!"

While there are no explicit references to sex in the novel, the descriptions of Hyde's pleasures are laced through with sensual imagery, and Jekyll's apologies are laced through with the imagery of repression. Recalling his first transformation under the influence of chemicals, for example, the doctor writes: "There was something strange in my sensations, something indescribably new and, from its very novelty, incredibly sweet. I felt younger, lighter, happier in body; within I was conscious of a heady recklessness, a current of disordered sensual images running like a millrace in my fancy, a solution of the bonds of obligation, an unknown but not an innocent freedom of the soul." That freedom is in marked contrast to the inhibitions of the public man, who describes himself as having lived "nine tenths a life of effort, virtue and control", a grim life marked by "restriction" and "renunciation".

With the aid of chemical hocus-pocus, the doctor contrives to split off his disruptive, socially unacceptable urges into the figure of Mr. Hyde, and yet the two remain one, bound together by shared memory and desire. No matter how stark the contrast between his public and private selves, between the upright doctor and the secret sinner, Jekyll insists that "I was radically both." Radically: at root. "I was no more myself when I laid aside restraint and plunged in shame, than when I laboured, in the eye of day, at the furtherance of knowledge or the relief of sorrow and suffering." The imagery in this passage is typical of the contrasts that run through the novel. Whereas Jekyll is a creature of the daylight, Hyde is a creature of the night. Whereas Jekyll is lethargic ("laboured"), Hyde is energetic ("plunged"). Whereas Jekyll is restrained, Hyde is free. The doctor appears only indoors, while his darker half wanders footloose "through wider labyrinths of lamplighted city". The moral dualism of good versus evil, and the psychological dualism of conscience versus instinct, is thus complicated by a pattern of imagery that makes Mr. Hyde out to be, if not more virtuous, then at least more dynamic, more engaging, more vibrantly alive than Dr. Jekyll.

Whenever we glimpse Edward Hyde, he is in motion, abrupt and restless. Henry Jekyll, by contrast, is languid, sickly, confined to his rooms. From childhood on, Stevenson himself suffered chronic sore throats, colds, and respiratory infections. In his letters he frequently complained of feeling prematurely aged, trapped, cut off from life by illness. In fact, while writing *The Strange Case of Dr. Jekyll and Mr. Hyde,* Stevenson was so weak from infection that he could not leave his bed, so feverish that he could not sleep without opium. "He was suffering from continual haemorrhages," his wife recalled, "and was hardly allowed to speak, his conversations being usually carried on by means of a slate and pencil." It is not surprising that a man so ill should create a healthy alter ego for his ailing doctor, that he should imagine an energetic self who is capable of acting out what the invalid can only dream.

Writing about his childhood impressions of Edinburgh, Stevenson emphasised the contrast between splendour and squalor, between the handsome townhouses and the ugly slums: "I seem to have been born with a sentiment of something moving in things of an infinite attraction and horror coupled." Mr. Hyde inspires just that ambivalent response of horror coupled with attraction. Like Long John Silver, Stevenson's famous villain from *Treasure Island,* Edward Hyde is the most commanding figure in his book, more intriguing than the upright Victorian gentlemen who surround him, partly redeemed from villainy by his energy, inventiveness, and daring.

Jekyll himself, beholding his altered face in the mirror, proclaims: "I was conscious of no repugnance, rather of a leap of welcome. This, too, was myself. It seemed natural and human. In my eyes it bore a livelier image of the spirit, it seemed more express and single, than the imperfect and divided countenance I had been hitherto accustomed to call mine." In the midst of apologising for his mischievous half, Jekyll remembers fondly "the comparative youth, the light step, leaping impulses and secret pleasures, that I had enjoyed in the disguise of Hyde". That liveliness and youthfulness cling to Hyde throughout the novel. He is so much younger than the doctor, in fact, that he could be taken for Jekyll's son. Indeed, in Stevenson's original manuscript, Mr. Utterson speculates that Hyde might be Jekyll's illegitimate child. Although that unseemly speculation was removed before the novel reached print, our version of the book still suggests that Hyde might be viewed as the rebellious, libertine son of an authoritarian father. "I was the first," Jekyll boasts, "that could plod in the public eye with a load of genial respectability, and in a moment, like a schoolboy, strip off these lendings and spring headlong into the sea of liberty." Summing up the relation between his two halves, the doctor writes that "Jekyll had more than a father's interest; Hyde had more than a son's indifference."

As a youth, Stevenson himself had brought on a family crisis by rejecting the engineering career his father had chosen for him, by dismissing his father's strict Calvinism, by scorning the family's genteel standards of behaviour, and by leading a bohemian life in the bars and dives of Edinburgh. One of Stevenson's poems about those rebellious years makes his younger self sound remarkably like Edward Hyde:

I walk the streets smoking my pipe
   and I love the dallying shopgirl
That leans with rounded stern to look at the fashions;
And I hate the bustling citizen,
The eager and hurrying man of affairs I hate,
Because he bears his intolerance writ on his face
And every movement and word of him tells me how much he
   hates me.

I love night in the city,
The lighted streets and the swinging gait of harlots.
I love cool pale morning,
In the empty bystreets,
With only here and there a female figure,
A slavey with lifted dress and a key in her hand,
A girl or two at play in a corner of wasteland
Tumbling and showing their legs and crying out to me
   loosely.

That is a more frank description of the sort of street where Hyde lives, a street of gin shops, low caffs, raggedy children, and "women of many different nationalities passing out, key in hand, to have a morning glass".

The novel is too decorous for the women to lift their skirts and utter loose cries, let alone to be called harlots, but they nonetheless give Hyde's neighborhood a mildly lascivious air.

In rejecting his father's religion, Stevenson was influenced in part by the English biologist Charles Darwin, whom he read while in university. Like his fellow Victorians, Stevenson learned from Darwin to link our sexual and aggressive impulses with our animal origins. In keeping with this view, Hyde is compared to an ape, a monkey, a growling beast. He strikes Utterson as "hardly human! Something troglodytic," a throwback to cave dwellers. Jekyll describes him as "the animal within me licking the chops of memory" and "drinking pleasure with bestial avidity." When the doctor wakes to find himself spontaneously changed into Hyde, he notices first the bestial hand: "lean, corded, knuckly, of a dusky pallor and thickly shaded with a swart growth of hair." Tales of metamorphosis—of shape-changing—are as old as literature, as old as myth, and many of them, including those about werewolves and vampires, reflect our deep dread of reverting to bestiality. The struggle between the human and the animal within us provides yet another way of understanding the painful division that lies at the heart of the novel.

The split between Dr. Jekyll and Mr. Hyde bears a richness of meanings that corresponds to the richness and ambiguity of our own experience. The pattern of contrasting images—day and night, public and private, instinct and conscience, splendor and squalor, age and youth, human and animal—cannot be reduced to the simple formula of good versus evil. The overtones of sensuality in the novel, the appealing vigor of Mr. Hyde, the hints of a son rebelling against his father, the indictment of a rigid social code—all help explain why Stevenson felt "dreadful" about laying bare "that damned old busines of the war in the members." But they also help explain why, a century later, we are still reading his novel. Like Dr. Jekyll, we are divided creatures, torn between contrary impulses, haunted by shadow selves.

Scott Russell Sanders
Indiana University
June 1991